CW00866977

HELLBORNE

THE ARC CHRONICLES BOOK 2

MATTHEW W. HARRILL

For my mum and dad, for all they have done, and for April Vine, because everybody needs an erotic author for a friend!

THE ARC CHRONICLES

PROLOGUE

The mechanical whine of planes, in the distant darkness as they taxied about Birmingham airport, mixed with the smell of jet fuel leant an eerie and somehow metallic aspect to the skeleton of what had once been a stronghold for humanity: The ARC hangar and base of operations in the Southern United States. They did not know it, but mankind relied on this shadowy organization. Not only to protect them from his kind, but also to keep the secrets buried, the masses ignorant of what existed beneath their feet, beyond the limits of their tiny minds. If they could comprehend the horrors spawning from their mere existence, they would wish they had never been born.

Asmodeus considered this as he stewed in frustration over the events of recent months. The plan had been ambitious, and never subtle, not by his standards. He had hoped it would end with the portal, meaning he could get back home and save what remained of his caste. No doubt, the others would have decimated his numbers in his absence. Abaddon, Mammon, Lucifer, Leviathan. All had the advantage while he worked to save them, but he had no illusions that the first thing they would do when they arrived would be to end him.

He took a moment to observe the figure at his side. One of his most bitter rivals, Belphegor had become his only ally in a world cut off from all they knew. When Satan had descended from Heaven, their alliance had endured beyond ages. Now it threatened to leave him alone, isolated.

In response to his gaze, Belphegor shivered, clutching with her one good arm at the other, almost completely frozen. She received the wound ignorantly making contact with one of the Nameless, the force Satan had kept in check over the millennia. Now, the wound threatened to destroy her if they could not return to their own realm in time. Even in the dark, her long blonde hair shimmered. To the mortals of this realm she was a beauty, a facet perpetuated by Asmodeus to instil lust in the easily influenced. To demonkind, she was a force to be feared: remorseless, calculating, and utterly without mercy. Asmodeus hoped she would become so again.

"Can we get on with this?" Belphegor's hiss came through teeth clenched in a grimace to prevent chattering.

"Hold out your arm," Asmodeus instructed.

Unclasping her frozen limb, Belphegor reached out with her good right arm. Carefully, Asmodeus folded the sleeve of her blouse back. Smiling, he avoided the steely-eyed gaze that reminded him above all, Belphegor admired fashion. Even in her dilapidated state, woe unto the being, mortal or otherwise, who ruined her favorite garment.

Since the collapse of the portals, inclement weather had ravaged the entire state of Alabama. From within the trench coat he had favored since then he produced a knife. About a foot in length, from tip to hilt, the blade glittered as it caught the light in the near-darkness. The knife was legendary.

Belphegor stepped away. "The Well of Souls," she said in part reverence, part horror.

Asmodeus laughed. "You need not fear for your existence my dear. The blade is corrupt. Iuvart saw to that in his lust for advancement, for which, I suspect, we have you to thank. There is nothing left on this mortal plane for us to fear. Not now the blade is stained with her blood."

Asmodeus turned the dagger, regarding it. There were dark stains amidst the conchoidal perfection of the blade. Dried blood. Her blood. "The only act the blade is good for on this side of the void is the very act they sought to prevent."

Trembling, Belphegor stretched her arm out. "You have a faith I am rapidly losing."

Saying no more, Asmodeus ran the razor-sharp edge of the blade along the inside of her forearm. Raising the knife, he regarded it for a moment before running it across his right palm.

"The blood of the most unholy, mixed with that of the sacrifice on the blade of the Well calls forth at will, not by chance," he intoned. "Return to us, born anew."

Asmodeus touched the dagger to the tarmac of the runway, a place still bearing the scars of a violent explosion. There was a brief flash, and a body materialized in mid-air, dropping to the ground with a thud. Asmodeus felt a rush of power through his body, filling him with ecstasy. By the look on her face, the same had happened to Belphegor.

"Like it?"

The answering look of lust on her face had nothing to do with his demonic force. "I feel stronger."

"And so you shall. For each of Hell's minions returning,

with your life used on the blade, you shall grow stronger. As I said before, there is nothing here for our kind to fear."

Belphegor gazed down to the body lying inert at their feet. "I want another."

"All in good time. There are many places we can raise you an army. We have a long road before us, though the destination is known. This is the first of a new breed. He has been called at will, by our blood and by that of the sacrifice. They may come as before now the way is open, but those we choose are ours without question."

Asmodeus drew his right foot back and kicked the body square in the ribs, causing the man to emit a groan. "You. Up."

Drawing deep breaths, the man stood. He was taller than both of them by a good six inches, with a barrel chest wrapped in a plaid shirt. Denim clung to legs under the swelling of his growing gut. He clenched his fists and glared at Asmodeus, his shoulders heaving. Teeth gnashed and his face began to distend, the proportions inhuman in nature.

"Enough," Asmodeus decided, and waved his hand. "You will only revert to your true form if and when I decide it, and not a moment sooner."

At the command, the man subsided, his face returning to normal. "Where am I?"

"You are at the place of your death, the site of your ascension, and rebirth. You have been brought back to serve us, and you shall do so with every fiber of your being."

The man clenched his fists. "I feel strong. I feel really strong. It worked as Lord Iuvart predicted." He raised his hands, punching the air, and roaring into the darkness. Then he paused and looked around. "The explosion. The plane. How long?"

"Five, maybe six months. What else do you feel?"

He closed his eyes, and pointed east. "There. I feel something tugging at me. What is it?"

"It works," Belphegor breathed in wonder.

Asmodeus could not suppress a satisfied smile. "It's a homing beacon of sorts. You are feeling the blood kindred to those the dagger's blade resurrected."

He stared at first Belphegor and then at Asmodeus. "I can feel you as well."

"There is more: you will feel when we call you, guide you. The first of a new breed you are; an army of demons meant to open the true gates of Hell."

"What do I do now?"

"You follow your instinct," Belphegor purred. "That other pulling, the insistent calling, it will lead you to your former wife and her lover. You should know she is with child. His child. We want you to hunt them down. Them, and all those with them."

Brian Ross rubbed his hands together, his eyes betraying the element of insanity dwelling deep within any demon constrained in mortal form.

"Perfect."

CHAPTER ONE

Eva Scott winced as Madden led her around the dance floor of the small inn doubling as the town hall for the residents of Unnaryd, in southern Sweden. A crowd of relative strangers cheered on in approval while a local elder played his nyckelharpa with gusto. Eva had asked for a traditional Swedish wedding and she had gotten it.

Madden leaned in, concerned. She smiled to indicate she was fine. Having him this close, Eva marvelled at the fact he was her husband. He was nothing less than dashing, dressed in a white tuxedo, with his long brown hair tied back. He was so tall she had to crane her neck to see his face. He was her personal hero. That he had been reborn not once but twice was an afterthought. Forgetting herself, she winced once more.

"The baby?"

Eva let her hand drop to her middle. The borrowed dress had been adjusted to cope with her swollen middle. It was unheard of in the village for anyone to be pregnant before the wedding, but these were special circumstances for a unique couple. The baby kicked her hand away in response to the motherly inquiry.

"No, she is fine. It's these damned coins they made me wear in my shoes. It's the smell of the food. It's all making me nauseous, but I'll survive."

Madden chuckled. "Well, you did ask for tradition. The gold and silver coins in shoes are a traditional wealth blessing."

"Invented no doubt by a torture merchant."

Madden twirled her slowly with hands still bandaged and slightly clawed from his ordeal on the mountain in Afghanistan now widely known as 'Mount Gehenna', after the biblical destination for those who were wicked. It had certainly earned its reputation with what had been dubbed 'The demon incursion' by all at Anges de la Résurrection des Chevaliers, or ARC.

Eva still woke up sweating many nights, the flames and boundless hordes of Hell's legions almost within touching distance, the demon Behemoth rising above her. She had crossed countries, endured numerous attempts on her life to find Madden, and ultimately they had witnessed the failure of their enemy by a miscalculation that cost them their victory. The demon in Madden had been ripped from within, he had been slow to recover, but recover he had, and now they belonged to each other.

Eva caught the eye of Swanson Guyomard as she completed a slow twirl, and invited him onto the floor. The descendant of the ARC founder, Jerome, and current council member grinned and stepped closer to them.

"If I may interrupt, I believe your wife wants to cut the rug with a fellow who can actually dance."

Madden laughed and handed her over. The tune changed and others joined them.

"You be careful, twinkle toes. She's delicate property. Besides, I will be in perfectly good hands."

"Without doubt," said his new dance partner as Swanson led Eva off in the opposite direction.

Dr Gila Ciranoush, ARC researcher and artifact expert of the Coptic Museum in Cairo, was an adept dancer. She would keep Madden safe. Eva trusted her with her life and certainly with her husband. Caught off guard by Swanson's skill, she groaned once more.

"Are you unwell?"

Eva threw out a look of mock ferocity. "I am heavily pregnant with the child of a man who used to be part demon, I am wearing coins in my shoes, and I have sore feet. Go figure."

Swanson laughed aloud. "Reap what you sew, tough lady. Suck it up!"

Eva couldn't help but smile. Since she could not contact her parents, he and Gila had acted as surrogate 'parents' for the coin-giving tradition.

All too quickly, the song ended to much cheering, bawdy comments in Swedish, and the raising of glasses containing what Eva had been told was a brand of local vodka. Eva threw her arms around Swanson's neck and hugged him as much as she was able. Leaving him to the tender mercies of one of the many beautiful young women who had seemingly materialized from the village for the party, Eva made her way to the table set for the wedding party.

Only one person sat there. Elaine Millet was Eva's friend, confidante, and bodyguard. In this world so readily ruled by men, it was a rare woman who could become all three. With her long red hair and matching temper, she appeared severe, but had a wicked sense of humour and a face that lilluminated when she smiled; she was a joy to be around.

"Not dancing?" Eva asked, letting out a long sigh of satisfaction as she leaned back into the heavily cushioned chair which had been provided for her.

"Not my thing. Besides, I can't take my focus away from you."

Unassuming and practical described Elaine perfectly. A former member of the assault squad housed at Mount Gehenna known as Legion, Eva had found her and struck up a conversation as they were returning from the near-cataclysm above. With Madden unconscious, both Gila and Swanson otherwise occupied, she had been very much left alone. Legion had sworn, to a man, to defend her, but Eva had chosen to keep Elaine close. Madden had a burly redhead named Rick Larrion, who lounged across the room from them earning a stare of disapproval from Elaine, he had chosen as his bodyguard.

Madden approached, and instantly Elaine sat straighter, a smile touching the corners of her mouth. He spared a grin for Elaine, oblivious to the fact she had taken a shine to him.

"My parents are leaving. Want to come see them off?"

"I would love to," she replied, holding her hand out and allowing him to help her stand.

"Coming, coppertop?" Madden added to Elaine, offering her his other hand.

"I don't need your help standing up, thank you very much," she replied, bristling at the comment.

Outside, it was a pleasant May afternoon. The sun was dipping behind a horizon of spruce and pine, the dark green of both creating the illusion of an impenetrable wall of green. There was a hint of a chill in the air, but Eva had Madden to keep her warm. Next to a range rover, an older but clearly active couple waited patiently. Christopher and Jana Scott were guests because they were ARC affiliates. They could be trusted to keep a secret, having been part of the organization for decades. They also worked for an American Senator.

Upon seeing her son, Jana let out a noise of pure delight and hugged them both. "Don't you two look like a picture. The perfect couple, and what a place for it."

"One could almost forget it's a glorified safe house," Christopher Scott said as he leaned on the car. "You kids stay safe." He got into the back of the car and waited.

The hurt on Madden's face was plain. "I understand," he said to his mother.

"You are a good man, Madden." Jana reached up to touch his face. "We are so very proud of you. Of you both. He just has difficulty sometimes accepting the truth."

To Eva, she said, "I was the ARC agent. He came from the Government. Chris will listen, but he sees Madden as the embodiment of everything that should be unreal. You have a demon in you."

"Had, Mother. Had."

"Be that as it may, everything that has happened in the last year has overwhelmed him. Cathy's death was almost too much for him. It was a major step for him to come here and he only did so because you are his son, or rather, you were his son. It is too much for him to imagine his own flesh would die and come back in such a way. Eva, you look out for Madden. I have been in the organization far too long to give any credence to the idea this is over."

With a kiss for her son, Jana Scott joined her husband and the Range Rover departed.

Madden stared after them, his face pale, his eyes wide.

Eva nudged him. "You coming back in, husband?"

Madden sighed. "No, I think I am going to walk for a while. Don't worry, I'll be back. Go on in. I don't want you catching a chill, not after all we have been through.

Madden wandered off, the stocky form of Rick Larrion detaching from the shadows of the hall to trail him.

"He should not have done that," Elaine cautioned.

"I understand."

"No, you don't," Elaine replied with a mysterious smile. Let's get you back in and you will find out."

In the hall, it very quickly became apparent to Eva that without Madden at her side, she was a target for all the local men. A line began to grow as more and more of them sought to give her a kiss. Rather than protect her, Elaine encouraged this with a smug smile. Eva began to panic as one elderly gentleman planted a kiss squarely on her lips and then began a lecture in Swedish, punctuated with many gesticulations. Not understanding a word of Swedish, Eva smiled graciously and nodded when she thought it was the right time.

As he shuffled off beyond the red and white banners draped about the tables, Eva looked at Elaine for an explanation.

"Don't ask me," she shrugged. "My Swedish isn't much better than yours."

"He said he admired your gusto in shouting louder than your husband during the ceremony, and he wishes he had a wife like you." A small rotund woman with elaborately braided brown hair and a mischievous twinkle in her eye sat down beside them.

Eva beamed a smile, recalling the declaration of their vows, and how the partner with the loudest voice was considered dominant. "Rikke, there you are. Was there more to what he said?"

"That is all I want to translate for you, Mrs. Scott." Rikke was nothing if not proper. "Still, your husband should re-join you before the next tradition of young men claiming an abandoned bride happens."

Eva began to panic glancing around the room for signs of movement. Nothing. She looked back at her two companions, and Elaine began to tremble with suppressed mirth.

"You monsters," she exclaimed, and both women burst out in peals of laughter.

"Were that true, my Eyvind would not have stood a chance." Rikke added, after they'd had a chance to catch their breath.

The door opened and Madden strolled in, to cheers and the raising of tankards. He spoke something in Swedish, and received more of the same. Grinning, he sat down and joined them. Eva took his hand and held it in her own. She couldn't remember ever being more at peace.

"So what did you say?"

Madden looked across at Rikke, who nodded in approval. "I asked the gents here if they had all managed to get enough of you. It seems you are very popular."

"You could say so. Still, now you are here, I only have my eyes on one man. Would you ladies excuse us, please?"

A brief look passed Elaine's face indicating she was less than pleased with this idea, but she rose from her chair. "Rikke, let us leave the lovebirds alone and see what trouble we can find for ourselves."

When their companions had moved away and been pulled onto the dance floor, Eva pulled Madden closer for a kiss, causing yet more riotous cheering. Yet, what she had sought she had found. A hesitancy. The passion was there, but it was forced, as if for her benefit.

"What is it?"

Madden blinked, caught off guard. "I don't understand. What is what?"

Eva pointed at herself. "Psychologist. I can tell these things. Besides, I have this magical little bundle of joy telling me there's a problem."

Madden balled his fist, thumping the table with repressed frustration. "Since Gehenna, since you saved me, I haven't felt right; it's as if I am connected to something just out of sight. There is an absence, Eva, if I am brutally honest. I think despite all the trouble it brought, despite all done to save me, I miss the demon."

"Do you regret how it has all turned out?"

"No, of course not. We are going to have a child. A beautiful child who, by all accounts, has something special going on already. Marrying you is the best thing I have ever done. It's just hard to adjust at times."

"And yet it's the reason we are here. We have the time to adapt to the world as it now is. You are unique. Not even Jesus was resurrected twice, and you are still here."

Madden raised his glass. "A toast, to Janus, wherever he may be. May Hell spare him eternal torment."

That was the crux of the matter. Madden was crippled and helpless while Janus had saved them, stabbing the demon Iuvart with the obsidian dagger before jumping through the portal to hell. It was a large cross for any man to bear, but they had all played their part.

"Eva?"

Her thoughts interrupted by the sound of his voice, she

came back to the present. Madden was in front of her, glass still raised.

"To Janus. May he rest in peace."

Eva raised her own glass in silent tribute and nodded. Janus Lohnes had saved her skin many times during the past year. She never truly understood him, but he was the one person missingshe would have had here. He was a guest of honour, absent or not.

Done with dancing, Swanson and Gila joined them. For two people so utterly different, they made a great team. Swanson, with his mousy blonde hair lounged, indolently in a seat, while Gila, wearing her usual black bob clipped up, missed nothing. Eva suspected this was by design.

"Is it really over?" Eva asked the select group around her.

"We have no reason to suspect otherwise," answered Gila, trying to be sincere. "Events are moving on. They don't appear to be hunting you any more, though you pop up in the occasional interest article. Everybody is aware that monumental events threatened to overtake us, but we are still here, and people are quick to forget. ARC has a good handle on the funnelling of information to the public."

"And what of you two?" Madden asked. "Do you go back to the same jobs?"

"There have been opportunities," Swanson admitted. "As you know, the Coptic community was heavily involved in the recent insurgency. A new Pope has been elected. They wanted me to stand."

Madden grinned. "Pope Swanson. Well, wouldn't the appointment have been nice."

"There's more. There is a great amount of interest in promoting Gila to the Council of Twelve. We shall see how that pans out."

The conversation continued, and Eva let her mind wander, comforted by the presence of those closest to her. She looked out of a nearby window, enjoying the sight of a healthy forest. But something was wrong. The sky darkened. A flock of starlings burst from the trees. Everybody around her was oblivious to this fact. Eva pointed, but they ignored her and carried on talking, the sound of their voices blurred and indistinct.

Outside, the darkened sky had become a deep, angry shade of red. Eva stood and walked to the window. The sky had begun to swirl, collapsing in on itself not fifty yards down the road from the hall. Cars left furrows in the dirt, as a force stronger than gravity sucked at them, pulling them in. The swirling became a vortex, a yawning maw screaming her name as it devoured everything it touched. The reek of carrion assaulted her nostrils, and the vortex flexed.

A titanic presence loomed on the other side of the hole in space. It exuded menace, directed solely at her. Even though the vortex was too small, it tried to shove its way through, roaring with unbridled rage. Eyes blacker than night beheld her. Fangs longer than she was tall gnashed from beneath snarling lips.

It roared, and she flinched. Hulking shoulders forced their way through into her reality, and it bellowed one word.

"EVA!"

CHAPTER TWO

Eva screamed and everybody in the room went silent.

In an instant, Madden was peering into her eyes. "Eva, what is it? What did you see?"

Beyond words, unsure of whether the vision had been real, but still smelling the stench of decayed flesh, Eva pointed at the window.

"There's something out there," warned Swanson, following her gaze.

Before anybody could stop him, Madden leapt to his feet, the force of his movement whipping the air past Eva's face. Gila tried to shout a warning, but Madden was out the door and outside the window in moments. He appeared in the distance, as if chasing something or someone, but then stopped and turned back. Approaching the window, he shrugged and mouthed the word 'Nothing'.

"So two of you saw something out there?" Madden asked when he re-entered the hall. He knelt next to Eva, holding her hand.

"There was somebody out there, peering in from the

side, when I heard Eva scream," Swanson stated. "I stake my reputation on it. Eva, what did you see?"

Sure now she was safe, Eva said, "Death. Fire. The end of this place. I saw the Behemoth. It hungers for me."

By the sudden increase in pulse, and the sweat on his hand, Eva knew he was incensed. Madden turned his rage on Swanson.

"You said we would be safe here! You said this was over!"

"Who knows what drove Eva to see what she did," Swanson countered. "I saw something, too. What it was, I cannot say. I thought it was a man."

Eva felt suddenly drained, and halted the argument before it became any more heated. "Madden, today has been the best day of my life, but I'm exhausted. Can we go home?"

He squeezed her hand in response. "Of course, we can."

That night Eva's dreams were haunted by the recent past. Iuvart, Behemoth, Brian. Other nameless faces and shapeless forms. All sought her. Portals sprang open and nightmares erupted from them, beings of twisted flesh screamed obscenities at her. Gibbous, drooling creatures with leather wings stretched impossibly thin over deformed skeletal protrusions hungered for her. Only one thing kept them from her. Her unborn child was a beacon of hope and, in times gone by, her most ardent protector. Somehow, the child within held them at bay.

In time, she woke, gasping for air and sweating profusely. Laying her arms around her middle she hugged her bump, aware that as was his preference lately, Madden would be up already.

"Thank you," she said to it, sure in the belief her gratitude was received.

Resting for a moment, Eva wondered what Madden was doing, until she heard two axes chopping wood outside.

She groaned as she stood, throwing her hands out to the wall to steady herself before making her way to the window. Throwing it open, she breathed in the chill of the early morning air, scented heavily with pine. Having adapted to many Nordic customs, she accepted the cold air was good for mother and baby alike. The two-toned call of a cuckoo echoed through the forest. Mornings were always her favorite time. The day was still so innocent.

Outside Madden and Eyvind were trading blows as they assaulted a pile of wood. Eyvind Moltke was an accountant by trade, but owned and ran the house with Rikke, hiding, by his own admission, persons of significant ARC interest. He was a heavy set man with dark, curly hair threatening to reach down his back. He wore a jacket unlike Madden who had stripped bare to the waist, covered in sweat, and glistening in the early morning.

Intense physical exercise had been a large part of his recuperation, and the way the muscles of his shoulders bunched under his skin, Eva could see the benefits of the therapy. He glanced up and waved, resuming his attack on the woodpile shortly thereafter.

Not wanting to distract him anymore, Eva washed and dressed, making her way down to the kitchen. Scents of breakfast assailed her as she opened the door. Toast, bacon, and the sweet scent of honey made her realize how truly famished she was.

Sitting at the table near the bay window offered a fantastic view of the road and forest beyond. She smiled at Gila who had a mouth full of honeyed oatmeal. The house was large enough that Eva and Madden shared it with both Eyvind and Rikke, as well as Swanson and Gila. In an instant, Rikke had poured her a large steaming mug of decaffeinated coffee and placed a large plate piled with toast and bacon under her nose. The combined smell of the two was enough to make her ignore her first sip of coffee.

Nodding thanks, Eva eyed the food, slathering butter all over the toast and placing a healthy amount of bacon between two slices.

"Bacon isn't the best food to be eating in such a quantity this late in your pregnancy," Gila warned.

Eva tilted her head to one side, seeking inward for any sign of warning. There was none.

"Baby says it is fine," she countered.

Gila shrugged. The answer was good enough for her.

In the preceding months, what could only be described as a force had protected Eva any number of times. It came from within, and grew stronger as the pregnancy advanced. Eva had been forced to reassess the limits of reality since meeting her current companions. Demons should not exist, yet they did. Her reasoning stretched now to include the idea that if evil existed then so did good. In short, Eva concluded she had found faith. What good that did her she had yet to determine.

Eva made short work of the food, and relaxed with the coffee.

"Feel better?" Gila moved to an adjacent seat so they could chat without shouting. The large whitewashed kitchen had a wood burning stove that crackled and spat as pine logs too full of resin burned down, enhancing the scent of the trees outside.

"I do, now," Eva admitted. "Not a good night's sleep. Being awake and exhausted is the easy option lately."

"You went through a hell of an ordeal, Eva."

"Yeah, literally," Eva agreed and the two women laughed. "Madden is right, though. There is something missing since the portal closed. He is the same man on the surface, yet there is an indefinable absence to him."

"You are aware of what defined Madden, and you saw part of that ripped away. He might still be that same man, but you have to seek those parts of him and bring them to the surface. He has a wife and soon, a child to protect. He just needs to remember that."

"He remembers that all too well," Madden said from the doorway. "But there is more to it than that. Eva is the qualified professional. With *what* do I protect my wife and unborn child beyond my irascible nature and a skill set unique to a demon that no longer exists? Where do we go now if not at the whim and difference of ARC? We may as well be prisoners for all that our cell is rustic and surrounded by forest. I'm gonna take a shower."

Not giving Eva a chance to placate him, Madden crossed the kitchen, slamming the door behind him. Eva winced at the noise.

"You need to make him see, Eva. Go after him. Do not let this fester." Gila's stare was deadly serious.

"What if he just doesn't want to?"

"Then all you fought for on that mountain is lost."

Perplexed at what she was supposed to do to convince Madden that there was more to life than being a reborn demon, Eva crept hesitantly up the stairs. The ancient carpet, worn and, in places, entirely bare, mixed with the scents of the aged pine beams to create an aroma straight from antiquity. The wooden steps creaked under foot, reminding Eva, if she needed such reminders, of her delicate condition. As she topped the stairs, the sound of water rushing from the showerhead indicated Madden was already in. She decided to wait for him to come to the bedroom.

Reaching for the handle, a noise gave Eva cause to wait. As quietly as she could, she put her ear to the door. Two people were talking. The words were indistinct, but Eva managed to pick out the words 'born' and 'master'.

She threw the door open to find Elaine rising up from the bed Eva shared with Madden.

"Elaine, what are you doing?"

Stone-faced, Elaine answered, "Tidying up after you; someone has to clear up this mess."

Eva peered into the room. It was spotless, exactly as it had been when she had left it not a half hour before.

"Who were you talking to? I heard voices."

"Don't you ever talk to yourself?" Came Elaine's more than defensive reply. "People seldom make sense. Sometimes it's the only way to get a decent answer, especially when nobody listens to you."

Elaine shouldered past, stomping down the stairs and muttering to herself.

Eva watched for a moment, bemused, and then turned back to the bedroom. Examining the bed, she found there was a clear impression of a body stretched out on the side Madden usually slept. Furthermore, there were impressions of a second person on her side.

The door creaked, and Eva jumped, her hands going to her belly in reflex.

Madden peered in. "Sorry, love, didn't mean to startle you."

"It's not you. Elaine was in here, apparently talking to herself."

Eva described the brief encounter while Madden stood in the doorway, a towel wrapped round his waist.

"Interesting," he concluded. "Has she ever done this before?"

"Not in all the time I have known her." Eva realized that purely by chance, she had stumbled on exactly the sort of cause that would make her husband forget his woes: a mystery.

"I will keep an eye on her and ask Rick to do the same. Maybe we can have Swanson dig a bit deeper."

"Be careful. It is probably nothing. God knows we have all had cause to become a bit unhinged in the past year. She's probably innocent. Everyone goes a bit mad at times."

Madden chuckled, and gently hugged her. The warmth in his bare muscles comforted her as never before. "I'll be down in a minute. Go have some more breakfast. You aren't eating enough." He swatted her rear and closed the door behind her.

Back in the kitchen, breakfast had become a crowded affair. Eyvind had joined his wife, and Swanson had appeared. They were crowded around the table. There was no sign of either Rick or Elaine.

"They are taking point outside," Swanson said when he caught Eva's eye. The look on his face said as plain as day he was aware something was up.

Eva smiled at Gila as she entered, and nodded. Resuming her place, she helped herself to another dose of bacon and thick, toasted bread.

Soon, Madden joined them and did the same.

"Better?" Swanson asked.

Madden shrugged. "It comes and goes. I have good moments and bad moments. I don't foresee any change."

"Well, let me put your mind hopefully at ease," Swanson offered. "Given your importance in the events recently played out, you can consider yourselves operatives of ARC, with all the benefits therein granted. You are unlikely to want for anything ever again since you basically saved this planet and every living soul on it. Once the media frenzy quietens down, we can discuss where we go from there."

"How much are you talking? Salary-wise?" Madden asked, earning a smack on the arm from Eva.

Swanson laughed. "Madden, the ARC budget is almost without limit. As such, we don't tend to think in terms of financial gain. Ask and it is yours, within reason, of course before you decide on a rocket car and solid gold house."

"What about jobs?" Eva asked. "Could I, for example, resume practicing psychology?"

"There is no reason to presume otherwise. ARC has facilities all over the planet. Our organization is split between the theological and the scientific. We have portal research, green energy, research, logistics, media, security, and global defense. You name it; we have it under our umbrella. Believe me; you two will be in great demand. I might recommend you not going back to Worcester though. There are more issues there than the consequences of a few escaped demons."

Eva shuddered at the thought of the detective who would not believe her, and of Brian, under the influence of gluttony, tearing a small child apart.

"What do you do? We never really covered that in all

our time together. I thought you were just some on-call hero type."

Swanson took a sip of his coffee. "For my sins, I am the ARC council member in charge of defense and tactics. My responsibilities include frontline threat response, portal monitoring, and of course now Legion, your own private army."

"And do all of your family sit on this council?" Madden asked, a touch of cynicism in his voice."

"Only my uncle, Daniel. He heads up Security and Global Response. On occasion, other members of my family have been involved, but only on merit. Obviously, Jerome founded ARC, and many of the council of twelve are descended from the original members."

"So why are you out here and not wherever your council is?" Madden continued.

"We have seven sitting members of the council so as to always ensure a vote. The remaining five are non-sitting and while they have to travel to the headquarters every so often, they can effect better change elsewhere."

"Such as your work in Cairo," Eva provided.

"Exactly," Swanson replied, his face animated."

Eva glanced around the table. Everybody had stopped eating to listen.

"Thanks to your recent involvement, we now have a much more complete record of portals to Hell and where they open. It seems across the world, portals began to spring into life at the anticipation of the scroll being completely accessed. Of course it was not, yet we have records of all, and footage of many. Some in the strangest of places. One opened up right over the Grand Canyon, if you can believe it. Lightning was hitting the ground all over the place. We have energy signatures the likes of which we have never before seen."

"Do you think this is what happened last time?" Eva asked.

"Maybe," replied Gila, "although mankind was not as prolific back in those days, and, as such, the detail was sketchy. Some wall art, ancient hieroglyphic passages that have been deciphered hint at a cataclysmic event in the ancient past. There are a few drawings too faint to make any meaning of. Mostly word of mouth carried the tale through the ages. But there is one source we now know to be irrefutable."

"The book of Revelations." Madden confirmed.

"Exactly," Gila said in triumph. "The scroll of judgment is real. The tale is real. These beings exist and now the whole world has seen it. You have seen it up close."

"Whether they choose to believe it is another matter entirely." Swanson added as he spread butter on yet more toast. He waved his knife in Eva's direction. "You, my dear, might well end up the focal point for a new religion."

"Great," Madden said in a sullen tone. "I get to become Joseph to your Mary."

"What you get to do, Mr. Madden Scott, is spend every waking moment on this earth at my side," Eva replied, and pointed at her belly. "With us, your family. What more could you want from your second stint, third even, on this earth?"

Gila put her hand on Madden's arm. "All of our research indicates only one other had the chance you do, to live a second life on earth, and he only did it for a day."

Madden stared in astonishment at Gila. "Are you saying Jesus was a hellbounce? That He rid himself of the demon?"

"Maybe He was the first hellbounce. Maybe he was the original."

There was a twinkle in Gila's eye and Eva could see she was playing with him. Madden caught on eventually, and the table erupted in laughter. Madden took her hand to reassure her, but Eva could not help but think there was a deeper meaning to Gila's tale, as if her story was not yet complete.

CHAPTER THREE

THEY REMAINED IN THE COTTAGE FOR A FEW WEEKS more, until in early May there arose the opportunity for a bit of exploration. Eva had grown increasingly restless as the latter stages of pregnancy began taking their toll. She was sitting on a bench in the sunshine one morning with Madden when Swanson drove up. He was in the battered old green Volvo truck he had been using during their exile.

"Morning kids, time for a field trip."

"Oh?" As tired as Eva was, she was nonetheless intrigued.

"There's a market festival, the 'Vårtorg', today in the nearby village. It has to do with flowers and fishing, so a bit for everybody. I thought you might fancy a change of scene."

"You bet," Eva replied at once, excited. "Who is going?"

"Elaine and Rick have gone on ahead to check on security. You know by now this village is mostly ARC. Well, the same cannot be said of Unnaryd. Still, it's remote out here. There shouldn't be any problems."

"And that's usually when the trouble starts," Madden added wryly. "When's the proper transport coming along?"

In a matter of moments, they were aboard the truck, Madden opting for the open air and a bale of hay as comfort so Eva and Gila could sit inside. As spartan inside as it was out, the 1965 truck jogged along at a merry pace.

"I don't understand," Gila commented. "We have access to all manner of vehicles, most of which are far more comfortable than this, yet you insist on driving this pile of crap."

"We are away from the technology," Swanson replied, patting the steering wheel. "Sometimes, I crave simplicity, and this truck defines it. A rare chance indeed it is to embrace the past. You will both see there is much to be said for a traditional, rural life. These people don't know the half of what is going on outside their village. This is the sort of existence we strive to protect."

They were no more than ten minutes through the winding road of the forest, with fleeting glimpses of the cerulean water of the majestic Lake Unnen on their left.

"That looks enormous," Eva breathed, when the trees disappeared momentarily.

"It is, indeed," Swanson agreed. "The locals fish it with care, and they barely make a dent in the marine population."

"What do they catch?" Madden asked through the open window behind them.

"Catfish, trout, eels mostly. You name it, they have probably worked out a way to farm it over the years. You will see a lot of their produce on show. It should be quite interesting."

Eva felt her already-squashed stomach lurch as they hit a pothole. "You can keep your fish. I'll stay near something more fragrant."

When they finally entered Unnaryd, Eva found herself surprised by what she saw.

"It's so pretty," she said admiring the houses painted a cheerful combination of reds and yellows."

"What did you expect?" Asked Madden.

"Some smelly little fishing village crowded up against the lake."

"Really? I find it hard to imagine anything would be ugly in this beautiful country."

Swanson parked the truck along what appeared to Eva to be the main street of Unnaryd, long and straight with a beautiful white church and more of the gorgeous houses in their riot of bright colors. It was made even more so by the clear blue skies above, the sunlight reflecting off the roofs, causing the buildings to glow. He led them toward the lake and into a field heaving with market stalls. Rick and Elaine waited to meet them, trying to look as inconspicuous as a mismatched couple in black combat gear could possibly look. The locals paid them no heed whatsoever.

"It is fine," Elaine announced. "The only thing here to fear is the over smoked fish."

"Well, there we have it," Swanson decided. "Go, you two. Have a look around. Enjoy the scenery. We have lunch reserved in an hour or so at a local restaurant."

Eva looked at Madden, who shrugged back, and they moved off.

The market was unlike anything Eva had ever seen. There were many traditional stalls, selling wooden trinkets and jewelery, but they paled into insignificance compared to the enormous displays put on by the flower sellers.

"Oh, look at this," Eva gasped in admiration as they came upon a display full of tiny white flowers. "They are gorgeous."

"Mayflowers," provided Elaine, pointing at the small star-shaped flower poking out hesitantly from between two huge leaves.

"And these?" Eva trailed her hand down a stem where two flowers hung opposite each other. She leaned over to smell the delicate pink blossoms, and was rewarded with a sweet scent so intoxicating as to be addictive. Eva did not want to step away.

"The Swedish Twinflower, their national bloom."

Eva turned to the woman behind the stall, a kindly old lady who had so many wrinkles in her sun-tanned skin, Eva suspected she had never spent a minute indoors.

"They are lovely, just the most beautiful flowers I have ever seen."

Eva expected no response, since it was highly unlikely the woman spoke any English. But that did not seem to matter. She smiled, came round to the front of the stall, said a few words in Swedish, and took the very blossom Eva had touched, pinning it to the front of her blouse.

Eva raised her hand to the flower, and on an impulse reached forward and hugged the woman. As she held her close, the woman spoke in her ear.

"Wear it and be safe always, even unto Perditions Flame."

Eva stood up. The woman nodded at her and waved

them on. She looked back, confused. Already, the old lady had disappeared in the press of the crowd.

"Ah, there you are," Madden said, leaning in to kiss her cheek. "We lost you for a moment. Where did you get that lovely flower?"

Eva reached up to touch the twinflower, confused. "The old lady. I..."

Madden smiled. "It's all good. Come on; let's keep exploring while we still can."

All too soon, Swanson appeared, waving them on.

"Come on, time for lunch. We can explore more, later. This market goes on well into the evening."

Turning away, he led them in what seemed to Eva a forced march across the field. It was not unpleasant. The lake was so calm it, looked like someone had laid a sheet of glass across the top. Indeed, for some strange reason, Eva felt she could walk across the surface should she but try. A feeling of peace and contentment radiated all around her.

As it was, she marvelled at the simplicity of the building Swanson led them. White walls, an enormous red wedged roof. The structure was simple, but it appeared so much more grand than everything else. A sign on the door read 'Fisk', which she took to mean fish.

Inside, Swanson ushered them all through the white fishmongers to a series of tables in the wood-beamed restaurant. A few other people were in the room, a man with black hair and two blonde women. Unusually, they watched Eva with what appeared to be alarm on their faces.

"You all right, love?" Madden asked her.

Eva sat down, leaning back as much as the wooden

chairs would allow. "Those people we passed. I swear they know me, or recognise me at least."

"Have you ever seen them before?" Swanson asked, leaning past Gila to have a look. Eva followed his gaze. The other party all had their heads down, appearing as if there was no greater concern for them at that moment than the meal on their plates.

"No. I have never seen them before. They weren't at the wedding otherwise you would have known it."

"Let's find out what is going on, then," Swanson decided.

As he was about to get up, a blonde waitress wearing a polo shirt bearing the name of the restaurant strolled up to them with a handful of menus. She took a breath to introduce herself, and then caught sight of Eva. Her face went pale, and the menus fell from her hands to the floor with a clatter.

"Okay, what? Who are you and how do you know me? What have I done that has everybody so spooked?"

"My... my name is Freya," said the waitress in the undulating rhythm of her slight Swedish accent. "I know you. You are the woman from the mountain of the fire. You are who they are seeking?"

Eva spread her hands wide in confusion, inviting comment from anybody else. "Who? Who is seeking me?"

"All manner of nut jobs probably," Madden replied.

Looking around the room in desperation, Freya floundered for an answer. Eva caught Elaine's eye, and Elaine nodded back.

"I think it is best if I show you."

Freya turned away, and with shaking hands, flicked on the screen of a nearby television. "We have a satellite dish," she said by way of explanation, but Eva's eyes were already drawn to the picture on the screen.

It was ABC world news, with the usual blue rotating logo in the bottom corner, but the presenter was not Jeanette Gibson, the media head of ARC. It was an unknown face, and from one square in the top right corner of the screen they described the action in the bigger panel to their left.

"As you can see from this footage, the events that were believed to have happened in the Hindu Kush range of Northern Afghanistan, were not just hearsay, but actual, real occurrences. The person in the middle of all this is believed to be Dr Eva Ross, a psychologist from Worcester, Massachusetts."

The portal erupted, and Behemoth clawed its way out. Eva shrieked, putting her hands up to her face. The fear came back to her in an instant.

Madden put his arms around her, and from within, the child glowed in response. The memories of that dreadful day remained far too strong.

"This appears to be what has been described as a 'demon' coming out of this gateway. If reports are to be believed, the creature was driven back and the gateway somehow closed. That this woman is Eva Ross cannot be denied. Her whereabouts are unknown, although it is believed she is currently hiding somewhere in southern Sweden."

The picture of Eva was the very same used in America when she was on the run from Gideon Homes, the man later known to be the demon prince, Iuvart.

"Another communication has been released from the group calling themselves 'The Convocation of the Sacred

Fire', calling for Dr Ross to reveal her whereabouts and surrender herself to their custody."

"What the hell?" Madden shouted at the screen.

"Shh!" Eva hushed him.

The screen faded to black, and a single flame lit the center of the darkness. The flame increased in intensity, and was replaced by a handsome man with tied-back blonde hair, and smart if slightly antiquated clothes.

"I am Nibiru, also called Zerachiel," he announced in a strong tenor voice, persuasive and full of confidence. "I am the planetary leader of the Convocation of the Sacred Fire. I am here to bring you a message of peace and of hope. This world is destined to become Heaven on earth, a permanent golden age in which all will find sanctuary, and fulfilment. Our brotherhood is vast, and we shall lead you to this age. For we have sought out, and almost found the one true planetary leader who will guide us and usher in the new Era."

Nibiru leaned forward, his face intent, but his tone still conversational. Eva found she was hanging on his every word.

"In your great America, only months ago, was conceived a child of pure light. The Messiah seeks to walk amongst us again. The light of the child shall shine forth, and become as bright as the sun at midday in a clear sky, a beacon for us all to follow. She shall come into her spiritual heritage under our guidance, for we will help her attain this and nothing can prevent it. America will become the keystone upon which we shall traverse the valley of sin, and despair, and find on the other side the Promised Land. Prosperity, success, beauty, peace. All shall be yours.

The child will follow in the footsteps of her forebears. Spiritual leaders such as Mary, mother of Jesus, Buddha, Metatron, Saint Germain. She shall lead you to a greater state of consciousness and move you forward in spiritual evolution beyond the confines of this planet. Be warned, if she is not found, expect the world as you know it to descend to this level of chaos."

A screen popped up in the corner of the television, showing corpses littered about a yard. The camera zoomed in, and it became apparent these were not human corpses. Distended heads, overgrown limbs, grotesque bodies in a sick parody of mankind. Each had a face frozen in a rictus of agony.

"This is your future."

Nibiru broke eye contact with the screen for a second and Eva regarded her fellows. Every one of them gazed at the television. The other party was in tears, and looked terrified. Swanson appeared analytical, but it was Elaine who surprised Eva. Her face was serene. At peace. What did this mean?

"Where do we find this child of light? This serene and Holy being? That is the challenge besetting mankind. For such as Mary was mother to the Christ light, so is Eva Ross mother to our new savior. Indications are she resides in Scandinavia. Eva Ross, are you watching this? Do you hear my message? What right has one person, in this day and age, to decide the fate of mankind? There are bigger risks than your personal safety now. You have stared into the abyss. You, like no other, understand what is to come. Bring your child; seek sanctuary in our holy refuge. We shall raise her to be a beacon for mankind."

The screen froze as the recording halted, a picture of her own face somehow merged in freeze-frame with Nibiru. After a moment, the newscast resumed, discussing her whereabouts with a map of Scandinavia.

Eva looked round the room once more. Those at the other table were staring at her in part-horror, part-reverence.

"What do you make of that?" Gila asked even as Swanson was on his phone, issuing orders, and demanding to know everything about the Convocation.

"Funny," Eva replied. "They say savior, why do I hear sacrifice?"

"Damn it!" Swanson burst out, slamming his phone to the table. "Those pictures were seen all over the world. All this anonymity has been for nothing. All these months of protection. Wasted."

Madden reached across the table to take her hand and the gesture warmed her. "Oh, I wouldn't say for nothing."

"Remember, Madden. It's time to step up to the plate. You are going to have to forget all your inadequacies and protect Eva. We are moving out. Halmstad first and then we get council orders. Honeymoon is over, people."

There was a moment of unrest as all at the table came to realize the implications of his comment, but for Eva it was deeper. Elaine hadn't been nodding at her, she realized. Freya, the waitress, had been standing directly behind her. Freya had put the report on. Elaine had been here before they arrived. But how could she prove it?

CHAPTER FOUR

"No. That cannot be!" Swanson shouted into his sat-phone. "Not now, dammit!"

They had been on the road for the better part of an hour, following dirt tracks and unheard of trails in order to lose anybody that might be following them. Eva was feeling quite uneasy and more than a little sick from the potholes and random lurching motions of the old Volvo truck. Still, at least she was inside. Madden was sliding all over the place in the back. Her back felt every vibration when he slammed into the side of the truck.

"What is it?" Asked Elaine, who was at the wheel.

Swanson ignored her and dialed a number on his phone.

"Gila, the vote has been brought forward. They are recalling the entire council. What? Yes. Benedict Garias. No, it can't wait. Not if you want to stand a chance. The game is on. Best get to Halmstad, quickly."

"Problems?" Eva asked.

"No. Yes. Possibly. We will know more when we get to the town ahead. We need to have a conference. We have to decide what to do and who is going to do it. But I need everybody in the same room. This is not a discussion for the airwaves or the general public. Elaine, step on it. Hotel Mårtenson; enough with the false trails."

Eva kept quiet. She knew Elaine well enough by now to know her friend hated being ignored, even if it was by her superiors. The tension in the truck was evidenced by the fact Elaine did exactly as she was told and rocketed the truck to the larger roads. Eva kept her hands round her middle and closed her eyes.

All too soon, Halmstad came into view. As they crested the hill, the picturesque city spread on both sides of the winding mouth of the Nissan river and framed with the abundant Swedish forest. Beyond it, the deep blue of the sea spanned into the distance, merging with the sky at the horizon to form an endless blue vista. They descended into the city for Eva to find the detail lived up to its promise. Fountains on the riverbanks sprayed crystalline beauty into the river, rainbows forming in the spray. A landlocked wooden ship was bedecked in flags, fluttering in the breeze. As they crossed the river, teams of eight rowed under the bridge, each encouraged on in Swedish by an enthusiastic coxen. But the air, it just smelled clean and fresh with a distinct Nordic crispness.

"I could live here," Eva admitted. "It makes Worcester seem so dank and backwards. Oh, what is that?"

They passed a church, with a needlepoint spire rising from a wide tower. It was spotless, yet looked ancient, as if time had frozen around it.

"Saint Nikolai church," Swanson advised. "Built in the fifteenth century when this was still part of Denmark. The borders were much more blurred back then. Mind you, this town is centuries older. Civilization has been in this part of the world for a very long time."

"Civilization does not mean culture," Elaine argued.

"While that may be true, it offers the inhabitants much more of an opportunity to achieve exactly that," countered Swanson.

"Nor does it mean spiritual enlightenment," Eva heard Elaine mutter to herself. Swanson appeared not to notice.

There was no time for further discussion while Elaine slowed the car to a stop outside a modern-looking hotel with white walls amidst the brickwork, a mix of the ancient and the modern.

The words 'First Hotel Mårtenson' shone in gilded lettering. Below, crowds of people filled the plaza, many with great mugs of frothy-topped beer in their hands.

"You have to give it to this country," Madden admitted as he helped open the door of the truck. "These people know how to drink. Fancy one, Swanson?"

"I'll go with you," Elaine said, smiling across at Madden.

"Nobody is going anywhere, yet," Swanson said in a tone which brooked no argument. "This is no longer a pleasure trip. Our hand has been forced."

Eva held Madden's hand as they walked into the lobby of the Mårtenson. It was very business-oriented. Leather seating and panelled wood flooring in various shades of brown were surrounded by works of contemporary art.

"Is this a hotel or an art gallery?" Eva whispered to Madden, who squeezed her hand in response.

"I won't let them force us to do anything we both don't agree to," he whispered back. "I don't care what the rewards are. You are pregnant and we are not tomb raiders."

Eva nodded. Madden was referring to the time Eva had visited an underground mausoleum while following the clues in the Nag Hamaddi scroll she had inadvertently recovered. She had nearly died in an encounter which had ruptured the roof, bringing tons of earth down on her.

Swanson led the party to a conference room, opening a rather grandiose mahogany door that somehow defied the delicate sensibility of the lobby. Inside, Gila waited next to Rick, who was now armed. His pistol was subtly hidden, but easily available at the small of his back.

Behind them stood an array of screens and speakers.

"The council members are waiting, if you will all please be seated," said Gila.

Eva took a seat between Gila and Madden on one side of the table. Swanson sat alone on the other side.

The screens flicked on, the middle showing a confer-ence table with seven people sitting around it. Two women and five men. On the screen to the left, Jeanette Gibson appeared, and smiled when Eva made eye contact. Another woman with black hair and an overly serious expression appeared in a window next to Jeanette. On the other side, an aging man appeared, dressed in a mint colored polo shirt, unlike everyone else, who appeared more formally dressed. There was no doubt in Eva's mind he was related.

"Swanson, you little scamp," he said in a deep voice tinged with a trace of a Dutch accent, "how fares my only nephew?"

Swanson nodded at the screen. "Uncle Daniel. It appears contrary to reports, we have somewhat of a situation."

"You could say so, lad," his uncle agreed.

"If we could possibly get started and save the pleasantries for later," said an elderly gentleman, "we have several situations to discuss. First, who are your companions?"

"Dr Gila Ciranoush, you all know already. Next to her is Dr Eva Scott and on the end, Madden Scott, her husband." Swanson turned to them. "May I present Dr Johan Klaas, head of the ARC Council of Twelve."

There had been an audible intake of breath at the mention of her and especially Madden. It was clear to Eva Swanson had been keeping secrets.

"You were at the wedding," Eva recalled aloud, causing a couple of the other council members to turn and glance at Klaas. "What were you doing there? Keeping an eye on Swanson?"

"Keeping an eye on you," Klaas replied. "Your reward for your part in Gehenna was anonymity, a chance at a peaceful rest and time to have and raise your offspring."

The way he said the last word left Eva in no doubt whatsoever of his meaning, and it irked her.

"You mean you wanted the demon growing inside me to have an isolated birth so you could take action if necessary."

"If need be, yes."

"Well, at least you are honest. I can respect *that*, if not your motive."

"Whatever our personal feelings, likes, and dislikes, we have bigger issues now. Jeanette, what have we learned about the Convocation of the Sacred Fire?"

A look of exasperation passed over Jeanette Gibson's face. "Not a lot. Most of it is guesswork. I can tell you 'Nibiru' refers to a dark planet, an anti-earth if you will. Zerachiel is the name of a fallen angel, not unlike Iuvart. Media wise, there is nothing of note."

"Gaspard, do you have anything to add?" Klaas turned to the man on his right, a man with thinning hair and tiny round spectacles.

He shuffled in his seat, clearly nervous. "Uhh, Gaspard Antroobus, head of Documents and Antiquities," he said with a nod, in an accent not unlike Swanson's uncle. "A great honor to meet you, Dr Ross. Suffice it to say, we have no items pertaining to this group, though clearly the names are known."

"There are rumours abounding in the various religions," interrupted a man on the other side of the conference table, Pakistani, if Eva judged correctly.

"Sejal Khawaja, Dr Ross. I head up Biblical Interpretation. The sight of a woman pinned on the threshold of Hell has sent shockwaves through the world, especially those who denigrate women to second class."

"Well good, then," said Madden. "About time somebody shook them up."

"No, Mr. Scott," said the woman next to Klaas, with white hair tied back in a severe bun behind a deceptively young face. "Not good at all. I am Margaret Anderson, deputy chair. Do you realize just how many enemies you have made by being in the wrong place at the wrong time?" The Canadian accent was strong and Eva picked up on it instantly.

"Those same religions now see you as a target. You are a woman in a position of strength, globally. You are a force to be reckoned with, whether you like it or not, whether the man to your side is a demon, was a demon, or may be a demon again in the future. ARC, through its association with you, needs to maintain control of this situation, and, thus far, it has been successful. Now, if other cults or religions start claiming you, we have not only a security issue, but a logistical nightmare."

"Look, I didn't ask for all this," said Eva, the accusations and responsibility all being levelled at her were becoming too much.

"No indeed, you did not. It seems your place in this was decided in the distant past." The voice on the screen came from the other side of the table. "Dr Ross, my name is Petra van Veld. I am Dutch and I head up the ARC Treasury division. I am the paymaster. I am responsible for logistics, building management, funding, and travel. Your little trip through America, Egypt, and Afghanistan was funded entirely by ARC and had my signoff. Solely because Swanson recommended we see your story to its fruition, your actions have cost tens of millions of dollars."

Eva shook her head, placing her hands on the coarse-grained oak table. "So are you saying I just followed your path and should be thankful? Did you know that was where I was going all along? Why did we not just go straight to the endgame?"

"Because the endgame is not played out yet, or you would not be here. Benedict, if you would?"

A thin man, with hands bordering on skeletal, raised a control, and pointed it in their direction. The screen went black for a moment, and Eva glanced at Swanson.

His face showed he was not impressed. He looked at Gila and said quietly, "Benedict Garias, naturally." He flicked a switch on the table's microphone array, and the unit switched off.

"Don't act surprised. He likes that the reaction. Benedict has suffered from throat cancer, and his voice is somewhat unusual."

Swanson flicked the microphones back on. The black screen remained.

"Now you have no doubt finished explaining my, shall we say affliction, may we continue?"

The voice made Eva's blood run cold. A sibilant whisper that sounded like death might be warm and cheery in comparison. There was no tone, no timbre. The screen then began to show detail as a satellite zoomed in. The red shape swelling on the screen was hauntingly familiar.

"We recently received this intel from one of my research departments: Emergence Tracking. What you are seeing is the signal we detect from an emergence, or as you have so colorfully coined the phrase, a 'Hellbounce'."

There was silence for a moment. Perhaps ten seconds later, though it seemed to Eva a lifetime, Swanson said, "Where was it located?"

"Birmingham Airport, Alabama."

The words hit Eva like a hammer fall. "Brian?"

Gila looked concerned, and Swanson dropped the pen he had been twirling in his fingers.

"How? The portals were all closed."

There was static from behind the angry red of the amorphous blob.

"Dr Ross," enquired an elderly voice, clearly South American in origin.

Eva looked to Swanson, who nodded encouragement. "Yes?"

"This is Jose Barroso-Partada, head of Grail. My department catalogues, stores, and analyses any object of significant historical or religious importance. Firstly, let me thank you for recovering the stolen Nag Hamaddi codices."

Eva blushed. "Well, all I really did was pick them up."

"Be that as it may, they were important to us, as Dr Gila

has no doubt explained. You have also seen much of what we do, and hold sacred. May I ask you to retell the tale of what happened shortly before the portal closed?"

Eva closed her eyes. After all these months, the images were still too vivid. Reds and blacks, swirling visions, endless hordes. She felt Madden take her hand, warm and secure.

"I was cut, my blood was running along the altar to where your Scroll of Judgement had been placed. As my blood touched the seals, they dissolved. Beings came through the portal and began to fight the ice forming in the sky. On the sixth seal, an enormous creature came through, and attacked the ARC troops. The seventh seal did not dissolve, and this prompted Iuvart to make a play for my child. Madden knocked the blade away, and shortly after Janus stabbed Iuvart with it. Janus asked for the scroll. I gave it to him, and he took them all through the portal."

"So in your opinion, Dr Ross, all the artifacts disappeared?"

"Yes."

"That should not have been possible, Dr Ross. In fact, it is well documented the knife cannot enter the domain."

"Why do you insist on calling me by my maiden name? We are married."

Johan Klaas leaned forward in his seat. "No, you are not. Until I sign the document authorizing your union with this creature, you are Eva Ross."

Madden stood, thrusting his chair back with one leg. He leaned forward to the camera. "What exactly is the meaning of this?"

Unperturbed, Klaas glared at him. "The meaning is simple. A marriage occurs between two humans. We have extensive information pointing to the fact you are not defined as human. You were, until recently, part demon. The offspring Dr Ross will soon bear has already been reported to have had an effect on this world, saving her life. Before you say it, it does not count as maternal instinct. That is your doing. There is no classification to define you now. However, we may be encouraged to amend our position if you do one small task for us."

Madden glowered across the table at Swanson.

"I didn't know this was in the cards," Swanson admitted. "It seems decisions are now being made all over without all parties involved."

"You forget yourself," Johan Klaas cautioned Swanson. "Your family name may have weight, and history, but it does not mean you can set your own rules and your agenda. The council requires you and Dr Ciranoush in Geneva. Consideration will begin on the replacement of the late Cathy Knott as the final non-sitting council seat on ARC."

"Cathy was on the council?" Madden burst out.

"She was, indeed, and out of respect for her, as well as your own situation, I hope you will accept your task and see it to its conclusion."

There was no avoiding this. Eva decided cooperation was the only solution. She had no card to play.

"What would you have us do?"

The screen changed once more, a map of a lake, with more of the glowing traces off to its right, concentrated in one spot.

"This is Lake Bodom, near Helsinki. As you can see, more of the demon trace has been spotted in this region. The council would have you travel there and investigate the source of this. Normally, we would send any agents in the area with you, but as you can see, Swanson has greater obligations. We will send you with your guards. They should be all the protection you need. Logistics have already been set in place. Given your somewhat unhealthy celebrity status, we have mixed up the travel arrangements. You shall not be going straight there, since that is what others would expect for somebody in your state of health."

"What of Brian?"

The screen changed back to the council. Jose Barroso-Partada had stood up and was pacing. "We believe although the Scroll is lost to us, the knife cannot pass through without some advanced witchery. It is the belief of the greatest minds at Grail that the knife is being used somehow to bring demonkind to earth. Furthermore, since your blood was on the knife, it could well be you may well act as a beacon for the creatures."

"And so your proposal is to send a woman nearly eight months pregnant into a nest of them?"

"Better to keep them all in one place, do you not think?" Mused Klaas. "You do not even need to worry about where the other emergence is headed. Our theories stem from the fact he has been making a direct line for you no matter where you are."

Eva's heart began to pound. She would never be able to fight him off. "Where is it now?"

"Great Britain. Moving at quite a pace. I would get underway and do so quickly, Dr Ross. Redemption is a costly business, and a perilous one. Especially for you."

The screen went blank, and Eva took a couple of deep breaths to steady her nerves. In the space of a day, she was right back in it.

CHAPTER FIVE

SWANSON WAVED HIS HANDS IN A GESTURE OF DEFEAT at the now-blank screen. "Well, I guess it's game over."

Any further comment was forestalled by the simultaneous beeping of everybody's phones. Eva glanced at Madden, wide-eyed in confusion.

"Orders and travel plans," Swanson said. "Whatever their position on your nuptials, you are now officially part of the team, and they have your details. I suggest we get a move on. There is nothing I can say about staying safe you don't already know. These two will look after the pair of you. Listen to them closely."

Gila hugged Eva hard. "If there is any way we can get to you, we will. You have our numbers. Call us if you need us."

"Good luck, yourselves," Eva replied.

Without another word, Gila and Swanson hurried out of the room, both of them looking at their phones and exchanging confused glances.

"What was that about?" Madden asked.

"If I was a gambler, I would lay odds Gila is being considered for the final place on the team."

"No time to discuss," Elaine intervened. "The council don't like to be kept waiting, and we should be off ourselves."

A warning feeling emanated from her middle as Eva nodded at Elaine and began to stand. Her protector did not trust her bodyguard.

Eva did not have more time to mull over where the issue lay with Elaine, as it turned out they were booked on a flight to Stockholm within the hour. All too quickly, they made their way to the local airport with Rick hurtling through traffic as if it were melting out of his way through sheer force of will. They did not even stop to go through the passenger terminal, Rick driving them right up to the stairs of a nondescript private jet complete with welcoming staff and carpet.

Inside the plane, Eva and Madden took seats at one of the two leather sofas attached to one side of the cabin. Rick and Elaine sat opposite, and waited in silence for take-off. The plane began to taxi almost as soon as they sat down, and they were airborne shortly after.

"Go on, then," said Eva. "Tell us what we don't know."

"More diversion tactics, I am afraid," answered Elaine. "We need anybody watching to believe we are travelling directly to Finland. There is a leak somewhere, even in an organization with the security of ARC. From Stockholm we go by ferry. We have the GPS coordinates on our phones. It will be straightforward to locate."

"Not quite the horse and buggy tactics I expected," said Madden.

"We just need to keep moving," Rick said as he toyed with his phone, flipping it up and catching it. "If hell-bounces are following you, they can only keep moving toward you, and only at the best speed they can attain. We are faster, and it's nearly impossible to run after a ferry in the middle of the Baltic Sea."

"It's strange, though," said Eva as a chill ran through her. "I feel as if somebody is watching me, even now." She looked out the window. Beneath the clouds, lakes and forests rushed by with little or no definition from their height. From that distance anybody could be observing the vapor trail of a small plane. Eva felt in her gut somebody was.

It only took just over an hour for them to reach Stockholm. As they flew northeast, the forests surrounding the numerous lakes began to give way to more and more urban surroundings. The city itself sprawled to the northwest over a series of islands and peninsulas, and it was onto one of these the plane touched down.

As Eva disembarked, a large sign in Swedish with English translation proclaimed 'Stockholm Bromma Airport'.

"It doesn't look any bigger than Halmstad," she observed, "although it's certainly warmer."

"It's comparable in size, but the popularity of this place is higher." Elaine replied, reading from her phone. "It seems the Swedish like small and boutique in many aspects of their lives. There is a bigger airport, but many shun it."

"So our advantage may be lost?" Rick asked.

Eva watched Elaine narrow her eyes briefly, as if assessing a rival. "It depends entirely on how the other side think. Past experience seems to indicate they don't do a lot of thinking. The minions at least."

"Trust us, Elaine," said Madden, we have seen their

thinkers, and if this is anything like last time, I would expect we are on some predetermined path, whether we know it or not."

Rick led them through the passenger terminal this time, a clean building with square patterned tiles underfoot and a welcoming demeanor to all. Eva felt like the people from Unnaryd had just been transplanted into a different environment.

Outside, the typical nondescript ARC off-roader was waiting for them. The vehicle was large in a bulky sense, full of power where it was needed, with darkened bulletproof.

"Nothing like anonymity," Eva said with a smile.

"Given our cargo, I would expect nothing less," added Madden. "What did you expect for our so called 'Messiah'? A donkey?"

"If we can, please," Elaine said as she ushered them into the vehicle, "our ferry leaves in little over an hour. Logistics don't like to leave us waiting around when there is an urgent task."

Before long, they were once again dodging traffic. Eva lowered the window so she could watch the scenery as they travelled along what passed for freeways. Much like Halmstad, the combination of picturesque buildings and grand rivers of darkest blue made for a stunning view.

As they drove along the shore of Lake Mälaren, a building appeared in front of them. To Eva, it was flaming red, with a hint of blue, and blazing gold on top as the sun shone down on it. The building grew as they closed in on it, majestic and stern in its architecture.

"What is that?"

"Stockholm City Hall," said Elaine. "The building hosts the Nobel Prize banquet and what you see shining are the three golden crowns, an ancient national symbol of the country."

Eva shuddered. "Forgive me if I am averse to anything glowing red and yellow."

As they closed in on the town hall, the traffic slowed to a crawl, and then eventually a near-stop as cars fought for a single lane of access. Eva began to feel confined, despite the open window. She watched the town hall as it crept ever closer, focusing on nothing else. The child within her was content, and wriggling for space, but no other warning came.

Eva jumped when a hand grabbed her own, and turned to Madden who was watching her with a very concerned look on his face.

"What is it? Uncomfortable?"

"No. I'm fine. I could practically live in one of these huge beasts. It's just the traffic. I was remembering Cairo."

"The demons chasing you in cars?" Elaine asked, interrupting her. "I read about that. The report says they crashed and were consumed."

"Consumed, yes," Madden confirmed, "but by what? If we are dealing with Hell, what is all this ice? Why does it keep taking the demons? Is the enemy of our enemy our friend, or just another enemy?"

"Some stories allege the core of Hell is ice," Rick said as he edged around a smaller vehicle to the evident frustration of the driver. "Dante's Inferno, for example. Maybe there is more fact to that story than fiction."

"He is out there, I can feel him. If what the council said is true, I can't imagine staying still for the rest of my life.

"Sounds like paranoia speaking," Madden said. "Being

thrown out there by ARC is likely to do that to anybody. Especially, with the limited information they have given us."

"We know what we need to," Elaine advised. "That way, secrets don't get leaked."

"Leaked to whom? Demons?" Eva unclipped her seat-belt. The confinement was getting to her. When she opened the door, Elaine reached out to her, taking hold of her arm.

"You will not get out."

"Oh? I think you will find I can do what I damned well please, to hell with ARC instructions. This traffic has stopped. I need to stretch my legs."

"Eva, don't," begged Madden, "please."

Saying no more, Eva stepped out into the fresh Stockholm air. The t-shirt she wore above the elasticized slacks announcing her pregnancy as clearly as the bump in front of her was scant protection from the breeze, but Eva had had enough of confined spaces.

Walking as quickly as she could, Eva approached the swarm of people. Many bore placards written in Swedish, but dotted amongst them were signs in English. One such sign had the slogan 'Repent! We are not yet safe!" written in red paint. The bearer was an unassuming young woman with brown hair and glasses, wearing a blue Berghaus walking jacket and a white bobble hat.

"Excuse me," asked Eva, "but what is going on here?"

The young woman smiled. "It is a rally, against the weirdness that happened a few months back. People believe there is something more to this and we are being kept in the dark, blinded by media, from the truth."

The girl, for Eva concluded she was not old enough to

be grown, was English judging from her accent. "And you came here just for answers?"

"Look, the public deserve the truth. Strange events, a complete cover up and then this 'Convocation of the Sacred Fire' taking over the airwaves? I am part of an action group formed to demonstrate until we get some answers. We are hitting every key location globally. Here, Geneva, the Vatican for example, any key center of science, history, or learning. Somebody knows. Where have you been? You missed everything. The world is on the threshold of Hell."

The portal loomed in Eva's vision. Hordes. Infinite in number, terrible beyond words to behold. Behemoth leering. "I've been... out of touch."

The girl looked at her with suspicion. "I'm Ali."

Eva shook the proffered hand and, without thinking said, "Eva."

"I knew it!" Ali crowed in triumph. "I was watching when the Convocation of the Sacred Fire put your face on television all over the world! But that was only the other day. They were right. You were so close."

Ali went on, spouting what was no doubt in her mind, some very useful and informative rhetoric, but Eva had already stopped listening. The mood of the crowd had changed almost the very second she had uttered her name. There was a shift of bodies, the beginning of a surge. A restlessness threatened to overcome her, until a solid thump from her unborn child brought her back to reality. The same feeling had overcome those around her judging by the looks now directed her way. Worse, dread rose within her as she tasted a scent absent for a number of months. Filled with the stench of carrion, the dry, dusty fog washed over her, causing a ripple as it passed through the air. The restlessness turned in a flash to anger. The demonstration was quickly becoming a mob. Bodies began to press in on her, and Eva was forced to shield her belly, from all of the jostling, with her arms. Shouts began to materialize as others in the crowd recognized her face.

"You! You're responsible for this!"

"Why didn't you stop them when you had the chance?"

"Where were you? Tell us what happened!"

A voice then drifted above the rage of the mob, chilling her to the very core, for she knew it well. "Maybe she should be taken to this Convocation. To save us all!"

Eva began to back away, looking over her shoulder for an escape route. The crowd was mostly in front of her, their hostility directed outward at her and, to a lesser extent, the police nearby. Something pulled at her and Eva found Ali had her right arm in a claw grip.

"You aren't leaving," Ali said in a voice no longer her own; a voice speaking with leering overtones of desire, of the need to dominate. *He* was here.

Fear threatened to overwhelm her, a panic even the child within her could not defend against. In a moment of clarity, the realization flight would not succeed hit home. As she had many times before, Eva turned to confront the malevolent presence of Brian Ross.

Peering into the eyes of Ali the demonstrator, a pawn in all of this, Eva sought the malicious spirit beyond. It hovered there, out of sight but ever present, around the crowd, influencing events.

"Oh yes I am. You could never possess me in life. However you have managed this, you won't have me."

The hand on her arm gripped tighter, pulling her close. A force ripped at her from behind and Eva found herself separated from her assailant. The force within the crowd snarled, and the mass of humanity reached in her direction.

"Just keep moving," Rick said from over her shoulder, and moved to cover her retreat.

The temperature of the crowd reached boiling point, and fists began to fly. Not having paid much attention to Rick in the past, Eva marvelled at how delicately such a brawny man carried himself. Fists flew, he avoided most, and deflected the rest. A regard for innocent humanity left many standing where they could have fallen as they made their escape.

The same could not be said of the police, who reacted to the threat in force. Shields and nightsticks were used freely.

"The cops, they are under the same influence," Eva shouted above the din.

Rick merely nodded and guided her back to the car where Madden and Elaine waited, concern on both their faces.

"Enjoy your walk?" Madden asked, his voice full of sarcasm and dripping acid.

"It's Brian. He's here."

"Go," Madden instructed Elaine, not taking his eyes from her for a second. "You don't want to get bogged down in this."

Even before their car had moved, Eva felt the crowd surge in their direction. She held onto Madden, gripping his hand as tightly as she did the seatbelt, and watched the oncoming wall of flesh. The police were unable to hold them back, and many had joined the roiling mob.

"Elaine!" Eva screamed as they broke ranks and ran for her.

"Hold on," Elaine responded and floored the truck, piling through abandoned motorbikes whose owners had seen the wisdom of getting out of there, or had joined the mob. Eva did not care which as long as it granted them a path away from the violence. The engine roared as Elaine forced them over the protesting metal, and Eva watched the advancing elements of their pursuers climb over the remaining traffic, the cloud of rage throbbing above them, full of Brian's malice.

Past the bikes, Elaine drove them down a path, scattering the confused pedestrians. The bridge was busy, the road packed, but the path let them escape. The mob behind was only a distant disturbance by the time they reached land again. Elaine steered them back to the road and checked her watch.

"Ten minutes. Twenty less than when you decided your own well-being was paramount. If we don't make the ferry, perhaps you would be happy to row us."

"Don't you understand what was going on back there?" Eva asked, put out by the hostile treatment.

Nobody replied. Madden still frowned at her, though there was relief written all over his face. Rick and Elaine looked forward, Elaine muttering under her breath. Eva swore she heard the word 'headstrong' but chose to say nothing.

Freed of traffic, the city flew by, and very quickly they had joined the tail end of a row of cars boarding a white and red colossus with the words 'Viking Line' painted in large white letters on the red bow.

Still in silence, they boarded, and Eva found her way to the passenger deck. She leaned up against the white railing, the early evening wind adding to the chill of the metal. Madden stood alongside, Rick and Elaine like ghosts a few steps behind them. With a meaty blast of its horn, the ferry edged into motion. There had been occasions over the past year where Eva had been relieved to the point of unbridled joy at escaping a situation. Even the hellhole on Mount Gehenna did not compare to this.

The ferry slipped out into the beginnings of the Stockholm archipelago, and Eva began watching the docks slide by. Her eyes met with a person standing on a concrete promontory sticking out into the water. Alone, passive, and studying her. He made no gesture, no move to advance. All relief was wiped away in an instant, as Eva uttered one word.

"Brian."

CHAPTER SIX

"Brian?" Madden followed her gaze to the shore. "I don't see anything."

"There, on the concrete jutting toward us, don't you see him?"

Madden leaned forward, his hands clasping the railing with such pressure Eva could hear the paint crack under them where the sea air raised bubbles on the metal. "I'm sorry, love. The dock there is empty."

What was going on? The sea air smelled fresh to her, the wind now biting as the ferry gathered pace. She could not be dreaming. And yet the child within her, her symbiotic protector, remained quiet. tThe silence, above all else, gave Eva cause to doubt her senses. On shore, Brian, evidently having come to some decision, began to pace along the dock. They were getting away. He had lost!

"Try rowing!" Eva taunted as she began to lose patience with the whole situation, not caring who heard her.

The figure on shore emitted a roar in response. "I shall do something better."

Despite his bulk, and the unfit state of his reanimated

mortal body, Brian executed a perfect dive, with barely a splash as he entered the water.

"No," Eva screamed, "he's coming!"

Eva held her breath, watching in mute horror as the vision sped along under the surface of the water, an eerie white light showing the path of his passage. He aimed directly for the ferry, but veered away at the last moment, shooting off ahead of them.

"He's gone ahead," said Eva, still watching what she perceived to be his wake. She moved forward, catching her feet on the uneven deck, but the force of her momentum coupled with Maddens hand guiding her, kept the balance.

"He is waiting for us." She turned to Madden, noting Rick and Elaine were still ghosting them. Far enough to maintain the illusion of privacy but close enough to listen, and to act. "I don't know why I am telling you this, anyway. You probably think I am insane."

This brought genuine amusement from Madden as he burst out laughing. "I died, was reborn a demon, had the monster ripped from me on a mountain covered in other demons as the world tried to end, and you consider your own sanity? Bless you Eva; you care too much for others and their opinions. Can we go inside now? Whatever is out there can stay in the water for all I care."

Eva detached herself from the railing. There was no sign of Brian, and the bump on her front was suddenly a burden. "I'm tired. This pregnancy is more taxing than I had ever thought possible. Let's go."

That night, despite the luxury the room afforded her, Eva slept fitfully. Her dreams were filled with flickering images of Madden, Elaine, and Iuvart. At one point, Elaine chased

Madden and caught him, each then tore the clothes off of the other, and proceeded to make furious love while Eva could not quite reach them to stop them, her legs paralyzed. Their child intruded on the dreams, present yet strangely apathetic, observing. Over all there loomed the brooding menace of an indefinable presence, one wishing her ill.It wanted her to know that fact.

When Eva awoke, she reached for Madden and found the crisp cotton sheets disturbed only be her own movements. Madden had not come to bed. There was a russet glow coming in through the small circular window which did nothing to ease her worries. With a groan, Eva pulled herself out of bed, threw on her heavy coat, shoved her swollen feet into her slippers and, not caring about her ragged state of dress, went in search of her husband.

She did not have far to go. As soon as Eva closed the door and turned, she could see him on the deck at the end of the corridor. He was leaning against the railing in a relaxed manner, talking to somebody. Eva tottered down toward him, feeling the deep rumble of the ferry's huge engines underfoot, and swaying with the roll of the waves.

Pushing through the door, she found Madden and Elaine laughing as Elaine tried to orient a map.

"You will never get the hang of it with only half the picture," Madden advised, as Elaine opened out the map to reveal the entire Baltic area.

Frustrated, Elaine dropped the map and brandished her phone, displaying a small map. "That's why we use these."

"Well, what happens when you run out of power?" Eva replied, causing Elaine to jump. Just for an instant, Elaine glared at her, a look filled with resentment and jealousy. Eva gathered the map and folded it until it showed what she presumed was an area around Stockholm.

"Not quite, love," Madden corrected her, refolding the map. "We are a little further along."

"How long was I asleep?"

"Better part of five hours. You missed a spectacular cruise through the islands of the Stockholm archipelago, cliffs as high as mountains and forests of lush pine, almost within touching distance. Along the coast we crept, until about half an hour ago, when we set into the deep water of the proper Baltic Sea. At least you were up in time to see the sunset."

Eva turned to regard the setting sun. Deep and red, staining the sky around it and turning the few wisps of cloud vivid shades of purple, it was stunning. Off behind them were the remnants of the outlying archipelago, the outstretched fingers of Sweden. In the twilight, a few gulls could be seen circling lazily above the water

"They say it never truly goes dark up here in the summer. Were we just another month or so later, we could have seen it."

"Maybe another time," Elaine replied, and for a moment Eva felt like she was the intruder, not the wife of the man standing beside her. What had happened in the few hours she had slept?

"Hungry?" Madden asked her, oblivious to the charm Elaine was trying to bamboozle him with.

It was their task. Elaine and Rick were there for guidance and protection. Yet, Eva felt she and Madden were prisoners on a forced march, and she did not know what to do.

"I would love some food," Eva replied at length, "and a walk with my husband in the fresh air. Alone."

Elaine opened her mouth to protest, and Eva forestalled her. "No, I won't hear another word on the subject. We are quite safe on this ship." She raised her own phone and waggled it at Elaine. "We have these; send us a text if you find it necessary."

Acutely aware Elaine was a cauldron of emotions at this moment, and fully as capable of violence as any of the prisoners she had worked with, Eva took a brave step turning her back on her guard, and felt better for it. Not prepared to give an inch, she kept walking, holding on to Madden for dear life as Elaine disappeared out of view behind other passengers.

"What was that all about?" Madden asked after a few moments of silence.

"Elaine has designs on you," Eva replied as Madden held a door open for her, an unconscious act of chivalry speaking volumes about the innocence of such a complicated soul.

"Really? Well, I can assure you they are in no way reciprocated. I'll see this is made clear."

"It already has been."

Madden paused mid stride, silently mouthing the words of the recent conversation. "Is that what the little command performance was about back there? Reducing her to the role of hired help?"

Eva chuckled. "There's so much more to it, dear. But essentially, you are right."

Madden led them into an open area containing duty free shopping. The area was packed with people desperate to get their fix of discounted tobacco and alcohol. Immediately, Eva was drawn to striped onesies being folded and put on show by a blonde woman dressed in the crew uniform of white shirt, and dark blue waistcoat and trousers.

"Oh, those are just darling. You know with everything

that has gone on, the wedding, and now this, I have never considered something as simple, yet necessary as baby clothes."

Madden picked up the garment, fingering it for a second. "Then, let this be the first of many."

He handed it to her. Eva ran her fingers over the smooth fabric. Smooth as a baby's skin might feel. She felt a wave of emotion begin to creep up on her, and her eyes began to fill with tears.

"I'm alright," she said in response to Madden's concerned look. "In fact, I'm better than alright. It's Strange."

Eva held her front, closing her eyes. The child was there again, watching over her, a note of concern and even panic feeding through the connection they shared. Eva sought to calm them both, taking deep breaths.

"When you come into this world, oh, the wonders I shall show you," Eva said aloud.

"Your wife," said a voice with a Swedish accent, "is she well?"

Eva opened her eyes to find the female crewmember staring at her, curiosity on her face and a slight smile on the corners of her mouth.

"I'm fine. Just pregnant. Sometimes it gets the better of me. Above all, I'm famished." She reached out to grab a packet with the label 'choklad' on the side and handed the garment to Madden. "Put the blue clothes back. We aren't going to need them. Get the red or the pink. Also, get this."

Eva tore the wrapper off and handed it to Madden, retaining the chocolate within. "Go, I want to eat already."

While Madden carried out his task, Eva wandered the store, edging around people while she nibbled on the dark and bitter bar she had opened. Every bite sent shivers down her spine. Other than the clothes, nothing else interested her. Alcohol was not an option, and the many perfumes just made her nauseous. By the time Madden returned, she was more than ready to leave.

"Got a text," he announced, and Eva looked at her own phone. Nothing. The game evidently was still afoot.

Eva popped the last of the chocolate into her mouth and led the way out of the shop. "Where to then?"

"You didn't get a message?"

Eva gave him a knowing look, causing Madden to make an 'o' shape with his lips as he comprehended. Eva leaned up to give him a quick kiss. "You are mine, Mr. Scott, and I intend to make sure everybody remembers."

Madden took her arm, ushering her down yet another hallway. "Why, yes Mrs. Scott, I do believe I am."

The restaurant turned out to be on the top deck of the ferry, up a central flight of stairs leading from the top of the ship right down to the cars.

Eva made her way ahead of Madden into a large room filled with tropical plants, slanted windows, and an array of plush seating strewn about a white pinstripe blue carpet. A few people were dotted about other tables. This was clearly not widely known about.

"Good choice," Eva approved aloud to Elaine, who sat at one of the tables, food already dished up on top.

Showing none of the earlier emotion, Elaine appeared completely under control, serene even. The feeling inside warned Eva, a warning she did not need.

"I have ordered the best they had to offer. You need to keep your strength up."

"Indeed. The Swedish term 'smorgasbord' barely

applies to this bounty." Eva took the seat opposite Elaine, Madden sitting beside her. The aroma was incredible, meats and sauces, sweet and pungent reached out to her, reaching inside and tempting her to taste them. "Care to take me on a tour?"

Elaine pointed at the plate closest to Eva. "Pickled Herring, meatballs with mash, Chanterelle mushrooms sautéed in cream, pancakes, pastries and milk to wash it down. I recommend the herring. High in essential oils. Good for..."

Every time the word 'herring' was mentioned, or Eva glanced in the direction of the fish, her baby kicked and a wave of nausea swept over her. Whimsically, she decided to do the one thing she knew bothered Elaine and interrupted her. "No, I think the mushrooms will suffice. Why don't you trade? I know how you loved the fish while we stayed in the cottage."

Not giving Elaine a moment to react, Eva leaned over and swapped the plates, all the while studying the woman opposite, a woman she thought she had known. As expected, the fury was still there, and through the brief glimpse of narrowed eyes was the understanding she was being set up.

Putting on her most innocent face, Eva began to tuck into the Chanterelle mushrooms. The golden delicacy was creamy and delicious, meaty and full of earthy goodness, as anything grown so close to the ground should be. For a moment, Eva forgot her troubles. The warning was still inside, but her child seemed to indicate a reluctant need to sleep. Then it hit her. The mushrooms were drugged, and not lightly so. The baby was taking another hit for her, drawing the drug into itself

Elaine responded by eating the herring, looking for all

intents and purposes like the cat that had just gotten the cream. Madden, still not on the same wavelength, picked at the pastries, unconcerned.

It was only when Rick burst in, that the situation became completely transparent. He marched over to Elaine and grabbed her by the shoulder.

"What is the meaning of this? There is no issue with the car."

Elaine tried to appear innocent. "I was told there was."

"By whom?"

Elaine waved her hand. "Oh, I can't recall the name."

"Let me guess," Eva said. "Elaine sent you on an errand when she was coming up to the restaurant."

"That is exactly the case. It is against protocol, but she insisted you were safe on this ship."

Her own words used against her. Elaine was nothing if not clever and resourceful.

"So I believed. But let's look at who I am safe with, and what I am safe from, a lesson in logic and observation, Elaine. When I got up earlier, and came out to see you on the deck, you expressed shock, and surprise."

Elaine started to comment, but driving the point home, Eva spoke over her. "Elaine, I'm a trained psychologist. Hide your emotions as you might try, I can nevertheless read you like a book. You are attracted to my husband. You can't deny it. He is not a bad specimen for sure, and he has a rather unique history. There is a lot to like about him. I would make the supposition you have been slipping a little something into my food, just like you attempted to do here."

Elaine turned to Madden. "I did no such thing."

Madden moved closer to Eva, putting his arm around her. The protective warmth gave her great reassurance. "You have insisted repeatedly on checking Eva when she has been asleep. You did so earlier. To make sure she gets her rest, in her late stage of pregnancy, you said."

"Ridiculous," she scoffed. "I'm sorry, but how can anybody sit here and listen to the word of somebody who is clearly having a mental breakdown. Seeing things. Really?"

"Oh, it gets worse," Eva admitted. "Not only do I see things, but it has become clear to me Madden is not the only one with an interesting side to them. You just wait until you meet my daughter. She contained whatever you dosed me with so I could be awake. She is aware of you even now; the mushrooms were covered in the same medicine. I don't know what your game is Elaine, but I am going to find out, and then Swanson will know your true intentions just as soon as I can tell him."

The challenge was evidently enough for Elaine, who, snarled, throwing her chair back, and leaping for Eva. Food scattered as the table was shoved sideways. And then a strange thing happened; Elaine hit an invisible wall, bouncing back across the table, where Rick plunged a taser into her neck, rending her unconscious. At the same time, Eva began to feel the familiar sense of proximity to Brian, yet it was somehow different. Sirens whooped and outside, people began to run.

Madden jumped up and ran across the room to the window. "People are gathering on the foredeck." He stepped through a door onto the small veranda in front of their restaurant and began shouting down at them.

Sparing a brief glance for Elaine, who lay in a heap and was having her hands cuffed by Rick, Eva put on her coat and followed Madden out.

"You speak English?" He yelled down at somebody below. "What's going on?"

The passenger on the deck below tried to shout back,

but yet more whooping of sirens prevented most of what they were saying. A pause in the noise allowed her to catch the tail end of a sentence.

"...get the survivors."

What had he done?

CHAPTER SEVEN

THE FERRY REMAINED AT ANCHOR FOR SEVERAL HOURS as the crew fished a succession of people in life jackets from the sea. At one point, an announcement nearly deafened Eva as the ship's captain asked for anybody with any sort of medical experience to come to the deck where they were holding their catch. Eva got up immediately.

"You don't have to do this," Madden cautioned her.

"I might not be a general practitioner, but I have basic medical training. It would be remiss of me to not offer aid. You two should come along. You never know when they might need a strong pair of hands."

"What do you want to do with her?" Rick indicated the Elaine's unconscious body.

"I still don't know what her ultimate game is." Eva looked at Madden, coveting him, wishing he could take her the way he had once done in a hotel in Worcester, half a world away. "Do what you need to, Rick. Bind her if necessary. Search her. If you find whatever she was giving me, dose her up good. Then come join us."

"Do you trust him?" Madden asked as he helped Eva

descend the many flights of stairs. The ferry was in absolute turmoil with people rushing in every direction.

"I have no reason not to. We have to trust someone here, and Elaine has proven she isn't trustworthy. The question is do you trust Rick?"

"He's a great guy. Yes. I trust him."

"That decides it, then. I trust you, you trust him. That's enough for me. I don't know what we are going to find down here, but Brian has had his hand in it."

"Out here? In the middle of the Baltic Sea? How is that even possible?"

Eva stopped in the corridor, causing several people behind to mutter at her in various languages. She turned to Madden, ignoring them, and leaning back against the frigid metal of a bulkhead to try and take some of the weight from her feet. "When you were... younger, did you feel deep down there was anything you could not accomplish?"

Madden caught on quickly, it appeared. "Fair point, love. Even with as little zip as I had, the world felt like it was at my feet."

"And with all we have seen, all we have recently accomplished, do you think others, given the right aid and direction, might not be equal to the task?"

Madden looked down at his hands. Still scarred but nonetheless improving. To force her point, Eva took one of his hands and stroked it, the scarred skin under her hands the only evidence of the injuries inflicted by contact with the Scroll of Judgement. She held his hand up to him.

"Think of what you have touched with these hands."

Madden looked down at the hand, then winked at her. "I am. Not right here, love."

Before Eva could express mock outrage at how her husband could take nothing seriously, a voice shouted, "Do you two want to get a room? Have mine! But get out the damned way!"

By the time Eva and Madden made it through the crowds, most of the survivors had been pulled aboard. Those awake were utterly disoriented, and to make things worse they all appeared to speak different languages. She counted twenty five in all, and over each was the reek of dust and decay that had until now determined a Hellbounce. The difference was this group did not appear to see her as a target.

"Sir, madam, you should not be down here," a polite but insistent young man in company uniform told them in Swede accented English. When he reached out to take Eva's arm to guide her away, Madden slapped it back.

"It's okay, I have medical experience. I'm here to help."

"And him?"

"I'm her husband," Madden growled. "I stay with her to stop wannabe authority figures from laying their hands on her."

The young man was about to take umbrage when a smartly dressed middle aged man with iron gray hair poking out from under his captains hat interjected.

"It is fine, Magnus. These people are welcome here and only want to help." The ship's captain turned to Eva. "My name is Svend Karlsson, Captain of the Amorella, pride of the Baltic fleet. I have been informed you might be of some use, and my company has passed down orders we are to be of any assistance you deem necessary."

Rick's considerable bulk appeared behind the captain. "I made some calls. We have friends nearby."

"Friends in high places, I would say," Captain Karlsson added. "Is there anything I can do to help?"

"Did you receive any mayday calls recently?" Madden asked.

"None at all. We are the only ferry on this particular route today."

These people, these hybrids of hell made Eva's fingers itch. "What has he unleashed? Tell me, Captain; is this area of any significance?"

Captain Karlsson became solemn. "It is indeed. About twenty years ago there was a disaster in this very area. A ferry called 'Estonia' sank and hundreds of lives were lost. Those rescued were taken to the nearby Island of Utö."

"So that's his game," Eva said to Madden, who turned to look out to sea. She empathised with him. As alien as the concept was, these mostly unconscious beings were not at fault for their rebirth. Eva felt the connection to everyone. They had been brought back the same way Brian had. They had something Madden now lacked, and it would be bound to affect him.

Eva put her hand on his shoulder, feeling the tension in his muscles. "You all right?"

"I'll live."

"A fact you have demonstrated repeatedly."

Madden smiled and pointed at the survivors. "You can never demonstrate without demons. I just wonder why there aren't more. And why summon them back and then leave them adrift?"

"Delaying tactic." Rick had approached them and now shielded their conversation with his bulk. "These people don't know what you know, and unless you want pandemonium on this ship, you will help ensure it stays that way. They will take these people to the nearest medical facility, and as it happens, that is a boon for us. Just convince the Captain to do what he has already half decided on."

Eva turned back to Captain Karlsson. "What do you have in terms of medical expertise?"

Karlsson spread his hands wide. "We do not have much. You, a medical doctor, and a surgeon. We have basic medical training and facilities for seasickness, but not a lot more."

"Then you need to get these people warm and indoors, and definitely on land. You can only do so much at sea, and these people are going to be mildly hypothermic or worse."

"Exactly what the doctor over there said to me." Karlsson pointed in the direction of a very elderly man trying to rub the arms of one of the semiconscious victims.

"Rick, see if you can help him. Captain, Utö is how far away?"

"Twenty miles more or less."

"What are you waiting for?"

"Yes you are right, doctor. Please, will you excuse me?"

As the captain disappeared in a hurry, Madden whispered, "Do you think we will get there in time to save them?"

Eva looked over the deck, with bodies everywhere. It was a death trap. "I only hope we do. If any of this lot are so badly injured the inevitable happens, if they lose control, or if the portals begin again, there won't be a ferry left to reach shore."

"Well, that's the thing about being a hellbounce," Madden observed as he put his arm around her shoulder. "Sooner or later, you always lose control."

After a few minutes, the engines began to whine as the ferry changed course, heading north east. Shortly, there followed an announcement as to their destination and an estimate they would arrive within a couple of hours and be there a few more while they attempted to help the survivors.

This created a combination of dissatisfaction mixed with sullen acceptance it was the right thing to do. Eva smiled politely when an elderly Canadian informed her he intended to storm the bridge and take over the ship. The Finnish leg of his retirement tour was at risk due to a tight schedule. Eva sympathized with him, but knowing the cargo they now carried, kept her eyes fixed north.

In time, a dark blur appeared on the horizon, becoming into a low island, barely poking out of the sea. Eva waited as close to the bow of the ship as she could, the wind biting and burning her skin raw, but the closer she was to land, the better she felt.

The ferry circled the island, and Eva was stunned at the unyielding collection of houses springing up on what was no more than a wide flat rock a few feet above sea level at most. There was a lighthouse on the center of the island, and another tower nearby dominating the skyline perhaps six stories high, but elsewhere, everything else was single story. Trees grew around the houses and provided a natural windbreak, and as stark as it all appeared, in the early morning sunshine the small community actually seemed fairly pleasant.

It was as the ferry was positioning itself in deeper water off the small harbor used by the islanders that a horrific shrieking from below deck made Eva lurch forward. Another alert sounded.

"What now?" Eva asked the open air.

"Ladies and gentlemen, we regret to inform you the ferry appears to have run aground. While every effort will be made to re-float and see you on your way, we must ask you kindly to take any belongings you can and depart for the nearby island. One of the local ferries will be docking alongside shortly and once we have secured those we rescued, we will endeavour to see you all ashore as soon as possible. Please be patient, and have no worry, we are not in any danger."

"Great." Eva turned to find Madden waiting patiently with Rick just behind him. "So we are off on a little side-trip?"

"A necessary one, so it seems," Madden replied.

"What's become of Elaine?"

"Thoroughly knocked out," said Rick. "It appears she was using Methaqualone administered through the skin to keep you sedated. She's a strong woman. I made sure she had plenty of it."

"Methaqualone," Eva pondered aloud. "That hasn't been around for decades."

"What is it?" Madden asked.

"They used to use it in the 70's and 80's. It was one of the many 'little pills' circulating around dance clubs. They induce euphoria, slow the heart rate, and relax muscles." Eva looked Madden straight in the eye. "And increase sexual arousal." To Rick, she added, "but I thought this stuff was banned?"

"It is widely used in Africa still, smoked with cannabis. ARC has an extensive pharmaceutical arm. It would not take much for Elaine to have procured some. She may have been carrying it even before Afghanistan. The application through the skin is new, though. We will definitely need to go ashore. Questions need answering."

"What answers can you possibly find here? It's a rock."

"You would be surprised what you can find in the middle of nowhere," Rick said, shrouded in an air of mystery. "Just remember who you now work for."

. . .

Given the events of the day, the unloading of the ferry was accomplished with remarkable ease. The feeling Eva had of Brian's proximity never left her, yet there was nothing worse than a slippery metal bridge joining their ferry to the small island boat coming out to meet them. As they cruised across the stunning expanse of light blue water that separated the ferry, on its shallow underwater ledge, from the island, Eva took in deep breaths of pure air, untainted but for the diesel of this one boat.

"You don't have to say it," Madden said from beside her. "I know exactly what you are thinking."

"Oh? Mind reader now?"

"You are thinking two things. First, this place looks like somebody built a model and transplanted it out in the ocean. Second, you are wondering where the trail ends. Where we are going to finally find a place so beautiful we can't travel awhile and find somewhere more perfect."

"You sure you don't still have some demon remnant in you? That was pretty much it."

"It was easy," Madden conceded. "Just the looks of amazement, amusement, and longing all in conflict on your face. You might be the psychologist, but you aren't good at keeping your cards close to your chest."

"I just wonder if I am the same person still? Who am I really? The sensible doctor? The paranoid mother to be? The international trouble seeking agent? The sacrifice and savior of a race? I don't know any more."

Madden gathered her in his arms, where Eva had always felt the most secure. "You are my wife and whoever you are, whoever you grow to become, you will be at my side." He leaned down and kissed her as passionately as the bump would allow. Eva held on for dear life.

"I would say get a room, but it's clear privacy won't help the situation," observed Rick. "Get ready; it's your turn to disembark once the survivors are in safe hands."

Getting the survivors ashore and safely ensconced in relative comfort proved easier than Eva had hoped. The entire community had been forewarned and were waiting either on the jetty surrounded by white sailboats, or on shore with blankets. It did not take long to get them in a low wooden building retro-fitted to serve as a makeshift medical center, and as Eva did not speak a word of Finnish, there was nothing she could do beyond watch.

At length, the doors were closed, and everybody not absolutely crucial excluded from the building. Captain Karlsson was last out and approached Eva.

He took her hand in his own, a strong grasp and not uncomfortable, the fabric of his sea-coat rustling as he shook.

"Thank you for your aid, it was most forthcoming of you."

"It was the least I could do. How is the ferry?"

Karlsson turned to look at his ship, a behemoth towering in the distance above the tiny island. "The hull is sound. We are just slightly aground. Two tugs are being sent from the neighboring island to assist. We should be afloat in no time at all. Still, anybody with desperate need is being air-lifted to Helsinki. Are you in need?"

"No, we have something else to do in the meantime."

"Well, don't wander off too far. A few hours and perhaps we will be underway again."

"Like we can wander off anywhere here," Madden said as they turned east and headed for the white building by the towers. In moments, they had passed by the few houses, all painted a rich shade of deep brown with white framing the windows. A dirt track led them to the three-story building. It seemed to Eva they had hardly even moved.

"So, this is the Utö Atmospheric and Marine Research Station," Rick informed them as they approached the building.

"Nice," Madden said in cynical tones. "Stuck on an island in the middle of nowhere predicting the weather."

Eva, however, was not fooled for a moment. She had noticed a glyph on the door. A stylised 'A' linked to a 'C' with a small 'r' in the middle. To anybody else, this would have looked like a series of random scratches, but Eva was not anybody else and had seen this before. In Cairo.

"Rick, what is this place?"

Rick smiled. A small mysterious smile, and opened the door.

CHAPTER EIGHT

Eva poked her head over Rick's shoulder hoping to see something magical. No such luck. Instead, she was led onto the ground floor of a very busy office. Two banks of desks, four deep, faced an enormous map of the world overlain with wind patterns and other meteorological data. In the middle of the desks was a large meeting desk, evidently hewn from a single piece of wood. To her right were banks of television screens showing satellite footage. Small windows in the opposite wall provided most of the lighting. The room reeked of unwashed bodies and office furniture. It could have been in the middle of Worcester.

"The Utö center, a utopia of meteorology." Madden announced in grand tones.

Eva groaned aloud. "Very good. How long have you been waiting to apply such razor-sharp wit?"

A woman walked toward them from the front screen, and Eva swore she looked familiar. Black hair hanging in a ponytail swished behind her. The black jacket and skirt made her look severe, but there was an air of expectation about her.

"Well, I knew you were in the area, but I never expected to have the pleasure." The words were spoken in a clear English accent, the crispness of the words instantly grating on Eva's nerves.

"Do I know you?"

"Not really, no. But you are familiar to me. You both are. My name is Zoe Larter."

"The one who stayed silent," said Madden.

"Indeed. Everybody else on the team is so eager to get their point across, stumbling to talk over each other. They don't realize the value of just listening. It helps weed out the valuable information from the majority of self-aggrandisement. Doctor Eva Ross, my but you are blooming."

Eva couldn't help but smile. "Thank you very much. If we can get this little peradventure out of the way, I'm looking forward to concentrating on what's important."

"So what brings you here? Chance, or intention?"

"A bit of both," Eva admitted. "Is there somewhere we can talk privately?"

"Certainly, come this way." Their host led the three of them from the floor and through a very secure door, the emblem again faint above it.

"This is not just a weather station," Eva decided aloud.

"You are indeed correct," Larter agreed. "Anges de la Réssurection des Chevaliers has roots in many places, and the World Meteorological Organization has very close ties. The ARC headquarters lies within their magnificent glass headquarters in Geneva. Have you seen it?"

"Must admit I have never been to Europe before now, so no."

The councilwoman led them down a corridor, the fluorescent lighting and white walls reminding Eva of the hospital she'd once worked in. The hospital nearly responsible for the end of her life. The floor sloped down, and the air steadily grew colder. Their footsteps echoed off the walls, giving Eva the feeling there were more than three of them here.

"Careful now, demon. This hallway might hurt if I understand your kind correctly."

Eva smiled at Madden as he strode purposefully forward.

"Ooh, ow," he said. "Tingles. Sort of itches."

"I don't know if you read the reports, Councilor, but Madden is demon-free since the mountain."

"We don't get a lot of information out here," she admitted. "Limited access only. In here, please."

Opening another door, the councilwoman led them into an underground office, the windows replaced by pseudo-imagery appearing to Eva as though it was trying to convey natural light, but was ultimately failing. The sea and horizon as depicted were just too clear. A large mahogany table with screens in its surface was surrounded by opulent gray leather chairs.

"So what is your issue?"

"Rick?"

Rick nodded at her and addressed the councilwoman. "We have cause to believe Elaine Millet has been attempting to poison Doctor Ross. I confiscated a large quantity of Methaqualone from her when it became apparent she was dosing Doctor Ross on a regular basis."

"To what end?"

Madden blushed. "It seems I was the object of her affections and she is somewhat infatuated with me. I think she just wanted to get me to herself."

"I can understand," Larter agreed, eyeing Madden up and down. "Quite some catch you have there."

Madden looked helpless for a second, and then buried his head in his hands. "I don't know how I do it," he mumbled.

Larter turned to Eva. "That is not all the good news you have, is it?"

"We picked up two dozen or so survivors of we know not what floating in the Baltic Sea, which is the reason we are here. They are hellbounces."

"Impossible," Larter replied. The words spoke of disbelief, but there was excitement behind them, or Eva was no psychologist.

"They all disappeared with the portals. Every last one."

"There is something different about these," Eva replied. "I can feel them. They might not know it yet, but I am pretty sure they can sense me, too. There is a connection."

"Do you know what it is?"

"You were on the conference call, lady," said Madden. "You may have said nothing but you were certainly listening. You know as much about the knife as any of them."

"The knife, and your blood contained thereon. But even if it is you would have to consider something needs to use the blade in some way to bring these creatures back."

"Brian, he's responsible." At the councilwoman's evident lack of comprehension, Eva elaborated. "My ex-husband, the red dot heading for us when we were in Sweden. He is a hellbounce, too."

"I didn't have access to all the information on screen. I said already we are somewhat limited in our connectivity here."

"My, but aren't we the poorer cousin," Mocked Madden.

"In some ways. But in others we have far more to offer than a Coptic museum. Let me show you what lies here."

Larter pressed a button and a wall dropped away, revealing a cavern filled with dimly-lit objects.

"Another repository," Eva breathed in wonder.

"Yes, and unlike your collection of scrolls, this is believed to be the finest collection in the world. It is filled to the brim with Norse relics."

"Such as?"

Larter pointed at a great stone ship in the middle of the room. "That is reputed to be Skibladnir, the ship belonging to the Norse god Freyr. Legend has it Skibladnir hit a rock and formed the island at the will of its captain, in order to preserve it. The cavern you see was where it was found. It has never been moved, barely even touched. Those making contact with it tended to lose their sanity soon after."

"A ship of the Gods?" Madden's tone was cynical.

"You don't believe?"

"I don't see why I should."

The councilwoman leaned forward in her chair, studying him. "A very odd attitude for somebody who has been to hell, returned, and has witnessed the unsealing of the Scroll of Judgement. How are these objects any less biblical?"

"Can we go in there?" Eva asked, her eyes transfixed by the treasure beyond the glass.

"Despite my warning? Certainly." Larter pressed a button on the desk and the glass slid noiselessly back.

"Rick, stay here," Eva warned, and taking Madden's hand climbed to her feet.

"Why me?" Madden asked.

Eva could sense the hesitation in his voice. "To prove you are still special."

She stepped into the cavern. As with Nag Hammaddi, and to an extent the chamber in Gideon's room, it was chilly, and well ventilated. The ship dominated the center of the cavern, perched with majestic authority on a natural stone plinth appearing to fuse it to the ground. The great serpent head, once carved of wood but now lithified with the rest of the ship, stood defiant at least four times Eva's height. Horn and a forked tongue reflected the dim lighting giving the appearance of life as the lights flickered.

There was much more in the musty-scented room. Several stone pillars had been placed along the far wall, and they drew Eva's attention. She peered at them in the gloom. They were covered in glyphs and carvings.

"Magnificent," Madden observed.

"Sacred, every last one," Larter observed from behind them. "Thorwald's Cross, from the Isle of Man in Britain. Over there is the Ledberg stone from Sweden. The others have a similar eminence. They all have one common trait, as does every item in this chamber."

"It has to be the end of the world," Eva guessed. "These ARC chambers are so full of doom."

"Exactly. It is known in Scandinavia as Ragnarök, the last battle of the Gods where the earth is engulfed in fire. Look about you and consider how the artifacts here are really similar in subject to what you have already seen, if somewhat differing physically."

Eva climbed aboard Skibladnir, Madden helping her up. She stood for a moment in the musty silence. There was warmth and a very low hum she could feel through the palms of her hands. Eva considered the danger, and only calm contentment radiated from her middle. She considered Madden, and strangely the feeling changed to amusement. Her child found his presence on this ship funny!

"What?" Madden said, and Eva began to laugh.

"Your hair, it's standing on end."

Madden touched his head to find his hair was raising from his head and untied the leather thong he had been using to keep his hair tied back. It billowed out like the sail of the magnificent ship on which they stood may once have done.

Eva laughed even more and turned to their host. "I am not sure why you were so amenable to letting us on such a potentially dangerous artifact, but we are quite safe."

The councilwoman remained firmly on the cavern floor. "It seems there is a little demon in your companion yet."

"Or I have been reborn so many times fate has decided to forget me," Madden admitted, parading around with his hair floating about him. "What's this?"

He picked up a spear from near the bow of the ship, and balanced it on his hand. "Perfect weighting," he said, and handed it to Eva.

She did the same, moving her hand under the spear as she admired the runes carved down its length. "I see what you mean, and it weighs nearly nothing."

Eva turned to see their host stood mouth agape. "Is something wrong?"

"The spear was fused to the ship. No method has been found by which it could be detached. It is believed to be Gungnir, the spear of Odin."

Eva dropped the spear at her feet on hearing this. The spear instantly turned the color of the stone. "That's not possible."

"The spear of Odin eh?" Madden said, a mad glint in his eye. "Pray tell, where do you store Mjölnir?" He struck a grand pose. "I want to see if I possess the power of Thor!"

"We don't have Mjölnir. We do have a couple of items of jewelry believed to be Draupnir, and Brisingamen, but nothing more."

"Nothing more?" Madden said as he climbed down and offered a hand to Eva so she could exit the ship. "You talk about mystical relics as if they were commonplace. Honey, if I were you, I would be more worried about the Norse Gods' reaction to you possessing all their junk than any end of the world."

"Have you ever read any of the ancient texts?" Larter asked, her voice full of irritation. "Here, have a look."

Larter picked a book from a nearby plinth, leafed through it a moment and handed it to Madden. "Read it aloud."

Madden squinted in the light for a moment. "It sates itself on the lifeblood of fated men, paints red the powers homes with crimson gore. Black become the sun's beams in summers that follow, the weather full of treachery." Madden looked up from the text. "Grim."

"Read on," the councilwoman encouraged him.

"Brothers will battle to death, sister's children incestuous. It is a harsh world, whoredom rife. An axe age, a sword age - shields will be cloven. An age of wind and an age of wolves before the world goes headlong. No man will have mercy on another."

"Now pass the book to Doctor Ross and have her read."

Madden did as bidden, and Eva nearly collapsed under the weight of the book. It stank of the ages, the pages appearing ready to crumble. Eva peered at the text. It was all in a foreign script, the letters formed ornately, more created than written.

"Where's the translation? I can't understand this."

Madden peered over her shoulder. "What do you mean? It's written in English."

"I beg to differ. What do you see on that line?" Bearing the weight of the book in one arm Eva pointed at a passage.

"It is the line about cloven shields, or words to such an effect."

'Madden, all I see is 'skildir ro klofnir'. How are you reading in English? Councilwoman what does this mean?"

"It means this man is definitely more than he thinks he is. Tell me, how long after you turned did you realize you were different?"

Madden sat on the second rung of the ladder to the ship. "I must admit, I knew from the very start my luck had changed. I sat there on the shore in Montego Bay, the rain belting down and the wind howling. As the police stared out at the wreck of the car and mangled ship we had hit, I never felt so alive. Anything I did from that moment onward had no consequence. I could walk into a bank, empty the registers, and as soon as I was out of sight, they forgot me. So, in answer to your question, it was almost instant. However, whatever happened to me, wherever I went, I was there a split second. These others have been there for two decades. It may be they are more disoriented."

Madden paused, his face expressing sudden compre-hension. "You want to know if you can make them safe before they realize what they are. That's why you let us in here. What are you? Another Ivor Sarch?"

"You wouldn't!" Eva added, outraged.

Larter folded her arms. "You fools. All this points to exactly the same event you witnessed in Afghanistan. We have original copies of all the classic Norse poems. They all point to what was so well-documented across the globe, and we need to be ready. Your actions deprived us of years of research. You think you saved the world with what you did? You delayed the inevitable, and Gehenna was just a skir-mish. Look at what you saw during those dark days. The portal, the sentinels. Behemoth. The Book of Revelations has passages kin to the documents in this room. The only difference being they are poetry and not Roman scripture. Our defense is as it always has been, through science. Now we have a chance to continue what we started. You are going nowhere, demon."

Larter's words were suddenly drowned out as the world erupted into chaos. Red lights began to flash and sirens blared.

Rick came running into the chamber, stopping well back of the boat. "The meteorological center is under attack!"

CHAPTER NINE

Eva hurried as best she could back into the conference room, the secure glass beginning to slide across before she had made it through. Madden narrowly avoided being trapped, jumping through at the last second. Having sensed the lack of sympathy towards their plight in the moments before the alarm, Eva suspected to trap him was Larter's intention; Madden was clearly still a prize.

Despite the cold, the room began to smell of sweat, a foul onion reek. A desperate look of panic had begun to show on their host's face. Today was not turning out as expected by all accounts.

"What can you tell us?"

Larter pressed a button under the table and a screen tilted up. It flickered into view to show a black and white scene of complete carnage in the room they had first passed through. Everything not attached to the floor had been tipped or smashed, the large screen at the front of the room showing evidence of violent abuse. There were a couple of bodies lying prone on the floor, but the majority of the action was centered on the door at the other end of the hallway.

"Looks like they want what you have," Eva said as the dozen or so enraged survivors beat at the door with whatever they had in hand.

"I would say it's safe to assume they know what they are," Madden added. "Where's the other way out?"

"There is no other way out," answered Larter. "This cavern was discovered and the island was appropriated by ARC. It was the ideal place to store artifacts, an island in the middle of nowhere, good for nothing but measuring the weather. It was an unknown and unheard of sanctuary against the end of days."

"Until a ferry sank in these waters twenty years ago," Eva countered.

"Before my time. We work with what we are given." As the councilwoman said this, Eva watched her. Larter still watched Madden like he was a prize.

"So what have we to arm ourselves?" Madden began to search the room and Eva helped him. There were few bar chairs and the table. The search ended quickly.

"At least we can bar the door," Madden said with a grin.

"What good will blocking ourselves in do? Remember who these people are?"

Larter examined the screen and despite her distrust, Eva joined her, studying the picture.

"The question is, do they know?"

"I would say so," Madden affirmed. "Look at what they are doing."

On the screen, one of the assailants had positioned himself by the door, facing in their direction. The rest of the group had moved to the other side of the room, out of view of the camera. The figure by the door began to shout at the unseen group, encouraging them to do something. After a brief pause, another figure, a woman, hurtled towards him brandishing a knife. She plunged it first into his middle and then her own.

"Oh no," Eva said. "Not good."

As both figures fell to the ground, two portals blinked into existence, swirling and angry. One was above the pair, the other directly where the door had been. The lens of the security camera began to frost over as the already-cold Baltic air was exposed to the frigid influence of the realm on the other side of the portal. Mist poured out into the room, carpeting the floor.

"No!" Eva yelled at the screen, frustrated by their impotent lack of action.

"Amazing!" Larter yelled after her, enjoying the moment. "Oh, don't give me your evil look," she added when Eva began to glare at her with disgust. "You know we are quite safe here."

"I admire *your* confidence," was Eva's sarcastic reply.

On the screen, the portals were glowing bright, and tentacles had begun to reach through. Dull and leathery, they grasped for their victims with slow, creeping single-mindedness. Wrapping about the legs of both, they began to drag them screaming into the icy infinity beyond. Eva's horror was akin to the councilwoman's level of fascination. She represented to them a greater danger than the demons outside. Despite Zoe Larter's level of seniority within ARC, she only had her ideals and preconceptions to guide her. If she had seen a portal, and what lay beyond in anything other than the controlled circumstances of Nag Hamaddi, there would be a different look on her face.

"Creeping death," Larter whispered as the tentacles tugged on the dying hybrids.

"For us all," Eva agreed, earning her a confused glance from Larter. "Do you not see what they are doing? Oh, he is so clever."

"Who? And what do you think they are doing?" For the first time, a hint of doubt had entered Larter's voice.

"Is there no sound on this?"

Larter hit a few buttons on the screen. "Nothing. The sound has been disabled."

"Open the door," Eva said to Madden, who stared back at her, seemingly questioning her sanity.

"The hallway has been sanctified, as with any repository of artifacts," Larter informed him. "Remember your tingling?" They can't make it down here."

"But we can still see and hear what is going on at the other end," he said, nodding in agreement. "I get you." Madden opened the door, wedging it ajar with one of the chairs.

From the other end of the hallway came groans and shrieks as metal protested.

Sparing a glance for the hallway, Eva concentrated on the screen. "The portal is doing the demons work for them. They positioned it right over the doorway they could not breach."

On screen, the doorway began to collapse as the tentacles pulled the demon corpse through the portal. An eruption of sound threatened to deafen Eva as the doorway disappeared entirely, sucked into the vortex. A scream of rage slammed into them, continual, threatening violence.

In the cacophony, Eva saw Madden mouth the word 'Demon' with a questioning look on his face. She shook her head, and mouthed back 'Portal'. This was all very wrong. The other portal remained, tentacles thrashing about wildly. The being on the other side had been thwarted, but by what?

More roars of anger threatened to shatter the glass in the fake windows, and on screen, Eva saw three of the hell-bounces dodge past the tentacles and make it to the now-ruined doorway.

"We need weapons," Madden managed to shout above the din. "Open the cavern!"

"No!" Eva contradicted him. "That is what they want! That is why they are here! Objects of power!"

"What?"

"To open something bigger! They are not here for us. They are here for what's in there! We need to find another way past them."

Rick held up the bottle, and their way out suddenly materialized.

Eva nodded in agreement. As a roar subsided, she managed to shout, "Smash the bottle! Use the Methaqualone to knock them all out. All those drugs should take care of even a half-human."

She stood to go with Rick, but Madden put his hand up. "You shouldn't be out there."

"Well, I'm sure as hell not staying here with her!" Eva countered. "We should all get out of here and lock this place up. Better yet, bury it forever. They know it's here now."

The councilwoman, having evidently come to a decision, also stood. "We go."

Rick led the way, Madden following next to Eva with Zoe Larter behind them.

Eva did not feel comfortable with the ARC councilor at her back; an instinct was confirmed by her child. Strangely though, there was still no feeling inside toward what was ahead, as if they were not walking into danger.

In the hallway, the three past the portal waited, one or more of them yelping as they touched an invisible barrier.

"Works," Larter said from behind Eva.

The roaring began to lessen as finally the other portal was satiated and began to close. At the broken doorway, there was a last flicker of an icy tentacle and the portal snapped shut with a pop.

When Rick paused, Eva said, "Don't stop. We can get pretty close before we have to dose them, and I want to see if we can get any answers."

Rick continued advancing until they were no more than a couple of steps away. The three men opposite waited with increasing agitation, attempting to reach through the sanctified barrier.

"Sorry old bean, you need to have the right hall pass," Madden taunted him. "There's nothing down this way you will ever see."

"Time will tell, human." The lead figure, an old man, said in halting English with a strong Eastern European accent. At the word 'human', the other two cackled.

"There's not a lot for you to be laughing about, from where I stand," Eva said. "You have seen what awaits you."

"Maybe," said the man on the right, brown-bearded and skinny, "but you have a different fate. I have a message for you, soulless creature. The Well of Souls has tasted your blood, and your soul is forfeit. With every one of us the master creates, we become your brother. That infestation in your womb cannot protect you because we are your kin. It will not warn you. It will not save you. Every one of us rising knows only you from the moment of our rising. Unseen peril lurks on the horizon of your life and you will walk into it as an innocent babe. The master wishes you to know you will find your end on the shore of the lake you seek. He is ahead of you. He knows everything."

"He doesn't know this!" The councilor launched forward, ripped the bottle from Rick's hand, and threw it at the feet of the three where it smashed, releasing the drug into the air.

Recognizing the danger, Eva stepped back before Madden began pulling her farther down the hallway with greater urgency, Rick dragging Zoe Larter behind them.

"Hold your breath," Rick urged from behind his free arm, letting Larter go as he sought to fight the fumes.

A roar from the other end of the hallway indicated the opening of another portal, followed by a rush of feet as more of the survivors entered. Upon seeing their quarry, they gave chase, but did not last long as they soon hit the invisible boundary marking the sanctified hallway. Meeting the cloud of drug-saturated air, more of them collapsed on top of the three original antagonists.

"So, Councilor, how do you plan on getting out of this one?" Madden asked, turning. "Hey? Where'd she go?"

At the end of the hallway, they heard the door to the conference room slam shut as Larter barricaded herself in.

"Great," Madden said. "That helps a bunch. Well, what do those of us *not* a complete coward do now?"

"Hold your breath for one," Rick advised. "The Methaqualone was concentrated and if it spreads back down here, we are all likely to end up on the floor. Doctor Scott, I did not tell you before, but the dose Elaine was applying was reaching lethal levels. You are lucky to be alive."

Eva held her middle, trying inside to convey love and gratitude. The feeling came back tenfold.

"*I know,*" a voice inside Eva's head appeared to whisper.

"Luck, maybe. Fate, definitely."

"Fate, from a doctor?" said Madden.

"There are forces controlling us we are not aware of, will probably never know." Eva admitted. "I am long past the idea I am in control of my own life."

From behind the growing pile of unconscious demon-hybrids there came another roaring. It was no rage of hellspawn. Eva picked out a new sound: human voices answered by what was surely the remainder of the survivors.

"Rescue?"

"Perhaps," Rick replied, pulling out a bandana and ripping it in two. "Put this over your nose and mouth. It will slow the effects of the drug." He held out the torn material to her.

Fate. The word still echoed in Eva's mind. Fate had seen her in worse places than this, in far worse situations definitely.

"You keep it. I don't need it. Madden take the other."

"Woman, are you crazy?" Madden tried to push his half of the bandana to her but Eva stepped away.

"Maybe I'm just a believer." Disentangling herself from Maddens attempts at restraint, Eva walked up the hallway once more. There was a cloying smell in the air, sickly and sweet. It must have been the Methaqualone. The demons did not move, but beyond the opening to the room, she could hear the dying sounds of violence. As she had hoped, the drug did not affect her, though her child had once again quietened. Eva begged forgiveness for asking the being within her to do this again.

"When you come into this world, I'm gonna spoil you rotten," she promised, and stepped into the now fog-filled room. Carefully avoiding the scattered furniture, she crept across the room. There was silence, but for broken masonry giving in to gravity. The moisture in the air settled on her clothes and exposed skin, quickly beginning to drench her. As Eva searched for the door she knew was there, she felt a sense of urgency. Madden and Rick were still in the tunnel with the drug in the air. She turned back and, as she did so tripped, catching herself on the floor with a jarring impact to her wrists and knees.

On reflex, she checked her middle. All was fine. As luck would have it, she could see daylight through a gap near the floor. The door. Scrambling to her feet, Eva took the final couple of steps to freedom and pulled the door open. Despite all she had been through, what stared back at her left her stunned.

CHAPTER TEN

Dozens of people stood outside, many with crude weapons in their hands, and several showing signs of injury. The ground was white, covered in several inches of ice, for a good thirty feet or more, encasing some of the nearby buildings and reaching up the nearby tower. In the frigid air, it looked like a permanent addition to the island. The ferry had moved slightly, a tug attached and slowly aiding it out of the shallow waters. Several of the crew slipped on the ice as they approached her, including Captain Karlsson. Eva grabbed hold of the door handle as if her life depended on it.

"There are two of my companions down there, in a hallway filled with knock-out gas. It needs ventilating."

"Get every window open," Karlsson ordered his crew, and then turned to her. "Are you well?"

Eva checked herself over. "A few aches and pains, bumps and scratches, but I should survive."

He pointed. "And the child?"

"Snug as a bug in a rug," she replied. "What happened out here?"

Karlsson's eye narrowed. "I think you could tell me, could you not?"

Eva looked around. Several of the islanders had already recognized her, and from the general hubbub, were telling their fellows.

"I am the one the cult invading the news is after. They believe my child to be some kind of savior. We are trying to travel incognito, if such a thing is possible any more. What happened here? I suggest those rescued from the sea, regained consciousness, decided they did not like their surroundings, and made for the meteorological center. It looks like some of these good people found exception to the lack of manners and took matters into their own hands. When one or more of the survivors was injured, something opened up in the air and took them. Something with long arms. Something turning the very air to ice. Close?"

Karlsson's face could not hide the fact she had pretty much nailed it. "How could you know?"

"Because she was the one saving all our asses on top of Mount Gehenna several months ago," Madden said as he and Rick emerged from the building. "But for her, some ice would be the least of your worries."

One of the locals, a young woman in her twenties with a weathered face and long black hair, yelled something at them. Eva looked at the captain.

"She asks what you are going to do about this. The state of Utö and the injuries sustained?"

"Me? I am going to do nothing. I don't have all the answers. I'm struggling with many of the questions. Tell them there is a person inside, locked in a conference room by her own hand, who is perfectly capable of organizing whatever these people need. Tell them to speak to her, if they can get her out of her shell."

"Tell them they had better bind those left, too or dispose of them," Madden added. "Unless they want more of the same."

Karlsson translated and the people moved into action.

When they were alone, Eva asked, "Is the ship clear?"

"Indeed. She wasn't too badly stuck. It took barely anything, though with all the shaking on this island she would have floated on her own, I think."

Good news. "Can we go?"

The captain appeared amused. "In a hurry?"

Eva waved her arm in the general direction of the worst ice. "What do you think? Several unconscious creatures with no logical reason for existence are inside this building. You have seen the reports, the ones they could not hide. I don't want to be anywhere near them when they wake up."

Eva watched Madden as the captain considered this. *"What is left inside of you?"* She thought. *"How can you do what you did in there if it's all gone. What if it never left?"*

"Time to leave," the Captain decided. "We have passengers; you are right."

Eva sighed as she remembered they had another demon to deal with on board.

The ferry resumed its course with no more hint of incident. Eva watched the tiny island disappear into the distance, only feeling secure once it was hidden from view.

Madden stood at her side, protective of her as only he could be. "Feel better now?" He asked, when she finally turned from view.

"Relieved. There were more on Utö than the obvious demons." Eva laughed. "Demons. Amazing how commonplace it all sounds."

"Only to those of us that are used to it. The incident probably frightened the wits out of those islanders."

"Did it? They looked pretty organized to me, more like a militia than a mere community of people. They handled it pretty effectively. No, there was more there than you noticed. How did you translate the book Zoe Larter gave you?"

Madden leaned on the railing, shaking his head. "Ragnarök? I honestly have no idea. The words just leaped out at me in English. I still doubt they were anything other."

"They weren't, and your ability was what put you in danger. Zoe Larter knew it the moment she laid eyes on you. If she hadn't locked herself in the chamber, I think she would have found a way to keep you down there." Eva leaned into him and he wrapped his arms around her, a buffer against the chill. "I'm afraid I would have never seen you again."

"Such situations are all in the past."

"Maybe. She has a hallway full of critters to play with, now. The look of lust on her face was scary. Not sexual lust, but I guess more of avarice. Those demons are her playthings, and you would have been the same. We need to find out more about her when we get the chance. God, I wish Gila and Swanson were with us."

Madden stroked her hair, making her back tingle and goose bumps appear on the exposed flesh of her arms. "Well, why don't you just phone them?"

"Elaine was the one with the sat phone. I can't emphasize just how much I don't want to rock *that* particular boat at this time."

"We are going to have to deal with her sooner or later, love. There is no way Rick will leave her stranded. She has a lot to answer for if nothing else. The ARC council will no doubt have questions about her motives."

"Oh, I know exactly what her motives are."

"Then why don't we use the situation to our advantage? Let me speak to Elaine, see if I can get hold of this phone from her. Maybe she will do things for me she is highly unlikely to do for you and Rick, given the right incentive."

Eva stepped back, shocked at the insinuation. "You wouldn't dare. We're married!"

"Yes we are, and our union is something I'll never take lightly. I think you are jumping to conclusions, Eva. Do not forget, we are once again in conflict with those bigger, stronger, and faster than we are. They hold all the advantages. As it appears, our own side is fragmented; those we can trust are very few in number. We have to do whatever it takes in order to make ends meet. You just remember whatever happens, I love you. You, and no other. Now let us find Rick and arrange this.

The remainder of the journey passed slowly for Eva. Not entirely convinced of Madden's intentions, she knew his charms would certainly work on Elaine.

By the time the modern elegance, coupled with the backdrop of huge industrial chimneys, of Helsinki crept into view, Eva was bordering on a state of panic. Elaine was still unconscious; Madden had helped Rick move her to their car. The ferry had taken most of the day to cross the remaining distance, and twilight was once again upon them.

As they waited in the bowels of the ferry to exit, Eva closed her eyes. "It must have been dreadful for them, dying by drowning."

"I agree," Madden said from the driver's seat. Rick had

elected to guard Elaine in case she came to, leaving Madden with the prospect of driving in a completely strange city. "There is no worse way to go."

Eva looked across at her husband. There was a horror in his eyes she had never considered. "Oh, Madden. I'm so sorry. I never thought before speaking."

"It's all right. You have heard my tale. I was never sure whether it was the water or the impact responsible for finishing me off. It was all so quick and I was back so soon. Blink and you miss it type of stuff. I never even found out what happened to the rest of the crew."

At the other end of the ferry, the ramp began to lower with a series of deep mechanic booms. Soon they would be on dry land. Eva realized she was holding her breath and forced herself to relax.

"Don't worry. I doubt we will have quite the same reception here." Madden winked and Eva forced herself to smile, if only for his benefit.

"I just want off of this ferry. This journey has been long enough."

In due course, the traffic emptied from the ferry and, aside from a brief stop in customs, where Rick disappeared and left two very apprehensive people staring at the bound and unconscious Elaine, they were soon driving the streets of Helsinki.

Rick directed them to a hotel, and once parked underneath in a mostly deserted car park, the two men carried Elaine into a service elevator.

When the lift stopped, Rick threw Elaine over one shoulder, and stepped confidently out. "ARC bolt hole," he said in response to Eva's unspoken enquiry.

"Naturally," she responded.

"There are two rooms here. Sealed off from the rest of the hotel. The elevator is the only way out. Whatever you have planned, it happens here or it doesn't happen."

Madden opened one door, and Rick entered, dumping the unconscious Elaine on one of the beds. Lifting an eyelid, he checked on her. "Still fairly deep, but it shouldn't be long."

Madden poked Elaine's shoulder. "Don't you guys have kits for this sort of thing? Chemicals to wake them up?"

"We are not spies, pal. Mission Impossible this ain't. Elaine acted on her own in procuring drugs. We are fighting demonkind, not studying them."

"Well, not all of you," said Eva. "I'm going to try and get some rest in the next room. Wake me if there's anything worth hearing." Eva opened the door to the adjoining room, leaving it ajar. There were two single beds. She took the nearest. After rearranging the pillows so her bump was supported, she closed her eyes. She had never had never been this tired. The thought had hardly registered before she dropped off.

At some point in the night, Eva awoke. The room was dark but for glimpses of light around the drawn curtains, keeping the ever-present dusk from tired eyes. Letting her senses adjust, she luxuriated in the comfort of the bed and the thick duvet kept her snug. The room smelled of new carpets, evidence of recently renovation. There also soundproofing, judging by the fact not one normal hotel sound could be heard.

Eva turned over, expecting to see Madden. His bed was

empty, completely untouched. Then she remembered why they were there. Part of his plan.

Trying to make as little noise as possible, Eva sat up, letting her eyes adjust. She noticed Rick's silhouette standing next to the door of the adjoining room when fully adjusted to the gloom. He raised his hand, indicating he had seen her, and then moved it over his mouth.

Eva nodded, and leaned back into the bed.

Making no noise whatsoever, Rick moved to her bed and leaned over the drawers to one side, indicating she should take what was there. It was an earpiece. Eva took it and placed it in her right ear.

Rick put his hand over his mouth once more and his voice spoke through the earpiece, rough, but sibilant as if he were not moving his mouth. "She is awake. No noise. Let's see how this plays out. I have no idea what he is going to say either."

Madden's voice interrupted any more of Rick's thoughts.

"Are you awake?"

Eva wanted to say 'yes', and nearly did so. It was hard to remember he was not talking to her.

Elaine groaned, the noise of somebody waking very slowly after an extended sleep. "Where am I? This doesn't feel like the ferry."

"A hotel in Helsinki."

"Ah. We made it then."

"We did. Why would you think otherwise?"

"Try leaving Eva alone with that hulk you have trailing round after you for a couple of hours and you might find out. I'm glad you are here now. Where are they?"

"In another room in the hotel. It was pretty full and we needed a place to crash. We are on our way to the lake."

"Bodom? Good. All the answers are there."

"They are?"

There was a pause. Elaine was still groggy, and perhaps unsure of exactly what she was saying.

"Well... yes, of course they are. The lake house is where they wanted us to go, after all."

"They did, didn't they? In the big house?"

"The glass house is wonderful. You will enjoy it. You belong there. Mmmm, that's nice."

Eva wanted to jump to her feet and burst into the room. Whatever he was doing to her was having the right effect. Rick held his hand up, ordering her still. He clearly knew what she was feeling.

"I don't know I would enjoy the company of demons any more now than I did when I had one in me," Madden admitted. "Elaine, what did you do with the sat phone? The ARC sat phone?"

"I threw it in the sea the second we were aboard. If you had access to external communication how could I spend any time with you? What I did, I did for your own good, Madden. I know you still have a demon in you. I'm drawn to it, as they said I would be. I suspect I would have been drawn to it before you died. It's always been there."

"Elaine, I'm sure I don't know what you mean."

The sound of Elaine stretching and attempting to appear seductive to her husband nearly drove Eva out of her mind.

"*Patience.*"

The warning from her child came just at the right time, as once again Eva was on the verge of standing, and ruining it all.

"I will take us all to a place where we can be safe. From

there, we can contact those who need to be told their future. Our future. Together."

"Elaine, I won't make any promises. I can't. I am married."

"No, you aren't. It was annulled. They didn't tell you? A free agent you are."

Eva's heart skipped a beat.

Rick moved his hand to his mouth. "Lies. She's getting desperate. They just haven't ratified it which is different. Elaine interprets events the way she wants to see them. Stay calm and let it play to its conclusion."

"Maybe," Madden concluded, "but if you want me, you will not touch Eva. That is my child she carries. You will behave as if this conversation never took place, until we reach our destination."

"For you beloved, anything."

More silence followed, an extended period during which Madden did not return. When he eventually did come through and close the door, Eva heard him whisper.

"Get another room. Unprotected. We need to be there before she wakes. Or this is for nothing."

Eva closed her eyes, feigning sleep. She felt Madden brush stray locks of hair from her face before he lay down on the bed next to hers. Her husband had hidden depths; every time there was nothing left to surprise her, he pulled another rabbit out of the hat.

CHAPTER ELEVEN

THE NEXT DAY FOUND EVA IN A DIFFERENT ROOM, having endured another move and interrupted sleep. As a result, they had slept in, and daylight intruded with luminous persistence until Eva had no choice but to rise.

The wall clock, once white but now stained and grubby with marks all over its roman numerals, ticked with increasing annoyance, reading just after eleven in the morning. Despite this, Eva felt much more at home with the familiar slammed doors and the smell of cooked food wafting in from a window unable to be completely shut.

Eva dressed as quietly as possible, but turned around at one point to find Madden awake and watching her.

She clutched her arms over her front, though she wore black trousers and a dark blue stretch top. "You should warn people when you are going to jump out on them, especially pregnant women."

"Why? I enjoy your shape and it's nothing I haven't seen before."

"My figure is not the point. You could scare me into labor and we aren't exactly in a safe place."

Madden stretched before sitting up. "Better here than many others I can think of. The top of a mountain, the shore of a lake."

Their impending trip worried her, but they were too close to ignore it. "You think they are out there?"

"Oh, most assuredly so. Yet, I think there is more to their plan than just isolation and death. We wouldn't be here otherwise."

Eva closed her eyes and concentrated. She could feel them out there, close, but not too close. "We may find out today."

Madden dressed and Eva took her turn at watching him. He might never volunteer every aspect of last night's encounter. Eva knew better than to press him for it. In his mind, she was sure, *he* thought he was doing the right thing.

"Hungry?" He asked when done.

"Starving. This little one is eating me alive."

"Then let us go find the others."

In the restaurant, they found Elaine and Rick enjoying a late brunch of cooked food, pastries, and coffee. It unnerved Eva somewhat as the whole scene was strangely civil. Was Elaine really so stupid to believe the chips were all falling into place?

The glance she stole at Madden indicated conveyed her feelings without a shadow of a doubt. "Welcome, both," she said in as friendly a voice as Eva had ever heard. "Please, won't you sit down and join us?"

Eva did as bidden, and continued to study Elaine. Her red hair was not tied back as usual, and hung down around her shoulders. There was also a trace of makeup on her face, and Eva had definitely never seen her foe made up before. The game was afoot, and Eva decided to play.

"How are you feeling?"

"I'm much better thanks. I must apologize most sincerely for my behavior over recent days. I haven't been myself."

Eva wanted to say 'I'll bet, you raving psycho' but instead, smiled sweetly and answered, "Think nothing of it. I am sure you were just trying to make sure I got my rest. I forget myself at times and am quite prone to overdoing it."

This appeared to relax Elaine, who settled into the meal, oblivious of the shared awareness around her. They lingered, making sure Elaine began to get restless, as they had agreed. It worked and despite the facade, she started to fidget, rubbing at the skin on her throat and the back of her hands in tell-tale signs of nervousness.

When this had gone on for another ten minutes or so, Madden said, "Right, then, time to be about business. We have plenty of daylight ahead of us, and the lake is only twenty miles away. What say we go find this little demon colony?"

Elaine jumped to her feet before she realized what she was doing, and then tried to cover up the impulse. There was far more to this trip than any of them knew. Any of them but Elaine.

Another city, another fast stop. Eva watched the buildings fly by as they traversed the highway taking them west towards the suburb of Espoo. A slate-gray sky brooded over-head. The forests beneath appeared cowed under the weight of pressure from above. What could have been beautiful views were obscured by distant murk.

The urban landscape gave way to open countryside interspersed with forest, and it was maybe half an hour before the glassy surface of water was visible in the distance. Following Rick's directions, Madden took the car off the main road, following an asphalt-covered lane not much bigger than a track through the forest.

"This is a dark road, a place of ancient death," said Elaine in a solemn voice. "Much violence was done to innocents here fifty years ago."

"Sounds fun," Madden replied as he turned the car down a track leading directly to the lake. "Care to elaborate?"

They stopped at a small beach sticking out into the water.

"Artificial?"

"This was built as a memorial to three children murdered in their sleep while camping on the shore of the lake. They were stabbed and bludgeoned. The blood was everywhere. The locals wanted this to bring happier memories to replace those more negative sentiments."

The thought of standing in the place of so much innocent death made Eva shiver. She took Madden's hand in her own and looked out over the calm water, searching the shoreline beyond. The horizon was hazy and indistinct, the surrounding green forest concealing any structures. It felt eerie to Eva.

"A fitting place for a host of demons. Did they ever find the killer?"

"They never confirmed who was responsible." Elaine spoke, but never turned her head, her eyes fixed on a distant point somewhere on the far north shore. "There were theories, and even a trial. Spies, local merchants, even the one surviving boy had the finger pointed at them. One did kill himself in the lake, confessing to the murders, but again, there was no proof."

Eva lost track of the rest of the conversation. A feeling made her stare across the lake, as if something was tugging at her, calling her onward.

"Eva?" She heard Madden say, his free hand upon her arm.

"They are out there," she replied.

"They are close," Elaine added, but there was another meaning behind her words.

"Where do we go then?" Eva pulled out her mobile phone, looking for the coordinates. The screen came up blank. She tried the power button, but still nothing.

"Strange, it was fully charged."

The rest of the party did the same, looks of confusion coming from Madden and Rick.

Elaine looked around at them in apparent innocence. "Mine's fine. Take a look." She held out the phone, and the screen showed the location of their destination, in much the same direction Elaine had been staring.

A sense of fatalism swept over Eva. "We aren't going to be able to avoid whatever is out there. We may as well get on with it."

Eva climbed back in the car, and watched as the rest followed her. Elaine was somewhat animated now and strolled very close to Madden, glancing at him as if oblivious to the rest of the world.

Madden drove at a crawl along the side of the lake, the road taking them close to the shore and deeper into the pine forest at regular intervals.

Eva tilted her mirror so she could keep an eye on Elaine. There were regular bouts of fidgeting, betraying the fact she was extremely agitated. Elaine attempted to cover this up by concentrating on the phone, playing with the screen and repeatedly tapping the buttons. When she wasn't doing this, she was gazing at Madden the way a child would stare at a desired toy.

Eventually, the road began to wind away from the lake.

"I guess we must have missed it," Madden admitted.

"No! Keep going," Elaine blurted. "There's a junction up ahead. We turn right."

The sense of familiarity with which Elaine said this was too much for Eva. "Madden, stop."

"No. Keep going!"

Madden looked at her and slowed the car to a complete halt. "What is it?"

Eva turned to look back at her companions. "Where are you taking us Elaine?"

Elaine tried to appear surprised. "I... I don't know what you mean. I've never been here before."

Madden laughed. "Yeah, sorry sweets but the sweet and innocent performance won't work with Eva. I thought you would have learned by now."

"She's stalling," Eva decided.

"But for what?" Madden asked.

The answer was not long in coming. Shadow blocked the light from behind their car as an object maneuvered close. A van, black with high sides, began to nudge them. After three of four attempts to elicit a response, the nudging became more insistent.

"Maybe you should go see what they want," Elaine suggested, her face now devoid of any emotion.

"Perhaps you should tell us what is going on and we will decide if speaking to someone trying to run us off the road is the prudent course of action," Eva retorted.

"Prudent or not, there is only one outcome here."

Madden chuckled. "She's been playing us from day one. Rick, want to deal with her?"

"Not a wise course of action," Elaine said. "I have done nothing here to warrant such an aggressive response. If you *do* decide on that route, I can promise both you gentlemen, you will not make it to the end of this road alive."

"What about me?" Eva asked, expecting only one outcome.

"Somebody wants to talk to you," came the smug answer.

There was a knock on Madden's window, and perhaps the biggest man Eva had ever seen, tall enough she couldn't see his face and muscled enough to fill the window, pointed at them, and then forward.

"I suggest you do what he wants," said Elaine.

Eva had had enough of looking at the woman, and turned to face the front. "Mad one," she said under her breath, but loud enough for Madden to hear. She clipped her seatbelt and pulled it tight. She knew Madden would never forget his first life as a street racer then getaway driver in Jamaica, and the name he had earned. She was also pretty sure not even ARC knew the reference, in fact she was counting on it. Such skill was now needed.

The mass of muscle outside rapped on the window once more.

"All right, all right," Madden said through gritted teeth and nodded. "I hope you realize what you are asking."

He began to edge away and the man outside stepped back and turned to signal the van forward. Madden planted his foot on the gas and suddenly they were off, racing down the road with forest and lake whistling by on either side.

"You may as well stop," Elaine said, calm as if they were

still stationary. "We have come too far for them to let you escape."

The van was distant, as the driver sought to catch them, but not completely out of touch. Eva concentrated on the road ahead, seeking anything possible to aid Madden in their escape. In a lucid moment, she realized there was nothing she could do or say to make a difference. A glance showed he was utterly in the zone, at one with the car.

The forest track veered to the left and in the distance, a flash of light revealed another van waiting in the middle of the road.

"We're screwed if we don't find a way off," Madden said, his eyes urgently seeking an alternative.

"There." Eva pointed to where a path opened into the forest on their right.

"And they called me mad," he muttered before slowing the car enough to turn.

The van behind caught up, and nudged their rear fender.

"No," Elaine called as the car swerved in response, but Madden threw the car right and then they were through, hurtling along a woodland path at sixty miles an hour.

"Hold tight," Madden advised.

"You think?" Eva replied, clutching her seat belt.

The van had attempted to follow them, but had very quickly became stuck. They were on their own and Madden relaxed, slowing somewhat.

"There, easy job."

"It's not over yet," Elaine taunted.

"Maybe not, but we are alone, and free of pursuit." Madden stopped the car and turned in his seat. "Now you can tell us what the hell is going on, or I can have Rick squeeze the truth out of you."

Elaine gazed back, calm. "Do as you will, it makes no difference now. My task is complete." She turned to Eva, and for an instant, the boiling rage appeared in her eyes. "Almost complete."

Eva jumped at the sudden shift in character. Elaine was not doing it by choice. "Madden, let's get out of here. I don't like this."

"What should we do with her?" Rick asked.

"Dump her. I have a feeling we haven't seen the end of her, but let's be rid of excess baggage." If Elaine could play the shock game, so could Eva, and the response was immediate. The dismissal of her importance threw Elaine into a rage, she attempted to lurch forward, and head butt Eva. Rick however was faster, catching Elaine, and pushing her out the door.

Wasting no time, Madden started the car, leaving a screaming and cursing Elaine in the mud behind.

"Shame we had to drop her off," Madden conceded. "She had the only working phone."

Rick grinned and waved his hand. In it was Elaine's phone. "Bet she never even knew it was taken. Not the most stable of women there."

After a few minutes, the track levelled out and the trees disappeared. Madden navigated them along a grass causeway between two fields as the lake glistened to their right. A few trees offered potential cover, but otherwise they were exposed.

"I don't like this," Madden said, echoing Eva's thoughts. "If they see us from the road ahead we're screwed. If I was still a demon, I could make us vanish."

"No. Don't ever say such a thing, Madden. There isn't any choice. We need to get out of here, ARC mandate or not. We're in trouble. We may have come seeking answers, but this looks like one big ploy from Elaine to get us here. We need to change the rules. Just head for the road, turn right, and drive like hell."

Madden nodded, taking them through the small copse at the convergence of the fields, and then north toward the road. As Eva had asked, the second they hit the road, he was off, swerving right, and gunning the throttle.

Eva watched the road in the side mirror to check they were alone. Nothing. Patches of forest broke up the fields around Lake Bodom, and they remained alone. Madden began to ease back as it became clear they were not being followed.

"Easy," he said with confidence. "Just like a stroll in the... oh no."

Eva glanced ahead. Three more vans had moved out of the woods and were now blocking the road. The only way out was down a track leading to the lake.

"Goddammit," Madden shouted as he looked behind them.

Her child cried out in warning, and Eva turned to see the van they thought they had escaped sauntering along the road. Elaine was at the wheel.

CHAPTER TWELVE

MADDEN HAD NO CHOICE. HELPLESS TO ACT IN ANY other way, he edged the car forward. Eva knew he had no choice.

"Rick, what is this?"

"I'm sorry Dr Scott; I have no knowledge of who this might be. All information indicated this area was deserted other than the small villages around the lake. Certainly no army about here."

This made Eva think. "Army?"

"Look at the size of them, love," said Madden. "Look at the organization."

"I didn't see a single weapon. And Elaine? What was her excuse for subservience when she tends to fury at the drop of a hat? There might be more to this than we are aware of. May I suggest an element of caution until we find out exactly what's going on?"

They were shepherded down a sharp right-hand turn back toward the lake. Trees opened out to well-tended fields beyond which lay forest so dense it appeared black. The vans kept them at a constant speed, boxing them in.

Eva peered about her. Their captors were uniform in size, all masked with grim faces. These people were implacable. Her attention was drawn from them as they neared the lake and entered the pine forest. Despite the daylight, Madden flicked on the headlights as the skies became dark in seconds.

The gloom abated as they neared the lake, and Eva's breath left her lungs in a single gasp. A huge structure perched on the edge of the lake. Three stories high, it was seemingly made entirely of glass "Beautiful," she whispered.

"You don't see such beauty every day," Madden agreed.

The vans pulled up in front of the structure. People wandered about inside in much the same way Eva had seen ant farms work as a child. She got out, not waiting for an invitation. The pungent pine scent was heavy and the structure was much more surreal because of it.

Madden joined her, as did Rick. Elaine exited the van and strolled over to the building's front door where a gathering awaited behind it. Elaine opened the door and bowed her head, and a procession of people, in what Eva could only describe as multi-coloured robes, strolled out to face her.

Eva glanced behind. The well-muscled men had formed an impenetrable wall of flesh. While all looked peaceful here, it was only the case on the surface.

The lead figure walked ahead of the group, and Eva realized it was a woman, albeit a tall one. Judging by her face, she appeared overcome with excitement, though she attempted to mask it with serenity. She stopped close to Eva and pulled back the hood of the bright blue robe she wore, allowing it to fall about her shoulders. Her blonde hair was tied back and her weather beaten face seemed in stark contrast to such a grand house. Her eyes were pale, and her gaze seemed to pierce through Eva as she approached.

She put her hands together, palms facing up on her chest, and bowed her head until the tip of her chin touched the points of her fingers.

"All life is one," she said in a rich voice, crisp tones full of intelligence.

"All life is one," those behind her intoned, and all waited expectantly, watching her.

Eva realized they expected the same of her, and not wanting to be rude, she formed the same movement and said, "All life is one... I guess."

The speaker broke into a smile. "I have found you, safe and hale. At last. I have dreamed of this moment and feared it would never come." She held her hands aloft, the sleeves of her robe slipping back up her arms. "She is a source of light, and Her light shall blaze forth, dazzling as the midday sun, across the nations of the earth!" Dropping her arms and pointing at Eva's belly she added, "You bear such light beneath your breast. It radiates Goodness, and connects us all."

"All life is one. Blessed is the vessel," intoned the followers.

Eva couldn't help but smile. "This is all very nice, and not what I expected, given the nature of our journey here, but who are you?"

The foremost of the followers, a short stocky man in a white robe stepped forward. "She is The Mahatma, Helen Cusins Prophet. Mistress of the Planetary Rebirth, Lady of the White Lodge. She is the Risen."

Her baby screamed caution, and Eva heeded it. A mere

shuffling of the feet from Madden was enough to indicate he understood all too well. Iuvart, the demon prince who had masqueraded as her boss Gideon Homes, had called the hellbounces by the very same name.

The white-robed man had not yet finished. Mistaking her concern for awe, he waited a moment and continued. "Beloved servant of most-Holy Nibiru, initiate of the seventh level, she has surpassed her negative karma and ascended beyond the understanding of mere mortals. She dwells on this plane until the Divine Plan is complete, until the Savior walks among us and the Golden Age has returned."

"The Convocation of the Sacred Fire," Eva said with growing understanding.

"All life is one," echoed the followers.

"But what do you want with me? Helen..."

The spokesman's arm shot out, grabbing her arm in an iron grip. The leader did nothing, smiling passively.

"You will refer to the Lady as Mistress, or Holy Risen." The look he gave her promised immediate and brutal retribution if this was violated.

Eva didn't miss a beat. "Mistress, if I may ask? For what reason am I here?"

"To be hidden, whole and hale, in this palace of crystal until the Holy day to come. The savior will be born again, and the golden age will dawn once more. Come; let me show you my house."

There was an audible gasp as the Risen put her arm about Eva's shoulder, leading her in through the glass doors. Clearly, the Risen was above such menial tasks.

Allowing herself to be led, Eva decided to press her luck. "Mistress, we came here looking for a site, a factory, a warehouse perhaps, on the edge of the lake."

"No child, you came here because you were called. The sanctuary we offer will see your child safely born. Tell me, how came you to our blessed manor?"

Eva glanced back at Elaine, who walked head bowed, red hair hanging over her face. There was the smallest of smirks on her lips. The betrayal by a woman she had considered a close friend suddenly reached boiling point. How dare Elaine do what she had done: the drugs and the clumsy attempts at seduction on her husband?

"It all started when your minion there drugged me in order to try and lay claim to my husband."

The Risen paused mid-stride, the soft blue slipper she wore hitting the glass floor with an audible 'slap'.

"Please, would you explain further what you mean?"

"Look at her face. See for yourself. She lusts after my husband. Lusts. Elaine used these men and vans to threaten us with violence. We were chased here, coerced into coming. We are not here by choice. Wrath, avarice, lust, and envy. These are all deadly sins. Are you not a holy order? Do you not abide here in the face of these sins? She has dealt heavily in them all."

The Risen rounded on Elaine, but Elaine's response was very alien. She raised her chin, imperious. "I was commanded to do so."

"By whom?" Demanded the acolyte in white.

"I have been in communion with Nibiru. He speaks with me in person. He instructs me. His will brought me to the actions needed to accomplish my goals."

"Impossible," countered the Risen, the first time she had spoken directly to Elaine. "You are a level one initiate, and as such, not capable of communion with the Planetary leader."

"All life is one," murmured some of the assembled

group, though many of them were clearly frightened and forgetting protocol. Elaine's announcement had evidently stunned them.

"Nonetheless, it is how it is," responded Elaine. "I have communed with Lord Nibiru in person. When can you claim to have done the same?"

"What you claim, you who are awash in sin, is baseless and irrelevant."

The warning signs were there. Elaine began to tense up as her 'leader' poured scorn on her claims. Eva had pushed the right buttons.

Without warning, Elaine jumped forward, hand extending to slap the Risen. Rick was quicker, catching her mid-act, her hand inches from the Risen's face.

"Always the little boy scout," Elaine struggled against Rick, but his vastly superior strength was more than enough. "When are you going to realize we are meant for more than servitude? They don't value you. When you die, as you inevitably will, do you think they will mourn you? Do you think they will remember your name? You are a pawn."

"I am what I choose to be," was all Rick said in reply.

The white-robed man stepped forward, his face red. "You dare raise your hand against the Risen?"

The Risen put both of her hands up in the air. "Enough. Peace, my children. Do not let your Karma suffer from the emotions of a momentous event." She turned to Elaine, whose hand was still locked in position by Rick. "My child, you believe you have spoken to the Nibiru. However misguided your belief, I ask you to retire to a contemplation chamber and meditate on your studies until you see the truth I, and those around you, see. You have been a long time gone, and have much to make up before your Karma becomes aligned. You have fulfilled your duty to the Convocation and to humanity through means of this gift. In time, you shall be rewarded."

Surprisingly, Elaine accepted this, and bowed her head. The risen nodded to Rick and he let her go. Elaine moved off but not before she ogled Madden once more, where Eva alone could see her do it. This was not over.

The Risen regarded Eva once more "As for you, child, there is no other community on this lake other than the Convocation. True positive Karmic meditation requires isolation and a symbiotic interaction with the environment around you. We would know if we lived in the same space as any full of such negativity."

They entered a large semi-circular room, faceted with panes of glass higher than Eva could reach. Lake Bodom stretched into the distance beyond, the sky at the horizon showing hints of purple as evening beckoned. Eva turned to see a different view of the lake from each glass pane. It made her catch her breath.

"Stunning, no?" The Risen clearly approved of mortal awe.

She turned to her followers. "Leave us."

White-robe made to protest but thought better of it. Sullen, he bowed and scraped his way back out of the room, sliding the glass door shut. He remained outside while Rick placed himself in the way of the door.

"In here, without the zealousness of my retinue, please call me Helen."

Eva perched on a large yellow sofa filled to bursting with yellow silk cushions. "Helen, are you really the same person? The Risen?"

The Risen laughed, a light, tinkling sound. "We all wear so many hats, my dear. Be sceptical, if it pleases you, but always remember yes, I am that woman, and everything she is responsible for."

"But you aren't from around here."

"Also true. I am English by birth, from a city in the West of the country. We all come from somewhere."

"And how did you end up here?"

The Risen leaned back, waving cheekily at her acolytes, who dropped to the floor. "They don't approve of me. What you really want to know is where you may end up, so you may affect a rescue. Your wish will simply not happen. We all have our orders. There are three departments in the Convocation. Here, Brazil, and Tibet. The center in Tibet is more a state of mind than a physical place. The city floats above the mountains, a karmic center reaching out all over the planet. When I shrug off this mortal shell, if I have not attained complete ascension, I will undergo trials. If I keep you here, I may pass there when the savior arrives. So, you see, you may make yourselves comfortable."

Eva turned from her host, rising to stand by Madden, who had not moved from the door to the lake.

"What do you think?" He asked.

Eva closed her eyes and reached forth, seeking for Brian's sensation. It pulsed to her left, a glow of rage. She pointed. "There. Out past the lake is where it is."

Eva turned to the Risen. "You have been misled if you believe you are alone in this place. I would say within ten miles of here, nests a source of evil so vile if it touches you, no amount of Karmic meditation will purify your soul."

The Risen smiled, and climbed to her feet. "I had heard the rumors about you. I just needed to see it for myself." She waved white-robe in. "It is confirmed. Send the cleaners."

He bowed, and left them.

Eva watched him move off with a purpose through the

glass mansion, only furniture eventually blocking sight of his actions. Wherever he passed, those around him became more animated, as if they had been waiting to take action.

"I must leave you now, but we will speak again in the days to come. When the Savior arrives, you and I will travel to Tibet, to enter dwellings more suitable to our station. Be at ease and take your comfort in my house. Glory awaits you Eva Ross. Glory awaits us all."

The Risen said nothing more, nodding pleasantly at Rick, but ignoring Madden entirely, and left in the same direction as white-robe.

Madden sat down where the Risen had been. "Just another day in the office," he laughed. "In the space of a day we have gone from being assaulted by demons on an island full of god weapons in the middle of nowhere to being made prisoner in a glass castle full of karmic wannabes."

Rick withdrew a steel implement from inside his jacket and tapped it on the glass. "Not a problem. We can go when you want."

Madden pursed his lips. Eva adored him when he tried to look decisive and thoughtful.

"We need the car. Eva can't run and once we make noise smashing through glass we won't have long. Besides, everybody here can see you."

Rick tested the glass. The dull ring of the metal made it sound thick. "Reinforced, but not impenetrable. The sun is going down. Let's wait until the moon rises high and reassess the situation. They say they are taking you to an invisible floating city?"

Madden put his arm about her shoulders, giving Eva warmth and the feeling of reassurance. "Wherever they think they are taking you, it can't be pleasant. I get a strange impression from these people."

"I'm sure it will be no less pleasant than standing on the threshold of Hell. You guys were nearby, but you didn't see what I witnessed. There was heat, but not warmth. It was a hunger, a rage, a force. It emanated from every creature, and from all around them. There were more of them writhing and cavorting on the other side of the portal than I think there are people on the planet. They all wanted in, with a kind of desperation. I don't know what part I saw, but I will bet it was just a brief glimpse. They still want in, and there is a force behind the ice still seeking them out. I can tell you if there is such a thing as redemption, I would love to seek it to avoid going there. Being stuck here is not going to help us at all. If there is no choice, going to their invisible city to have my baby in safety is preferable to waiting around to see what happens if another portal opens."

Madden looked shocked. "You want to accept their offer?"

Eva touched his face, running her forefinger down the line of his jaw. "No. We haven't gone through everything for me to be held against my will and have our child raised to be a deity because someone says I should. Whatever happens here, we need to get this done, and find safety, and then I will decide. If you remember, we were supposed to be living in the cottage. We were supposed to be at peace. This shows we will never be able to afford time at peace, not unless a larger task is accomplished, or we just walk away and ignore it all."

Madden looked around, and began to tap his fingers on the sofa in amusement. "Well, we are in a big glass building with no easy way of escape. I can't demon us into obscurity, though it appears I can read foreign languages pretty well. You know for a fact there are a dozen sets of eyes on us just waiting for Rick to assault the window. I am sure robes will flock from a dozen different places outside when we do, and outside there somewhere, your ex-husband is roaming around with a wild pack of hellbounces, all who can smell your blood from any place on earth. I would say our options are limited."

Eva nodded, lost in thought. She barely noticed when the first pain spasmed through her belly, so preoccupied was she with their predicament. The second hit her like a jolt, and she cried out.

"Madden!"

Eva clutched at her belly.

"Eva, what is it?"

"The baby!"

CHAPTER THIRTEEN

EVA REACHED FOR HER BELLY. IT HAD GONE HARD AS A rock.

"Something's wrong!" She cried.

In the periphery of her vision, Madden floundered. "What...I..."

Rick was there in a moment. He looked her over once. "Doctor Scott, listen to me. You need to breathe. Slowly, regularly. You are panicking and will pass out if you do not. Breathe."

Eva forced herself to inhale. The effort against the cramps in her stomach was nearly more than she could manage.

"And again. Breathe."

Another breath, a little easier.

"Breathe, breathe, breathe."

With each breath, the pain subsided and did not return. When she was able, she lay down on the sofa, her head in Madden's lap. It was clear he was shaken by her episode, and was grateful to be able to comfort her. Eva clutched his hand to reinforce her appreciation.

"Feel better?" Rick asked.

"I'm not in labor," she decided aloud. The baby radiated contentment.

"When was the last time you had anything to drink?"

Eva chuckled. "Good point. I'm just dehydrated."

"Will you two please explain what's going on?" Madden asked. "Are you having the baby or not?"

"I'm not, love."

Rick sat opposite them. "What your wife is experiencing is known as 'Braxton Hicks' contractions. A sort of pre labor preparation."

As Madden's face once again went white, Eva added, "False contractions can happen from six weeks into the pregnancy until the end. I'm not having the baby Madden. Of course, it's not to say I won't soon. I am eight months after all. It can be triggered more acutely when one hasn't had liquids in a while."

"And you haven't had a drink since breakfast. Well I can remedy your condition in a second."

Madden stood and began to bash at the glass into the hallway, waving at those members of the Convocation in nearby rooms. Soon a group of three opened the door.

"All life is one," they intoned.

"Screw your chants," Madden growled. "My wife is unwell and needs nourishment. Food and especially water."

One of the three made to object and Madden cut him off. "Don't you even think about quoting meditation or Karma at me. Instead, consider how much positive Karma you will get from serving the Vessel, mother of the Savior."

The three acolytes set off at a dead run.

. . .

In due time, two of the Convocation delivered refreshment to the three of them. Red-robed and hooded, they kept their heads down as they brought in a tray of fruit and jugs of water. The sun had gone down while they waited, and every moment built up Eva's nerves. Lights glowed steadily, turning the mansion into one great beacon. Eva closed her eyes as refreshments were served, taking deep breaths and attempting to remain calm. In silence, she drank several glasses of water while Madden and Rick hovered protectively. It was ice-cold and refreshing. The fruit she chose was sharp, bordering on bitter, an orange on the outside, but deep purple in the middle.

"Thank you," Eva said in genuine gratitude, feeling much better already.

"Think nothing of it," replied a rich male voice from beneath the cowl of the nearest robe. "We live to serve the Vessel."

He turned to join his fellow, a slighter figure with the lines of a woman.

"Wait. I know your voice. Who are you?"

The figure turned back, bringing his hands up to pull the cowl from over his face. A neatly trimmed blonde beard and mustache framed a face too pretty to be male. His golden hair swept back left eyes watching her like a hawk. Piercing eyes that she was sure she had seen once before.

"I was called Zerachiel in a former existence. The mortals here know me as Nibiru. You are so close, Eva Ross, to finding out the entire truth. You will know me by another name before the end."

He watched her for a moment, his gaze lingering on her belly as if he tried to stare through the skin to find what lay beneath. There was a hunger in his face, along with anticipation. With no more words, he turned and left, sliding the glass door shut. The other figure accompanied him, and pulling back her cowl, Elaine, her face bearing her own brand of hunger, watched Madden.

"One gets the husband, the other the wife." Madden observed, but had no more chance to speak when, from the other side of the mansion, there was a loud smash. The lights went out.

"There are people outside," Rick said, positioning himself in one of the corners. "Stay where you are."

Eva did not need to be told twice. She remained still, Madden at her side. "Where are they coming from?"

"It appears right out of the lake."

In front of them, several figures rose from the still water and approached the mansion intently, passing their room and moving around to their right. Eva felt each one of them as they passed.

"They are hellbounce."

The door behind slid open and the white-robed acolyte leaned in.

"What did you do? Why did you come here?"

"What do you mean?" Madden answered. "We were led here by one of your own. What's happened?"

"The cleaners. Those sent out to rid the nearby center of the evil. They never returned, and now this. I should kill you now, and be rid of the problem before they destroy everything."

Teeth clenched, he launched at Eva, brawny arms reaching for her. Rick intercepted him and the two rolled on the floor, wrestling for position. It was a mismatch. Using his superior weight and strength, Rick gained the advantage and with deadly force wrenched the neck of the acolyte to one side. The crunch told its own story, and the acolyte dropped to the ground, lifeless.

"There's our way out," Madden said.

Eva stood. For a moment, she was lightheaded and had to lean on Madden. "Hope we don't have to jump around too often," she said with a smile more for him than anything.

"Put this on," Rick instructed her, handing her the white robe.

Eva did as told, wrinkling her nose. "This stinks. Do their acolytes ever wash?"

"It might just save your life. Put the hood up, then you don't look like a heavily pregnant woman, just another cultist."

"What about you two?"

"It's dark. We will chance it."

Rick led the way, back down the hallway they had come along previously, in the direction of their car. Behind them there were yet more crashes as large panes of glass erupted. More and more screams could be heard as the demons found their peaceful hosts. Lights flickered overhead as somebody sought to restore power, but soon it became unnecessary. Over the screams, came a roar of rage, of endless hunger. The side of the mansion nearest the lake lit up bright as daylight in the dusk, the swirling mass, a fractured vision through a thousand cracked panes of glass. The entire building shuddered.

"Somebody has killed a demon?" Asked Madden. "With their bare hands? This lot wouldn't know how."

"Great place to have a quake," said Rick, attempting to hurry them along.

Eva looked about her. Above, bodies were thrown everywhere as the mansion's structure lurched in response to the portal. Glass floors shattered, shards falling all about them. Blood from countless wounded bodies flowed down the walls. In the distance, the glass began to frost, emphasizing the portal. Eva tried her best to move with haste.

"The tentacles! They are doing this," she shouted above the din.

Nobody replied. The outer doors were within reach and they were alone. The three captives hurried toward the doors, swinging ajar in the chaos. In moments, they were through. Eva's heart pounded with the exertion, and then her stomach dropped.

"Where's the car?" Madden called.

Behind them the mansion lurched again, sending shards of glass in every direction. Eva beckoned to her companions and stumbled in the direction of the woods at the far side of the clearing.

"Get behind the trees," she called. "At least we won't get hit by glass while you figure out how to escape."

They hid in a grove a few feet into the general woodland. It was freezing, and Eva quickly began to shiver, despite the thick robe.

"We have to find something now," Madden shouted above the noise. "She's not going to last out here. None of us are."

"The car has a tracking device in it," Rick called back. "If I can get one of these damned phones working we will be able to find it."

Eva watched the building shake and shatter, afraid they were not far enough away. The impact of the portal could be felt through the ground, and the stygian light show would be visible for miles across the lake. The terror began to defeat even her reasoning.

"There are hundreds of hellbounces out there! We have to get out of here now!" Eva turned and attempted to pull herself past a barrage of pine branches. It was tough going and she did not get very far very fast. The unforgiving trees scratched at her face and roots tried to trap her feet.

"Eva! Come back!" Madden shouted, but any further words were lost as a massive concussion lay waste to the Convocation's mansion, causing glass to shoot through the air and the building to collapse in on itself.

Silence followed. If anybody was left alive in what was left of the death trap, Eva wasn't going to waste any time over them.

Several car alarms sounded off to her left, the other side of what must have been the road they had driven in on.

"Got it!" Rick shouted. "Doctor Scott, come back."

Obediently, Eva made her way back to Rick, Madden embracing her with a fierce passion as she caught up with him.

"Best get over there quickly. The house will be a beacon for the demons."

Eva sought calm with a deep breath, closing her eyes. There was a dwindling sensation, only getting fainter. "They are leaving. The hellbounces are moving away to the southwest."

Both Madden and Rick stopped walking and turned to her. "What?"

"I don't know. Maybe they think they got me."

Madden shook his head, "No way. I wish more than anything the Demons are gone. Yet why would they seek you out only to leave? You can feel them. You have evidence they are aware of your existence. I don't buy it."

"And how do you qualify the explosion?" Rick asked.

"I have some ideas. I want to think about it first. Let's find the car and get out of here.

. . .

The car was in a garage down a small lane, partially obscured by the trees. In the otherwise silent night, the garage was easy to find. As they passed the ruins of the house, Madden stopped to stare.

"My god, one side of it is completely gone. Do you think she escaped? It all happened so quickly."

The tang of blood wafted through the night air, mixing with the pine scent to form a smell Eva could describe in no other way than 'unnatural'.

"To be brutally honest it wasn't the first thing on my mind. Come on, we have to get out of here."

Madden sniffed. "So much for their Karma. Fat lot of good it did them."

As if to emphasise the point, the remains of the mansion shifted under its own weight, glass cascading in a series of tinkles over the superstructure. A multi-faceted grave hiding nothing.

The garage was open, and although the side facing the mansion was peppered with glass shards, many sticking through the corrugated iron sides, the ARC car and two vans were unharmed.

"I'll drive," Madden volunteered. "You two sit in the back and figure out what Elaine did to them. One wrong turn out here and who knows where we will end up."

Eva wasn't going to argue, and found her way into the car with a bit of help from Rick. The engine purred into life at the first attempt, and soon Madden had them creeping through the darkness, clearly choosing caution over urgency.

"So what did you mean about the explosion?"

Eva put down the shell of the phone. Her fiddling hadn't made any difference. "The knife they cut my arms with on Gehenna. When Swanson, Gila, and I found it in the vaults in Qena, we were attacked by hellbounces. I stabbed one with the knife, and it exploded, bringing half the roof down with it. A similar thing happened in Afghanistan when we were coming after you. Unfortunately, I sort of alerted Alexander the Great's reborn army to my location that time." Eva laughed, a little insanity creeping into her voice.

"I know," Madden sympathized. "It's strange how you can make such an outlandish tale sound normal."

"What is normal nowadays?" Rick added.

"So it was the same knife, but you said when you saw your ex, he was wielding it."

"And he told me every demon he raises knows me because of my blood on the blade."

"So why is a hellbounce killing other hellbounces in such a manner?"

Eva turned to watch the impressions of trees passing by in the dim moonlight. She had no real perspective as to their speed, and in the warmth of the car, she began to doze.

"I don't know. He was a lunatic when he was alive. I can imagine a journey to hell and back only makes someone worse. If he has to answer to whoever gifted him with the blade though, and they are anything like Iuvart, I can only see an icy future for Brian Ross."

"Unless Brian is now the master."

"Got it!" Rick exclaimed. He held up the phone. The screen was bright, a nest of red pulsing to the southeast of their position.

"What was the problem?" Madden asked, keeping his head forward and eyes on the road.

"Simple really. Elaine removed the SIM cards from the phones. What she has on her phone is a clone of the app we use on the ARC network, modified to be close enough to convince the casual eye but programmable with any location you desire."

"Clever," Eva replied. "How did you recognize the difference?"

Rick waved the phone like a conductor's baton. "I created the original program. I was in Cairo with Swanson working on the technology when you first came to our attention."

He reached over the back of his seat, retrieving a small black case. "There are always more secrets. Elaine did not know everything."

Unzipping the case, he flipped it open to reveal a wealth of micro-technology. In moments, he had a small chip inserted in the phone and closed the cover with a click.

Instantly, the phone began to buzz, red lights flashing from beneath the keys. Rick pressed the speaker button.

"Yes, sir?"

"Rick?" It was Swanson.

"Well, you are a pleasant voice to hear," Eva chipped in.

"As timely as the angel of death," Madden added.

"Well, it's a relief to hear your voices, too. Tell me you have something I can use. We are in a bit of a predicament."

CHAPTER FOURTEEN

"WHAT'S HAPPENED?" EVA ASKED. THE STRAIN IN Swanson's voice was well hidden but definitely present. "Is it Gila?"

"Not exactly, but sort of. The campaign does not go well for us. It seems the council is split right down the middle regarding the selection. The portal research of Ivor Sarch has become an important piece of the puzzle here, impressing many of the senior council figures. They see a future, power, and technological development. The fools can't comprehend we are once again living in biblical times."

"How do you see the split?"

Eva could imagine Swanson ticking off his fingers.

"I believe Jose Partada, Gaspard Antroobus and, of course, Jeanette will side with my uncle and I for Gila. Benedict Garias and his underling Zoe Larter are automatic for Ivor Sarch since they are basically his sponsors. As for the rest, well Sejal Khwaja, I suspect fears for his position if Gila comes on board. She really is very talented at what she does and is a very capable administrator. He sees a rival.

Petra van Veld doesn't appear to be able to see beyond the end of her ledgers, and the research offers the potential for a vast cash flow. Margaret Anderson has always been dead-set against the idea of too much Guyomard influence. She voted against my appointment, and took defeat heavily as the previous head of the council. She stepped down in protest but the vote stood. We have no ally in her. She would rather disrupt."

"So Margaret makes the situation an even score," Eva concluded. "Yet you haven't mentioned the head of the council."

"Margaret Anderson has the ear of Johan Klaas and, we suspect, a lot more," interceded Rick.

"That's right," Swanson agreed. "So the logical assumption is unless we can provide irrefutable evidence swaying the council in the other direction, Sarch gets the nod."

"Well, we can only tell you what we have been through thus far, and you can make of it what you will."

"I see you have been to the location. Odd position though. I would have expected you to be on your way back to Helsinki."

"We haven't made it there yet."

There was a pause. "Who's driving?"

"Madden," Eva supplied.

"Madden find a spot to pull over, somewhere hidden from view of the road."

"Okay, bear with me here."

It took them a couple of minutes, but Madden managed to locate a track down which he reversed the car long enough the road disappeared behind the forest.

"Done. Now want to tell me why we are hiding?"

"I don't want you going there in the dark. Rumour is the facility will be bad enough in the day. Besides, it appears you have some rest to get and information to pass on, and I want you to have your wits about you. Now, let's get started."

Madden flicked a switch, enabling the front two seats to swivel in place and face the back seats. When they were all settled, he said, "Where do you want us to begin?"

"How about a brief overview of what's happened?"

Eva picked up the phone, holding it near her mouth. "Well to sum it up, Elaine was drugging me, we got assaulted on an island in the Baltic Sea where Zoe Larter tried to make Madden a permanent resident with all the other Norse God weapons you have hidden there, and then we were imprisoned by the Convocation of the Sacred Fire. Brief enough for you?"

Another pause, then, "Maybe you had better start at the beginning, in detail."

"You sure you have long enough to listen?"

"If it is important, I have all night. Besides, you are going nowhere until daylight so you may as well make yourselves comfortable."

"Well it pretty much is as it is," Madden said, taking over the conversation. "It transpires Elaine's been slipping Eva doses of Methaqualone to keep her asleep."

" Methaqualone is illegal. Wiped out in the 80's. Why would you do such a thing, Elaine? That's monstrous."

"Sorry bud, Elaine isn't here. We will get to why in good time. Under the pretence she was keeping my wife asleep for her own health, Elaine was actually keeping her out of the way so she could prey on me. It seems our steadfast bodyguard had designs on me. Romantic designs."

Eva smiled sympathetically at her husband. It was clear it disgusted him to have to admit what had transpired. For such an apparent rascal, he was a complete innocent at times.

"That could have made the situation awkward," said Swanson.

"It was dealt with on the ferry from Stockholm, sir," Rick replied. "However, we are jumping ahead of ourselves."

"Indeed," Eva added. "Brian has been making a nuisance of himself the entire journey."

"So it is definitely him? Has he taken any direct action against you?"

"Not as such, no. I can feel his movements, as I can of any hellbounce created with the obsidian blade."

"Ah yes, the dagger. Gila believes it is known as 'The Well of Souls'. The reason for the name might go some way towards explaining why you experience such feelings."

This concerned Eva. "Are you saying my soul is trapped in this dagger?"

"I don't believe so. Gila put it that the dagger retains the essence of those it cuts. That dagger is thousands of years old. You have a rather extended family it seems. You can feel them, and they you. It's also possible you might be able to sense them through time, though information governing the facts is rather sketchy. So what happened?"

"He stirred up a mob protesting against withholding information in Stockholm."

"Outside the Nobel banquet hall. I am aware of it."

"He also appeared to me on the docks as the ferry departed, his usual Brian self, boasting of how he was always watching me and such. Nobody else could see him beside me. We think he was responsible for raising the presumed survivors of the Estonia disaster since I could feel every one of them. It appeared coincidence, but we were too close to Utö."

"A hellbounce returned and a rogue member of our forces. Unfortunately, it is nothing I can use, not to make light of your situation. These things have both happened before and as much as we had hoped no more demonkind would come through, one can only accept the inevitable."

Eva took a couple of deep breaths, holding back the retort on her lips. It had not felt quite so unimportant at the time, but Swanson, as always, appeared to look at the bigger picture.

"What happened on Utö?"

"The ship landed, so we could move the survivors to medical facilities. There was no way I was going to tell them what they were dealing with. The weather center there is where we met Zoe Larter, and she was very interested in Madden."

"How so?"

Madden shrugged as Eva glanced at him. He still had no idea. "I started reading from a text kept in the sanctified storage. It was old Swedish."

"Impressive," came the approving tone from the phone.

"I was reading it in English."

"And you think this is related to your previous state?"

"Well, it has to be. I didn't study languages when I was in school. In fact, if I'm honest, I didn't study much of anything. My parents always overlooked my faults and I had the sort of attitude where I was right and the teachers were wrong. It wasn't conducive to a strong educational background."

"We might have to run some more tests at some point. It is interesting you are left that particular legacy of all things.

Can you think of any situation where your aptitude for translation has been used elsewhere?"

"Not in the least, pal. But if I see everything in a language I recognize, how would I know any differently?"

"Larter was all over him," Eva interjected before the conversation took to wrong a turn. "In a similar way to Elaine, but she was more like she had found a prize than lusting after him. It appeared the hellbounces had been raised specifically to go after the Utö cache. They came at us but were turned back by the sanctified hallway combined with the drugs. Brian, or whoever is pulling the strings, got us there for a reason. As it is, many of them were incapacitated and Larter got her prize. I think she was there because something like this was bound to happen. I suspect she is in cahoots with whoever gave Brian the idea to resurrect dead ferry victims."

"Can you prove it? Evidence of collusion would go a long way toward helping with the vote."

"The only proof would be on Utö, if any is still there. Listen Swanson, we know you all have your secrets, but if the ARC council is sending us on foolhardy missions and we are blinded by ignorance, it might be useful to divulge a tidbit from time to time."

"Explain."

"The population of Utö were a little too well-prepared when the fight came. The islanders have seen such action in the past, mark my words. You are clearly well aware of what is hidden there. Maybe we could have used some of the relics to our advantage?"

"Trust me, when you get to Geneva, all will be made clear."

"I was hoping to go back to Sweden." Eva's heart sank at this announcement.

"Not safe anymore. Now, tell me about the lake. You appear to be safe now."

Eva stretched, feeling the smooth material of the ceiling with the backs of her hands. The car for all of its apparent luxury was confining when one had a bump on the front of them. "If you tell me you knew Elaine was a member of the Convocation of the Sacred Flame, I think I'll scream."

"No, such information had never been disclosed to me, or anyone else, I think."

Eva glanced at Rick, who shrugged, his face totally innocent.

"Probably best if I take over here, sir," Rick said. "Elaine had altered my sensor-app so it showed a completely different source from the satellite feed. You might want to check the software on the ARC network with such information in mind. She had us drive straight to the local Convocation headquarters with a little chase thrown in for good measure. She wasn't pleased to be separated from Madden, but had to accept the commands of her order. I think she was Convocation before she was ARC, though she didn't appear to fit in."

"That might help us some – challenging a ratified council decision. Somebody approved her appointment and there will be ultimate responsibility."

"As long as it doesn't lead back to you," Madden quipped.

"Oh, it will not lead back to me. I can promise you. So how did you escape?"

"It was the damndest thing, sir. Hellbounces. They came from the lake, and attacked the building we were held in, the Convocation manor. Somebody fought back and a portal opened. The beast within shook the building apart and then there was a detonation which killed everybody.

We were the only three to get out alive. The building was flattened."

"What sort of detonation?" Swanson asked.

"The type happening when someone takes a holy relic and plunges it into the embodiment of sin." Eva replied. "Swanson, I think Brian has been dispatching his own creations. I have no idea why he would do this. Unless there is a greater plan. You have to stop them finding portals by whatever means possible. What if they keep one open and whatever is on the other side finally decides it's time to step through?"

"You let me worry about such eventualities. I will speak with Gila and see what we can come up with. This is what I want you to do. Get some rest. I absolutely do not want you going near the true location in the dark. Get in, look around, get out. If there is any cause to doubt what you are doing, leave. When you are done, call me for further instructions. I will meet you tomorrow afternoon."

"You are going to come here?"

"This is too important to leave you to chance. I will put the wheels in motion to see if we can't stop Ivor Sarch from joining the council. Gila and I have a lot of work to do. Try to sleep."

The phone went dead, and Eva looked at both of her companions. "I don't know about you two, but I'm beat. I'm gonna try."

"Do so," Rick advised. "I'm going to work on these phones some more. Maybe they can tell us what else Elaine was up to."

Eva turned her head to one side, and now really feeling the strains of the day, watched Madden watching her until her eyes began to close.

. . .

Before Eva knew it, the sun was rising again. Both of her companions were deeply asleep so she slipped out of the car and saw to her ablutions in the privacy of the woods. The silence was broken only by the occasional call of a raven, and the far-off honk of an elk. The crisp morning air and the glistening of the sun through the foliage was beautiful. The sunshine fell on her face and Eva remained still, starting to doze off again without even realizing it. Grumbles from within indicated she was ravenous, and even her child, though happy, implied a slight dissatisfaction at her irregular feeding. '*Look after me by looking after yourself*' was the phrase seeming to radiate from her core.

Eva made her way back to the car to find Madden and Rick both standing outside looking in different directions.

"Afraid to shout?"

"After last night, definitely." Madden replied. "Next time, don't wander so far away."

He was only looking out for her, so Eva let the comment slide. "Are we ready to go?"

"Not until you get some coffee and bagels into you, doctor Scott." Rick replied, proffering both.

"Oh Rick, you are a gem. Almost enough to make a woman want to leave her husband!"

Madden scowled.

It didn't take much time for the three of them to make the track look as though they had never been there. The ground was still hard so tire tracks were minimal. Eva had moved far enough away from the car any disturbance she had made was disguised by nature. The only beings moving out in these woods had four legs.

As Rick edged them out onto the road, Eva found she was full of nerves.

"It's far enough away for our being here to not seem a coincidence, right?" She whispered.

Both Madden and Rick watched the road from the front of the car. There was a faint wisp of smoke in the sky behind them.

"We could be here all day," Madden whispered back.

"Just watch the trees," said Rick. "The road will be empty. It's the hidden eyes I'm looking for."

At length Rick must have concluded, as he edged the car out and they resumed their journey around the lake.

With Swanson's warning echoing in her thoughts, Eva watched the road, turning as best she could to look behind. They were headed into God only knew what peril and this time there was nothing to prevent them getting there.

The trees disappeared on their right to reveal the mirror like surface of Lake Bodom, not a ripple on it. The morning was abnormally quiet. Eva wished for a rock to disturb the pristine quiet. In the distance, there was more smoke, but the mansion was hidden from view.

They began to edge away from the lake and for a moment, Eva tried to relax, without much success. The lake, its history, recent events; it was a terror, sinister in its placidity.

"There. Turn right," indicated Madden, his eyes fixed on the screen of his phone. "It leads directly where we need to go."

Eva looked in the direction they were headed. More trees. "Strange how when all these roads are practically woodland tracks this one is covered in asphalt. Recently laid too, by the looks of it."

"Indeed," Rick agreed.

The road continued arrow-straight for a couple of miles, heading through dense patches of pines mixed with enormous hardwoods. Their passing caused more than one flock of birds to take startled flight, and once they had to slow for a panicked deer to skip out of the way. At length, they came to a chained gate, the only evident entry point in a fence about eight feet high, and covered with barbed wire and nasty-looking caltrops welded to the top. The fence stretched off into the distance.

"Break-in it is, then," Madden decided aloud and got out, striding with purpose to the gate, a large wrench in one hand. Wrapping the chain around, he attempted to snap the links by sheer brute force.

Eva and Rick walked up to find him red-faced and gasping.

"May I suggest an alternative?" Rick asked.

Madden nodded. "Chain's...too...thick," he gasped.

Rick withdrew what appeared to Eva to be a small piece of twisted metal on a handle, and proceeded to insert it into the heavy steel padlock keeping the gate secure. Shortly, there was a loud click and the padlock popped open. He did the same for the main lock on the gate and in moments, they were swinging the gates open.

"Part of your ARC training?" She asked.

"As a youngster, I had a fairly unusual background. I could bench-press three hundred pounds, was a pretty mean hacker, and a burglar with all the appropriate skills. You aren't the only one with a story to tell, Madden."

Getting back in the car, a thought struck Eva. Deep down, she didn't appear to know anybody around her. They all had secrets. Rick took the wheel and they edged past the gates, Madden getting out in order to maintain the illusion the gates were still locked by closing them.

The trees spread back to provide an open space in which there were a few buildings dotted about. There were piles of what looked like refuse spread all over the ground outside the building.

Madden grabbed her hand. "Wait here. Whatever you do, stay in the car."

He climbed out and knelt to examine one of the nearer piles. As he rose and turned, he looked like he had seen a ghost.

"What?" Eva called. "What is it?"

Madden walked back, stumbling on the dirt. When he reached the car, he leaned on the hood, taking deep breaths.

"Madden? What's wrong?"

"Those piles aren't trash. Dear God Eva, they're bodies."

CHAPTER FIFTEEN

EVA STUMBLED ABOUT THE YARD, UNSEEING. SHE could not focus on the ground, for everywhere lay remains of what had once been people. A long time ago, she admitted, but people nonetheless. A furnace lay open in front of her, the reinforced iron doors left ajar, and half-cremated bodies hanging out.

When she closed her eyes, the smell still assaulted her, making her want to retch. Charred flesh and the putrid stench of decomposing bodies invaded her every time she drew breath; the sickly-sweet aroma filling her with regret she had eaten any food at all.

It had been too much for both Madden and Rick, the two of them emptying the contents of their stomachs within moments of witnessing the ghastly scene. They both wandered off in different directions, Rick examining the piles of bodies, Madden standing by the lake, staring off into the distance.

Eva chose to join her husband, since the lake provided at least some respite from what was behind them. She approached, and put her arm around his waist. He responded in kind, being careful not to squeeze her.

"How are you, love?" He didn't turn his head.

"Wishing we were captured in a mountain of glass rather than witnessing what's behind us. I never thought such horrors could be found in the modern world. Whoever did this must be brought to account for their actions."

"Maybe that's why we were sent here: to reveal this to the world. Remind them the situation is not as bad as they might think it is; there are always those worse off."

Madden pointed across the lake to his right and Eva followed his gaze.

"The mansion," he said, his voice revealing the strange lassitude descending over them all.

In the distance, flocks of large black birds swirled lazily as they settled to pick over the remains of the Convocation. The sky was growing black over the destroyed building as more and more birds read the signs in the air and joined for the macabre feast. There was still smoke, but no flashing police lights, no other sign of activity.

"Nobody's going to miss them," Eva observed.

"Nobody knew they were there," Madden agreed. "I'll bet the glass mansion just showed the trees behind where it was exposed. At night who is going to be out on the horror-lake to see them? I'll tell you one thing though, the hell-bounces must have come from here. Why else would we be standing here now? They must have done this."

"Would you two come look at this please?" Rick called.

Fearing another look at the enclosure, Eva clutched Madden's arm. He turned and guided her back toward Rick. Every footstep had her fearing she was going to step on an appendage. She kept her eyes down, her head turned into his shoulder.

"What is it?" Madden asked, his tone neutral, but with a frosty edge.

"There is more here than meets the eye at first glance."

"How can this carnage be of any benefit? Look at this place. It's chaos incarnate. It is a death camp like those we have seen everywhere it seems over the last century."

"As I said, at first glance, take a closer look."

Rick shifted what Eva presumed by the noise to be a body, the soft thump as it fell off the pile making her wince.

"Do you see?"

"Holy crap! He's... I mean it looks like... Eva love, you are going to want to see this."

"No."

"Trust me, love, this might well make you reassess the situation."

With a great sense of hesitancy, Eva turned her head from Madden to look at the ground in front of her. A body lay face-up, features stretched beyond human dimensions. The face was a depiction of agony, but despite the deformities, the face burned into her. It was a face she had seen before. The remnants of clothes were the very same he had worn in prison.

"That's Harold Fronhouse, the cannibal from Worcester."

"You know him?" Madden's face betrayed his surprise. Even Rick raised an eyebrow.

"He was a patient, my patient, at the hospital back home in Worcester. In many ways, he is responsible for my feet being set on the path leading me here. He got into the mind of a grad student in my department, causing her to nearly have a nervous breakdown. She should not have been in there with us. He was the reason I began to doubt Gideon Homes."

Eva turned to Rick, suspicious. "Of all the bodies, why did you choose this one?"

"Look around you. They are everywhere." Rick moved to another pile and dragged a body from one side, flipping it over. The cadaver made a sigh as decomposing gases escaped and forced dead vocal chords to resonate. The skull was stretched to the point the head looked to be reminiscent of what could only be called 'little green men'. It caused Eva to reassess what she was seeing.

"This isn't a death camp. It's waste disposal."

"Indeed," Madden agreed, "but waste disposal from what?"

Now she was aware of what she was seeing, she looked upon the enclosure with a different perspective. This wasn't a travesty. This was not cruelty and torture. This was a collection of evil no longer hurting those still alive. It was still grotesque, but at least there appeared to be a purpose.

"All of demon kind was sucked back into hell when the portal closed. Harold was a hellbounce from before." Eva looked up at Madden. "Like you. How was he preserved?"

"How did they stop the portal from claiming me on Nag Hamaddi?"

"Technology. They had machines keeping the portal open."

"All right, then. Who developed these machines?"

"Benedict Garias," answered Rick. "He is the council head for Technology, Demon Tracking, and Emergence Research. Nag Hamaddi was his pet project and Ivor Sarch is his prodigy. If anybody would know, it would be him."

"I don't think Benedict Garias is likely to let us join his inner circle, not unless he gets me on a table and carved into small pieces first." Madden kicked the corpse of Fronhouse so it was face down. "Zoe Larter looked at me the exact same way, as a lab rat just free of its cage."

"Well, why don't we see what else we can find here?" Eva asked.

"Come, look at this," Rick suggested. It's kind of interesting."

Rick led them over to a place where the fence emerged from the woodland. The fence had several large holes at ground level. Around the fence were the remains of several bodies. They were, fortunately, so decimated Eva could not use what was left to form a decent image in her mind.

"These were human," Rick observed.

"They broke in here first, and then came at us across the lake," Eva surmised. "Why would they do such a thing?"

Madden looked around them. "A sense of injustice to demons?"

Eva arched an eyebrow at her husband. "Feeling compassion?"

"Who knows what they feel? I never had much of a sense of kinship when I was one. I was a target. I spent most of the time after my resurrection like a rabbit staring into the headlights of an oncoming car."

"The demons you were tasked to investigate weren't those attacking last night if your theory about the dagger is correct," said Rick.

"Right," agreed Eva. "I could feel them nearing me. When we were shown images of this compound by the council, there was nothing. Those hellbounce were only created in the past few weeks."

"So you are saying the attack on the compound was intentional, to bring you here?"

Eva nodded at her husband. "That's exactly how I perceive it. Someone wanted us here."

"Well, there's nothing out here telling us why. How about we take a look in the overly obvious trap behind us?"

The building to which Madden referred had been painted green and was uniform in color, except where the paint had charred to black around the furnace. A chute led out into the lake from the shore side of the building. It was one story in height, and Eva figured there could not be much inside since it was only the length of three or four the houses on her street back home.

Rick led the way, finding a door with its lock bashed in on the opposite side from the entrance to the compound. He opened it just a crack, using the flat end of a crowbar.

Peering inside for a moment, he looked back at them.

"Deserted." He opened the door farther, causing it to shriek on its protesting hinges.

"If anybody is in there, they know they aren't alone now," Madden observed.

"And they had best watch out as your fearsome reputation precedes you," Rick replied with a wicked grin. "This entrance hasn't been used in a while. I would say whoever was in here has been using a different exit. This is just for show.

Inside, the furnace dominated the open space, taking up well over a quarter of the floor. Paper was strewn everywhere, seats tipped over and the majority of the open space covered in rubbish. Doors hung off their hinges, and even the skylights in the ceiling showed signs of abuse, the glass cracked within the frames.

"This place has been completely trashed," Madden said.

"Great deduction, Sherlock," Rick replied, his face deadpan.

Eva couldn't help but laugh. "Well, it was funny," she said when Madden glared at her.

"Go ahead," he said in mock defeat. "Just steal my wife from under my nose. Take my watch while you are... Hey!"

Madden pulled the sleeve of his shirt up to reveal a bare wrist. "It was there before," he said to Eva, who laughed yet more.

Rick held the watch up from behind Madden. "Pickpocket, remember? How about we search the rest of this room, Dr Scott?"

Trying to keep a straight face for the sake of Madden's pride, Eva followed Rick past the furnace.

"It looks like they brought the bodies in here, and the ashes were disposed of by road," Eva said.

"Maybe the two groups of workers never caught sight of each other, Rick agreed. "Anonymity and all that."

"But why the bodies outside? It doesn't make any sense."

"Perhaps somebody was overloading the furnace," suggested Madden. "If you consider your friend out there, and the time when there was most likely to be demons on the earth, it was just before the portals closed. To me, it all ties in perfectly."

Eva nodded in thought. Madden was absolutely right. "But the question remains, who was doing this?"

"What's 'Westlabs?'" Rick asked as he peered down at the side of a box on the floor.

"Westlabs? Why do you ask?"

"It's all over this rubbish. There are blueprints here for a building, laboratories, conference rooms, and the like. All are stamped with the same name."

A feeling of dread began to creep over Eva. Had she really been within touching distance of such malevolence for so long?

"Westlabs is a massive research company." She looked at Madden. "Their headquarters is in Worcester, on the Biotech park adjacent to the State Hospital where I worked."

"How close to the hospital?" Madden asked, clearly remembering the night, they fled Worcester.

"You could see the building for miles. It is enormous, a massive glass monstrosity. It can't be more than a hundred feet from where you found me."

"What is the betting this is a disposal point for West-labs?" Rick asked.

"Well, they are a global power, to be sure. But no, it couldn't be. Why this far away, and in such an awkward place?"

"Not like they would want to advertise something appearing akin to genocide on their own doorstep," countered Madden.

"True, and a place like this would explain the massive turnover of patients. I never thought to question why so many came and went. Prisoners were always being trans-ferred around. It could be the reason this is empty is someone was on to them."

"Nah, this company would be slick, and well-orga-nized," Rick said as he fished through the documentation. "They left here in a hurry."

He reached up and pressed a button on the wall. Yellow warning lights began to flash and an entire section of the wall lifted to reveal a dock. A cold breeze wafted in off the surface of the lake, causing Eva to look down. She put her hand to her mouth. Bodies bobbed face down in the water, nudging the dock with the slight ripples in the lake.

Rick grabbed one with a boathook, bringing it about and flipping the body so it was face up. Bloated and pale, it was still recognizable.

"It doesn't look like those slaughtered outside were the only victims. Know him?"

Eva stared at the pale face, lips blue and veins full of cold blood prominent. The clothes he wore were unaltered, merely soaked.

"Abel Slocum. One of the hospital guards. He was there the night we escaped. In all honesty, I thought he had been killed by the inmates when they were released." Eva turned away from the corpse. "I guess I was wrong."

As Eva looked the other way while Rick examined the body further, she saw a flash of yellow through the glass of a window into an, as yet, unexplored room.

"There's someone inside," she said, staring straight ahead, her lips barely moving.

Madden edged along the wall of the room, on the far side of the dock, while Eva watched his progress. He ducked beneath the window and came to a halt at the door.

Rick finished prodding the guard and moved to examine another, a lot closer to the door. When both looked her way, she said, "Nothing,"

Rick silently counted to three and both men kicked at the door, sending it flying off its hinges. They followed the door into the room, and the screaming began.

Eva waited outside, and shortly Rick and Madden emerged, both holding a frantically struggling blonde woman between them. She kicked at Rick, who appeared unmoved by her assault. Madden held her firm.

Between the shrieks, Eva made out words. This woman

had been scared witless and was having trouble focusing. Stepping in close, Eva measured the woman, and as she turned her face towards Rick once more, slapped her hard on the face.

The effect was instantaneous. The woman stopped screaming and stared at Eva, eyes red and face puffy from extended bouts of crying. "Where am I?" She said this in an accent not unlike Eva's own. This woman was from Worcester. Eva tried to hide her surprise.

"House of death is the best description coming to mind," Eva replied. "Who are you? How did you end up in such a grisly place?"

Still shaking, the woman gave them a suspicious look. "My name is Florentina. I work here. I should be the one asking you the questions. How did you come by this facility? It's completely off the grid."

"Not completely," countered Rick. "There are organizations bigger than Westlabs, with far more resource."

"You mean like ARC? Are you with them? Are you ARC operatives?"

Eva was thrown by the response. "How do you know about ARC?"

"It's all over social media networks, rumors a body known as ARC is the reason the truth is being hidden from the public."

"You seem to be a fairly integral part of our truth," accused Madden.

"I am well-paid for what I do, but then anybody would be for living in this hellhole."

"And what you do... Florentina, you know what it is you have been destroying here and the potential danger you have been in?"

"It is... was necessary. I dispose of the carcasses for

Westlabs. Well, I did until we were overrun last night."
Florentina looked past them to the carnage inside the building. "They came from nowhere. They overran the guards
and broke into the furnace room, then just started tearing
the place apart. I hid in the office, under the table. I haven't
moved in about eight hours. Do you think I'm just highly-
strung? Everybody on the disposal team knew what they
were doing. We have advanced technology decades with the
research."

"What research?" Pressed Madden. He had demonstrated in the past he was not happy with his lot in life as it
stood, but even when he had been a demon, he had rarely
been as helpless as the time Eva had found him in Egypt.

"I'm not at liberty to say," Florentina answered in a
defiant tone. "I was never invited to the inner sanctum."

"Why here?" Eva waved her hand round the room.
"There must have been a thousand isolated places closer to
home."

At this, Florentina became reluctant to say more, hesi-
tating a couple of times before speaking. "It's... I mean to
say it's not my place to answer that question. I'm no policy-
maker. They live in better offices than I do. Why don't you
go ask them?"

There was an aspect of this Eva felt was suspicious.
Florentina was too familiar to let her wander far, Eva
decided. She pulled Rick's phone from his pocket and
flicked it on, handing it back to him.

"Call the boss. He wants answers and I think we are in
a position to deliver."

"What do you want me to tell him?"

Eva looked at Madden and a smile crept round the
corners of her mouth. "Tell him I'm going home."

CHAPTER SIXTEEN

"Yes sir, I can confirm positive identification of multiple individuals, all pointing to the Worcester facility. There is more, sir. We have one alive."

Rick paused, straining to hear the voice on the other end. "Yes, sir."

He handed Eva the phone. "He wants to talk to you."

Eva put the phone to her ear, stepping away from her companions. "It's me."

"You took a great risk in calling in front of a captive. There wasn't supposed to be anybody left alive there."

"Swan..."

"Don't use my name! We have no record of this person. According to the Westlabs employment records nobody called Florentina has ever worked there and they have employed a lot of people. She must be an agent. Step very carefully, Eva."

"Sorry, sir."

"Are you able to go outside?"

"One second." Eva waved the phone in the direction of

the men, and nodded her head indicating she was going back out.

She held her breath as she walked past the carnage of the incinerator, though outside in the morning sunshine, the carcasses of demons were not a much better alternative. The stench was overpowering.

"Okay I'm out," she said with a sleeved hand covering her nose and mouth. "What is it?"

"Switch the speaker on, and activate the camera. I want to see some of this for myself."

Eva did as bidden, and panned the phone round, paying particular attention to the closest mound of bodies. Once done, she turned the screen back so she could see Swanson. He was walking along a path surrounded by trees, behind which stood the biggest glass building Eva had ever seen. Given the previous evening's excursion, Eva didn't approve of so much glass in one place.

"Park?"

"Privacy," Swanson confirmed. "It looks to me as though it's all started again. Would you agree?"

"No, Swanson. It's not starting again. It never stopped. This is just a new chapter. Another battle in the same war. These bodies, this company. We've come all this way just to have them point us right back to the beginning. I may as well have never left."

"I don't think you really mean that, Eva. Look at all you have accomplished, all you have endured and triumphed over. Look at what is to come, the things literally right in front of you."

Eva glanced down at her swollen middle. She couldn't help but smile at the prospect of meeting her daughter. "Little Hellbender here has no idea the trouble she's causing. It might be the first thing I do when we meet. Give her a sound scolding, and then my heartfelt thanks. She has saved my skin more times than I can count."

"So you have no doubts as to your next destination."

"How could I? Someone somewhere wants me back in Worcester. We need to find out where all this is coming from and perhaps we can get Gila elected at the same time. I have to go home."

Eva returned to the office to find Madden and Rick looking at each other, completely dumbstruck. They turned to greet her as one.

"Swanson is arranging a flight for us at Helskinki Malmi airport. We have to get there and wait. Rick, Swanson says you know what to do, yes?"

Both men stared at her, mute.

"What is it?"

"Did she pass you?"

Eva then realized the cause of perplexion for both men: Florentina was gone.

"No, she did not. I have been on the phone the entire time. What happened?"

Madden answered. "We were discussing Westlabs. Florentina was telling us about the clock tower near the Westlabs facility, how beautiful it is. We must have glanced at each other for some reason."

"Hunger," Rick added. "I was suddenly starving, and would have eaten anything. I actually think I was sizing you up Madden."

Madden laughed sheepishly. "Me, too, actually. Then we turned and she was gone."

"Just like magic," said Eva, unimpressed. "And you don't remember anything else?"

"Her arm," said Madden, holding his hand up. "It was freezing."

"How so?"

"We were just trying to figure out why when you returned. Give me your arm."

Eva held her arm out, and as Madden touched it, several things happened. Eva felt the icy chill on Madden's hand pierce her arm. The baby screamed out both in pain and warning, and a force not seen since the lab complex in Cairo shoved Madden away. Everybody ended up on the floor.

"What the hell was that?" Moaned Madden as he propped himself up.

"I don't know," Eva replied, "but by the reaction of this little one you had better not touch me until your hand warms up, and we should get out of here right now."

Eva sat with Madden in the back of the ARC vehicle waiting for Rick. She was no more eager to stay than her husband, but both understood the necessity of Rick's actions.

He emerged from the building, rolled blueprints under one arm, a case stuffed with papers in his other hand. He dumped all this in the trunk.

As Rick took the wheel, he said, "Time enough to sort through our collection of junk on the way back."

"Are we locking the building up?"

Rick glanced over his shoulder at her as he reversed the car. "Not much point. Swanson knows protocol. I'd say we have about three minutes to get out of here."

"Until what?"

"This location is vaporized. Now let me drive."

Eva kept her mouth shut, looking to the sky for any sign of impending doom. The car sped down the road by which they had entered, Rick only stopping to shut the gates.

"Can't have any random stranger entering this place by accident," he said when Madden questioned the time it took. Once done, Rick floored it, taking them quickly out of the area. In moments, there was a brief roar of a distant engine, and Eva ducked on reflex when the entire area behind them lit up like a colossal bonfire. The ground rumbled and the trees bent as a shockwave slammed into the back of the car, the heat touching Eva through the window. Rick did not slow at all, taking them on roads bordering a nearby golf course, the members of which, to a man, stood mute, watching the idyllic distant scenery light up like a torch. Eva concluded they would never remember a lone car fleeing from the very same direction.

When they made it to the main highway, and Rick visibly relaxed, Eva began to ask questions.

"You knew they were going to launch a weapon," she accused.

"I did, Dr Scott. There would have been no point in warning you. It would have only served to cause undue panic and you needed to be focused."

"What was in it?" Madden was turned, watching the distant inferno. "Seemed nasty."

"Imagine a tomahawk missile carrying something made from a smart bomb and thermite plasma and you get pretty close. There are all sorts of little nasties ARC has prepared and this one will incinerate anything it touches. There won't be anything left by now, and if we ever suffer an incursion like Gehenna again, I wouldn't want to be the enemy."

Rick stayed silent as they drove into the outskirts of Helsinki. She didn't know the people going about their lives, yet Eva felt a kinship and worried for them.

She felt a hand on her leg, and turned to her husband.

"You can't save them all, love."

Eva leaned in to him, savoring the close contact. "I can't help but want to. What have all these people done to deserve what could happen to them?"

They passed the main airport in Helsinki, Eva watching it creep by on their left. Once it disappeared behind them, she assumed they would end up in some provincial little backwater with turf for a strip and a single-prop engine plane would take her to somewhere ARC controlled.

As it transpired, she was almost right. After a couple of right turns, another airport materialized out of the middle of a series of industrial estates.

"Oh, that's beautiful," Eva murmured.

Woods, isolating it from the industry beyond, bordered the airport. Several runways latticed together and, at one end, what she presumed to be the terminal was topped by a white circular tower several stories high.

"Helsinki Malmi," Rick declared. "An airport solely for flight training. There hasn't been a regular service out of this port in over sixty years."

"Unless you work for ARC," said Eva.

"Unless you work for ARC," agreed Rick. "Where better for us to leave than an airport with no service? Anybody watching will presume you are heading to the nearest large airport, whereas we shall sit here and wait."

"Don't you have a plane ready? I thought ARC were omnipresent."

"We have transport in most places. Sometimes, we have to make do. It will suit our needs. Elaine had us on course for God knows where, but the Convocation wouldn't come here. They tried to avoid detection by blending in. Our destination is fifteen hours flight time. It's about twelve here now, so that would make it about three when we arrive. Give some time for refuelling and that puts it about four. Get some rest while you can. With the six hour time difference, we are going to be reaching their end about one in the morning."

Abandoning the car to the mercies of the Finnish climate, Rick grabbed their bags and led Eva and Madden through the very ancient, if well-maintained, terminal. The unused check-in desks with their small signs spoke of a much more personal era when air travel was restricted to the rich and famous, a luxury rather than a convenience. While not overly busy, Eva noted a good number of people going about their business with quiet efficiency, much how it must have been when still a proper airport half a century before.

The air outside was filled with normal activity as training flights took off and landed at regular intervals, the style of plane varying from the small single prop variety to jets of various sizes.

"It's all very cosmopolitan," she observed.

"They are lucky," said Rick. "Hardly anywhere do you get such facilities dedicated to training pilots. They take full advantage. I think we will wait here."

Rick sat them down on a series of very plush yet worn orange seats seemingly built decades ago, but with Eva's current state of body were very well received. Madden disappeared and returned shortly after with food and drink, and in no time at all, Eva was comfortably full. The baby drowsed within, wriggling from time to time as she stretched her limbs, and Eva began to watch the people walking across the terminal.

Face merged with face as Eva began to nod off. The noise of many small engines served to make her drowsy and she realized just how tired she had become. It appeared to Eva that as she watched people would turn and glance at her as they passed, as if she were an unusual attraction. The foot-traffic increased in volume, and she tried to focus on individuals. What she saw startled her. Brian glanced at her as he passed, all bulk and anger. She tried to follow him but the crowd swallowed him up. Then Elaine walked by, the smirk on her face now revealed for all to see. Eva tried to stand, but a pressure prevented her. The baby was calm though all of this. It must have been all right.

Gideon came walking toward her. Eva tensed to run, but was held in place now by hands from behind the seat. Panicking, she turned to free herself. The muscular demons from atop the mountain...

"No!" She cried, but the demons held her fast. The seat upon which she was held remained the only point of reference as the floor fell away, and she plummeted down, all the while Gideon, or Iuvart, closed in on her. The ground caught up with a 'thud' and she was atop the mountain once again. Iuvart, in all his deadly glory, menaced her with a grin, and Eva screamed in defiance. Iuvart stepped aside, and Behemoth, all horns and fire reached a massive paw toward her stomach, twisting and clawing. Behind it, through an angry red swirling portal, swarmed the infinite masses of hell's legions, every one of them hungering to devour her. Behemoth touched her stomach and pain erupted.

"Eva!" The monster roared.

"Eva!"

She twisted to escape. One of the demons holding her loosened its grip and she pulled an arm away. Behemoth swiped for her face. Darkness. A feeling of urgency.

"Eva! Wake up!" The voice was not demonic in nature, but female, and familiar. Eva struggled to consciousness.

She found herself staring into the concerned eyes of Gila Ciranoush, face worried, dark hair framing her face and as beautiful as always. Eva gasped, and reached forward, clasping her friend in an embrace. It was then she felt more than just relief. The baby pulsed a warning to her, and she felt the presence of hellbounces beyond count.

"We have to get out of here. Brian is back, and he's brought company."

"How many?"

Eva looked at her friend, one of the few she could trust, in the eye. "All of them, I think."

"Come on, we have to get you out of here." Gila grabbed one hand and helped Eva to her feet. "The boys have packed the plane, and we are just about refuelled."

"What are you doing here?"

Gila smiled. "You are far too important to be let loose to wander the earth alone. Look at the trouble you have gotten in."

"How long have I been asleep? We weren't supposed to be leaving for hours."

"Plane first, questions later," Gila urged, and hurried her out onto the runway where a plane painted entirely black waited. The steps were down.

"Eva!" Roared a voice, and Eva turned.

"Oh, Hell. It's Brian!"

Her ex-husband came running through the crowd with

what seemed an army at his heels. They spread out behind him, inflicting injury on anyone who didn't have the sense to get out of the way.

Eva hurried as best she could toward the steps. They seemed so close and yet miles away. The engines whined into life as she reached the steps, and a black blur whipped by her as she reached out to climb.

"Come on!" Madden yelled, as he took her hand. "He knows what he's doing!"

Eva turned to see Rick bowl into Brian, the both of them rolling over the tarmac as they tussled. The rest of the hellbounces watched, crowing with delight as their leader was engaged in battle.

Brian had brute strength, more than he had ever had as a human, but, despite his size, Rick matched him with skill. Years of weights gave him a very apparent strength of his own, and the tussle soon became a grappling match.

"What's he thinking?" Eva said aloud.

"Simple," Swanson answered from behind her. "Encourage him to lose control and release the demon thus limiting his shelf-life, or wound him to the point where a portal opens and swallows him whole. Watch carefully."

Eva tried to concentrate on the fighting pair. Rick was animated, his mouth moving constantly. Brian erupted with bellows of rage, but the demon remained leashed. At some point, a decision was reached, and despite Brian's bulk, Rick raised him aloft and rammed his opponent head first into the runway.

There was an audible crack, and even from this distance, Eva could see the blood. Rick wasted no time and sprinted for the plane. Behind him, the air misted as it swirled and coalesced into a portal.

Howls of defeat emanated from the gathered crowd of

demons, quickly replaced by screams of rage from the portal. Brian didn't wait around. As the portal widened and the tentacles began to slip through, he put on a burst of speed Eva never thought possible, and disappeared around the side of the terminal.

"Go," Rick shouted, as he reached the steps. "Who knows what that thing will come after now."

Eva made space for Rick to sit down. "Couldn't quite get him to demon up?"

Rick took a few deep breaths before replying, his eyes on Madden "He's waiting for something, and I was not it. He's a hellbounce. Sooner or later, you always lose control."

CHAPTER SEVENTEEN

Eva's reunion with her friends was muted, but full of relief. She embraced Swanson now they had the chance to without peril, and she sat quietly as the others talked.

"You okay?" Gila whispered from her side while Rick described the scene in the mansion.

"I'm fine. A little on edge, but not as tired as I feared I would be. How long was I asleep?"

"About seven hours."

The time lapse startled Eva. She rubbed at her face with her free hand; the skin was rough and flakes came away in her hand. "I'd kill for some moisturiser."

Gila placed her own hand over Eva's. "One benefit you gain when working for ARC. You are never without supplies." She stood, dragging Eva with her. "If you gentlemen will excuse us, we are going to freshen up."

The three men all gave various comments of assent and continued to pour over the blueprints Rick had retrieved from the compound. Gila led Eva to the rear of the jet where they passed through a doorway into a room with a bed.

"Oh, that looks like heaven."

"Go nuts," Gila replied. "We have quite the journey ahead of us, and Swanson insisted we take a private jet with such comforts you would probably need."

"Face first," Eva decided.

Gila opened a cabinet bursting with lotions and creams.

Eva had to stop herself from grabbing handfuls and settled on a simple moisturiser. "You can't believe how bad it has been to go without this. Frigid arctic air, breezes, the constant sunshine; I'm surprised with the pregnancy I even look like me."

"You are radiant," Gila approved. "Pregnancy suits you, just as motherhood will also."

Eva smoothed the cream over her face, working it in gently. There was a slight sting where the wind had burned the skin raw on her cheeks, but otherwise she felt totally invigorated.

"Never leave home without it," she advised, and promptly put the moisturiser into her bag. "What about you? Ever considered a child of your own?"

Gila blushed. "Once perhaps. I had a boyfriend for many years, but the work got in the way. You can imagine now, with the potential council position and the work I have in the museum, there doesn't leave a lot of time for anything else."

"Sometimes I feel the same way. My own career seemed to rotate around my husband rather than the other way around."

"And look where such an approach has gotten you. I would have killed for normality of any type, but now it looks like we are destined to never find peace."

Eva smiled, resigned to her fate. "People have to make hard choices, and it appears we are those who have been chosen."

Gila reached over and took her arm, rolling the sleeve back to where Iuvart had cut a six pointed star into her arm. The scar was puckered and livid, rising red above the smooth white skin. "Not always willingly. I know the dreams haunting you, Eva. I was not on the altar that day, but I was nearby. I can't pretend to remember it the way you do, but let me assure you, I share the same dreams. Trust me, you are not alone."

Gila gave her shoulder a reassuring squeeze and left Eva to herself in the cabin. The bed was so soft and comfortable Eva couldn't help but try it out. Positioning a pillow under the bump for support, she lay on her side and despite all the previous rest, was quickly asleep.

When Eva awoke, the plane was still in flight. Feeling hungry, she climbed off the bed and assaulted the cabinet full of toiletries. It helped to remember she was a woman for a time, rather than a vessel bearing a child to fruition.

When she felt clean and decent, she opened the door and entered the main cabin.

"Well, it's about time!" Madden said, rising to greet her with a kiss. "You could sleep through Judgement Day!"

"I could? How long was I asleep this time?"

"We are about two hours fight from Worcester."

Eva tried to calculate this in her head. They had fifteen hours flight, give or take, so the maths was easy.

"I have slept half a day?"

Madden laughed. "And the rest of the time, love. We

left you to it. I don't think anybody realized just how tired you were."

"I think with the pregnancy, the stress of the past few days, and the drugs Elaine was feeding you, your body just needed time to recover," said Gila. "With that in mind..."

Gila stood and pressed the lid on a large chest by the table at which they were gathered. It popped open with a click, and Eva was assaulted by such a mix of sights and smells she went weak at the knees. Cooked breakfast, fresh fruit, cereals, coffee; it was heaven.

"Oh. I want that." Eva helped herself to a small portion of everything, fried eggs, juice, and all the meat she could manage. She realized she should have felt queasy for just looking at this, but she was ravenous after such a long sleep, and the baby reminded her of this fact, kneeing her in the stomach.

Between mouthfuls, Eva asked, "So what happened? We haven't been flying all that time."

"We refuelled at an airport in England before crossing the Atlantic. This plane's good, but the range has its limits."

"Oh yes? Whereabouts?"

Madden looked across at Swanson. "Where'd you say? Bristol?"

Swanson nodded. "Home of Blackbeard himself, and of an ARC legend, Isembard Kingdom Brunel. Without him, many of the advances in the organization's scientific history would have remained unrealized. You slept through the whole landing, but it was dark; you didn't miss anything. As it is, we should be landing around midmorning local time."

"So what about you guys, what did I miss in updates?"

"Not a lot, love," said Madden. "We mostly slept ourselves. Just not in such blatant luxury."

"This plane used to belong to some rock star," Swanson

said. "I can think of worse ways to travel. Anyway, I guess you want to know everything."

Eva nodded. "Always. First off, why are you here and not hustling for votes?"

"Well, as I said to you on the phone, we pretty much know who is voting where. The loyalties are quite well defined. Remaining in Geneva would leave us stagnating and getting us nowhere. Coming out here with you, on the other hand, might lead to information preventing Ivor Sarch from becoming the next member of the Council. The politics of the situation is dominated by the fact his research into portals was providing more than information on the realm below. He was on the verge of developing a sustaining energy source, a type of fusion if you will; a solution benefitting all mankind."

Eva slammed her cutlery down. "But at what cost? If his fusion comes by keeping a portal open, what is to stop one of those creatures on the other side from attempting to pass through? I was not the only one on Mount Gehenna. Are these other councilmembers blind?"

"Besides their own greed, several have no concept of the true situation. We all know Gila here is infinitely more qualified to take a position on the Council than Ivor Sarch, and we know why. However, they are the ones in charge, and they perceive any threat to their position as one would consider a rabid dog: it must be put down. The fact of the matter is, Ivor Sarch does not represent a viable threat as long as he remains under Benedict Garias."

"And what about this Garias? What is his play?"

"He seeks to muddy the waters as much as humanly possible," Gila answered as she toyed with her mug of coffee, twisting the handle one way and then reversing it. "It was also better for us to get out of Geneva for our own safety right now. We have allies who are not in the line of fire, and they are safe. Swanson's uncle, for example."

Swanson laughed. "My uncle Daniel is such an uncaring agent of chaos, none of them would dare cross him. They don't know what he is going to do from one day to the next. However, we are a more obvious target. ARC might seem the military behemoth and scientific think tank, but at the end of the day, it, like any big corporation, has its factions. We need to keep it together, at least long enough to see off this threat, and then after? Who knows?"

Eva resumed eating, and watched as Madden helped himself to a serving of the cooked food, piling bacon and sausages on his plate.

"What? Don't you give me anything about how bad this is; I've been to Hell and back. I deserve a little comfort food."

Eva smiled. Madden was right, of course. If anybody had earned the right for a heart-attacks worth of calories, it was he. "So where is the world in all this? What's happening out there that doesn't involve mad cults and reborn demons?"

Gila slid a laptop onto the table, pressing one of the keys to start a slide show. A series of mountains appeared.

"The world is waking up to the fact there is something amiss. They are arguing and debating on a massive level, but these pictures show it all."

"What am I seeing?"

"Those mountains were covered in snow last year, ranges supposed to be producing glaciers. The snow is melting, and sea levels are rising."

"But that's been happening for centuries. They call it global warming."

"A phrase coined by my grandfather, Wilfred, when he

was head of the ARC council," said Swanson. "It was part of an ARC initiative to keep the populace of the earth in the dark. Back then, hellbounces were few and far between, not much more common than the story you once read about Jerome and his encounter in Africa. It really has only been in the last few years this has gotten out of control. My grandfather led a project designed purely for one reason: to convince the world global warming was a natural phenomenon. There is plenty of evidence to back the theory. The amount of carbon stored in the form of oil and coal that dates back to the Cretaceous Period in geological history, for example. The idea this is now being released and creating an echo of a long-dead atmosphere was an easy fiction to maintain. The truth is a much bitterer pill to swallow."

Gila tapped a code into the laptop, and a series of graphs popped up.

"This shows the rate of warming on the earth. There is a supposition to be made here, a scientific leap of faith, if you will. The earth is warming because hell is quite literally freezing over. We presume hell to be a place of fire and brimstone, of pressure and friction. Look at who is probably going there."

"And who has been," Madden added, winking at Gila.

"However briefly," Eva jumped in to defend him before anybody could say anything.

Gila smiled and reached out to take Madden's hand, giving it a squeeze. "We are all friends here, Eva. There is no judgement on this plane. Madden was no saint in life; in his first life. But, consider this fact; as Hell's minion, your husband did more good than he probably did before he went there. People can change."

Gila pointed back to the chart on the laptop. "If we take

into account what we know about Hell as a realm, and the age of the documents, be it biblical records, the lost scrolls, whatever. Add the rate of warming on this planet and the increasing ferocity of the portals whenever a demon on this plane is injured, there is a different story being told. This is not the re-release of carbon into the atmosphere from the Cretaceous. This is intentional, a balancing of atmospheres." Gila closed the laptop.

"The numbers coming through the portal," Eva said in a whisper. The army isn't an invasion."

"This is the preparation of the earth for demon colonisation."

There was silence in the plane, the whine of the engines the only noise, as Eva watched everybody consider the enormity of what Gila had just concluded. What was there anyone could say? Eva placed her cutlery on the now-empty plate, glad she had already eaten for she now had a serious lack of appetite.

"There's more," said Gila. "It is difficult to hear, but if we are the only people who listen then that's a start. What you saw through the portal, Leviathan's army, the Twelve Lost Tribes, is as limitless as it seemed, and the tribes are just a fraction, a mere trickle of water compared to the flood to follow. What we saw before? That was Magellan. That was Columbus, John Cabot, and Captain Cook; discovering a new land. We all know they are the trailblazers, I think nobody has really been in a position to admit there is more to come."

"How do you know?" Eva asked the gathered group. "They went on forever, a seething mass of bodies."

"It's a simple case of statistics," said Swanson. "Forget theology and religious beliefs. Let's assume your average Joe in his lifetime is likely to engage in some act of sin, be it coveting his neighbour's wife or stepping on a cockroach. Murder is murder after all. Let us assume their heinous acts mean they are sucked into hell instead of the rapture that many spend their lives praying for. How many have gone to Hell? How few have gone to heaven? The global death rate is an average of eight deaths per thousand of population as it stands. So, for six billion people that's forty seven million deaths. If only one percent of them are going the wrong way, and we think it's highly likely it is a far greater number, you end up with half a million demons in one year. Minimum."

"That's a lot of assumption."

Gila pressed a button on the laptop, the screen flicking to a series of graphs. "It's what we have to go on, but the facts fit the theory. Imagine this: half a million demons in one year. How many years has this been going on? I am sorry Eva, but the countless numbers you saw were more akin to a squadron if the figures are in any way accurate. They are still preparing to come through despite the setback, and now they have found a new weapon."

"The dagger."

"Right. The addition of your blood on the dagger has them in some sort of religious ecstasy from what we have seen. They have had it from the moment it was lost. We scoured the mountainside and presumed it gone."

"And you are here for my protection? I'm sorry Gila; this is just spiralling out of control."

Swanson leaned forward. "We are here for your protection, your intelligence, and your local knowledge. Your boss Gideon Homes was ARC before he was corrupted and possessed by Iuvart. You were to be recruited to join the organization as his successor. It is very clear from Bodom demonkind is aware of the Westlabs project. We need to find out what Homes knew or at least learned after that point in time."

"Can you get us in there?" Madden asked.

"Getting into the company is the easy part," replied Swanson. "Westlabs has been desperate for ARC affiliation for years. I have booked us a tour of the facility with an implication ARC might be interested in purchasing a stake in the company. We have a meeting tomorrow and it's up to you to convince them."

"What do I have to do with it?" Eva asked.

"You are listed as Gideon Homes' replacement at Worcester State. You might not know them, but they are fully aware of you."

"Great. I don't know who I would rather deal with: demons or corporates."

CHAPTER EIGHTEEN

THE ANTICIPATION GREW WITHIN HER AS EVA WATCHED from the window of the private jet. They had crossed the Atlantic coast moments ago, Cape Cod evoking memories of vacations past. Now the scenery was so familiar. Once they passed the urban sprawl of Boston on their right and followed the Massachusetts turnpike west, every town brought Eva closer to her home, and the possible horrors awaiting them. When Worcester crept into view, they were on approach and only a few thousand feet in the air.

"It looks so familiar, and yet so surreal from this height, like someone built a model," she observed.

"Don't remain detached for too long, Dr Scott," Rick advised, prompting Eva to turn to Swanson.

"They said pending the outcome of the delivery of your report," he said in reference to their marriage. "You aren't coming home, not yet."

In many ways, this comment relived Eva. In others, it was yet another hurdle to overcome.

Madden reached across to buckle her in. "Make sure

your trays are locked and in the upright position." Eva looked at her husband and smiled at his attempt to ease her nerves.

The landing was brief and uneventful. Eva's nerves were frayed and despite what anybody said, nothing made her feel better. The feeling changed when she stepped out of the plane. The sights, the sounds of traffic, even the smell were far less alien than she was used to, and Eva began to settle as the sense of belonging overtook her trepidation.

Swanson guided their party through the terminal, using his accreditation to fast track them whenever necessary. In moments, they were outside, being bundled into a black Chrysler Grand Voyager. Eva forwent the usual comments about the quality of their transportation, realizing she was becoming far too accustomed to this standard.

Eva's heart quickened when she realized where she was. "Pleasant Street," she said.

Madden peered past her out of the window. "Houses, woods, flowers, picket fences. Looks nice enough to me. Typical suburbia."

Downtown Worcester began to grow in the distance, and worryingly, she knew they were headed straight for it.

"Where are we staying?" She asked.

"The Hilton Garden Inn," Swanson replied, as offhandedly as Eva thought was possible.

"No. We can't go there. Too many bad memories."

"Not all bad, I hope," Madden replied.

Eva smiled at him, but her heart wasn't in it. "No, in retrospect, not all bad. But given the situation and what happened after..."

"Your history is the very reason we are going there,"

Said Swanson. "Eva, we are your friends. We are here for a very good reason, one of which could affect the outcome of every life on this planet. You need a clear head, you need closure, and you need to realize there is more than your own situation to concern you now. It might help you to see people have moved on since last autumn. If nothing else, it might give us a bit more of an inkling into your psyche."

Eva felt slightly offended. "I thought I had been quite candid with you."

Gila reached forward from the seat behind and touched Eva's arm in sympathy. "I think what our not so subtle colleague is trying to say is hearing a tale is not the same as experiencing it first-hand. Yours is one of the most important tales since Jerome himself founded Anges de la Résurrection des Chevaliers. It is not over, but the likelihood it will end here is very slim. We are here for you."

"Fine, well it doesn't look like I have much choice in the matter. Where to first on this tour of doom?"

Swanson grinned. "I'm thirsty. Anybody fancy a drink?"

Eva had to give Swanson his due. Outside, it appeared nothing had changed to Moynagh's Irish Bar, the panelled wooden walls plastered with signs for Miller Lite and Guinness. Eva was the first to enter, and stood blocking the entrance as soon as she opened the door. The inside could not have been more different. Gone were the roughly sanded wooden floors and the stained wooden bar. Slate tiles were topped with stainless steel, on both tables and serving counter. Bottles hung down behind the bar, but nowhere near as many in number. The stale beer smell had been replaced with a kind of sterile soap smell. It was true to say Moynagh's had seen better days.

"If you don't mind?" Swanson asked from behind her, and Eva came back to herself.

"Sorry. You weren't kidding. How did you know about this?"

"You think walls covered with blood could disappear without refurbishment?" He replied.

"What blood? When we left, everybody was cavorting in an orgy."

Swanson pointed with his right hand in an open invitation to move along and Eva did so. As she reached the end of the bar, she stopped, causing Madden to bump into her back.

"Here. The TV. It was here at the end of the bar. I was having a drink and you sat beside me. Jeanette Gibson was on the news." Eva turned to Madden, gazing into those deep blue eyes as if it were the first time she had ever really seen him.

"Hoodoo," she said, and kissed him soundly.

Caught off guard by Eva's comment, Madden was slow to react but warmed to the task quickly, causing her legs to turn to jelly.

"Hoodoo? Magic Hoodoo?" Gila asked when they finally came up for air.

"It was the first thing we ever talked about," Eva said, excited she could now remember the conversation.

The barman approached from a door behind the bar, the same slightly rotund, bearded man in his thirties from the last visit, and Eva lowered her voice. "It was regarding something we should not talk about in front of strangers."

"We are not strangers, Eva Scott," the barman said in an Irish brogue. "At least not in the way you think."

Swanson shook his hand. "Eva, this is Steve Collins, owner of Moynagh's."

Steve nodded in her direction. "Passion plunge?"

Eva laughed. The drink offered was what she had been drinking to forget her woes when Madden had entered her life. She patted her belly, tight and full.

"I think it would be remiss of me to have one of those. Give me a couple of months and maybe, I will."

"If you will please all come with me, there are safer places to talk than this." Steve turned and led them down the hallway from which he had emerged. Stepping through a doorway, he held it open until everybody had passed through, shutting it and locking the door with several bolts. He then crossed the room and opened a hidden door in one of the wall panels.

Eva looked at Madden in confusion. What had they found?

He shrugged and walked through. Eva could not see what the source was, but there was an audible gasp and more than one cry of panic from the room beyond.

"Demon!" Shouted a voice, and chair legs scraped on the wooden floor as those inside prepared for conflict.

"No, stop!"

Eva pushed inside, past Madden, fully prepared to defend him. Three men, in the process of standing, paused as they saw her.

"It's you," said a tall young man with a mop of floppy blonde hair, the building rage on his face evaporating in an instant.

"It's me," Eva agreed. "Who am I?"

The young man stepped back, revealing a wall behind him covered in newspaper cuttings.

Eva moved around the room to the wall. It was all there: her entire movements from the moment she left Worcester, tracked in hearsay and conjecture all the way to Birmingham, Alabama. Police reports, news clippings. There were even snippets about Egypt, and the now-famous long shot of the mountaintop in Afghanistan. Amidst all were photos of Madden, and other demons, many being those Eva had encountered on her travels.

"I don't understand," she said. "How come you have all of this here?"

"Eva, this group is what's left of the night you last visited." Swanson moved around the table. "Steve, you have already met. He took over the lease when the previous owner died of a heart attack. The tall man there with the glasses is Ben Bird, his fiancée Jodie is sitting next to him. We have April and Devon Vine, and Mike and Alison Mitchell."

All six of them nodded or smiled in greeting.

"You all have a very special bond," Swanson continued. "You have been in the presence of a demon prince and survived unaffected. Given the insanity spreading across the world, your shared experience is a rare boon."

"What about the demon?" April asked. "What is he doing here?"

"He's not a demon," Eva protested. "I was there. I saw it ripped from him, as he lay unconscious. He was a hell-bounce, barely. The demon aspect was what saved him."

"Trust me, it hurt like hell, conscious or not. I don't recommend it to any of you." Madden turned to Swanson. "Eva is right. What are they doing here, and why all the secrecy?"

"They are an ARC cell, keeping tabs on your home town," Swanson said, taking a seat.

Eva looked to Gila, who shook her head. "First I heard of it."

"What do the names Asmodeus and Belphegor mean to you, Dr Scott?" Asked Devon Vine, a well-muscled man in his early forties judging by the salt and pepper hair and the few wrinkles Eva could see on his face.

"Two of the principle demons in Hell. I learned of their pre-eminence in Egypt. Belphegor is linked with gluttony." It suddenly dawned on her.

"And Asmodeus with lust," Madden finished.

"Two of Hell's chieftains in the same place, not ripping each other to shreds?" Swanson moved to the wall covered with information. "Tell me Eva, what do you remember about that night now?"

"Most of it doesn't bear repeating."

"Oh, I don't know," cooed the woman Swanson had identified as Alison. "Bad things happened, but there was also a lot of good. Look at yourself as an example. You must be due soon."

Eva could not help but smile. "A few weeks. I haven't kept track."

"Four," Gila and Swanson said simultaneously.

"Sorry," Swanson added, "It's an ARC priority to see you come to term."

"Great. I escape the Convocation and still end up tracked. So all the intimacy aside, there was this guy staring at me. He had piercing eyes, like a hawk. I think if Madden hadn't plonked his sorry hide down next to me, I would have ended up with him. He had blonde hair, but it didn't really fit, like it was a wig. There's no more, sorry. I was very distracted."

Swanson pushed a pin in a map at the center of the wall. "And the day you witnessed the slaughter?"

Eva had tried her best to forget the little girl, that poor, poor child; the sounds of bones cracking, the blood, the mindless need to consume and Brian revealing his true self. Tears welled up at the mere thought of it. Eva swore she could smell the blood.

"There was a woman. A blonde woman. She led the girl into the slaughter. She... hang on." Eva turned to Madden.

"That's where I know her from. The blonde woman, Florentina. It was her. It was the very same person."

Madden held up his hand. "Still cold. It's never healed."

Eva looked down at her arm, exposing the flesh by the scarred star. There was no change. The flesh was still healthy.

A warning glance from Rick cautioned Eva to silence. It was apparent the group around the table were not privy to the information about Bodom. Eva stuck to local references.

"Is it even possible this... that we were contrived?"

"You have learned of your ancestry during your travels. You are a Child of David; *the* Child of David. These demons believe with every ounce you were chosen to bring forth a key, as it appears your ancestors did. Madden, it appears was crucial in this. They needed a demon retaining enough humanity to move in the normal world. They wanted you to become pregnant. What better way than to overcome you with feelings of lust?"

"But we left. We were alone all night."

"No, you weren't," Ben Bird countered. The gangly youth opened a folder and passed a series of time-stamped photos to Eva. They showed her and Madden from various angles, and not long after, a single figure with dark hair loitering outside their bedroom.

"You had a spiritual ménage-a-trois whether you intended to or not."

Swanson slid the photos to Madden, who picked them up and stared at each in turn. "Asmodeus wanted to ensure the deal was sealed. He spared no chance you wouldn't end up together. It would appear Iuvart was also aware of this fact."

"How better to keep me close than to work with me."

"Indeed. It would also appear Iuvart has undergone various guises in the past, and each individual was possessed in time. "I know who he subverted," Eva said, her eyes lost in the vision of a dark room with a small window and six pedestals, each with decaying corpses on them. "I will take you to them, but first I want to go home. There are items dear to me I could not pack when I fled. If I am not coming back here, I want to know they are safe and accounted for, if Brian didn't destroy or sell them."

"We have time, but not a lot. They want you, and they still want your child, Eva. Remember, you may be a 'Child of David', but Iuvart, right at the end, was utterly convinced once he knew you were not the one; your child is the key. They thought being pregnant would be enough, that it would change you sufficiently to open the scroll. All it did was make them realize they were one step away, and the dagger is the key to intentional hellbounces."

"Are you saying they are all sitting around waiting for Eva to give birth?" Madden asked, incredulous.

"I am saying more, my friend. I am saying all the forces arrayed against us, on this world and the next, are awaiting the moment of truth, when you produce the one being able to link the various planes together permanently. We need to hide you if we can, and the information gathered here will help if we can be where the other guy is not. Trust me when

I say you will not be alone whenever and wherever you have your baby."

"Do we have time to be hanging around here if my imminent birthing is so crucial?"

Swanson smiled, a thin, grim, fatalistic type of a smile. "We do, just don't go into labor for a few days yet."

CHAPTER NINETEEN

For an hour or so, Eva got to know her fellow survivors in the security of their haven while drinks were served. Each of them had a steely resolve, a backbone the likes of which Eva had witnessed in many of her recent acquaintances. They knew there was something bigger than the worth of their own lives, and they embraced this fact with every fiber of their beings. How soon after meeting Janus had ARC descended on Worcester, or was it her friend, Dr Mohammed El-Rafi? Could it have even been before then? Her activities had been fairly well tracked from the word 'go'.

A slight resentment began to build as Eva came to realize they might have been able to whisk her out of her various perilous encounters. She remained more and more silent as resentment blossomed into anger. Eventually, she could not remain in the room any longer.

"If you will excuse me," she said, and stood, walking out of the locked room and down the hallway, back into the bar before anybody had the chance to stop her.

Throwing the door open and walking into the mild air

of early June, she shed her outer clothing, unmindful of the cars passing with honking horns as their idiot owners thought they were getting a free show.

Overcome somewhat, she put her hands on the side of the Chrysler, taking deep breaths. The baby was low now, and her inner communication had been rare of late.

"You all right, love?"

Madden's tentative and entirely expected question was inevitable given the love they shared, but it just heightened the tension. It wasn't his fault, though. He was as much a victim as anybody.

"Do you realize they could have saved us at any point from here to Birmingham? They knew. The pain, the terror. It was all an experiment in observation."

"I know."

This stopped Eva in her tracks. Astonished, she just stared for a moment. "You knew?"

Madden made a face revealing his inner conflict, biting at his lip. "That's not really what I meant. I know now. I didn't know before. The moment you stood up, it all clicked into place. Am I mad? Well, maybe a little dissatisfied. These people deal in secrets. The CIA and NSA combined do not keep as many secrets as this lot. But no, what happened has happened for a reason. That we are learning about it so late in the day tugs at our sense of righteousness, and yet look at what you have as a result. A husband, a child. Moreover, we are still here. They could have plucked us at any time, but we are stronger for it. Call it fate, call it Karma, whichever. We were destined to do what we were destined to do. Nobody told us we had to like it."

Madden's comments, and his fatalistic acceptance of reality as he saw it served to take the wind out of Eva's sails completely.

"I never knew you thought about it in such a way."

"You never asked, love. Janus saw us safe and despite all the trials, we are still standing. Where there's life there's hope."

Eva just sagged against him, her arms about his neck. "I just want it all over."

The door opened, and Gila came out, followed by Rick and Swanson. Eva stepped away from Madden.

"We good here?" Swanson asked.

"As much as every fiber in my being cries out to say no, we are fine. How anything can be fine in this screwed up world, I have no idea."

"Okay then. Next stop, your house."

Eva watched with detached bemusement as they drove along roads she had known all her life, in a city now alien to her.

"It all seems so structured, so orderly," observed Gila, who was now sitting beside her. "Cairo is nothing like this."

"Cairo has character though," said Eva. "This is Plantation Street. It's just sort of drab and soulless."

Gila laughed. "Believe me, it's tropical to somebody who has never seen the like."

"Well, then you are going to love my house. It's the epitome of tropical. Rick turn right at the next intersection and it's the seventh house on the left."

Northboro Street, a place Eva never thought she would be visiting again. The trees were in full bloom, the weather pleasant enough to set off a riot of green. A few cars dotted the road, and a woman pushed a stroller along the sidewalk. Everybody would be at work about now so it was a good time to visit, especially given the manner of her previous departure. Eva clenched her fists, finding her palms unsurprisingly sweaty.

The houses crept by, seemingly slower and slower until the white-painted wooden structure which was once Eva's own home came into view. The grass was overgrown, and the bushes had become infested with brambles in the months she had been absent. Otherwise, it didn't look much different from the time she had fled.

Madden climbed out and held the door open for Eva. "Welcome home."

Eva touched Madden's face as she passed, the stubble on his chin catching her hair in the breeze. "What you see is a building. My home is wherever you are."

"Eva?" Called a familiar voice from behind her. "Eva Ross?"

Eva turned at the sound of her name, looking past Swanson to see the woman with the stroller. She did not have to look for long, but there had been so many changes.

"Jenny?"

Rick moved to intercept, but Eva put her hand on his chest. "No Rick, its fine. Jenny, how are you?"

Tears came to the former grad student's eyes. "I'm a mom, Eva. I have a little boy."

"I can see. When?"

"Three weeks ago. After you left the hospital, it was crazy. Gideon was raging. He was beside himself, with everybody out looking for you. I tried to help, but they chased me away."

"Who? The staff?"

"No, the prisoners. Gideon was using them as a brute squad and they were listening to him. They weren't trying to escape. Worse, they wore guards' uniforms. All the reports about the escaped prisoners was a front. They were still there."

"That explains a lot," Swanson said. "We never could work out why a bunch of murderous crazies were suddenly so well-hidden."

"And how they turned up in Finland," Eva agreed, forgetting for a moment who she was with.

"Would you show us your boy?" Gila asked, distracting Jenny.

Jenny folded the hood back so they could see the baby. She gazed on the little round face of a baby boy; what stared back at her caused her to catch her breath. It was expected given the last time Eva had seen Jenny, at the door of her own house telling her husband she was pregnant, but to see the result right here in front of her...

"He looks like a little angel," Eva said, fighting to hold back the tears.

"You wait until he's awake. He's a stocky little boy. Just like his dad. I named my son Daniel, after him. I walk by the house every day in the hope his father might have returned. I wait a while, but nothing. He hasn't been here since just after you left Worcester."

Eva didn't know what was worse. The fact Brian had attempted to imprison her or his web of lies to this poor girl, who was innocent of all wrongdoing. Eva was suddenly awash with guilt.

"Jenny, I'm so sorry you have to find out this way, but I think it's best you know the truth, and you hear it from me. Dan, the child's father. He wasn't who you thought he was."

A look of confusion stained Jenny's face. This girl was a shell of the vivacious young woman she should have become.

"I don't understand. How would you know this? Dan and I were in love."

Blind faith was dangerous in the wrong hands. "Jenny, the reason I know is the reason we're here today. This is my house. The man you called Dan was Brian Ross, my husband."

Jenny was dumbstruck. Clearly clawing for something, she looked at Madden and Swanson. "But... but aren't one of you her husband?"

Madden nodded. "I am. We married in Sweden less than a month ago. Eva speaks the truth, young lady. Brian Ross was a very dangerous individual who had her imprisoned in this house the last time you saw him."

"He had a gun pointed at me when he spoke to you on the porch, Jenny. One word from me and I was dead, and probably you, as well."

"Why do you keep referring to him in the past tense?"

"He died, Jenny." Eva reached out to console her former protégé, but Jenny jerked away, stepping out of range.

"I don't believe you."

"Young lady, what you believe or do not believe is immaterial," Swanson said, his brisk tone indicating he had lost patience with this conversation. "Brian Ross died last year on the runway at Birmingham International Airport in Birmingham, Alabama. He climbed onto the wing of a plane, and a missile hit the plane. If it is any consolation, he was staggeringly insane at the time."

"How... how do you know this?"

"Would you really like to know? Would it help you to understand your, our, place in the world by gaining this information? You should rejoice in the knowledge all Brian Ross did to you was get you pregnant. He has done far worse to others. I can tell you it all, but if I do this will be the last time you see this street, this town. You no doubt have a family who are supporting you; can you live without them the rest of your life? Can you bear the burden of knowing they think you and your son dead after you just disappear?"

Jenny retreated behind her stroller, the boy-child within still contentedly asleep.

"Who are you to be saying such things? You can't threaten me."

"These are not threats, young lady. These are no idle boasts. These are facts. This is how it is. We are not here to paint the doorframes and mow the grass. Were we not needed here, you would never have seen us."

Jenny looked at Eva. "It's true. Sometimes the truth can be hard. Believe me, Jenny when I say my eyes have been opened. There is a much bigger world out there than anyone in this city believes, and one of these days, it might just come to visit. When the day comes, I suggest..."

Rick coughed, and Eva went silent. She had gotten too close to having Jenny incarcerated as it was.

"Who are you, Eva? In fact, who are all of you? Are you feds? Spies?"

Madden stepped forward, looking at the child, content and blissfully unaware. "I wonder if such innocent peace is what it will be like for us, love."

He looked up at Jenny. "We are the good guys. That's all you really need to know. Some of us have a way with words you would feel being dragged up against a cactus is a less prickly solution, but we all serve the same master, all aim for the same goal.

To be confronted by this strange collection of individuals must have been too much for Jenny. As the words sank in, fear began to replace the loneliness and self-pity hanging about her like an aura.

"I've got to go, Daniel will need feeding soon, and I have to walk all the way. I live on Hamilton Street now," Jenny said, referring to a road over a mile to the South. She turned to leave.

"Wait," Eva called after the retreating girl. "Why are you there? Do you want a ride?"

"My parents threw me out when I told them I was pregnant. I'm at a friend's house, right now. Penance. I'll walk."

Eva stared after her for a moment, dumbfounded. Then she rounded on Swanson.

"What the hell were you doing?"

"It's called the cold light of day. We aren't here to resume old friendships. The point of all this is to show you that aside from the fact that you are probably the single-most important person on this entire planet, you cannot come back here and act like you have been away on vacation. Say what you will, and I know you are mad with the Organization for putting your lives at risk, but up to this point you have shown strong moral character and a willingness to make the right choice when necessary. Don't start ruining a perfect record."

"But you shattered her life into a million pieces. Who knows if she will ever come out from the bombshell you just dropped on her."

"You are not the only psychologist here, Eva. You have to also remember basic, ordinary people have problems can be extrapolated as easily as a criminal mind would be to you. The girl is living a delusion. She comes here, standing outside this house for who knows how long each day, hoping against hope a man who is now a demon and is pursuing you across Europe is going to open the door and welcome her in with open arms. At worst, she will not believe a word anybody here has said, come back here day after day, and be utterly lost to the world. At best, she will wake up, realise she is making a fool of herself and mistreating her child through neglect. She will look at this place one more time and come to understand nobody is ever coming back, and if she has any sense throw a gas can through the window and burn it to the ground."

"She will not! This is my house!"

Exasperated, Swanson raised his hands to the sky. "Exactly the point I have been attempting to make! It is not your house. You do not live here any longer. You can have any place in the world but if you wish to see those you care about safe once we have done this you... will... never... return."

Eva took a few steps away from the argument, trying to make sense of it all. "I want something from you in return for this."

"Don't you always. What is it?"

"If we survive whatever happens in the near future, if we prevail. I want you to sort out Jenny like you have sorted those out at the bar. In many ways she is a demon survivor, though she does not know it."

"We can't go supporting every waif and stray affected by this conflict."

"No, but you can support a young woman whose entire existence was turned upside down by association with Iuvart, a hospital full of hellbounces, and ultimately the one person giving us grief. If you can't help her, watch me walk away right now."

Eva stared at Swanson, daring him to argue further. He was a firm friend, and she would follow his guidance, but in this, he had to see sense.

"All right," he said at length. "On your terms. If we all survive, I will personally ensure your young friend is looked after. Now can we get in the house?"

Satisfied now she had won the concession from him, Eva turned towards the shell of memories contained in her home. In truth, she was reluctant to enter, and held Madden's hand as she crossed the yard.

As she stepped up to the porch, she remained silent. Brian was not here. They had seen him in Finland only a day or so ago, yet his ghost loomed about the place, shrouding the happy memories, few as they were.

"The door isn't shut," Madden said, and pushed it open. "Oh my."

Eva strained to look past Madden into her house. When she eventually did so, what she saw broke her heart.

CHAPTER TWENTY

THE INSIDE OF THE HOUSE HAD BEEN COMPLETELY gutted, the walls stripped of everything resembling decoration. Flaked paint clung to the wooden panelling, and mold crept over every surface. Brickwork from the foundation of the house protruded into the hallway, and the ceiling had been all but dismantled in a frenzied hunt for who knew what. The building once called her home was now a haven for woodworm and a myriad of small insects, many of which scuttled, upon being disturbed, in search of darkness.

"Eva, you shouldn't go in there," warned Madden. "Look at the state of the place. It's not safe, especially for someone in your condition."

She could not believe what she was seeing. "No, I have to. If you all want me to truly move beyond this, I have to. You don't have to come in with me if you don't want to."

"We go in," Swanson decided to Eva's surprise. "We came all this way for you. I want to see what you see."

Eva flashed a grateful smile at Swanson. The man had surprising hidden depths when he chose to reveal them. She turned back to the hallway.

"Me first, then you, Gila, Swanson, Rick," said Madden.

Eva made to object and Madden held up his hand. "I don't want to hear it, love. I want you surrounded and protected at all times. If something is going to happen, I want it to happen to me first. This place is a death trap.

Eva barely had time for her heart to burst with pride at the Madden's chivalry as he immediately turned and stepped into the hallway. She followed, right on his heels.

The floor was solid enough, being cement under the scraps of ruined linoleum. There was a strange smell about the place, bitter and pungent. It was hard to breathe easily.

Rick bent down and flicked a small dark object. "Rat feces. Judging by the prolific spread and the stench of urine, the building is infested."

"Where are they then?" Gila picked up a wooden shard and poked at the wall. A fragment of plaster crumbled off, dust spraying everywhere as it hit the floor and shattered. "This house is wrong. We should leave now."

"Not until I get what I came for, if it is still here." Eva pushed Madden ahead of her and moved down the hallway. To their right, the door to the living room hung on its bottom hinge, the other rusted away. Madden pushed through and sent the door clattering to the floor. Inside, what had once been a beautiful white-painted room full of warmth and joy, was now a wreck. Soot from the open fire stained the wall above the chimney, white showing through where flakes of plaster had fallen off. One of the windows was still boarded up in haphazard fashion, the light dim as it attempted to permeate the mildew-stained glass. There were fist-sized holes all across one of the walls. The rat-stink was stronger here.

"Somebody was pissed," Madden observed. "No guesses needed as to whom."

Gila walked over to the window, tugging at one of the planks nailed across. "Was this him?"

"He wanted me to live in here, caged. I was to be the mother for Jenny's baby, to bring him up in here. Unfortunately, Brian already appeared unhinged. Let's face it, with what he did here, he could not have held me for long. Brian was flitting from idea to idea regarding my incarceration. I have no idea what had led to his descent into madness other than the fact he was slipping and I did not see it. The fall was just so rapid."

"I suspect he had a little help, given what we have found out about you."

Eva hated to admit Swanson was right, but the evidence just racked up. She took Madden's hand.

"Come on, we have to get upstairs, if the stairs haven't rotted through by now."

The stairs mercifully were in a fairly solid state. They creaked in the silence of the crypt house as Eva climbed them, Madden at her side. She swore she could her scratching around her in the walls.

"Does anybody else hear the noise?" Asked Gila.

"Scratching?"

Gila frowned. "No, an odd thudding."

"Just scratching here."

Swanson peered around suspiciously. "I suspect we may not want to hang around in here. This place just seems wrong."

At the top of the stairs, Eva started to sweat. There were gaps in the floorboards through which she could see the floor below.

"You can wait here," Madden offered, as he leaned on the wall. Eva turned to tell Madden what she thought of his expert advice, but there was a crack, and all Eva saw was Madden's face as he went through the rotten wall.

"Madden!" She screamed, clutching at his hand, but he disappeared in a cloud of splinters and rotten dust. Rick held her fast as the crashing continued. They waited in silence, listening for some sign of him as the dust began to settle.

"I'm okay, somehow," he called up. "I think I'm in a basement. Would you know it, I landed on a couch."

"Wait there," Swanson called. "I'm coming down for you. Rick, get Eva where she wants to go and then let's get out of this diseased shell."

Swanson disappeared back down the stairs.

"No," Eva tried to call, but the scratching came back. The look on Gila's face said she had heard it, too.

"Hurry," she said to Rick, who began to lead them around the safe spots on the landing.

Eva's eyes were drawn to the gaps in the floorboards, yawning and hungry for her to lose her footing. More than once, she slipped on loose wood already checked by Rick. Somebody was playing with her.

"This room?" Rick asked, indicating a faded green door to their right.

Eva nodded, not trusting herself to speak, and Rick pushed the door open.

From the hallway, she could see the massive hole in the floor, leading down to the kitchen. On the right of the room, the wall was relatively untouched.

"Not a chance," Rick warned, denying Eva access. "You tell me what you want and I'll get it."

"There's a panel on the wall, about two feet up. Smash it and reach through."

Hugging the wall, Rick did as bidden and one swift punch and grab later revealed a handful of jewelry.

"Really?" Rick asked, and then yelled as the wood gave way beneath him. Another clatter and crash; Eva's heart was in her mouth.

As one, she and Gila jumped forward, the Egyptian holding her shoulder.

Rick lay flat on his back, the sturdy dinner table having broken his fall. In his right hand, he clutched at the jewels.

"I always wondered what it would be like to be slammed through a table," he said, clearly winded, and then his eyes widened. "Dr Scott, I suggest you get down here. Quickly. Use the stairs."

Eva backed out of the room and attempted to retrace her steps. The wood seemed to have shifted and was twice as dangerous. Gila went down one hole, Eva grabbing her hand and pulling her back. The scratches returned; a million claws desperate for something softer than wood to rend. This time a shallow thumping accompanied it.

"Run," Eva whispered.

Gila stared at her, incredulous. "What?"

"Do it. Run!"

Eva launched into a waddling trot, her belly making it difficult to move fast. Given no choice, Gila followed on her heels. It was not a moment too soon. The scratching rose in volume to the point of becoming painful, and the floorboards behind the women began to disintegrate as they passed, clattering to the floor below.

Eva paused at the top of the stairs and turned back. The entire floor had disappeared in a cloud of dust.

"Don't stop," Gila urged, and together they descended.

Madden and Swanson met them at the bottom of the

stairs, Madden helping Eva along while Swanson did the same for Gila.

"The rats, they are in the walls, all of them."

"Not just in the walls," said Madden, and the stairs to the basement began to boil as the floor came alive with vermin.

Gila screamed, and they wasted no more time watching as they sought a way out.

"Hallway is blocked," Eva shouted above the noise of the rats, now poking through holes in the wall in addition to the mass of bodies seeking them from below. "The floor fell through. Kitchen. We need to get Rick and there's a door."

The hallway was now full of rubble, broken wood, and wriggling forms. Eva shivered as she felt a chill wash over her, causing goose pimples to stand on her arms. There was a conscious anger in this building, and it was directed at her.

Swanson and Madden cleared the way, kicking rats aside, the nasty little creatures squealing at them with blood-red eyes. They reached the kitchen, and Eva heard the thumping again. By the looks on their faces, all of her companions heard the same.

Madden ushered her into the kitchen and there was a snarl in the air.

"Duck!" Eva cried, and everybody dropped to the floor as shards of broken floorboard flew through the spot they had just vacated. The entire upper story of the house began to shudder and collapse, the only saving grace being there was nothing else above them.

Eva cradled her unborn child against the floor until Madden helped her up. She tried to find her inner peace, the communion allowing her child to act, but nothing returned. It caused Eva to worry.

"Get Rick," she shouted, pointing at their guard prone on the table. "We will get the door."

Madden turned to help Rick up, and stopped, staring in the same direction at the opposite wall.

"Eva!"

She turned to follow their gaze. On the opposite wall, perhaps the only unblemished wall in the entire house, were smeared the words 'Nowhere to hide'. Several broken and bloody rats lay in a heap beneath the words.

Rick groaned as Madden helped him up, his face pale.

"He's concussed, probably with a few cracked ribs," Madden called above the noise. "We have to get him out."

"Get the door, I want to try something."

"Quick," Madden advised Swanson. "I've seen that contrary look in her eyes before."

Eva turned from them. The snarling she could not be sure anybody else heard, but she suspected she knew the source. Something here contributed to Brian's downfall. He had to have had help in his descent into madness. She glared at the collapsing hallway, daring something to manifest.

"I'm not scared of you." She threw the challenge at the house with all the scorn she could muster.

"Don't you know who I am? Don't you feel what I have been through? I have stood on the threshold of Hell itself and defied it. You think I am going to fear your little tantrum?"

The walls of the house groaned in response. Rat squeaks became shrill squeals. A pressure began to build, and behind it Eva sensed an anger ready to explode.

"Go on, try it. I dare you. Bring the walls down about us. Crush us into oblivion. Do you think you will suffer anything but an eternity of torment if you do? Look to your elders, impotent demonling. You want to scare me? The time for fear has passed. You had your chance. Iuvart had his chance. Behemoth had its chance. Where are they now? Rotting in the pit of Hell, gnawing their claws in vain because they got it wrong, just like you got it wrong."

"Eva," Swanson yelled as he pried the nailed planks from the door, "what are you doing?"

Eva grinned. "Delivering a few *home* truths."

She turned back to the house, the floorboards were shaking now, loose nails popping out and flying past her. Wind began to gust about them

"You might think you are safe, but I don't know about the rest of us."

"Just work on the door." Eva turned back to the house, taking a step toward the doorway.

"Why don't you come out where we can all see you? Why don't you stop hiding in the shadows and face me? What are you afraid of, pitiful hellworm? Do you think to pit your rage against a mere mortal, a pregnant woman, and it won't be enough? Or are you so weak and feeble you can't even beat me down?"

The snarling became a roar of anger, and the whole house shuddered. Plaster shook around them, and the untouched wall began to bend and contort as their tormentor gained form. Above the words, a head twisted from side to side as teeth attempted to rend the wall and allow the creature access. Claws pushed forward in an effort to break through.

Confident now, Eva stepped up to the wall. "You can't even manage to break a wall. What are you? A demon that found his way back but is not a hellbounce? You're pitiful. How insignificant you must be."

The writing behind the wall intensified at a spot closest to Eva. The wall began to grow cold, frosting over.

"Done!" Called Swanson, yanking the door open. "Let's get out of here."

Eva didn't move. This was not what she had expected. The wall continued to freeze, and then the swirling became the pounding she had heard before. The rats all began to scream in pain, a high-pitched piercing wail. Cracks began to appear in the wall.

"Eva!" Madden yelled, and grabbed her hand, pulling at her.

Eva resisted, her eyes locked on the wall. She moved grudgingly, watching as she was pulled through the door. At the last moment, the wall burst asunder, and tentacles, razor-edged and wildly swirling reached through. They grasped in blind desperation for the quarry taunting them.

"What the hell?" Madden exclaimed, watching from beside her. "The portal only appears when a demon is injured."

Madden turned to Rick. "Anything you're not telling us?"

Barely able to draw a breath, Rick sagged between Gila and Swanson, shaking his head.

"No it couldn't be him. Look at the manner of the incursion. If it were Rick, the portal, if you can assume it is the same entity, would have sprung open earlier."

"The game has changed," Swanson concluded. "Get back now."

The five of them moved out of range of the house, which now began to collapse in much the same way as the Convocation mansion in Finland.

Rick held his hand up to Eva. "Hope it was worth it," he wheezed.

Eva gratefully accepted the jewels, even as the house collapsed behind them. "My father gave these to me; the only possession given to me by someone other than Brian. He would fly into a rage if anybody gave me anything, so I hid them."

Eva stared at the rubble. There was no sign of the tentacles, no trace of ice. All the house meant to me, the only memory I wish to carry away is my life was always full of secrets."

"Well, then you can carry those secrets to a jail cell," said a voice in the distance behind them. "Freeze! Hands up, all of you!"

CHAPTER TWENTY-ONE

EVA TURNED TO THE SOURCE OF THE VOICE, BEMUSED. At the side of the road, two squad cars had parked with lights off. Drivers were sitting in both, and in front stood a silver haired man with horn-rimmed glasses and an ill-fitting blue suit reeking of cheap tailoring. A man Eva recognized all too well.

"Detective Mike Caruso," Eva said. "Isn't this a pleasure? Trousers still don't fit I see."

Caruso had his handgun leveled at them. "I said hands up!"

"Really?" Madden replied. "You are actually going to do this?"

"Yes, I really am. Eva Ross, I am arresting you on the suspicion of the murders of Jane Doe and Brian Ross, false imprisonment, and resisting arrest. If there's any way I can link you, I'll do you for the murder of Brian Ross as well."

Down the road, Eva noticed a shape attempting to remain anonymous.

"Jenny. She didn't go home, after all. Poor girl."

"If this is how she starts to deal with reality, it's a start."

Swanson earned a glare from Gila, but Eva knew he was right. If this scene did not prove anything to the girl, she would never move on.

Rick shook his head and attempted to move forward, still seeking to protect them.

"No Rick, don't. There's nothing you can do here. He is going to take whatever course of action he deems necessary, no matter how dumb he looks."

The fact five people were facing him down completely unafraid despite the gun pointed at them was slowly beginning to register with Caruso. He looked uncertain.

Behind them, the house collapsed in one final cacophony of noise, dust erupting everywhere. Eva held her sleeve over her mouth until the breeze had cleared the worst of it.

"Anything?"

Madden turned and took a couple of steps back.

"You move once more mister and I shoot."

Eva stepped back to join her husband, ignoring the detective as if he were simply beneath notice.

"No tentacles, no rats. It seems as if you are now the target of more than idiot cops."

Eva felt a chill down her neck. Would it ever end? "I saw a demon in the wall. The tentacles used it to open a portal here."

She turned back to Swanson. "You know what today's lesson is?"

"Unfortunately, yes. Any demon we injure isn't being destroyed, it's being captured. They are experimenting like Garias and his team. It could also mean hell has already been conquered from beyond."

"More," Madden added. "You can't injure or maim any demon emerging here."

"Because if we do, we are only providing more access to those beyond," Gila concluded.

"Make the call," Swanson instructed her. "We have enough to, if not to shut them out of the vote, at least close down the experiments."

Gila pulled out her phone and pressed a single key. "This is Agent Ciranoush. I am confirming ARC protocol six-four-six is now in effect. Destroy only."

Madden grinned. Eva could sense his amusement.

"You would do well to smile, given the irony of the name." Gila put her phone away. "Protocol six-four-six was set up to deal with you, should you have ever lost control. Total incineration. Fortunately we never needed it."

Behind them, another car pulled up. The short form of Tina Svinsky, all bustle and wild blonde hair wrapped up in a tight black suit, emerged.

"Mike, stop," she shouted in what sounded like an order.

Caruso glanced in her direction, the gun unmoving. "Captain, we need to do this. We lost the chance last year and it cost us."

"No, Mike, we don't. There was never anything more than circumstantial evidence. Stand down."

"Actually, if you don't mind Captain Svinsky, I would love to hear his proof. Congratulations on your promotion, by the way. I'm sure it was well deserved."

Svinsky inclined her head in acknowledgement. "It looks like congratulations are in order for you, too. Is this the cause of it?" Svinsky pointed at Madden.

"Tina Svinsky, Madden Scott. Let's just say things have changed for the better."

"I'm aware of most of it, I'm sure. Privileges of rank."

Caruso in the meantime was staring at Madden anew. "This is him, the rapist?"

Madden glowered at the term, but Eva stepped in. "It wasn't rape. Not in the standard meaning of the word."

He raised his handgun again. "Got you on wasting police time and false accusation then."

Svinsky shook her head. Clearly, this was not the first time this had happened. "Mike, you don't have them on anything. We are letting them leave."

Eva glared at Caruso. "We watched you as you followed us all the way from here to Alabama. Every news article they showed on ABC. You were there. You, Brian... and Iuvart. You followed us with the creature... man trying to kill us."

The realization hit her, and Eva grabbed Swanson's arm. "You knew what they were doing, and it was your way of warning us."

"Not me, personally, but it is a tactic of Media where necessary. Jeanette is quite inventive. During your flight from Worcester, I had no clue as to your existence and the trouble you would end up causing."

Caruso, in the meantime, had refused to stand down. "They are killers. They should be locked up."

"I'm sorry, Detective," Eva replied. "You are wrong. In the days to come I hope you will see this."

Svinsky pulled out her phone and dialed. "Sir, we have a situation. Yes, we have tried. Let me pass you over."

She passed the phone to Caruso. "It's the Chief. He wants to speak to you."

Caruso grabbed her phone with his free hand, visibly angry at the diversion. "What?"

His face began to pale as he stared at Eva, and at one point he flinched, and stared at the phone.

"Yes, sir." Caruso eventually growled and handed the phone back to his superior.

Saying nothing, Caruso stared at her, and Eva understood, despite no fault of her own, she had just made an enemy. After a few seconds of this, he turned and walked away, not acknowledging them as he climbed into his car and drove off. At a nod from Svinsky, the uniformed cops followed him.

Svinsky approached, a look of regret on her face. "I'm afraid there's not a lot of time left on the force for Mike. He was gone for weeks after you, and despite what happened here, he wouldn't believe anything other than it was your fault. Mike Caruso has taken down every mark he ever set his sights on. It made for one dedicated officer. But in the last year or so, particularly in the months leading up to your phone call, he has been somewhat distant. There have been local cases too where his judgement and associations have been called into question. It's another story for another time."

Eva looked to Swanson for guidance. It was clear the police Captain knew some of what was going on. He nodded imperceptibly. His facial expression practically shouted 'Not for discussion in public'. Secrets. Always secrets.

"It was his association with Gideon Homes. Let us say, in my professional opinion as a criminal psychologist, it clouded his judgement.

Svinsky smiled at the jibe. "What about your personal opinion?"

"He fell in with the wrong crowd. I think you know what I mean."

Svinsky inclined her head. "Councilor Guyomard,

everything is set for tomorrow. We will be on the watch from a distance."

"Thank you, Captain. Should events go awry, look to Miss Ciranoush or Dr Scott for direction. Beyond those two, I would be tempted to leave you in Madden's capable hands."

Svinsky gazed at Madden and her face hardened.

"What? I'm no longer a hellbounce. I'm about as useful as a candle with no wick. Besides, you would never have seen me before. If you have access to the knowledge I believe you do, you will come to understand I was small fry. I was the least consequential cog in the engine."

"Self-effacing to the end," Svinsky observed. "I've read your file, and have seen what you did, what you nearly sacrificed. You are as much a hero as any person here, but from my perspective, you had the ability to become the ultimate criminal. Imagine the crimes of no consequence you could, might have, gotten away with. The man nobody remembers is the man who has everything at his disposal."

"It might seem that way, Captain. There is not a person on this planet who at some point in their lives doesn't entertain the notion of what they could do if invisible. The novelty wears off rather quickly. I had money, jewelry," Madden looked to Eva and she felt every ounce of love in his stare, "women. Whatever you could wish for, I had it. However, the price is eternal anonymity, whether you like it or not. I could pour out my heart, tell my life's story to a person just to have them turn away, and look back at somebody they had never laid eyes on. It was a lonely existence. I became a nomad. Those who recognized me did so because they had known me all my life. Can you imagine living with a group of people who see everybody around them suffer from selective amnesia? Can you imagine the questions? I would rather be alone than suffer memory loss again. Fortunately, I do not have to. Not anymore."

Eva's heart just burst with pride. Madden had never been this candid with others before.

Svinsky evidently agreed. "If this group trusts you to lead then who am I to argue? I will contact the group and inform them of our movements. April will take care of the rest."

Eva watched in silence as Svinsky turned and left, leaving them in the spring sunshine. Larks sang above, and in the distance, children could be heard playing outside. The city was full of life and the destruction behind them seemed somewhat out of place. If the supernatural violence on her own doorstep was an example of what was to come, Eva swore silently, she would die before her city fell to ruin.

Rick groaned, bringing their attention back to the immediate.

"He's hurt," said Swanson, being careful not to hold the big man too tightly.

"I'll be fine," Rick growled in response. "Just need a bit of rest."

Swanson looked to Eva. "You done now?"

"What else is there left but a tomb of memories and the hospital? You know where I would rather be anyway. It's certainly not here."

"World is your oyster," Swanson agreed. "Let's get him seen to."

The majority of the afternoon was spent in an emergency room with various doctors poking at Rick, who endured the constant attention with his usual stoic impassivity. The conclusion was he had sustained bruising but not much more. The flat faces of the doctors at Rick's comment about bulk being good for something showed they were not amused.

As it was, Eva found she preferred the stench of rush-hour fumes to the stomach-turning sterile hospital environment. The baby had no feeling on the matter, and this began to make Eva worry.

They fought their way through the crowded streets to find the Hilton Garden Inn. As part of her recuperation from twisted memories, Eva boldly entered the lobby, strolling up to the bar and ordering a whisky from the very hesitant barkeep. She looked around as she held the glass. It was identical, not a seat out of place.

"So what happened here?" Gila asked, gently removing the glass of amber liquid from her hand, and placing it behind on the bar.

"Various events. Here at the bar was where Gideon spoke to me. I had no idea he was Iuvart back then, though there was definitely something wrong. The barkeep pointed me in the direction of Moynagh's from this very spot. Over there, by the front door was where Brian came in, still covered in blood and gore. He stood, shouting for me, ordering me to come down and then threatening when I would not. There was a fight and he left." Eva pointed to the staircase in the middle of the room, white underneath, with black twisted metal bannisters all the way up to the first floor. "I hid up there. He never saw me, couldn't find me. If today's Brian had been in the lobby, I wouldn't have stood a chance."

"Tell me about this room in the hospital," Swanson asked, pulling out a chair at a nearby table and inviting Eva to sit down.

She refused the offer, her eyes suddenly became heavy

and Eva was reminded she was both hungry and tired. This was her town though, and her rules.

"I'm starting to tire, Swanson. You will have to be satisfied with the knowledge the room was near identical to the room in Egypt, and protected in much the same way judging by what I witnessed. With that in mind, what was there when I left should still be there now, and will certainly be there in the morning. You could go look if you wish, but I'm sure we would all feel a lot safer if we all stayed together awhile longer. It can keep. Have a drink, have some food. I am headed for my bedroom, room service, my husband, and sleep. In that order."

"I'll bet," said Madden. It's been a long day, not uneventful, and you are carrying an extra person around."

"Rooms have been sorted, exactly as you would want them Eva," said Swanson. "We're all on the same floor. Suffice it to say, they have removed the crime scene tape from your door by now."

"What about him?" Eva indicated the slumbering form of Rick, blissfully unaware of his surroundings thanks to the after effects of the medication given at the hospital.

"Don't worry, we will get four or five of these strong young people to help us get him upstairs and he will be right as rain in the morning. I'm not going anywhere. You get your rest."

Eva looked at her husband. His eyes betrayed the fact he was not anticipating this moment, replaying the last night they'd spent together in this hotel in his mind. She reached up and pulled his head close, kissing his warm lips, reminding him of what he had because of the very night he feared to remember.

"I'm not the only one who needs to put things behind them you know."

CHAPTER TWENTY-TWO

Eva opened her eyes after a night of blessed slumber. Daylight streamed in, highlighting the ever-present motes of dust. The scent of stale cooked food made her stomach growl, and she noticed the barely-touched meal Madden had ordered still on the trolley. She must have dropped off before the bellboy arrived. The patter of droplets on tiles indicated her husband was in the bathroom.

Madden. She remembered the name, and it brought a smile to her lips.

"Madden," she tried the word aloud. "Madden. Madden. Madden."

"Yes, love?" He called, pulling the door open as he wrestled with a towel, his still-wet hair plastered down his face.

Eva giggled. "You look a state."

"Well, you called; I came."

Eva patted her belly, hard as rock, full with child. "I know. That's what got us into this mess in the first place."

He grinned and dried vigorously with the towel sending

his hair into a whipping frenzy. "Nice you remember my name this time."

"I was just thinking the same thing. It is a better memory rather than a bitter memory. How are the hands?"

Madden dropped the towel and flexed both hands. The scarring was barely visible. "Strangely good. Almost completely healed."

Eva rose, and once she got her balance, joined him near the bathroom. She took his left hand and examined it. As he had said, the scarring left by the Scroll of Judgement when carried by Madden at Iuvart's behest was almost completely gone; faint white lines remained with a trace of scar tissue.

"I think you retain more of your past self than even you would care to believe. Stop ogling me and get dressed. We have a lot ahead of us and I'm hungry."

"Well, if you had done anything other than snore at the bellboy maybe you wouldn't be quite so famished." Madden danced out the way of Eva's mock swat, her hand only finding air.

"Breakfast awaits."

Swanson and Gila waited for them in the restaurant, the former having located a private area for them. The smells of breakfast, as always, threatened to overwhelm Eva. Her experiences in Europe demonstrated whatever America couldn't do by refined quality, they more than made up for with sheer bulk.

"I'm surprised they found any room for plates," she observed, eyeing the mountain of blueberry pancakes in particular.

Flashing an amused smile, Gila said, "What was the comment, Swanson? If you had to wait but a moment longer for Eva to decide what she wanted to eat, it would not be because of the menu?"

Swanson had the good grace to look embarrassed. "I want us to have as much time at the hospital as possible. If we can get started?"

Rick joined them shortly after, wincing as he moved, but easing somewhat as he polished off enough food, it seemed to Eva, for three people.

"It's fuel for healing," was all he would say.

Perhaps half an hour later, they were in the Chrysler, traversing the bustling Worcester streets towards the hospital. Beyond Worcester State stood the home of Westlabs, a giant glass mountain, designed by some architect or other. As they crept along Clocktower Drive, Eva's memories came flooding back.

"This wasn't real, was it? All my work here was a sham."

"Only if you consider it that way," Gila replied. "As a scholar, I would provide this counter-argument: everything you were taught, every demon you unwittingly assessed led you to this point in time, and this place in the world. Every moment of fear you experienced buttressed you against Gehenna."

"What did Gehenna buttress me against?"

Nobody answered her question. Nobody knew. Yet.

Swanson parked outside the former Worcester State Hospital, the building evidently having remained empty since its evacuation.

Eva climbed out of the car, and paused. The morning was cloudy, a brisk wind thrusting streaks of cloud through the sky at a pace fast enough to make Eva feel she was stood underneath an enormous vortex. Or portal. Several black-ops ARC operatives waited inside the entrance.

"You have been busy," she said.

"A lot of it you know already. After you fled with Madden, Iuvart went headlong in pursuit of you and left this place open. Most of it. I would suggest whatever deal was in place with Westlabs involved many of those same prisoners disappearing. A month or more went by before ARC secured the building, and it has been kept watertight ever since."

"You took control of this place, in the midst of a media storm?" Madden appeared as impressed as he did disbelieving. "How did you manage to keep the journalists out?"

Swanson tapped the side of his nose with his index finger. "Quietly. Under the radar. Westlabs was just interested in the science. They were like hyenas, gobbling down any scraps of development they could, trying to make sense of the secrets. Problem is, they are all about the science, and you know in this fight, science is only half the battle. ARC is science *and* faith. Once they took the test subjects, they were not interested in empty offices or the decaying shells of medieval buildings."

"We however, find all sorts of treasures in such places," Gila added, leading them up the steps into the hospital.

Eva hesitated upon entering. "This is where I really met you," she said to her husband, and turned to Swanson.

"I was being chased down by two of the inmates. Fronhouse was one of them. Madden saved me."

Eva knelt down to look at the tiles. Despite there being a thorough cleaning of the room, the grouting between the tiles was still stained brown from dried blood.

"One of them had his head caved in right here. I had come up from the basement."

"Not a great place to be in a nest of demons."

"I disagree. I was trapped upstairs. Gideon... Iuvart had control of the security doors from his office. I jumped down the laundry chute to escape. It was a pile of dirty socks or take my chances with some very unsavory individuals. You never did explain how you found me, Madden."

He shook his head. "I have no idea, love. It might have been instinct, like Brian and the knife. I just knew where you were from the moment I left the hotel. I wandered around for the remainder of the day, aimless, but always knowing in the back of my head exactly where you were."

"Like Dracula when he has bitten a victim," Gila explained. "The most famous hellbounce on record. Incredible powers of persuasion."

Eva stared at Gila, mouth agape. By the silence in the room, she could tell her husband's look mirrored hers.

"Every day the world is a little less black and white than you believe it to be, eh?" Swanson swiped a black plastic card on the security sensor of the door, causing a high-pitched beep and the door to pop open.

"That's new," Eva said, noticing the door for the first time.

"Wouldn't be much point securing this place and leaving it as is. Anybody could get in. Rick, you wait here. We will be enough for Eva this time."

Eva kept her eyes forward as they walked the halls of her former workplace and potential prison. Everything had been cleaned but the memories still remained. In her state of late-pregnancy, the steep wooden stairs up to their offices were a challenge, but they had time on their side. She paused for a moment to catch her breath at her old office door, hand reaching out to push it open. The comfortable sofa would be there, plush and welcoming.

"It's empty," Swanson said, before she could complete the movement. "Everything was removed for study."

"All of my stuff?"

"Everything not nailed down in this entire building. I am sure you can understand why."

Eva wanted to take umbrage at this fact, but she merely nodded. They would have wanted to research every aspect regarding Iuvart, and how he could have immersed himself in society so completely, fooling everybody.

Gideon's office was secured by another electronic lock, and Eva presumed Swanson had the only pass. The door popped open and he led them in.

The office was much like Eva remembered it. Gideon's wooden chair and desk, the old leather seat opposite, cracked and brown, covered in dust. The cabinet.

"This is different. Afraid to touch an item touched by a demon?"

"Until we returned here with you, this room was sacrosanct. If it leads to what you have described, then it is as important as Nag Hamaddi or Utö."

"It's where my journey really started," Eva agreed, approaching the cabinet. "Was this locked when you got here?"

"Yes, according to the reports."

"He tidied up first then. His actions beg the question why when he couldn't get beyond."

"For show? It's not tidy." Madden pulled out a sheath of documents from a drawer, folded and protected with plastic. Ripping the plastic open he unfolded sets of blueprints very similar to those Eva had seen in Finland.

"Westlabs." Madden placed the blueprints on Gideon's desk and rotated the sheet towards them.

"Looks like a laboratory, but separated from the rest of

the building. Also a tunnel runs underground from this point to somewhere outside the building, but there's no orientation on here." This got the rest of them to looking around the room, though Eva's attention was locked on the cabinet. She stepped close to examine it.

"It's safe to assume it comes in this direction," Madden elaborated from behind her. "Too much coincidence. Hospital full of lunatics, many of whom end up in exactly same place as we do."

"Here we go," Swanson announced, pulling up the false bottom of a drawer. Spreading a wealth of documentation on the desk, he sorted through the papers. "Inmates past and... well... past. Records of what look like the past hospital administrators and more blueprints. The tunnel ends in the basement of this building."

Eva recalled her escape the last time she had been in this building. "It's dark down there. In all honesty, I was too busy trying to avoid everybody to worry about what was behind doors number one two and three. What are the administrator names there?"

Swanson shuffled through the paper. "Buckland, Grouse, Andrews... a few others."

Eva flicked at a few of the sheets, sifting through them but seeing nothing. "I find it hard to believe Iuvart left all this around for somebody to find it."

"This was his power base, his nest, for decades. He felt secure here. With absolute control, he had no need to protect what was his. Once you evaded him, you became his sole focus, his obsession. But I..."

Caught mid-sentence, Swanson turned to Madden. "Not Eva, you."

"Makes sense," Madden agreed. "A near-powerless demon to bear his scroll. Eva was just a means to an end."

"It's time I showed you what we came here to see," she said. "We need to get Iuvart's cabinet open. The lock has changed since I was here last. He must have known."

Madden stepped up and took hold of the cabinet, straining to move it.

"You can't. It's built into the wall."

"I can get through the lock," Rick said from the doorway, lock picks already to hand. "I had a feeling you would need me."

Crossing the room in what could only be called a delicate state; Rick winced visibly when he knelt in front of the doors. Eva did likewise in unconscious sympathy. Yet despite his damaged ribs, his hands worked just fine.

In seconds, the lock clicked and the metal doors swung open, squeaking on unoiled hinges.

Eva peered in, anticipating the cache of drugs, but unsurprised when she found it empty. The cabinet had been sterilized, the stink of bleach still strong after all this time. She turned to Swanson.

"Not us."

"Okay, well hold your breath regardless."

Recalling her last visit, Eva reached into the back of the cabinet, tugging on the top shelf. As before, the door slid open, revealing the bricked corridor to the tombs beyond.

The carrion stench wafted through an instant after the door opened. Even forearmed with the knowledge this would happen, in her particular state, Eva couldn't help but retch.

Madden stuck his arm into the space ahead. "No breeze, yet still the scent flows."

"Decompositional build-up of gases," Gila said, taking the lead.

Madden followed, and Swanson indicated Eva should

go through third, while he unleashed a flashlight as bright as daylight behind her.

"Strange," Madden observed as he walked along the narrow corridor. "It feels cold in here. I think this passageway is still sanctified. Were I still demon, I think this would hurt."

"It appears to be based on the same design," Swanson agreed. "Actually, I think this is another."

"Well, if the design is correct, Iuvart could never have gotten in here."

"I don't believe he did," Eva said, running her fingers down the smooth cobbles sitting between the crumbling mortar. "I think he was guarding it."

"From what?" Madden asked.

"Maybe not so much from what but 'for whom'," answered Gila. "Possibly he knew this room to contain the very documents you brought to us, but he could not retrieve them. He sent people in there to bring them out, those who were utterly dominated by him, those who would not be missed because they were always going to die."

"And they chose to remain there rather than give in to his demands," added Eva.

Madden turned to argue this point and Eva forestalled him with a hand on his chest. "Trust me, they chose to remain here."

Gila led the way into the small room, and it was as if nothing had changed. Except for the fact she was with three of the people she trusted most on this Earth, she would have been terrified beyond the edge of her sanity. The narrow window allowed a sliver of light into the room, but Swanson's beaming torch soon made up for any lack of daylight.

Gila went straight for the altar, while Swanson checked the corpses. Nothing had changed. Each body still rested in to their various stages of decomposition. Eva stayed close to her husband, wishing against wish she would never have to spend another second in such a place as this.

"These markings on this altar; they look sort of familiar."

Madden approached the altar and Eva followed. He cocked his head to one side, and she could see his mouth moving silently as he read the words.

"Rosier." Madden started to speak, then paused and looked around at the rest of them. "And Garias."

CHAPTER TWENTY-THREE

THE DAY SEEMED MUCH GREYER WHEN EVA EMERGED from the hospital. The trees were a darker mix of green and brown, the sun dimmer. She held onto Madden's arm, still chilled from the contact with Florentina, yet it was still Madden even if it lacked warmth. She reached up to his elbow. The cold had spread.

"So that's how you do it," Swanson said to Madden.

"Just about. I can't explain it, and to be honest, I don't know how long it's been going on. I see things I presume are in English, and I read them."

"What you were reading wasn't in any known language Madden," Gila said, stopping him. She pressed a button on her tablet computer.

"Those are Satanic glyphs."

Madden peered at the screen. "'If willing and worthy, he shall rise again.' I don't get it."

"We really need to get him to a research facility," Gila said to Swanson. "Imagine what unwritten languages he could decipher."

"The wall read Rosier and Garias," Swanson shot back,

changing the subject. "Why don't we concentrate on that the names to begin with?"

"Rosier," Gila mused. "Another demon prince, second in command in dominions, has the ability to convince mortals of pretty much whatever he wants. He's not written about much."

"And Garias? His name is written on the wall in demonic glyphs. He is a sitting member of the council, permanently in Geneva."

Eva opened the door to her car, not prepared to stand up discussing this any longer. The seats were much more comfortable, and she had begun to experience discomfort. She sensed her time was close.

"How long has he been located there?"

"Twenty years."

"Well, isn't it conceivable he could have been here before then?"

Swanson turned to her from the front of the car, mouth agape.

"Seriously? You never considered this? Didn't you say somebody on the inside took the Nag Hamaddi scrolls from your archives?"

This led Gila to look to Madden for an explanation.

"No, he couldn't read the scrolls when we had them. They were Holy and they burned him."

"How did you know I would ask?"

Eva smiled. "Your new-found revelation."

Rick started the car, and they moved off along Clock-tower Drive, Swanson signaling to the black-ops.

"You didn't tell them about the tunnel." Eva fussed with her clothes, attempting to get comfortable; the baby pressed down in all the wrong places.

"No need. They started searching the second it was

revealed. Chances are they will reach Westlabs before we do."

The glass palace of science dominated the skyline, ever-present behind them as they drove away from the hospital for what Eva hoped was the last time. It felt as though she could not escape the place this close to it.

The drive only took moments. A quick hop onto Plantation Street and another left and they were in the parking lot. Ten stories high, the enormity of the building made Eva feel insignificant this close up. She began to have flashbacks of the Convocation.

"Ants in an ant-farm. A false nest with an ugly secret at its core."

"You're thinking what I'm thinking," Madden said. "I don't like the look of it either, but it does beg the question 'What does the Convocation have to do with this place?'"

"I'm done with coincidences," Eva decided aloud in response to the unspoken question on Swanson's face. "People in glass houses shouldn't play with demons. When we are done I'm living in a cave."

"She's right," Madden agreed. "Last time we were in a place like this it came down about our ears and nearly killed us, and this might have a... rebirth lab at its core? No thank you." Eva avoided using the word 'demon' as they approached a group of people emerging from the main entrance.

"Is one of you gentlemen, Swanson Guyomard?" A blonde woman with extravagant black eyelashes and long blonde hair, looking expectantly at Madden, asked.

"That would be me," Madden affirmed before Swanson had a chance to react, holding out his hand. "And you would be?"

"Shaney Warner, Mr. West's personal assistant."

"And what a lucky man he must be," Madden said through a smile before he raised her hand to his lips and brushed it with a kiss.

Shaney giggled, all eyes for Madden. "And your companions?"

"Dr Eva Ross, from Worcester State, and my associates, Dr Elga Noy, Richard Jones and Dr Benedict Garias."

Madden said this in such an offhand way nobody reacted before Shaney.

"Ohh," she breathed at Swanson. "Benedict Garias, the great man himself. This is an honour. Mr. West will be so stoked you sent two such senior representatives."

"You know us?" Swanson asked in a voice like a wheeze, clearly still unsure of how to react. His eyes threw daggers at Madden

"By reputation. Your associates, Doctors Sarch and Larter have been instrumental in certain projects I believe you are aware of."

Swanson nodded. "Indeed. It is the potential success of those projects determining the extent of our association with your company. However, let us not discuss such delicate matters out here on the steps. Too many ears." His voice had changed to the sibilant whisper responsible for chilling Eva back in Halmstadt.

"By all means. May I introduce to you to some of the board. Dana O'Neill and Bob Wainwright."

Shaney indicated and a couple shuffled forward, mumbling greetings. They could not have been more different. Bob Wainwright was skinny, taller than Gideon, with a beaked nose and thinning hair. Dana O'Neill, in complete contrast, was short, blonde and corpulent with a shock of blonde hair and shiny, mistreated skin. The trait they shared Eva spotted instantly before anybody could notice: they were both absolutely terrified of Madden.

"We aren't due to meet with Mark for a while yet," Shaney said to Madden, seemingly oblivious to the fear of her colleagues. "Would you like a tour?"

"If it can be brief," Eva answered. "I'm sure you can appreciate someone in my position wants to get to the heart of the matter."

The annoyance was well hidden, but the tension at the corners of her eyes betrayed the fact Shaney was irritated at Eva taking the lead. This was repaid in kind by her taking Madden to the fore and walking off at what could only be called a brisk pace. Determined not to be bested, Eva strode to keep up.

Shaney led them past an enormous reception desk manned by no less than four women, and through several sets of secure doors. Eva followed with Rick guiding her. Swanson and Gila entertained the execs at the back. They paused in a hallway full of large glass windows reeking of sterilizing chemicals. On one side, a host of scientists in white lab coats, all bearing the blue 'W' emblem of the company, worked diligently with pipettes, petri dishes and microscopes. On the other, a large open-plan room almost entirely white was sparsely populated with tables and what looked like the beginnings of a satellite.

"Now as Dr Ross is already aware, Worcester is an established leader in cutting-edge technologies. The Mass-achusetts Biotechnology Research Park is testament to that achievement, and the principal reason Westlabs made its choice to locate our headquarters here. As well as ourselves, notable companies such as Greene Bioresearch, Enhanced

Cell Technology, and Apollo Bioresearch have made their homes here, creating a veritable think tank for innovation and progress. The park is over a hundred acres in size and is closely associated with the University of Massachusetts and many satellite companies who have grown to support the incumbent behemoths."

Madden put on his most impressed face. Eva prayed Shaney was buying the act. She had no idea where he was going with this.

Not knowing anything about Benedict Garias, Eva was surprised to hear Swanson hiss, "What about portal technology? We came to discuss your advances." She presumed Benedict Garias was somewhat more direct than the rest of the council.

Shaney checked the hallway, and the rooms to either side. "These are the labs for public tours. Certain precautions are needed for research of a more... delicate nature. Your organization is known to us, and I daresay through your associates us to you, Mr. Garias. Such discussions are not ideal in public."

"Come now," Swanson rasped. "The money you have received in unofficial funding should be more than enough to compensate for my questions."

"Well, I like the look of it so far," Madden decided aloud. "You've got the space science going on over there, and the lab rats playing chemistry on the other side. It's all very research-oriented. My colleague however is correct in his questioning. We have travelled from Geneva to see what you have to offer. Our time is limited."

"And so it should be," said a voice from down the hallway.

Eva turned to see a heavyset man with a shock of gray

hair parted to one side and youthful features strolling towards them with an easy gait. He wore a fine cut, dark gray suit and as he reached them, Eva couldn't help but notice his pale green eyes. He stopped beside Shaney and put his arm about her waist in an easy manner. Shaney squeaked as he clearly touched a spot he should not have.

"You are not here for an interview after all." He held a hand out which Madden shook. "Mark West. CEO, Westlabs."

Eva held her hand out as West reached her. "Eva Ross, I know you by reputation. Gideon Homes was a great loss to Worcester State, and I expect you will make a worthy successor. I look forward to continuing our partnership." He looked her up and down. "It looks like you are already in a partnership of your own. Congratulations."

"Thank you," she replied, glowing. "Judging by current form, this one's going to be a right little demon."

This caused Madden to cough and Swanson to start making choking noises.

West just laughed aloud, a strange high-pitched titter, sounding completely alien coming from a man his size. "Aren't they all? My kids all started off like hellions, but properly broken in and trained, they can all become champions."

The comment was even stranger than the laugh. Eva smiled to hide her confusion, not trusting herself to look at her companions. Maybe this was a test?

"Shall we?" asked Shaney, indicating the door through which West had joined them.

"Capital idea," West replied, leading the way.

Shaney again grabbed Madden, but this time Eva earned a glare of jealousy as West fell in beside her.

"We have a different tour for VIPs." His voice was

conspiratorial. "Another entirely for you and your companions."

They passed through the doors into another hallway between labs, but this time Shaney turned and held her hand on a glass screen. A red light scanned her palm and silently the glass slid to one side.

"Nice," Madden admired.

"Like Star Trek, eh?" West replied, obviously proud.

"Only for the prettiest of hands," Madden replied, flirting openly with Shaney.

Eva bit her tongue. This was not like her husband, so he was playing a role. What struck her most was West's glowing approval. Chauvinist, she decided.

Their host led them through a lab crammed with equipment. Shelves piled with documentation. Rack after rack of small glass vials. Beakers covered with foil. The real work was done here.

A door opened and Eva found herself led into a concrete stairwell. Down one flight of stairs and West keyed in a combination to a security pad by a heavy metal door. A yellow warning light rotated upon completion and the door began to move outwards.

"That's some door," Madden admired as it continued to move outwards, revealing a thickness of over two feet.

"Some subjects require much more attention." West signalled to his executives. "And privacy. Go."

Wainwright and O'Neill turned without a word, and stumbled as they fell over themselves to get away.

West watched them leave. "Useless. Why do I even bother with a board? It's all a facade anyway. If you will, Dr Ross?"

The door had halted its ponderous revolution and a

three foot gap revealed a room bedecked with maroon furnishings beyond.

Eva stepped through. There was a large table, with seats for twenty, cabinets, and computers off to one side of the room. "An office?"

"Indeed. Secure down under the ground floor. You never know when the anti-vivisectionists are going to get creative and try targeting us. I don't like to take chances. In addition, it's the only place I can have a little ostentation. My wife hates anything not digital. These are my kids." West indicated several paintings on the wall.

"Horses?"

"You might say I have a passion for them. Take the board to the Kentucky Derby each May. I own horses. My favorite, Wormwood Tincture, came in second this year, at the wire and by a nose."

"Colorful name," Eva observed.

"There is of course another reason for having this room down here. It's one of the reasons the board is so jittery. The lab is adjacent." West turned to regard Swanson. "Benedict, I presume your presence here shows sufficient commitment for your organization to enter into a fully-fledged partnership, as you do with many others?"

"Are all the conditions met?" Swanson asked.

"The financials are more than sufficient. Westlabs has a market value of well in excess of fifty billion dollars with a share price on the increase. We are the next big thing. The board are puppets, the mass majority of the shares and stock options held in my name. The portal science is ready. We can turn man into monster without causing the dimensional rips. Your man Sarch provided the final piece of the puzzle when he delivered his hulking idiot to us with the dagger that resurrects demons."

West turned to Eva, and the look in his eyes had changed from genial host to a mixture of greed and dark desire.

"Most importantly, Lord Iuvart has taken a new host and we can rip the abomination from within the vessel and use the savior the way he was meant to be used, for the good of all mankind."

CHAPTER TWENTY-FOUR

For the first time ever, Eva considered 'What would Iuvart do?' Mark West held her by the shoulders and stared at her eyes, trying to see into her soul. She stared back at him, attempting to affect an air of superiority hoping against hope she was behaving as she should. How did he know about the Convocation in such a way to use those exact words? The broadcasts? They were never too specific were they?

Eva said the one phrase she hoped such an obvious megalomaniac would want to hear: "You have served well. You shall be next. Eternal life."

"Yes!" West cheered, pumping the air.

"We need to see the lab," Swanson pressed. "There's more to ARC approval than our Lord's acceptance."

West looked back at her. Afraid to say anything, she inclined her head at Swanson, indicating he was taking the lead.

"Very well. The laboratory it is." West reached beneath the end of the desk and depressed what Eva assumed to be a hidden switch. One of the maroon wall panels jumped back and slid to one side revealing a black door with a small circular window.

"Please, won't you go ahead? I'd hate to ruin the view by standing in your way. This lab really needs to be seen in all its splendor the first time you view it. Shaney, if you would please?"

The blonde assistant stepped forward, swiped a card over a sensor, causing the door to pop ajar, and lights beyond to illuminate the room beyond.

Madden took the lead, the rest of them following him in and when she got a first glimpse of the lab, Eva's heart nearly stopped.

"What the hell?" Swanson blurted, losing all trace of the character he had been attempting to portray.

Eva had a hard time trying to comprehend the scene in front of her. Demons, everywhere. All of them inanimate, dead. All of them dissected to some extent. Many were missing pieces entirely, an arm, eyes or part of a face. All were caught mid or post emergence, features stretched in obvious agony.

"Impressive, isn't it," West called from behind them. "And now, the best part."

There was a heavy 'thunk' behind them and Eva turned to see the door had closed. West's face filled the window, a small smile of smug satisfaction across his face.

"What is the meaning..."

"You can dispense with the act, Dr Ross. I am well aware Iuvart perished in Afghanistan. As for these others, well they are clearly not who they seem to be which is of no consequence. You are where I can find you, and a quick call to the real Benedict Garias will identify your companions. Be assured though, we need the savior and not the vessel.

You are most certainly in the right place until we deliver your child to the Lord Nibiru."

West turned and made a cutting signal across his throat. The lights began to fade and the wall closed across the hidden door leaving them trapped.

The darkness was absolute. This far into the core of West-labs there was no use screaming, or causing a fuss. Who knew what other tricks could be played on them. Eva edged to her right, trying to find a nearby table to lean on, and squealed when she touched a moving object.

"Relax," said Rick's voice. "Just me."

"How's it coming?" Swanson asked from somewhere to her left.

"Just give me a moment more. There. Got it."

A small light blinked on, growing in intensity until Eva was forced to look away, visual echoes of the light leaving her dazzled. The light grew until the whole laboratory was again lit, if not quite to the same extent as before. The light was somewhat eerie, with a sickly green tint. It threw the demon experiments into a different perspective, making them appear waxy and somehow unreal.

"You planned this," Eva accused Swanson.

He had the credit to look sheepish. "Actually, we both did. We needed a way in here, and I'm the only one who knows Benedict."

"Why couldn't you tell me?"

"We wanted your reaction to be natural. If Mark West thought you actually **were** Iuvart, he might still be here with us. As it was, we needed him out of the way. We learned some more interesting facts as part of this decep-tion. Mark West does not know you are married. He does know about the Convocation of the Sacred Flame. His admission suggests that there are more parties involved in this than was first apparent."

"You appear very nonchalant for somebody trapped in a box under the ground."

Swanson smiled. "Nobody is ever completely trapped. Still, we have work to do. We have more than enough evidence to use against Ivor Sarch, but a little more can't hurt. Our host is most likely in contact with Benedict as we speak, so probably best to move quickly."

"This could have been me," Madden said, peering at one semi-formed demon with its arms extended at impossible angles above its head, chest bulging as if it was about to rip the human host apart from the inside.

"It very nearly was, a number of times. How you retained your self-control is beyond me." Eva put her arm around Madden's waist as they looked at the corpse. He responded in kind, his arm about her shoulder.

"Ivor Sarch wanted it to be you," Swanson agreed. "He wasn't as sure of himself before Gehenna. If you meet him again, he will prove a vastly different character."

Eva recalled the officious jailer she had met at Nag Hamaddi. Cold and calculating.

"I can't think he's changed for the better."

"There are two types of people on the council: those who see the role as a responsibility, and those who just enjoy the power. The 'behind the scenes manipulation' of money and people is an aphrodisiac to many, and ARC is capable of manipulation for gain better than any organization on the planet."

"Which are you?" Eva asked.

Swanson remained completely straight-faced. "A bit of both. I can guarantee you Benedict, Zoe Larter, and if elected, Ivor Sarch, are not benevolent people. They are in the game to control others."

He turned away from her to place a small box on the side of a terminal back. The screen flicked on, and data began to appear.

"What have you found?" Eva enquired.

"Magnetic security override. Clever little beast. There's not a computer on earth this hack couldn't worm its way into. Ah, perfect. Here we go."

Eva left Madden staring at the demon-corpse and joined Swanson at the terminal. Maps flashed up in quick succession.

"Birmingham, Egypt, wait isn't that..."

"Afghanistan," Swanson completed for her. "It seems we are not the only ones to have been doing research on the portal events. In fact, given ARC has been keeping the public in the dark regarding these momentous events, it stands to reason this research came from us, and that means Sarch."

"Looks like we have been led right down the path of resurrection," observed Eva.

Swanson clicked through a few more files while Eva looked on. "Yes, I thought as much, too, or they followed you and picked up the scraps. Here we go. The same technology used to mask the demons in Egypt is being used on this room. You could fill it with hellbounces and they could rip each other apart, and not a portal would open. This place is one big vivisection lab."

"But who's going to miss a few people already dead, eh?" Madden said.

"Look for Finland in those files," Eva urged Swanson.

"No need. It's all over the place in here. The Lake

Bodom facility is exactly as you suspected: a disposal point for their used experiments. From across the world."

Swanson hit a key and a printer blurred into life, printing off an endless sequence of pages.

"Maps," he said by way of explanation. Somebody has been producing a very comprehensive list of all portal occurrences. I also found something you are going to find very interesting."

Swanson leafed through the printed paper and handed Eva a bunch of documents.

"Transfer requests. From my hospital. Wait, these are in my name."

"Countersigned by Gideon Homes, and every one of them authorizing the local police force to transfer prisoners between facilities. Look who was responsible for most of them."

Eva scanned down the paper until a familiar name leapt out at her. "Michael Caruso. How many of these prisoners never made it to their destination? How many times did he look the other way?"

"He may be like you, a dupe. According to these documents, you are as guilty of this as he is, yet we all know you haven't even been here. Oh, this is interesting. A video clip."

Swanson opened the file and Eva beheld a film of the very lab they were now trapped in.

"Test subject six-zero-six. The aim of the test is complete emergence from the human host."

A tall figure stepped into view. Short, gray hair, intense, staring eyes framed by spectacles.

"Ivor Sarch," Madden growled. He certainly had no love for one of his former jailors.

Sarch stepped forward and began to speak.

"Ultimately the protective shielding will allow us to harness a portal and keep it anchored in this reality while drawing power from its source. Before we do this, it is the proposal of Westlabs we demonstrate the effectiveness of shielding from portal incursion. As we are led to believe, the portals do not come from the lower realm but a place beyond. As is true with the test subjects used, this reality causes discomfort, even pain in extreme circumstances. The effect on the being coming through the portal is profoundly magnified to the point of fatality."

Sarch stepped back to reveal a series of tentacles hanging limp on a table situated behind where Eva was now standing. She turned to see if they were still there. Only another rictus demon carcass stared back at her, although there were clear markings on the table indicating they had once been there. The metal was scarred, etched as if by acid.

"However," Sarch continued, "this does not end the function of this creature's existence. Gideon, if you would please."

A grinning Gideon Homes, much more like Iuvart than her former mentor, approached the table and held his hands out over the table.

"As you can see, those pure of blood have no effect. However, when a test subject is introduced, even the lifeless form reacts. This serves to demonstrate a twofold conclusion. First, the mere presence of impurity allows reanimation. Second, the technology used to protect these experiments is beyond reproach, secure, and as such, ARC should consider this proposal."

Ivor Sarch stepped back as two burly men in white Westlabs lab coats shepherded one of the prisoners from Worcester State into view. Clearly not aware of his impending fate, the hellbounce glanced at the camera and smirked. Behind them, the tentacles began to twitch.

"You know him?" Madden whispered.

"No. Not a prisoner I ever met," replied Eva.

Swanson was flicking through a manifest. "I'm not at all surprised. They were pulling prisoners from all over the state and beyond as hospitals were closing. No, let me correct myself. They were closing hospitals in order to transfer the prisoners. They have been at this for at least a decade."

On the screen, the tentacles had begun to writhe, snapping against their bonds with mindless ferocity. The two orderlies grabbed the prisoner by his arms, and flipped him onto the table. The tentacles struck where it was possible to do so, doubling back on themselves to pierce their victim who began to scream. The camera focused in on the face of the prisoner, who screamed in pain. His mouth as wide as humanly possible, the noise he made was a high-pitched human wail overlain with something deeper, far more primal. His eyes widened, and continued to do so, the skin bulging and then stretching taut over elongated bones. The mouth reached wider and wider, the jaw distending. Gila turned away from the screen. Eve felt herself gripped by the scene. Never had she been this close to the transformation in safety. The scream became a roar as the transformation climaxed, his eyes rolling back in his head until only red orbs remained. Teeth became fangs and more demon now than man, the being fought upward to the camera, his visage filling the screen.

The film stopped, frozen on that dreadful mask of pain and fury.

"No more?" Eva asked.

"The footage ends there," Swanson confirmed. "You

can see the experiment was either a resounding success or a spectacular failure, depending on your point of view." He powered down the computer and turned away.

"You not looking further?"

"No need. Whatever Westlabs knows, ARC now knows. Another benefit of our little gizmo. This is our test subject right here. Judge for yourself the results."

Eva tried to will herself the courage to examine the misshapen lump of flesh lying prone in eternal agony, but the thought it might have been Madden on the slab was too much for her.

"I can't. I'm maybe days from giving birth, and all I see around me is the rebirth of evil. I just want out of here."

Swanson began to speak, but as he did, a series of loud metallic thumps interrupted him. The clanging repeated several times and Eva hid behind Madden.

Rick moved to the source of the noise, followed by Gila. After a moment, the pair of them began to shift one of the metallic worktables away from the wall. Rick searched and eventually flipped up a panel revealing a switch. Pressing one caused swirling yellow warning lights to rotate in the ceiling, and a series of electronic locks clicked into motion.

"Stay back," Rick warned when a motorized humming began to accompany the shifting of a wall. A gap began to appear. As soon as the gap was wide enough to put an arm through, the muzzle of an automatic gun appeared, pointed directly at him.

Rick raised his hands.

CHAPTER TWENTY-FIVE

THE GUN WAVED IN A THREATENING MANNER, indicating Rick should stand back. Eva hardly dared breathe. Trapped in a nest full of corpses underground and now they were going to be shot?

Rick continued to step back until he was next to Swanson, waiting with patience Eva assumed was feigned.

A flashlight shined through the gap as it widened enough to reveal a member of the ARC black ops. He stepped through and lowered his weapon as he recognized those in front of him.

"Sir," he acknowledged Swanson.

"Agent. You found the tunnel, then."

"Through the back-end of a furnace in the hospitals basement. Cleverly-disguised, but not hidden from your standard portable radar scanner. It's amazing to see how readily a door wants to open when encouraged by a block of c-four."

"You weren't tapping with your gun?" Eva asked the agent.

"No ma'am," he said in crisp, clipped tones, and she

realized he was South African. "What you heard was several different explosions. That is a door not meant to be opened from the outside. Chances are if you had no access to the panel it would have remained shut permanently."

The door had finished opening and behind the lead agent a squad of ARC special-ops lined up in the tunnel, each covered in a veritable arsenal of weaponry, which gleamed and glinted in the glow of Rick's light.

"What is the situation here, sir?" The agent asked Swanson.

"Fairly dire. They locked us in here, so you can expect a hostile reception when they return."

"Let's get you moving then, sir." The agent handed a walkie-talkie to Swanson and then regarded Eva for a moment. "Dr Scott are you going to be okay with the tunnel? Conditions are treacherous."

Eva flashed a grin. "I've had worse."

The agent grinned back. "So I read. Alpha team move up and secure the perimeter. Bravo team escort the hostages back to the hospital. Don't you worry, ma'am. Once we secure this door, nothing is getting through."

He helped Eva into the tunnel and Madden quickly joined her, holding her arm possessively.

"Jealous of a little courtesy?"

"You were flirting with him," Madden accused her.

"Oh no, I was just playing my role effectively," she cut back. To emphasise her point, Eva turned back and waved at the agent, who saluted. "Like you were earlier with Shaney Warner."

The last words Eva heard the agent say as the door shut were, "Douse that damned light. Night vision..."

· · ·

"Will they be all right?" Eva asked Swanson as the second team led them back through the tunnel.

"They know what they are doing," Swanson answered.

"All the demons in there are dead," Madden elaborated. "Those guys have all their weapons and armor. What's the worst that can happen: lab technicians with scalpels?"

Eva looked around the tunnel. In the shadowy light of the gun mounts, the bricks revealed they were not new. There were copious cobwebs hanging as spiders made home in the cracks, and in many places dried roots and moss hung down from the ceiling. She ran her finger across the mortar and it crumbled at her touch.

"This tunnel is ancient."

"Possibly as old as the civil war," informed the nearest agent, a short man with a mustache and goatee under his helmet.

"Looks like it's been well maintained," Madden said as he looked at the floor.

Eva followed his gaze. Wheel marks in the dust, many footprints leading in both directions. "And used continually: little or no build-up of grime on the floor."

"They needed their specimens clean for experimentation," Madden assumed.

"Whatever they have been doing here, it's safe to assume it has been in progress for a long time."

The radio Swanson carried crackled into life.

"Beta team this is Alpha leader. We have a situation here. Hope you are clear of the tunnel."

"We are en route, please elaborate," came the response. They all stopped to focus on the radio.

"The outer door is open. We have barred the inner door as well as the tunnel, but they are pretty insistent. We – wait! Look out!"

There was an explosion, followed by gunfire.

"Two by two cover formation," the leader shouted. "Hold the door. Hold the door!"

"Alpha team, report!" Swanson shouted, but the only noise returning to them was gunfire.

Then all fell silent.

"They've dropped back. Looks like private security, heavily armed. Must have been a dozen of them. We dropped six or seven and moved back to the inner door. Better defensive position. What... what is... There's something blocking the light in the doorway. Dear God it's huge... Fire! FIRE!"

More gunfire but the only answer was a roar, not of pain, but of rage.

"Alpha team," Swanson said to the radio. "Come in. Alpha team! Report!"

Gunfire answered them, followed by screams. "Two down! We are falling back. Get out of there! Get out..."

Another roar, bestial in nature, there was a scream and a tearing. Eva shuddered as the slow grinding clicks of a body being dismembered, bones pulled apart and the cartilage separated with agonizing deliberateness, echoed down the tunnel.

There was nothing more from the team, who had perished. Eva looked at Madden, whose face was a mask of horror. There was a guttural breathing from the radio, slathering and liquid-filled. Then a bang on the door, which echoed a second later from back down the tunnel.

"Get out of here now," ordered the team leader. "We split. Two hold the tunnel, other two escort you. Go!"

In the second everybody had paused, Madden grabbed Eva's arm, and began to pull her along.

"You heard those noises. You know what they have

there. A tunnel is NOT the place to be trapped when it breaks through."

It couldn't be. Demonkind had been eradicated, and Brian had been fixated on her in Europe. But how long had he been back before he crossed the ocean?

"A demon? But..."

"Eva. Move now, think later. Our child. She's defenseless. She needs our protection."

This brought Eva round. "Of course." Supporting her belly with one arm, Eva allowed herself to be led down the brickwork tunnel, the shadows threatening to become demons of their own.

"Tunnels," she said in disgust. "Why does it always have to be tunnels?"

The demon roared again and began to pummel the door with a regular rhythm. The noise started to change as the door buckled, the strange twofold effect coming from the radio and the distant echoes.

"How far is this?" Eva shouted over the noise.

"About four hundred feet, ma'am," the agent replied, his back turned.

"How far along are we?"

The door screamed as metal was ripped from metal. "Not far enough."

The demon fell silent, but the radio betrayed movement, heavy feet thudding down steps.

Eva stopped and looked back. The tunnel was pitch black outside of the agents' light. She thought she saw red eyes glaring at her for a second, and then the frequency of the steps increased.

"It's coming!" The agent shouted. "Run! Run!"

Forgetting she was pregnant, Eva broke for the other end of the tunnel. Her four companions maintained pace alongside, Rick lighting the way once more. Roars from behind indicated the demon sensed it was losing its quarry. The door appeared in next to no time, another heavy metal contraption left open by the special ops. Eva jumped through, Madden close on her heels. When the rest had made it, Rick maneuvered the door shut to the sound of gunfire.

"But the team?" Eva asked, pointing at the tunnel.

"Knew what they were doing and were prepared to make the ultimate sacrifice," Swanson finished.

They all flinched when an explosion rocked the tunnel, Madden protecting her with his body. God, how her middle ached.

"What now?" Eva shouted, beginning to panic.

Rick put his finger over his lips, and nodded toward the door.

Silence. Had the explosion gotten the demon?

A shuffling, and then a low growl indicated this was not the case.

"Go," Swanson whispered, looking like he was preparing to remain.

"No," Gila urged. "You come with us."

Strangely, Swanson acceded to this request. "Eva, lead us out. Quickly."

The furnace was halfway along the horseshoe-shaped basement hallway, and Eva made sure the door was locked securely as Rick passed by, the last of her diminishing team. For good measure, she hit the button firing up the furnace. If it even worked, she had no idea. Eva did not wait around to find out.

Eva headed to the right and up the stairs, as she had done nine months before. As she exited onto the ground floor, she heard gunshots, and Madden pulled her gently but firmly to the floor where Swanson and Gila were kneeling behind the questionable safety of the former hospital's reception desk. Eva glanced above the desk. One ARC agent lay unmoving on the floor, blood pooling about him. Three more held flanking positions on each side of the entrance, ducking, and returning fire in rotation.

"We're under attack!" Swanson shouted above the noise of bullets shattering glass.

"You don't say. Who?"

"Probably the same lot from Westlabs."

The tunnel. They had made the connection and sought to cut off the only means of escape.

"They've spoken to Benedict Garias. It's the only way we can be sure they have the security to kill us."

"You heard Mark West! They want you alive."

"Maybe, maybe not. I'm full term. They could pull the baby from me with minimal damage. We need to get to the one place that can stop all this. Swanson, we need to get to the Council in Geneva."

Eva fell silent as a roar shattered her train of thought. Even the ARC agents turned.

"We need to get out of here now, or it's all over," Swanson decided. "Rick, join the battle."

"Piece," Rick commanded, holding his hand out.

Without looking, one of the agents pulled a handgun from a holster at his hip and threw it at Rick, who caught it and brought the gun to bear in one movement. Eva had never seen the like. Instead of containment and wounding as the other agents had been attempting, Rick threw himself into the fight, picking the private army off one by one.

The onslaught demanded caution from their assailants as Rick tore through their number, and there was a lull as several armor-clad mercenaries pulled back behind cars already riddled with bullet holes.

The pause did not last long though, and soon it was as if Rick had made no difference.

Another roar from the floor below accompanied the smashing of doors.

"It's found a way through. Swanson, we have to get out of here or we are all dead."

Swanson nodded in agreement as another hail of bullets threatened to overwhelm the agents in front. There was glass all over the floor now, so crawling was out of the question. The doors at least were not blocked.

"Die hiding, or die fighting," Madden said, and stood up. He hurdled the desk and entered the kill zone, grabbing the assault rifle from the dead agent.

As one, the other remaining agents and Rick joined, and the four men concentrated their fire on the nearest car. The gunfire ceased as the Westlabs security ducked for cover.

"Now!" Swanson yelled, and Eva jumped to her feet, instantly regretting the act as inertia threatened to suck her baby out of her then and there. Gila helped her along, and they squeezed through the shattered door frames.

Gunfire was exchanged from both sides and Eva tried to hold her nose against the acrid stench. Muzzles flashed all around and she concentrated on making herself as small as possible.

Then Madden fell as if poleaxed.

"Madden? Madden!"

Eva dropped to her knees while the agents surrounded them. She rolled her husband onto his back, finding blood soaking through his shirt from his right arm. Swanson picked up the rifle and fired off a volley, but the mercenaries had already turned away to face a new threat.

Mixed in with the gunfire was the sound of sirens. Lots of sirens.

Madden yelled in pain. Eva took a closer look.

"Clean wound. Straight through. Hang on."

Eva ripped a strip of material from his shirt and tied it tight about his arm, causing him to scream in pain again.

"Don't be such a baby. You've had worse."

"Easy for you to say," Madden replied through clenched teeth.

The Westlabs men had engaged the cops in a firefight, and were mown down in seconds. When everything went quiet, she stuck her head out from behind the wall they were using as cover, to find what must have amounted to nearly the entire Worcester police department as well as two SWAT teams, all armed and armoured.

Tina Svinsky waved them over to where she and detective Caruso were standing. Swanson and Rick grabbed Madden, and the five of them made their way to the protection of the police.

Another roar followed them and the doors to the hospital burst asunder: a creature from nightmares hulked in the doorway.

Eyes black of night, and backward-curved horns ending alongside a jaw formed from tattered shreds of flesh. It had no discernible nose or ears, but a long pointed tongue lolled about as it moved its head from side to side and sniffed. Covered in hair, it must have been eight feet in height, and it raised paws ending in vicious claws to either side and bellowed at them, curved yellow fangs easily six inches long visible even form this distance in its mouth.

"See what your ignorance and corruption has birthed, detective," Eva said without looking as the demon stared straight at her, drooling.

"Me?"

"Your name is on all the documents allowing the movement of prisoners. The same movement used to bring about this monstrosity."

Caruso paled visibly. "It was nothing. Just a few felons. I would never..."

"Well, you did, detective!" Swanson shouted. "This is ultimately your doing. The end of the world, all for cash. Is this what you hoped would happen? Maybe the end of all of us? No link to trace back to you?"

"But I didn't mean to... Oh God, what have I done?"

The demon roared and started to approach.

"Don't ask God," Eva said as she moved back past the detective, her husband on her arm. "Ask our friend over there."

CHAPTER TWENTY-SIX

THE ASSEMBLED FORCE OPENED FIRE ON THE DEMON, the creature bellowing in fury as bullets pounded it. After the first volley, it took another step forward and roared again in defiance, a strange mix of throaty roar and high-pitched squeal. Eva was forced to let go of Madden and cover her ears with her hands.

"Go!" Swanson mouthed at her, but Eva paused, looking back at the monster.

It crouched, arms spread wide and leered at her, teeth bared in the demon approximation of a grin. Hunching, the demon prepared to leap right for her and in that moment, even the portal on Mount Gehenna never seemed as final.

"No!" Yelled a voice, and Mike Caruso, a shotgun leveled, jumped in its path.

"Get out of here Dr Ross. Don't let this mad act of an idiot be in vain!" Caruso began to fire at the demon, pumping off shots as fast as he could. One hit it in the eye and unlike the seemingly impervious skin, the eyeball erupted in a splash of black gore.

The demon threw its head back in pain, the sound so

high-pitched all those with weapons were forced to drop them. But not Mike Caruso. His ears ruptured and bleeding, he continued to scream obscenities at the demon, until he was forced to reload.

As he paused, the demon lunged forward and skewered him with one paw, the talons reaching through and up from his back in an explosion of red. The detective hung limp, all life eradicated.

"Look!" Gila pointed. All around the demon fog began to billow.

"Keep it penned in," Swanson ordered. "Fire everything you have."

By now, Eva and Madden were behind the armed forces and out of immediate danger. This gave her a chance to pause and observe. Several clumps of the air around the demon were shimmering, the air stretching and bending. As before, Eva felt the hostility.

"This is the same as before. Different portals."

"A new way through," Madden said through clenched teeth. "Come on."

"No, I have to see this."

The armed forces were keeping the demon, confused by semi-blindness, at bay. The air froze and four portals burst open, each with a writhing demon on the end of a tentacle. The four tentacles didn't grope randomly toward their prey as before, but instead struck straight for the demon, wrapping about its limbs and wrenching. The demon had a moment to scream before it was quartered, each segment pulled into a portal in a rain of black ichor. The last sight of the demon was of its head, tongue still lolling and its remaining eye fixed balefully on Eva as it was pulled through. The portals winked out.

"We have to go," Swanson said, trying to take her arm.

Eva shrugged off the attempt. "There was no noise. Something has changed."

"We can discuss it on the plane."

"But..."

Swanson rounded on her. "Eva, we have to go. Your time at home is over, and proves beyond any reasonable doubt this is not going to end. But consider this thought: isn't it funny how something always happens to distract us, and keep us misdirected? I have seen into the heart of the organization my own ancestors originated and found corruption festering. We have to get to the heart of ARC. We need to get to Geneva."

Time. It was all they had. Jumping forward, slipping backward. Eva's body had begun to rebel against her strict control. The strength of will was no longer sufficient. Whereas the journey to America had been pleasant enough, with a chance to rest and somehow adjust, the thrust forward in time coupled with the recent events at Westlabs left her exhausted and not quite aware of reality.

There was a lot of discussion and not a little argument on the plane. Eva sat there numb to it all, her body trying to throw all her depleting reserves of energy into sustaining her baby during its final days in the womb. The baby pressed low, head against her cervix. Eva closed her eyes and sought the communion so strong during the early days of the pregnancy, but it was absent.

It felt as though she was wearing noise-cancelling headphones reducing her companions to mimes. They waved arms, got in each other's faces, parted in apparent anger and then later resumed the same cycle.

Before she knew it, the plane had begun to descend,

slate-gray skies over early-morning Geneva reflecting off the great lake to the north of the runway. Where the time had gone, Eva could not fathom.

They avoided the masses, a heavy black limousine meeting them at the steps of the plane. Armed security was everywhere, helmeted ARC soldiers with machine guns cordoning off large areas of the runway.

Eva found herself quickly ensconced in the back of the limousine, a bandaged Madden and Gila alongside her. A bank of screens rose to one side, all showing news and financials.

"Feels more like a tank than a car," Eva said, emerging from her stupor to comment while she shifted to a more comfortable position.

"Funny you should say so," Swanson said from the front of the car. "It's a Mercedes S600 armored limousine, with all the toys. ARC acquired this vehicle from some eastern European crime boss a few years ago. Turns out they had it stolen to order. The boss of Daimler had it custom fitted to be one of the most secure vehicles on the road. He went visiting an office in Stuttgart, and they loaded it into a lorry right there in the street. By the time we recovered it, he had left the company, and nobody wanted it. We keep it here to use for very important people."

Eva didn't smile. She was too detached. She appreciated the compliment nonetheless.

"It's nice to know what you think of me."

"Oh it's safe to say, at this moment, there is nobody on this planet more important than you, Eva. I wish we had the time to take you to the Castle at the other end of the lake. You would love it."

"Maybe after hellbender here has set foot on the earth."

Eva lapsed into silence, the grandeur of one of the most important cities in the world lost on her.

The journey through Geneva was much like that of any other city to one too numb to appreciate the finer details of architecture. Helsinki, Stockholm, Worcester, Cairo, Birmingham. All eruptions of concrete in different formations. All memories full of shadowed alleys and lurking dangers.

"You base your organization in the most influential of cities," Madden observed. "How do you keep it secret?"

"Well, secret is a relative term," Swanson replied. "Look about you. Each and every building here hosts one organization or another holding secrets. They gather here because they gravitate towards those with the biggest mysteries, those with the most to hide. ARC was here before all of them, growing quietly in the background. Much as it is today. Unlike the U.N. or the World Bank, we do not advertise our presence. You know what sort of panic would ensue if the whole world knew what we knew. We are the ultimate media blanket."

"So where are you based?"

"They are based in the World Meteorological Organization building," Eva interrupted Swanson while fidgeting to get comfortable. The pressure inside was becoming immense. She felt like she was going to burst.

"The weather station, the meteorological outpost on Utö, was not what it seemed. What does everybody take for granted; it affects us all and is part of our daily lives? What organization would nobody bat an eye at no matter where they emerged? Weather."

"Very true," Swanson agreed. "The WMO is nearly a hundred and fifty years old, and came into being when past

ARC agents needed a more formal cover. We share the headquarters with them, the Intergovernmental Panel for Climate Change and the Geneva Center for Security Policy. Rather, they are allowed to fill the parts of the building we give them access to."

"Sounds like you have all the key players right where you want them."

Swanson looked at Gila, "Almost."

Shortly, their route took them along a wide avenue lined on one side with trees. Eva perked up at this.

"The park you spoke to me from. I recognize the trees."

"Indeed, you have a good memory and an excellent eye."

Madden leaned over and patted her thigh. "Some say she has two."

This prompted her to giggle, despite herself.

"I can only apologize for what is going to come next," Swanson said, all levity lost from his voice. "It wasn't on purpose."

Eva looked at him in confusion until a glass building dwarfing the Westlabs architecture came into view. She groaned.

"Always glass. How many of these portals does it take to destroy a building of such a scale do you think?"

"Hopefully not enough. It was built to be impregnable. The glass isn't really glass, but a form of scientifically manufactured crystal that shatters into tiny harmless pieces. It's a mess to clean up, but the cost of human life is much higher."

"You speak as though you have experienced this."

"Through bitter experience," Swanson admitted. "The

technology was developed in response to an encounter with a portal."

"Well, then how does your stance make you any better than Ivor Sarch?"

Swanson looked her in the eye, and Eva could see he was utterly serious. "Because I perceive the bigger picture, and don't seek dominion."

The car pulled into an underground garage, the lights wan and sickly, not unlike the portals Eva now saw everywhere. The car stopped outside the entrance to a hallway wide enough for several people to walk with their arms stretched and Rick opened the door for Eva.

A hand reached for her and she took it, the grip firm. An elderly gentleman with a surprisingly youthful face under a shock of white hair and black, bushy eyebrows stared at her.

"Well, if I had known you would be ten times as beautiful in real life as you were on screen I might have made an effort." He made an effort to brush his black polo shirt free of imaginary dirt.

Eva had to look at her host for a few moments before the name hit her.

"Daniel? Daniel Guyomard?"

"The one and very same," he said with a twinkle in his eye. "And this must be your husband, the demon. Welcome."

"Demon no longer," said Madden, shaking Daniel's hand.

"Ah, but one doesn't have to have always gone to Hell to be a demon." Daniel winked at him. "And here she is, the lady of the moment, the newest councilmember if those imbeciles up there listen to reason instead of money. Miss Gila Ciranoush, dear heart, how are you?"

Gila took Daniel by both hands and kissed his cheeks. "I

am well, a trifle nervous but very relieved to be here, given all that has recently happened."

"Still breaking the rules and contravening tradition, Uncle?" Swanson stepped forward with a handshake becoming a bear hug.

Daniel looked down at his clothes. "These rags? Nobody is going to force me to put on a suit. Why? Because screw you, that's why. That's what I tell Johan. Nobody forces anything on a Guyomard! What difference is a jacket if Hell spills over to Earth?"

"Popular as ever then, Uncle?"

Daniel snorted. "Those idiots wouldn't know sense if it slapped them in the face. It takes the likes of us to keep them in check, son. As it stands, the vote is close, but what changes? If you are as canny as I know you are, you have worked out our allies and those opposed. Ivor Sarch has a good chance, but I think we have the upper hand. Did you find anything of use on your travels?"

Swanson recounted the information gathered by Eva and Madden in Scandinavia, adding to it his own experiences with them from Helsinki onward as Daniel led them down the tunnel into the heart of ARC. The Westlabs description caused Swanson's uncle to regard her with utter seriousness and not a little sympathy as the incident played out through Swanson's words.

"I wish you had stayed away in all honesty," he concluded, and pressed a button to call a lift.

Eva thought on this for a moment as they waited for the elevator doors to open. "No, I have to disagree. Any psychologist can preach about the benefits of closure. You have to move on in order to accomplish your goals. If I had not gone back, I would never have a reason to stay away. As it is, I have to say it feels like we have been led on some global wild goose chase."

"We came back sooner than anticipated," Swanson elaborated. "Somebody here is up to something, and the coincidences, the Convocation, the hellbounces. They somehow tie in together. We have seen more than enough to convince us Zoe Larter and Benedict Garias are tied into more than just research. I think they are tied in with the Convocation. I just can't see how."

"So what is your plan? Just rush in and hope to throw Garias off balance?"

"Uncle, he was part of the Westlabs deal. Ivor Sarch was on camera with Iuvart, a demon prince, experimenting on hellbounces. Iuvart was not the leading force from what we saw. How much do we know about him? Where is he from? What did he do before ARC? It looks like he was in Westlabs but why?"

"You have to pace this. Test the waters and reveal it at the right time. As it stands, there is a Council meeting later this morning. They are going to debate the election of the new councilmember for the umpteenth time. Of course, now we have the entire Council in one place."

"They are all here then? Larter too?"

Daniel Guyomard laughed an enormous guffaw quite disproportionate to the situation. "Oh especially that one. She wouldn't miss the chance to crown her new sibling," Daniel turned to Madden, "and to eye up her prize."

Eva leaned into Madden, suddenly possessive of him.

"Miss Larter will leave very disappointed. He's going nowhere with her."

Madden put his arm around her in support. Eva was thankful for this. All this standing after so much travel had left her quite lightheaded.

The elevator doors opened, revealing an enormous foyer looking out from what appeared to be the middle of the building over the park opposite. They must have been ten or twelve floors up. Enormous glass doors across the hall were closed, and this prompted Daniel to call over to the receptionist.

"Danielle, why are the doors shut?"

The woman behind the desk, a neat brunette with gold-rimmed glasses looked up.

"They have been in session for the past half-hour, Councilor Guyomard. They have instructed you and your guests to attend at your earliest convenience."

"Strange. Who rescheduled the meeting?"

"Councilor Garias, sir."

CHAPTER TWENTY-SEVEN

SWANSON THREW THE DOORS OPEN WITH SUCH FORCE they swung all the way open and hit the inside of the Council chamber with a loud 'bang'.

"Dramatic," Daniel Guyomard under his breath where only Eva could hear. "Stay quiet dear and let's see how this plays out."

Eva followed Daniel into the chamber, Madden on her other side, Gila and Rick behind. She recognized the chamber as the room on the television screens when the Council had last conferred during their stay in Halmstad. The room was large and round, a circular table its focus beneath a circular bank of lights glowing like the underside of a UFO. Seats surrounded the table, all but two filled. A row of aluminium seats were pressed up against the far wall. Ignoring those at the table, Eva walked with all the arrogance she could muster and crossed the room to sit down, her stomach aching.

Swanson had already stormed ahead, where a mixture of expressions greeted him: fearful, delighted, and smug.

"What is the meaning of this?" Swanson demanded,

pointing at one of the council. "Why does he sit at this table?"

The man in question was none other than Ivor Sarch himself, dark-lensed glasses lending a sinister aspect to an already nasty demeanor. He reeked of smugness. It threatened to turn Eva's stomach.

"You will display appropriate behaviour in this chamber, Councilor Guyomard," shot back Johan Klaas, rising from his seat on the far side of the table. "You should remember exactly where you are."

"Where I am is on a Council convened by my direct ancestor who decreed all available persons of the ARC council should be present in order for a vote to be passed governing the election of new members."

"And they were," Zoe Larter said from beside Benedict Garias, her dark eyes flashing suppressed anger. "Even those you sought to have isolated on an island in the middle of nowhere. The entire Council was recalled for the vote, and you and Dr Ciranoush decided once you were here, your time was better spent elsewhere. As you rightly said, 'all available persons'. You and your uncle were not available. The vote has been passed with a majority of six votes for, three against."

Sarch rose from his seat, strode slowly around the table, his tall frame wide and imposing. He ignored Eva, but paused to look at Madden before turning to Swanson. His face wore an expression of avarice, as if he regarded Madden as 'the one that got away'.

"Welcome to our council, brother. I look forward to resuming my experimentation with the approval of all who sit at my table."

His voice was now slow and deliberate. Benedict Garias was a highly-intelligent man, his accent undetectable. This man did not want anybody to know his origins.

Eva watched the rest of the council as the two men stood off against one another. It was easy to guess what had happened purely from the looks on their faces. Petra van Veld saw money; Anderson saw a threat and Klaas went along with her. Gaspard Antroobus was out for himself, looking at Gila like a gazelle saw a lion. Strange it was this way around. It was exactly as Swanson had predicted it might go. Their allies were their allies but it appeared their opposition was divided.

"This will never be your table," Swanson countered.

"It will never be yours," Klaas tried to refocus the attention on himself. "You are insubordinate, Swanson. Living off your family name will only take you so far. It will win you no allies here."

"We have evidence this man has been working in league with our enemy."

Swanson nodded to Rick, who inserted a flash drive into the side of a large screen on the opposite side of the room to Eva.

The video played, the commentary the same as before, but blasted from a dozen hidden speakers around the room. Eva moved her hands to her ears, only to drop them when the baby wriggled in a most uncomfortable way. Clutching her middle, but trying to make no issue of the fact, she endured the presentation.

Sarch betrayed no small amusement at her predicament as he took his seat, mouthing the words of the presentation at her as his younger self tortured the hellbounce.

When the film ended, Sarch raised his hands to either side in a gesture of innocence.

"Did I not promise you results in my presentation? Do

we not have a stable portal open even now being worked upon to convert energy to a usable state?"

"You were working with Gideon Homes, who was marked by dozens of witnesses, not the least the members of Legion, to be the Demon Iuvart." Swanson's accusation was accurate, but the comment had no effect on most of those around the table.

"This was years before he was turned," Sarch retorted. "Westlabs was in its infancy when we began work on the ARC portal technology. Gideon Homes approached us, and we leapt at the chance. It was a medical holy grail, working on something so bizarre.

A strange feeling came over Eva, as if her eyes were being closed while still awake. The baby did something it had not for weeks now, and gave her a strong mental jolt. Instantly sober, Eva beheld every member of the council aside from Swanson nodding along with Ivor Sarch. They were listening to him, and they were believing him!

"Then how do you explain the shielding being used to protect hellbounces..."

"Swanson we do not recognise such a word in ARC," Johan Klass stood to face his younger colleague down. "It was a word coined on a whim, by somebody with no experience in ARC protocol. It is no better than slang and we are a scientific organization. We have no use for slang. We call them 'emergences'."

Caught short by the interruption, Swanson turned to Eva.

She nodded her assent. She was fine with the proceedings. Whether Johan Klaas was under the influence of Ivor Sarch, or whether he genuinely believed what he was saying, the man clearly had not dealt with anybody of a contrary opinion in years. He saw Swanson as a threat.

"The shielding developed to protect *hellbounces* was used to bring a demon fully from its human host. We flew here directly from a gun battle with Westlabs' hired mercenaries where this happened."

Swanson nodded to Rick, who now played footage of their escape from Westlabs and the tunnel. In great detail, the hulking demon brute smashed its way out of the disused hospital and fought the Worcester Police. Mike Caruso came into view with a shotgun and as much as Eva regretted the inevitable course of action, it nonetheless came to pass in gruesome detail.

As the portals opened and the demon was ripped asunder, there were differing reactions from around the table: a couple of the Council gasped, Johan Klaas stood up and back as he beheld the stygian violence. Benedict Garias and Zoe Larter sat quietly, and Ivor Sarch's eyes sparkled.

"How is this linked to your previous evidence?" Garias asked in his deathly hiss.

Eva stood, despite her body's repeated protests to the contrary. "It is linked because the very lab where the film was made is connected to the hospital in which I worked."

Eva thrust a finger at Sarch. "The same hospital where the man in your film, described as a trueblood, was my boss. The same hospital where the last five chief administrators were entombed in a room inaccessible to the self-same man you claim was uncorrupted. The same hospital where the missing Nag Hamaddi scrolls were once hidden. We have evidence of the pain it causes the most insignificant of demons to gain access to such a room. He could never have made it in there, and those he sent in were all men of such principle they would not come out."

"All coincidence," Sarch scoffed.

"You did not witness any of this," Garias wheezed. "You

were presented with a scene, and jumped to your own conclusions both the first time you saw the room, and when you revisited it."

This was crazy. All the evidence to hand and these bureaucrats were shooting her down at every opportunity. Eva began to falter as her belly spasmed and started to ache.

"Do you require a moment?" Margaret Anderson asked, genuine concern on her face. The opposition gloated at her apparent weakness.

"Thank you, no. I haven't waited all this time for answers from you people just for a little discomfort to stop me at the end. You, Johan Klaas, you said you would release the document ratifying our marriage once we had been to Lake Bodom and reported our findings. You have had them, why don't you keep your end of the bargain?"

Klaas bristled visibly at talked to in such a manner. He looked like he'd been taken to task for an action he thought he'd had the right to take. Eva had scored a point catching him off guard.

"Why don't you present your findings to the entire council, so we may deliberate on them?"

He was a slime ball, and Eva was a mouse in a nest of vipers. Would they care about the demons? Doubtful. She decided to stick to the facts.

"Elaine Millet drugged me. Repeatedly. This was personal: she was after my husband, or so I believed. It transpired she was a member of the Convocation of the Sacred Fire, and had been planted in your organization with the aim of securing me before I gave birth. We learned this when we were abducted and taken to one of their holding facilities, an isolated glass mansion not more than a couple of miles from the location you tasked us to investigate."

"You were asked to look for demons, not cults." Klass interrupted.

"You sent me to Finland and I was abducted," Eva shot back. "This is on you. I was ordered, blackmailed if you will, into this mission of yours. When we rescued survivors from an apparent sunken ship, they turned out to have been resurrected by the same creature supposedly chasing around after me. I find it somewhat ironic it was a portal that ultimately meant we could escape. The only source for portals now should be anything Brian has created. When we found the source of the demonic readings, a survivor pointed us to Westlabs. Furthermore, we found blueprints for the laboratory you saw in the first film. The facility was a cremation ground for failed experiments. Hellbounces were piled up all over the place.

After Brian finally emerged and chased us out of the country, we headed for Westlabs itself. A tunnel exists between the hospital I worked at and the laboratory hidden in Westlabs."

"Crazy talk," denounced Ivor Sarch. Many around him nodded in agreement. Eva was not fazed. Whatever he had on the others was not working on her.

"Really? We were all IN it. Two squads of ARC special-ops died so we could escape. The demon you saw earlier followed us down it and disposed of them all, but not until after Mark West himself gloated about the fact my child could be ripped from my womb and delivered up to the Lord Nibiru. Now why would such a man make such a claim if he was the CEO of an above-board medical research company? He knew your director here."

Eva pointed at Benedict Garias, whose frail old frame still exuded confidence. "All we found led us back here."

"You can see there is more than enough evidence to

cause another vote," Daniel Guyomard concluded. "I propose we..."

"You will do no such thing," Garias whispered. "Young lady, it is clear to all here you have missed the vocation of 'storyteller'. We are on this council because we believe, and understand how important this body is in preserving the earth. We have a long-term strategy. There are elements to it you will not approve of. Demon vivisection and portal study may be two fundamentals less than sanguine to you, but nonetheless need to happen. All of the icons who have represented humankind through the ages would be for nothing if we did not undertake the gruesome tasks lesser men are not prepared to do. This body is immense. Far bigger than a few people who would live off their family name. I propose we file this report for study at a later date."

Eva looked aghast at the table as enough nodded their heads in agreement. Swanson actually appeared helpless. Eva took a deep breath as her back throbbed.

"How dare you sit there and act as if this was nothing of consequence. Have you heard nothing I have said? I stood there on the threshold of Hell, not in a comfortable leather seat in Geneva. I looked into the abyss, and staring back at me was an army of limitless capacity. And it damned well nearly made it through. What saved you? Luck. Somebody miscalculated. Even a demon, it seems, can make mistakes."

There was a betrayal of emotion from Ivor Sarch. Just a flicker, and suddenly it all made sense. Anybody who put their all into an undertaking hated to have it questioned. Intuition made the leap to logic, and Eva made ready to unmask her foe.

"I was not the one. My blood was not quite right. One generation off to be exact. They believed it to be my child. They still believe it, and you sit there and grill me like I am on trial? What about you? If ARC is everything I believe it is meant to be, and you stand at the head of all tables then why are you so impotent to act?

There was more as you well know. We have learned this much: something worse than Hell, something beyond it. The force unseen hunts the demons. It is now using them as keys to open directly into this world. We saw it happen in my own house in Worcester. Demonkind is trying with great urgency to come to Earth. They are not trying to initiate conquest. They are trying to escape it. If we are overwhelmed and whatever is chasing them comes here, tentacles and all, do you think you can defeat it? Sitting in your chairs in this plush office? This may be the last bastion of mankind at some future date, but for now, for God's sake, act like there is still a world out there."

Eva put her hand to her brow to find she was sweating excessively. Her entire body seemed to throb, and her legs trembled.

"Such fervor, young lady," Garias said, mocking her despite the whispering eeriness of his voice. "You sound like you have found religion."

Eva stared straight at him. The time had come.

"Maybe I have. I found that my husband, for ratified or not, my husband he is in my heart and mind, could read any language as if it were English. An after effect of his demonization. In the hidden room adjacent to Gideon's office there was writing on the wall, a demon glyph. Iuvart had the administrators of the office trapped in there until they recovered the texts for him but they feared for what would happen. They left you a message. Two words: Garias and Ro...ohh."

The ARC council stared at her in collective confusion.

Madden jumped up with a grunt and put his free hand on her shoulder. "Eva, what is it?"

The sudden pain was so intense it made her see red. She clutched her hands to her swollen midriff, her legs threatening to buckle.

"The baby. It's coming."

CHAPTER TWENTY-EIGHT

THE PAIN WAS BLINDING. ALTHOUGH EVA KNEW ALL about the mechanics of childbirth, nothing had prepared her for the electrifying sensations now ripping through her middle. In an instant, questions flooded into her mind simultaneously. *Will I die? Will it survive? What if it's deformed? What if I can't cope? What is this world into which I release new life?*

The questions threatened to overwhelm her, causing her mind as much pain as her body already was experiencing. Eva cleared her mind. The scientific approach. One issue at a time. Logically. She began to breathe, even and slow.

"Steady Eva, breathe. Easy now."

Eva opened her eyes and looked up. The council hadn't moved a muscle, regarding her as some sort of oddity. Madden blocked their view, probably an intentional thing. What worried Eva was the look on his face. It was the one aspect Eva hoped he would never show. If he was a hell-bounce, Eva had no doubt Madden would be a demon, for he had completely lost all semblance of control.

Eva reached out and put her right hand on his left shoulder to steady herself. The contraction had passed.

"Damn, that hurt."

"We need to get her to a hospital."

"No need," Zoe Larter replied. "We have our own medical facilities right here. I'll just..."

"No, you damn well won't," Eva growled in interruption, causing Larter to jump. The voice coming out of her mouth didn't sound anything like her own.

"You tried to abduct my husband. Deny it all you will. If you hadn't been provided with an abundance of demon flesh you would have found a way to keep your claws on him. I will not have this child in a place where you can get to her. I'd rather give birth in a dirt-filled alleyway."

Eva turned to Swanson. "Find me somewhere else, and for God's sake, call an ambulance!"

Swanson was on his phone in moments, and Eva turned from the rest of the Council, ignoring them intentionally, despite their repeated calls about her well-being. Leaning on Madden for support, she followed her husband out of the chamber.

What followed seemed to take forever. The elevator couldn't have been slower if it tried.

"Is there anything we can do?" Gila asked, and in that moment, Eva really felt for her friend. She had been denied her rightful place at the pinnacle of this organization by corrupt skulduggery, and Gila was only interested in the state of others.

Another contraction started. Eva moaned aloud, her middle feeling on fire.

Madden yelled along with her, and Eva looked up to see she had grabbed near his bullet wound, squeezing tight.

"You think a healing wound is painful? You should try this once or twice."

"I nearly did," Madden replied, and suddenly to Eva the pain of the contraction did not concern her as much. He was panicking and causing a fuss for her sake, not because he was worried.

"You are bringing life into the world. Pure, wonderful life. I nearly ended mine on several occasions when what was inside me attempted to escape. I have you to thank for my continuing existence."

Despite the pain, despite the fact her body was repositioning itself to expel the tiny life form and change her world forever, Eva smiled at him.

The elevator bell rang, and the doors slid open. With her entourage of Swanson, Madden, Gila, and Rick, Eva shuffled in.

"The next contraction was only a couple of minutes after the first," Gila observed. "You don't have long."

"Good. I want this over."

Swanson switched his phone off and grinned for a moment. "There will be an ambulance there by the time we get downstairs."

"Thank you," Eva said, exuding relief. "How long will it take to get there?"

"Maybe ten minutes. The Geneva University facility is not too far away, but in midday traffic who knows? Look. Before you start to worry, you will be in an ambulance in probably the most sterile city in the entire world! There is nothing to worry about."

Another wave of pain hit her, and Eva dropped to her knees before Swanson and Rick caught her.

"I don't know if we are going to make it," Swanson said, only to receive a smack on his arm from Gila.

"Men. So full of well-meaning honesty they forget we just want to hear everything's going to be all right. That contraction was a minute."

"Is it? Is it going to be all right?"

"Eva, how many women throughout history have given birth to allow the human race to proliferate to the population it has reached? A population of over six billion. Such a number means that within the last century if not less there have been six billion occurrences of exactly what you are going through. Each of them in a similar pain as their body prepares for childbirth. Each of them different and unique in their own ways for sure, but what they all had in common was the birth of a life which is exactly what they had in common with you."

Gila always made sense. "How did I ever get by without you?"

Her friend looked at Madden, pale-faced and threatening to shake, and smiled. "I think you did pretty well until then."

The elevator opened to the tunnel, at the end of which lights flashed from a waiting ambulance. Eva took only a couple of steps before her legs gave way. Nobody had hold of her this time and she collapsed to the floor. A warm damp feeling spread down her legs, and as Madden and Rick helped her up, she looked down in fear. Clear liquid gushed everywhere, flooding the ceramic tiles flooring the tunnel and making the footing treacherous.

"Sorry," Eva said, too embarrassed to look anybody in the face.

"Her water broke. No blood," Gila confirmed. "This little one wants out in a hurry."

One of the medics from the ambulance came charging down the tunnel with a folded wheelchair. He was tall, well-muscled with a deep tan and black curly hair. His chiseled jaw would have been more at home on the cover of a magazine than in a medic uniform.

"Ah, do not worry," he said in a strong French accent. "These things 'appen. My colleague will attend. Congratulations, Madame, perhaps you would like to take a ride?"

Nodding in silent thanks, Eva was placed in the chair and whisked along the tunnel toward the ambulance. A shorter figure, clearly female, hurtled past to the puddle behind. For an instant, Eva wondered if there wasn't something familiar about the way the woman moved, but then they were past her and at the ambulance.

A third medic, a young woman with hair so pale as to almost be white awaited them in the ambulance.

"Looks like you are getting the five star treatment," Madden approved.

The young lady helped Eva into the ambulance, where Eva lay on a bed covered in green sheeting.

"Don't worry Madame, you will be safe now. We can deliver in here if necessary."

"I'd really rather not if I can... ow!" Another contraction made Eva shudder and she took long, slow breaths helped to alleviate some of the pain.

The medic banged on the inside of the ambulance. "Allez!"

"We'll follow behind," Swanson shouted around the closing door, leaving Madden crouched on a drop-down seat while the Medic attended to her.

The door slammed shut, and the ambulance shot forward, causing Eva to lurch somewhat. Panicked, she looked to the medic for reassurance.

"It might be a bumpy ride, but we shall get you there. Just hold on please. If it is acceptable, I need to check how much time we have, how far along you are."

Eva nodded, and under the cover of a blanket disrobed her bottom half. Breathing deeply, Eva closed her eyes while the medic examined her, the pain in her middle more than enough to offset what would, in any other circumstance, be the ultimate invasion of her personal privacy.

"Am I all right?"

The medic popped her head up from between Eva's legs. "Oh yes, quite fine. You are about five centimeters dilated. Coming along nicely."

"I wish I could feel as positive as you do. What's your name?"

The medic pulled off the latex gloves she had been using and dumped them in a waste bin attached to the side of the ambulance.

"My name is Nina. Nina Hesse."

Eva forced a smile to her own face. The medic was so cheerful. "You've done this a lot?"

"Oh yes. One thing is inevitable in this job: people always are having babies."

"And nothing is out of the ordinary?"

"No, all is quite fine." The medic blinked, staring at the panel on the far side of the ambulance, just left of where Madden was crouching. "I thought I saw something. It must be nothing."

"What?" Eva asked. "What did you see?"

The medic shrugged. "It looked like a face. Maybe I do need a break."

Eva looked to her husband. "Madden..."

Madden jumped up and away from the panel. "Not here. Not now. Where are we?"

The medic slid open the small window up above Eva's head and peered out. "We are on Avenue du Mail. It is not too far. Just Boulevard du Pont-d'Arve and a few streets to the hospital."

"We have to get out of here, now."

The panel opposite began to yawn open and this time Eva saw the face in a white sheen. Skeletal, screaming in silence and twisting as it tried to gain purchase in reality. It turned to regard her, reptilian tendrils writhing over its surface where tentacles held the demon fast in whatever Hell it resided. Frost began to glisten on the inside of the ambulance.

Eva saw a panic button, and pressed it. In an instant, the sirens blared and the ambulance surged forwards. Eva lay back, pouring her every thought into breathing steadily, and holding on until the absolute last moment.

"What's going on out there?" Eva asked Madden.

Madden clambered over and looked out the window. "There's... there's portals everywhere, trying to open. The semblance of faces. Skulls, ungodly things. All twisting and writhing. Eva, I think they know we are here. This can't be by chance."

The ambulance lurched to the right and Eva nearly came off the stretcher.

"Ahh!" She yelled and arched her back, putting her hands underneath to support it. The pain went on and on, her middle feeling like it was going to rupture. Pressed hard against the metal separating the drivers from their passengers, Eva had no choice but to let her back drop down. The pressure on her head was too intense. The pain went on and on.

An ethereal skull passed through the middle of the ambulance leaving a trail of mist as it failed to gain a foothold in reality. The ambulance was clearly moving too fast for the portals, but they did not stop appearing.

"That was a big contraction, no?" The medic checked her once more. "You are fully dilated, Madame. This baby wants out in a rush."

"Not here," Eva growled. "Not now."

The sky went dark, and Eva closed her eyes, awaiting the inevitable. A portal would yawn open for her and she would enter, falling endlessly as her soul was stripped from her in every tortuous way possible. Iuvart would be waiting for her, foremost among her tormentors; she was sure. She felt for the heat heralding the mouth of Hell, or indeed the ice and grasping appendages that might precede her being sucked beyond a fiery endlessness into an icy nothingness.

"Here we are," the medic announced. "Lie back, now."

Eva groaned as another wave of pain threatened to split her in two, and she reached for Madden's hand.

He wasn't there.

"Madden? Madden!"

"He's outside," the medic advised, and pulled the stretcher out onto unfolding wheels.

A crowd of strangers, doctors, surgeons, nurses all met them and for a moment, Eva forgot entirely about being pregnant. Struck by her sense of modesty, all she could think about was covering up.

A quick series of orders in French and the gathered team split up, running through different doorways.

"Dr Scott, I am Dr Pascal Cotterell," said a male voice in clipped tones, the French accent ever so slight.

"Madden, where is he? I want my husband."

"He's on his way," Gila replied. "He has some paper-work to do but it will only take a moment."

Gila was good, and meant well, but her voice betrayed

the fact she had no idea where Madden had gone.

"Get him here. I want my husband!"

"Madame, the baby is crowning. He is almost ready to be delivered."

With an effort that caused her an immense amount of pain, Eva attempted to cross her legs, only partially managing to do so.

She grunted, tears of effort running down her face, chilling against the breeze. "If you don't find my husband and get him here right now, then this damned baby ain't coming out!"

The staff around her, to a man, looked helpless. They passed through a set of doors and one of the doctors turned to Gila and held up his hand in apology.

"Non, je suis désolé."

"She comes!" Eva shouted. "If you useless lot can't find my husband, then my sister is coming through."

The doctor looked at the two of them, and Eva could feel him comparing like for like.

"She is not..."

"She is because I say she is. Who is having this baby?"

"Clearly you, by all the noise you are making," said Madden from the doorway.

Eva gasped, and reached for him. "The pressure..."

"It's all right. You are doing fine. Almost done now." Madden's voice was soothing, and Eva concentrated on his words above all else in the room. All of a sudden, Eva knew the time was right for her child to come into the world. There was so much to show her, so much to teach.

The pressure built, the pain of the contraction started, different this time, encouraging rather than alarming her. Eva pushed with all the strength she could muster, reaching through the pain to connect with her child, and screamed...

CHAPTER TWENTY-NINE

A TINY VOICE ADDED ITS CRY TO THE HUBBUB IN THE delivery suite. A voice in single clear note, full of gusto, determined to be heard. Everything stopped as people looked. The cry grew in strength, and a voice spoke to Eva.

'*I am here. We are both safe.*'

Her bottom half was completely numb from the exertion, but Eva soon forgot as Dr Cotterell handed her the child, umbilical cord still hanging from her belly, a small shock of brown hair on her head. She looked perfect. In a moment of complete awe, Eva wondered how on earth they had both made it to this stage. She gazed at the tiny human, still in the throes of her birth cry, and the strangest thing happened. As soon as they beheld each other, her daughter stopped crying, and regarded her. The eyes opened, and unlike the dark, unfocussed eyes of a new born, the irises were pale green, and focussed on her in an instant. Adult eyes in a baby. An ancient soul resided in her daughter and, safe in the moment, Eva knew she would do anything in her power to protect her.

"Would you look at that," Gila said, wiping away tears

as the medics clamped off the cord and offered the cut to Madden.

Madden stood up from the bed, where he had been watching the scene unfold through glistening eyes of his own.

"No, it's fine. You guys are the experts. You can do it."

The doctors took her daughter away for a moment, cleaning and measuring. For one so suddenly thrust into a world full of myriad sensations from the warm security of the womb, she endured it all with good grace.

"Seven and a half pounds in weight, and quite a long baby. She is going to be tall," said Dr Cotterell as he handed the baby to Madden. "Those eyes. We are going to need to run some tests. I have never seen the like."

"You will do no such thing," Eva contradicted. "Our little lady has unique parentage. She was bound to have a little something special about her." Eva glared at Madden, her love for him making it nearly impossible to maintain the façade. "Lucky for you she didn't come out with horns and a forked tail."

Madden looked sheepish at this, and attempted to change the subject. "What are you going to call her?"

"Don't you want a say?"

Madden brushed a lock of sweat-drenched hair from her face. "With all you have been through, I would never presume to take the choice away from you."

"I hadn't really given it any thought. I liked names of my family such as Samantha and Jessica, even Patricia." The face of the medic who had helped her in the ambulance flashed in her mind. Pale green eyes, almost albino hair.

"Nina. After the girl in the ambulance."

It felt right. All the questions Eva had asked herself the

moment she had gone into what seemed a remarkably quick labour were now answered.

'*Will I die?* No. *Will she survive?* She will flourish. *What if she's deformed?* She is more beautiful than I had ever imagined. *What if I can't cope?* I can do anything now. *What is this world into which I release new life?* It is a world in peril, but then isn't it always? Her life will be defined by the choices she makes.

"May I show her to the guys?" Madden asked nobody in particular?

"If you wish, just do not go any further out than the other side of the suite. We have some work to do tidying up your wife so we need a little time."

During the next few days, due to what Eva presumed was ARC influence, Eva remained in what could only be described as a 'plush' private apartment in the hospital with her husband and daughter. Bright from hidden lighting, the room had a huge double bed and a beautiful mahogany crib beside it, for Nina. With a private bathroom and a view looking out across lush green parks to the distant United Nations buildings, it was far more a hotel suite than a hospital ward.

Eva spent every waking moment with her daughter. The changes arriving with the birth were momentous, and so profound it had changed her completely. No longer did she worry about the future; her future lay in front of her, wriggling and kicking in her sleep, dressed head to toe in a beautiful pink onesie. Nina was remarkably content, watching Eva almost constantly when she was awake, implying with the slightest of noises she needed attending to. In truth, Eva knew in most cases before it got too far. The connection was fiercely strong.

Madden was an absolute rock during this period. Content to hold Nina whenever he was allowed, he was nonetheless present almost all of the time.

It was during one of these rare moments when Eva was happy to hand Nina over a thought occurred to her.

"What did happen when we got here? They said you had forms to fill in."

Rocking Nina, Madden smiled ruefully. "In truth, I was terrified. It just hit me. The portals, watching you helpless, the mad urgency of it all. Suddenly it was too much for me and I panicked. I just found a bench nearby and sat down."

This was a new sensation for Eva, seeing her husband genuinely vulnerable. By his own admission, too. In the past, even through their most dire moments, the vulnerability had stemmed from his strengths, and had been forced upon him

"I'm glad you made it in time."

Madden stood up and began to bounce instinctively on his feet, soothing his daughter. Nina was completely content, but Eva wasn't going to tell him.

"In truth, I wasn't going to, but then this guy sat down next to me. I have no idea where he came from but he asked me what I was doing there and having no reason not to, I told him. He said he had five kids, and he was here for his sixth. He said the moment of birth was the most incredible moment of his life, and he hadn't missed a single birth. He suggested I would regret it if I missed it, and suddenly I only wanted to be next to you. I thanked him and rushed to you. The rest is history."

Eva smiled. "I'm relieved you came. The guy sounds like a guardian angel. Who was he?"

"A huge black guy. I mean he was stacked. Big beard, enormous hair, but he had a way of talking that belied his looks, as if the whole world made sense to him on a different level. He was called Velos or something similar. He called his name after me as I was running to find you."

The door opened and Swanson peeked in. "Not disturbing you are we?" He whispered.

"No, not at all," Eva replied. "I find it hard to believe Nina could ever be disturbed. It can't be this easy for everybody."

Gila came in close on Swanson's heels and went immediately to Madden, who handed Nina over. Gila turned back the edges of the blanket wrapping Nina and gave her a kiss.

"Sorry to intrude, but we have to talk business," she said, stroking Nina's tiny face with the back of one finger.

Eva could feel Nina was awake, and regarding Gila, who was the one person not related directly to them who remained utterly unfazed by the eyes.

"Business?"

"It's not much really, but it might lead somewhere." Swanson collapsed into one of the upholstered chairs beside the bed. There were lines on his face new since the meeting of the Council.

"You haven't slept," Eva accused.

Swanson rubbed at his temple with one hand. "I have, a little."

"Yeah, no more than a couple of hours in three days," said Gila in between cooing at Nina.

"I will sleep when you are on the council, Sarch is in jail and CERN is locked down."

"CERN? The particle smashing place?"

"The same. You know it's nearby? It appears significant

funding has been directed in the direction of the Large Hadron Collider, much more than is reasonable. We have been trying to track the source, but it's proving troublesome."

"Let me guess," Madden said, "Garias?"

Swanson nodded, apparently ready to nod off. "It's his department, and he has it sealed watertight. I suspect it's the reason we were led on this merry chase, just to keep us away from Geneva and whatever is happening behind the scenes."

"Can we help?" Eva asked, concerned by this new development.

"Yes," Swanson replied. "You can carry on doing what you're doing. Take care of this beautiful child. We didn't get you this far to start concerning yourself about others all of a sudden. Rick will take care of you. Everyone's in safe hands. What could possibly go wrong?"

A few more days passed, and despite the utter contentment of and with her daughter, an uneasiness began to gnaw at Eva. Were they in the right place for all the wrong reasons? Nothing appeared out of the ordinary on any news channel. The new ABC news anchor, obviously an ARC plant to replace Jeanette Gibson while she was here in Geneva, was concise and informative, but the escalation Eva expected was not happening. Paranoia began to set in. Eva's dreams began once again to haunt her. Sleep became a rarity.

It was six nights after the birth of her daughter. Eva had finally succumbed to exhaustion after two days without rest, and was having a very vivid dream about Nina. Just out of reach, Nina held her hand out toward her mother, eyes calm and always trusting.

Eva stretched to her absolute limit, but there was always a barrier there. In time, her child began to age, hair growing longer, strawberry blonde and curly. The hand remained stretched until Nina closed and withdrew it.

'Too far, Mother. You will always find me. I will be safe.'

Eva started awake and clutched at the sheets she was entangled in, sweat drenched, and hot. Early morning light shone in from across the park, the sun not yet above the mountains to the east. Her head was fuzzy, her eyes gritty. Every breath came labored. She put her right hand on her chest, willing her heart to slow. Her breasts felt heavy, as good an indicator as any it was time to nurse her daughter. Eva pushed herself out of bed, feeling the plush carpet nonetheless cold and pleasant underfoot, and crossed the dark room to her daughter's crib.

She gazed down on the small blanket-wrapped bundle containing her daughter, and smiled in contentment. Sound asleep. It would be a shame to wake her, but necessary. Eva reached down, placing her hands on either side of the blanket, and lifted. There was no weight. The blanket unravelled, revealing another blanket bundled within.

Refusing to believe, Eva began to dig at the bedclothes in the crib. Nothing. She threw the sheets behind her, pulling the mattress up and hurling it atop the growing pile. When only the frame remained, she began searching the rest of the room, her only thought to find her daughter. Blind panic overcame her, and Eva tore apart cushions and smashed through closet doors.

When nothing was left, Eva looked at the bathroom. Only a bottle of shampoo and a bar of soap. Her heart pounded dangerously close to its limit, and she began to pull breath in gasps. Where was everybody?

"Help! HELP!!" She screamed, not knowing what else to do. There was no response. Where was everybody?

Eva ran to the door. Rick was always outside, especially since Swanson's visit. He hands had begun to shake, and her fingers slipped off the metal handle as she clawed at it impotently as she tried to open the door.

"Rick! Help me! My... My baby..."

Eva eventually managed to get the door open, the handle slick with sweat and blood. As she pulled the door inwards, it was forced open by the dead weight of a body leaning against it. Eva's first coherent thought was a detached wondering at how there could be so much blood followed an instant later by the realization the body belonged to her guard and friend.

She crouched down next to him. "Rick, oh Rick. What have they done to you?"

There was a gurgling noise as blood froth erupted from his mouth. Rick opened one of his damaged eyes and fixed it upon her. Gasping with his ebbing life, he reached up and grabbed her head, pulling it to his mouth, and whispered one word.

Eva's blood ran cold. Rick's breath rattled in his throat one last time, and the life left his eye, his body sagging as it succumbed to his extensive injuries.

Eva ran her hands over his torso, trying to find out what had been done. Even with his size, the broken ribs were unmistakeable. There was a dent in the wall opposite that must have been made by his body, the plasterboard crushed and broken. Blood trails smeared across the floor showed he had been trying to get to her, and had been for some time as a lot of it was dry, black, and crusted.

In one hand, Rick held his radio. Remembering her situation and understanding with acid precision she was now

MATTHEW W. HARRILL

alone and unprotected, Eva began to scream Madden's name into the radio, switching channels and depressing all of the buttons, no matter who heard her.

It did not take long. The door down the hallway burst open as Madden came hurtling in, several orderlies behind him. He stopped in front of their suite, where Eva still had the radio jammed on 'transmit'.

His face mirrored her own. Complete disbelief.

"Eva... What the hell..?"

"Madden. They've taken the baby! They've taken Nina!"

Eva held her hands tight and began to rock. She knew she was going into shock, and wanted to hold it all together, but she had no idea what to do.

Madden dashed into their room, and was back out again in an instant.

"Where?" He shouted at one of the orderlies, and the man pointed to an emergency exit, the plastic seal tampered with and made to look as if it were untouched.

"Call the police!" He shouted at her, and shouldered through the doors, leaving them swinging in his wake.

Swanson and Gila entered the hallway from the same direction as Madden had come. The look on their faces mirrored his own anguish. Gila put her hand to her mouth, and Swanson reached down to pick Eva from the floor.

"What are you doing here? They took my baby. My Nina. My daughter."

"We know," Swanson replied solemnly. "I think we have a problem."

Eva was about to scream a reply about a Goddamned problem when Swanson pried the radio from her hand.

"This is Swanson. Level ten lockdown. All key points in

300

and around Geneva. Nothing gets in or out." He knelt and folded Rick's arms reverently over his ruined body.

"Rest well, old friend. May we never see you again."

Standing, he turned back to Eva, who watched him expectantly. Why had he given her no answers?

"There is a communique coming through. We are trying everything to find Nina. Come in here, Eva."

She followed Swanson, her feet tripping over the detritus of her frenzied search. Eva was dimly aware of Gila holding her hand, but she watched as Swanson flicked the television on.

The ages-old ABC circular logo and music. Jeanette Gibson appeared on screen.

"This is a message received only moments ago from the Convocation of the Sacred Fire:

'We have found the next Messiah. He is among us. He is being taken to a place of safety where he shall be raised with the knowledge and the values of the Nibiru until he steps amongst you once more as leader.'

Contrary to the statement, this is the kidnapping of a child. No more."

Jeanette leaned forward, as if she was looking Eva right in the eye. "Swanson, they are headed to CERN! Seek out Orpheus. We calculate there is very little time left before she is beyond your reach. Hurry! Now!"

CHAPTER THIRTY

THE NEWS WAS AS BIZARRE AS IT WAS EXPECTED. EVA dropped to the bed, now flaccid amid the destruction she so recently wreaked.

"Naturally," she said, staring towards the husk of the crib. "Why wouldn't you? A newborn baby. Hell is the first place they are gonna want to visit. Imagine the conversation at school: 'What did you do this weekend Nina? Well, miss, I went to Hell and played ball with Cerberus, threw brimstone in the river Styxx.'"

Eva turned to Swanson. "You said you knew about this."

Swanson opened his attaché case and pulled out several files, each marked 'ARC: Eyes only' in red. He handed them to her.

Eva began to flick through the topmost. It contained drawings of an enormous circular device and a series of complex calculations. "I'm sorry, I have no idea what this is."

"Those are schematics and formula for a particle accelerator. ARC has been betrayed. The Large Hadron Collider at CERN was a major energy project financed in part by us and developed by some of the greatest minds in history, many of whom were ARC operatives.

But was more to the project than we expected. They will deny this of course, but from what I can see, Benedict Garias and Zoe Larter and at least Ivor Sarch, if not others, have been complicit in using the machine to attempt to open and control a portal."

"It just smashes atoms though?" Eva was confused, and tried hard to understand Swanson's point. He always had a reason for saying and doing what he did. "How is this going to help find Nina? We should be out there now."

"If you fail to prepare, prepare to fail," Swanson admonished her. "Where would you go? The machine is nearly thirty miles in length. If the Hadron Collider is where the abductor is taking your daughter, we need a starting point."

Madden walked in, frustration and failure mixed all over his face. "What part of CERN is closest? They got away. There's a trail of dead or dying guards reaching from here to one of the loading bays downstairs."

Eva stood. "We go then, to CERN."

"No doubt," Swanson agreed. "But where would you have us look?"

Eva held up one of the diagrams from the folder she had been examining. "Here. The CERN control center, near Meyrin. According to the map, it's only a few miles out of Geneva. Surely that would be the perfect place to look?"

"I'm telling you they won't have gotten so far," Swanson persisted. "The security measures are absolute."

"I beg to differ." Madden pointed back down the stairs. "Not from what witnesses say. There were two of them, a muscular man who carried something wrapped in his arms, and a woman."

It all made sense. "Elaine." Eva spoke the word as if it burned her tongue to speak it, and her ears to hear it.

Everybody stopped.

"What did you say?" Madden asked.

"Elaine," Eva repeated. "I opened the door, and Rick fell in. He was badly beaten, but he was still alive. He whispered one word to me before he succumbed to injuries. Elaine."

"I guess she's stronger than she looks," Gila mused.

"And immune to shards of glass," Madden agreed. "I guess we weren't the only ones to get out of the mansion with our lives. But who is the other person?"

Eva was having a hard time trying to hold it together, but this discussion and analysis: it just wound her up and got her nowhere.

"It's Elaine. She has Nina. If anybody can get out of the city, it's Elaine. Can we at least get to this control center? I need to do something. You don't even sound surprised to find out she's alive."

"Love, you only have a name. It makes sense, I know. Are you not groggy the way you were when she drugged you before? Are you not separated from the one thing you are certain helped you during those times? Eva, I want her back as much as you, but if we take the wrong course of action now, we might lose her forever."

With the decision made, the next few moments were a blur for Eva. A cacophony of organized shouting with the iron tang of Rick's blood on the floor. She could never get used to the sight of it, despite everything she had been through. She stopped to glare at her companions as they hustled her past the body of their former protector.

"Do have no respect?" She shouted.

"It's your decision to leave, Eva." Swanson answered. "You want to find your daughter or not?"

Unhinged slightly by having the onus put back on her, Eva glanced at the black body bag and nodded.

Taking the movement as assent, Madden grabbed her with his good arm and they rushed back out the way they had entered some days before.

Being naturally fit, Eva had mostly recovered from the stresses of labor, and deep down welcomed the chance to be active. The loss of her child would affect her profoundly if she let it. She had to hold it together.

The black armored Mercedes awaited them at the front of the hospital, and they bundled in taking whatever space was available, the leather seating cold and hard now Eva had nothing in life to celebrate.

"How far?" she asked as they sped off.

"It's just a few miles to the control center, but who knows how much more if they have moved beyond? Our quarry knows where they are going. We only have the clues they leave to guide us." Swanson waved the documents at them. "This. It reveals so much. We knew about the project aimed at a sustained incursion into Hell. What we didn't know about was the dedication they have to their cause."

Blank looks all around led Swanson to elaborate. "Did any of you take chemistry at school?"

"I did, when I attended," admitted Madden.

"Okay, well opening a portal to Hell is at its most-base level a chemical reaction. Ivor Sarch has been searching for a way to sustain that reaction. In chemistry, you use a match to light a piece of magnesium ribbon and watch it combust. It burns super-hot. However, if you want to make a form of thermite using sulphur and iron filings, a match will not suffice to start the reaction. You have to use the magnesium as a fuse."

Swanson turned to Eva, genuine compassion in his eyes. "I think he, or somebody associated with him, has procured his fuse."

"Nina?"

"Torturing a hellbounce produces the desired effect for a temporary incursion to wherever the ice realm lies. But for the most part it ends. What if there is no hellbounce? Madden, the energy you contained as your former self, well it was like nothing else on this earth; made nuclear fusion look like a store brand supermarket battery. What they accomplished on Nag Hamaddi was small fry. They wanted Afghanistan. They want all sorts of places, which is the real reason all these ARC facilities exist wherever a portal has been recorded, or is expected."

Gila took over at this point. "You are an unexpected factor in their plans. Both of you. As such, they have been forced to reveal their hand sooner than they hoped to. They wanted to keep the Gehenna portal open, but through sheer luck you found a way to close it."

"You think Benedict Garias is going to use my daughter to open a portal to Hell?"

"Unfortunately, no," said Swanson. "What you did was force them to get Ivor Sarch elected. His ascension allowed access to records pointing to these financial transactions. These records were found hidden deep in other movements of currency. We are talking trillions, people. Bodom was a mask designed for us to look the other way. You can guarantee Nina was not expected. I think whoever is ultimately behind this is taking advantage of the situation. It seems while Benedict and his cronies have the tools and the power, they didn't have the key. Elaine, or whoever is really behind this, does."

"No, that's not it," Eva said, remembering the mountaintop. "That's not what it's about at all."

Eva looked out at the city of Geneva flying past as they hurtled along the highway. Blue signs labeled 'Route de Meyrin' in white directed the heavy traffic toward CERN; the warning and the lockdown had not worked. Those who were not fleeing the area, were headed towards the cryptic promise of adventure and danger. How little the ordinary people of the world really knew. This would play out amongst crowds of innocents who knew nothing about the dangers around them.

"This so-called sensor called 'Orpheus'. What do we know about it?"

Gila pulled out her tablet and tapped a couple of keys. "What we know about the sensor is not much more than the name. It's apparently an instrument to read energy fluctuations in the Large Hadron Collider. However, in legend, Orpheus was a singer who attempted to rescue his wife, Eurydice, from the underworld. He entered through a cave, and went as far as Tartarus in his quest." Gila looked up. "That doesn't bode well."

"But it is appropriate. You see they wanted my blood to open the Scroll of Judgement. It worked enough to almost stabilize the portal on Gehenna. Sarch figured the secret. It's not about getting there. Whoever is behind this knows the answer. It's never been about mere kidnap. They intend to take Nina into Hell, find the seal, and finish the ritual."

The remainder of their journey was a fight with traffic. Contrary to her nature, Eva settled into a quiet state of acceptance of her fate. All about them, vans bearing media logos jostled for position on the mad rush to CERN. Once they had turned off the Route de Meyrin, the road lost a lane, and progress became painful. When, in time, the pale buildings of the CERN control center began to peek over the surrounding woodland, traffic was at a standstill. The short road leading from the highway to the CERN security gate was surrounded by military, and in front of the blockade, a media circus had erupted on a large field to the left.

Swanson solved the traffic problem by ordering the driver across this field, and right through the middle of the melee. A jolt brought Eva back to the present as the car jumped off a curb to land right in front of the assault-rifle wielding squad.

To a man, they peeled back, allowing the car to pass and reforming the line just as soon as they had. The car took a series of left turns and pulled up in the shadow of the gray building Eva had seen from the road.

"Welcome to CERN," Swanson said as he opened the door.

Eva stepped out and looked about. The building itself was very unassuming. Only a couple of stories high, a few steps led to a functional glass door. This place was all about science, not about pageantry.

A few people could be spotted at the windows as they gawked at the distant media circus. More had been waiting through the glass doors for the newcomers to arrive.

"Director Guyomard," one woman said in an English accent as they pushed through. "What's going on out there? We knew the latest upgrade would generate interest, but what's going on out there is lunacy."

Eva regarded the woman, who studied her back. Tall, with a wealth of brown hair tied loosely at the back, she wore a brown silk blouse and suit skirt; a woman who liked style but never put it above a towering intellect.

"You are her. The woman off the television," she accused.

"Dr Eva Scott, may I present Dr Ruth Grimshaw, chief administrator of the Super LHC project at CERN."

"Super?"

Ruth Grimshaw held out her hand, and Eva shook it. "The hadron collider has been upgraded. A scientific experiment is only as good as its last results, and over time, the likelihood of new discoveries diminishes if the constants remain the same. We are in the completion stage of an upgrade process that allows significantly higher power inputs to the collider. That means faster beams, bigger smashes, more detailed analysis. Who knows what lies beyond the boundary of our understanding: The next Higgs boson discovery or something much more profound?"

Eva could not help but shake her head at this comment. If what Swanson said were true then the next discovery these poor dupes made would not see them long in this world.

"You doubt this?"

Eva looked up, blushing as she realized the woman had not, for a second, taken her eyes off her.

"We aren't here because you are on the verge of something momentous." Eva closed her eyes and took several deep breaths. It was hard to keep it together, and doubly frustrating when presented with this. There was a pit aching deep within her. Loneliness, for despite all those around her, the maternal bond was strong and secure.

"Our five day old daughter has been kidnapped and we believe she has been brought here," Madden supplied.

Finally, a look of confusion crossed the face of Ruth

Grimshaw. "Why would somebody do such a horrific thing, and then bring them here? There's nowhere to hide a child in a building full of scientists."

"We were hoping you might have some answers since all our information pointed in this direction. Tell me, Dr Grimshaw, what do you know about a sensor project called 'Orpheus'?"

Ruth Grimshaw's eyes narrowed, and she ushered the other scientists out of earshot.

"That project was top secret. A sensor larger than any other with more instrumentation on it than anything used on any previous particle accelerator, either here, or in America. But the project was mothballed; caught up in red tape. We had even begun looking into possible excavation sites, but the cost was too great. Your own organization pulled the plug, Director Guyomard."

"I'm very sorry to hear it. Nevertheless, I would appreciate any information you could dredge up about the project. It could be of vital use to us at this time."

"I wish I could help," Grimshaw said. "It was only the other day one of your colleagues, Zoe Larter, came in and made exactly the same request. Naturally, who were we to oppose our paymasters?"

"Who were you indeed, but masters of your own fate?" Eva said, her tone scathing.

The administrator opened her mouth to retort, but as she did so, a door slammed open about ten feet behind her, down the sterile white hallway. Several men came dashing through.

"Dr Grimshaw!" One shouted, a rotund man with greasy hair and jeans clearly suited to a thinner frame. "You have to come quick! The children. They are misbehaving!"

"What do you mean? We don't begin operating for another week."

"Nevertheless, somebody has begun the power-up process for the Super Proton Synchrotron and the Large Hadron Collider, and we have no control over either. We're locked out!"

CHAPTER THIRTY-ONE

The entrance to the Control Center became a flurry of motion as Ruth Grimshaw, despite her obviously feminine demeanour, broke into a run. Everybody followed, and Eva was left fearing whiplash as Madden yanked her arm and she was forced to keep up.

"Coincidence?" He said between breaths as they ran down the hallway.

"I think not," she agreed.

"Right. 'Strange things are afoot at the Circle K'," he said, quoting *Bill and Ted's Excellent Adventure*, one of Eva's favorite movies as a child. The movie had taken a very unlikely couple of young men and, via some very unorthodox science, introduced them to people they would never have met otherwise, and places they otherwise would never have been. She smiled as she concluded without her husband, her own 'Excellent Adventure' would not have happened.

"You picked a perfect time to come visit," Ruth muttered as they followed her into a very grand room housing monitors of various descriptions on every conceivable wall. The floor was dominated by four circular banks of instruments, with enough space for thirty of forty people to have stood and watched in the middle of each.

"Mission Control," Ruth announced. "Welcome to the heart of CERN."

The majority of the population in the enormous room, easily half the size of a football field, kept their eyes on the instruments in front of them, many tapping away with feverish futility. A few looked around at the newcomers with panicked faces.

Ruth Grimshaw approached the nearest of the circular bays and put her hand on the shoulder of a black-haired man in a short-sleeved white shirt.

"Henri,"

The man in question jumped in response. He turned to say something to Ruth, and then seeing the rest of them stood up from his seat.

"Dr Henri Nesdez, may I introduce you to Swanson Guyomard and his entourage."

Nesdez's face blanched upon hearing Swanson's name, but his voice betrayed no alarm.

"Bonjour, Monsieur Guyomard. How can I help?" The strength of his accent spoke to Eva of a man who was much more at home speaking his native language.

"You can begin by telling us what's going on here," Swanson said, shaking hands with Nesdez.

"In simple terms, we are locked out of the particle accelerators."

"Your description doesn't sound in any way simple," Gila observed.

"An astute observation. Take a look here."

Nesdez led them into the ring of monitors, sweeping his hand broadly around the screens.

Eva followed. Nothing made any sense to her. Cameras showed live footage of the underground collider and the myriad of machinery designed to keep it intact. Nothing moved underground wherever it was. Graphic dials continued to move slowly upwards through mostly green wedges, towards orange, and eventual red sections.

"You will see here nothing of significance. All the charts are normal, power levels are within their limits. The problem begins when you try to understand the purpose of what is in front of you. Imagine, if you will, this entire experiment is a rail network, the beams are trains and the particles within are passengers. Your rail network will have controllers ensuring the trains do not crash. If the controllers cannot control..."

"...then you have one almighty crash," Madden finished.

"Indeed. The beams themselves are tricky, but with so many crossing simultaneously this could prove disastrous."

As if to emphasise his point, Nesdez flicked open the plastic cover on the dashboard in front of him. The words read 'Cut Power' next to a large red button. Nesdez slammed the heel of his hand on the button. Nothing changed.

"Not good," said Madden.

"Agreed. The problem is the amount of power the colliders are drawing. For its size, the Large Hadron Collider is an incredibly delicate piece of technology, and very expensive to run. If the power levels keep increasing, the coolant systems could rupture and the whole circuit could explode. It takes a lot of power to keep a system operating at near absolute zero."

Ruth put her hand on Pascal's shoulder. "Add the fact we have recently completed upgrades to make the system even more powerful, and we have a bigger problem. We don't know the limits."

Eva spoke up. "Who has the knowledge and authority to do such a thing?"

Ruth waved her hand about the room. "You are looking at the collective genius of CERN here, and it appears we are powerless."

"You need to check it. Check it all. They have my baby."

Confused, since he had not been party to the reason they had come in the first place, Pascal stood to protest. "Madame, these are two circuits of seven and twenty-seven kilometres in tunnels deep under solid rock. If there is a rupture, we cannot contain it; that is why the instrumentation is all here."

"Well, you are not driving this train any more, are you, *monsieur*? Who is in control now? Where are they? Elaine has my daughter and she came towards this very building."

"Maybe she wasn't coming here," Swanson deliberated. "She must be nearby, but she was only a few minutes in front of us. Why don't we try to calculate where the collider crosses with..."

The lights of the control room winked out, followed shortly by the screens. There were shouts of alarm and panic. Eva clutched to Madden's good arm.

"Everybody stay calm!" Ruth Grimshaw instructed above the noise. "Everybody..."

Then a sound louder than the collective cries of a room full of scientists caused a chill down Eva's spine. She felt Madden squeeze her hand so hard he threatened to break bones.

The noise was the chilling wail of a baby in distress. Betrayal, abandonment, loss. The feelings washed over Eva simultaneously and she threatened to drop to her knees. Where was it coming from?

The answer came as two of the main screens on the front wall powered up and cameras focused in on several people standing in a group. Behind them was an enormous construction. Octagonal in shape, with metal sheeting welded at equal points all focussing in on a circular section maybe eight feet in diameter at the center. A walkway had been built atop a set of winding metal stairs so somebody could approach the nexus of the machine.

"That's not like any sensor I've ever seen," Ruth Grimshaw declared. "Where's it hidden? Locate it."

This caused a flurry of activity around the instruments, the population of the control center colliding in the dark as they ran for information.

Eva ignored the rest of them, focused only on the small figure, arms and legs fighting for freedom, meaninglessly bumping off the arms of the woman holding her. Elaine held Nina not as a mother would hold their newborn child, but rather as a victor would hold a trophy. The lack of compassion on the face of a woman she once called 'friend' disgusted her. But Nina lived. For now, her daughter's existence was the only thought in Eva's mind.

Her vision widened to take in the rest of the figures on the screen, and her breath caught in her throat.

"I know the woman.s Florentina from Westlabs. But what's wrong with her?"

On screen, Florentina stood to one side of the group, her right arm glinting as if it were crystalline. She was shivering uncontrollably, looking at times as though she was having a fit.

Eva took Madden's own wounded arm, rolling up the

sleeve. Where the hand had been cold, spots of the same material glinted in the light of the screens.

"It's not a problem," he whispered. "I'll get it looked at."

"By the time you do, Madden Scott, you will have suffered the same fate as my mistress," Elaine taunted, stepping forward. "It is not an easy pain to bear."

Elaine held Nina aloft. "Behold! As prophesized by the Lord Nibiru, I have delivered to the world my child; the savior is among us again. I will take the child to a place of sanctuary where she shall grow strong, and with the knowledge the planetary leader Lord Nibiru imparts unto her she will return, and the Golden Age will dawn. She is the sacrifice. One life for billions. The continuation of the human race is her responsibility and like the Christ child, she will fall and rise again."

"She's a lunatic," Eva said, beyond caring that anybody could hear her. "How did we miss the God-complex?"

Elaine thrust Nina to the figure behind her and stepped forward. "You miss everything because you do not believe, Eva Scott. You have no faith. You just stumble from one situation to the next, relying on others to free you from your insignificant predicament. How are you going to escape this? I have the child you stole from me. You will tell those your truths about me; I do not like having words put in my mouth. Here is the truth. Madden has always loved me. From the moment I held him dying in my arms on Mount Gehenna, he loved me. I pulled him back from the brink, gave him hope. I kept him out of Hell a second time. You have never been worthy of him, and I will prove this to you. He will come for me. Wherever I go he will come for me."

Eva looked to Madden, and his expression spoke volumes: Fury at Elaine for the lies being spread, and the kidnapping of their daughter. Disappointment she had cause ever to suspect infidelity.

On the screen, the character behind Elaine placed his hand on her shoulder and she became compliant once more. Stepping back, she took Nina from him and held her the way a child would hold a doll, like a possession she didn't quite know how to handle.

The shadowy figure stepped into the light, and Eva's stomach sank as she recognised the raptor's gaze. The eyes that had stared at her all evening in a bar in Worcester now regarded her over the video link. Blonde hair, an attractive face, a shirt undone enough to reveal an ample supply of muscle. He smirked at her.

"You see how easy it is?" He said in a seductive voice, pulling at her, wanting to hear more of it; he was the source of Lust and Eva did everything she could to force the fact from her mind.

"Put lesser creatures together, and they spawn. Take what is theirs, and they are wronged. End their existence, and they lament. This is the way of the pathogen called humanity. You infect each other with your so-called ideals and principles, but where does it get you? Gluttony, wrath, lust, sloth. These are not sins. These are facts. They define what it is you bloodsacks really are: the imperfect creation of a blinkered Divinity."

"This isn't just being broadcast here," Gila whispered, holding up her tablet. On the screen the very same picture showed, but with the CNN logo.

"They've hijacked everything," she added.

"The nameless waits in Hell for you all, for sinners you are. Every one of you watching me now. You shall know me. You shall know my kind before this is over. Eva Scott, and those watching me from close by, know this:

Your mysterious organization counts for nothing. You protect these people and all you do is hide from them the truth. Hell is coming to Earth."

"ARC," he sneered. "Anges de la Résurrection des Chevaliers. What angels are you? What knights have you resurrected? You direct the finance and science of your entire planet to stopping us, and for what? For who? For humanity? You all make your best efforts at getting to Hell every day of your lives. You pretend to be pious, and nod your head in the direction of false idols, yet even the most Holy of you practice sin. You will all swell our ranks at the end."

The stranger raised his hands about him. "You even name your instruments of science after those within my domain. This? Orpheus? The man who challenged the underworld to reclaim his wife? How poetic. How futile. He joined us eons ago. But this child: this child will end all of your suffering. The breach will be sealed. Those who come from Beyond will be contained and then my minions will turn their attention towards humanity. This will be our Eden, not yours."

The stranger reached out of view and grabbed a woman who had a permanently-startled look on her face.

"My God," uttered an astonished Swanson. He looked to Gila. "That's..."

"Tell the world your name," ordered the stranger, his hand tight around the woman's neck.

"My... my name is Zoe Larter. I am a councilmember, one of the leaders of ARC. I can confirm what you see behind you is real, and everything as... my Lord Nibiru says is true. We developed the technology to harness the power of Hell, but not for this. It was a clean energy source. It was..."

The sentence never ended as the stranger tightened his grip and whoever was watching heard bones crunch in Larter's neck. There was a look of confusion on her face, just the briefest glimpse of pain, and then her head dropped to one side, her hair hanging limp across her face.

Screams of shock ran around the CERN control room. As Eva looked about her, she could see everybody was transfixed. The air stank of sweat as the air conditioning had failed with the rest of the instruments. Eva fancied this was not the only foul smell in the room.

"And look what you uncovered in your greed, your selfish quest for power. By trying to save yourselves, by trying to make your lives more meaningful, you have given us exactly what we needed. In birthing this child, Eva Scott, you have given us exactly what we needed."

He held up a vial of almost transparent liquid, and then passed it over to Elaine, who disappeared off camera, leaving the plaintive cries of Nina as the only evidence she had ever been there. "This child is the saviour, not of mankind, but of every demon in Hell. When one drop of this amniotic fluid is introduced into this machine, your wildest dreams will come true. You will witness a stable portal, one with the ability to cross both ways. The end of days is upon you."

The stranger continued to rave about what would happen, walking from side to side, not unlike a caged lion gone slightly mad. Most of the room was still transfixed by the spectacle, but one of the engineers slid up between Eva and Swanson, whispering to him.

"It is time you saw what future awaits you," the stranger decided, and the camera zoomed out to give a wider view of the room.

"I am Asmodeus, and you will all bow before me."

The strangers form shimmered, growing significantly larger. When the shimmering ended, the dark-haired handsome stranger was gone. A thing of nightmares remained, and people in the Control Center began to scream. Some, though still transfixed by the image on the screen, began to edge away.

Red eyes glowed at them from under burnished metal armor, or was it skin? Horns curved up above the head, the metal etched with swirls and detailed carvings. Shoulders covered in the same material bore spikes, or were they bone spurs? Heavily knotted muscles were enmeshed in more of the same, and as the creature glowered at them, everything moved, threatening to expand. It appeared the only limit to Asmodeous' size was the limit he imposed on himself.

A rattle came from deep within the creature.

'Is there air in Hell? Is it breathing?' Eva considered.

Asmodeus opened his mouth, revealing a maw lined with razor-sharp teeth. The demon in Worcester had been a crude shape, a mindless thug of a beast compared to what was now in front of them. Hellbounces were only a means to an end, Eva realized. If true demons were like these two, what hope did they have?

Off to one side, Nina began to wail once more. Asmodeus turned from them and reached out with impossibly long arms. Bringing Nina back into view, he regarded her for a moment, and then ran one clawed finger across her forehead and down her face. The wailing stopped, and Nina stared at Asmodeus, her strangely adult eyes clear and steady.

Asmodeus turned to the screen once more, the rattling increased as he prepared to speak. When a voice issued from the depths of the creature, it was ear splitting in volume, and several people dropped to the floor in agony. Nina remained calm, unaffected.

"This is your Testament. Today is your Judgement Day, your rapture. I am Asmodeus, and my brethren will soon be among you. Pray to your God. He will not hear you. He cannot act. He is without voice. Your time is at an end, ours is at hand. When this portal opens, all open. The gateway on Gehenna will be like a gentle dream compared with what is to come. Look upon the face of your destroyer, minions of Earth, and know despair. Your own people led you to this fate, and because of them, you will all become mine." Asmodeus reached toward them, crushing whatever was filming him, and the feedback blew the speakers in the Control Room. The room plunged once more into darkness.

CHAPTER THIRTY-TWO

Power was slow in returning to the Control Room. Eva remained completely still, cradling her belly by reflex as if Nina were still being carried. Madden held her, and she could feel the tension in his touch. He was stressed but trying his best not to let anybody know.

In time, monitors began to flick back on and the lighting faded back into being. The room came back into view; although the same in size and structure, it was now utterly different than before the lights had gone down. The previously calm scientists and experts were now huddled in groups, terrified. From the smell, several had soiled themselves. Most of those had fled. A few were beyond reason, rocking in their seats, staring at nothing. Some had passed out entirely. The resemblance between this scene and the aftermath of the little girl's murder in Worcester was uncanny, if for very different reasons. One noticeable similarity was their world as they knew it had ended, much as Eva's had that gory day.

Swanson's phone blared to life, the ringtone making many of those contemplating their own future jump.

Swanson himself gazed at the screen announcing the caller as if reluctant to answer, before reluctantly accepting the call.

"Yes? It is. Yes, we are. Understood."

Swanson motioned to Eva, Madden and Gila. "This is for all of us to hear. Come close."

Everybody crowded in, Swanson attempting to shield them from the rest of the crowded room. He put the phone on speaker.

"We are listening," he said.

"Good," came Jeanette Gibson's American accent from the speaker. From the clipped tone of one word, it was clear she too was shaken up.

"I'll be brief. Stay away from here, Swanson. Most of Geneva is on lockdown, as per your orders. ARC has taken it a step further and we aren't even being allowed out of the building. If you have need, use the retreat."

"What about Garias?" Eva asked.

"He's gone. Rumour has it he disappeared around the same time Zoe Larter was taken. Ivor Sarch is also missing, although I'm sure his absence is not a shock to anybody. Johan Klaas has ordered a complete security blackout for the near future. I think they finally realize they have been played. Your uncle is trying to keep things together, but you are better off free to act by being out of here for now. Is there anything you need of me?"

Madden leaned in. "What's it like out there? We still have to rescue Nina."

"I would say act quickly, for all of our sakes. As you well know Madden, Asmodeus' broadcast was not limited to your current location. It seems somebody has been using the ARC internal network against us, and the signal went global. Anyone in the region knows CERN is the place to be, whatever happens next. Many will flee, but more will be attracted by the chaos, and not necessarily the right types. Be careful. ARC has been infiltrated to the highest level. Your list of those you can trust is going to be small. One thing is evident: Benedict Garias might have thought he was the one using misdirection, but there is an agent in the background using him like a pawn. I think we have seen them revealed. All my hopes, Eva."

The phone went dead, and Eva found many of those in the room staring at her. She was the target of the broadcast, so therefore she must be the one to provide the solutions. Fortunately, her list of those she could trust extended to three very capable people around her.

Swanson began to issue orders to those about him. Simple things concerning hygiene and order. Henri Nesdez remained seated, his head in his hands, his shoulders shaking as he sobbed.

Eva was still contemplating the meaning of this when she noticed the unremarkable man who had been talking to Swanson during Asmodeus' unveiling approach with documents rolled up under one arm.

"Director Guyomard, we have located the source of this broadcast. It's the same place the beams are due to collide if our calculations are correct."

"Where, man?"

"About five miles to the South, there is an access point to where the Large Hadron Collider crosses the Super Proton Synchrotron."

"And this is not general knowledge?"

The engineer peeked over Swanson's shoulder at the people transfixed in front. "No, sir. I found the records locked away in the personal files of Dr Henri Nesdez. Forces are en route. Here, and there also."

"Keep that last bit quiet," Swanson said as he leaned over to Eva. "Give me those maps."

Swanson unrolled the documents, placing them on a nearby table. Everyone involved with what had recently happened gathered and looked at the maps. They showed a large schematic of the accelerators, and where they intersected.

"Here," Swanson said, pointing to a spot to the South. "This is where the access point is. What is that? Woodland?"

He laid another map, geographical this time, atop the first map. "There. In woodland near the Route de l'Europe. Where are those satellite photos?"

The aide handed over a folder of photos, spilling them onto the table. Eva grabbed one and studied it.

"Here? There appears to be a new road."

Swanson peered at the picture. "Looks like a tunnel. Let's go."

"Wait," Ruth Grimshaw shouted from across the room. "You can't leave yet. You don't know what you are looking for."

"Yes, we do," Swanson shouted back. "We have it all here in these documents, found in the possession of your good friend Dr Henri Nesdez. Orpheus isn't the detector. Orpheus IS the upgrade; the injector system designed as far as we know to fire the beams into the Large Hadron Collider. And yet from this schematic, it appears detection is not this machines intended purpose. We are going down there to take a look."

Ruth Grimshaw began to walk towards them. "On whose authority?"

A grim smile spread across Swanson's face, one with absolutely no humour in his eyes.

"That would be mine."

"You can't go down there. That is restricted access. I have complete autonomy. You have no rights to force us..."

"Complete autonomy given by who?" Eva cut in. "By an organization with Benedict Garias as its benefactor? She's stalling us."

"If you attempt to intervene, I will have you detained," Ruth added, and then Swanson pierced the air with a whistle.

In seconds, the Control Room was swamped with ARC special ops, wreathed in black, each bearing an automatic weapon.

"Lock this place down," Swanson ordered, and the agents began to shepherd the scientists across the room. Nesdez began to protest, but then his face went blank and he allowed himself to be led.

"Continue," Swanson asked the agent who had provided the documents.

"Here." He pointed at the map where the two circuits merged. "This is the point where the two circuits interconnect, where the Synchroproton has boosted matter to inject into the Collider. It is a point of massive power convergence. It is also the place where an extra entrance was recently constructed, as Dr Scott correctly pointed out on the satellite image. If you want to locate the child, and the source of the broadcast, underground is a very good place to start."

"Well, what are we waiting for?" Madden said, letting Eva go. "My daughter is there."

"Two squads with us," Swanson ordered. "The rest, detail these science folk. I suspect we will find more than one sympathizer for the Convocation of the Sacred Fire."

. . .

With the decision made, Eva found herself whisked back out of the Control Center as quickly as she had entered it. There was only one thought in her mind: find Nina. There was a sensation to the South. Eva wanted to believe it was her daughter reaching out, but in reality, it was probably that part of her psyche rejecting abandonment, and would not, could not let go. Every step brought her closer. Every moment meant she was farther away.

The agent who had supplied the information sat in their car, with Gila relegated to the following ARC special-ops van, the third in their little convoy behind the armored Mercedes and another van packed with security in the lead. Outside, ARC security had descended on the complex in force. A wave of black had everybody lined up.

In the car, Swanson shuffled through the maps the ARC agent had provided.

"Gotta say, pal, I've no idea what you were talking about with all those drawings." Madden peered at the schematics. "How do you come to such conclusions?"

"By being nosy. Look here," The agent pointed at a series of circuits surrounding the Large Hadron Collider in what Eva presumed was the tunnel.

"These are power relays keeping the supercoolers working around the circuit. They ensure the particle streams maintain an even velocity around the collider. Look at this one now: this is the Orpheus upgrade."

"They don't go anywhere," Madden observed. "They just end."

"Exactly. What this tells me is there are extra junctions, in the guise of a shutdown system with the ability to throw the power to this point here, but there is no outlet for the energy. Why would you have a circuit this size with such a sudden termination?"

"Because what the energy is feeding has no termination in this reality," Eva concluded. "They are actually doing it, Madden. This is no fantasy."

Madden turned to Swanson. "Floor it?"

"Everybody hold on," Swanson agreed, and spoke into his radio. "We have maybe twenty minutes until full acceleration is achieved. Double time it."

The convoy raced out of the CERN complex, ploughing through the media scrum, forcing journalists and onlookers alike to dive for safety. There were bigger issues and Eva was thankful her family was once again the focus; it was the only way she would see her daughter again. The cars turned left onto the highway and after just a moment, took another right on to a single-laned track through pastureland into a dense forest of beech and oak, gnarled and ancient.

As they sped through the forest, Swanson's radio crackled.

"It's Gila. According to one of the guys in here there's a shortcut on the left as we exit the forest. The track should take us right to these co-ordinates."

Swanson turned to Eva. "Your call."

Eva had no right to order these people about. She hesitated.

"Car one. Take the track. Secure the entrance and we will circle about and come from the other direction."

"Oui, monsieur," said a different voice, and the car in front began to surge ahead.

As the woodland began to thin, Eva watched with trepidation for the track on the left. As it appeared, the lead car swerved without slowing, and drifted onto the track.

"Nice," Madden admired, causing Swanson to grin.

"If we get through this, remind me to sign you up for advanced combat driving," Swanson said.

"If we get through this, I'll be teaching it," Madden replied.

It was perhaps thirty seconds later they turned left onto the road Eva recognized as having taken them through the main CERN complex on route to the control center.

The radio crackled into life again.

"More directions, Gila?" Swanson asked, attempting to appear jovial.

"Not me," she replied, before an ear-splitting scream erupted from the radio.

Eva stared at the screen, flashing numbers indicating the radio channel attempting to communicate. Gunfire erupted, the noise drowning out most of what was being said.

"Amb... There must be thr... Will try to hold... *Mon Dieu,* look at the size..."

Eva closed her eyes and took a deep breath. Suddenly, it hit home how much danger they were all in.

"We should've brought more soldiers," Madden said ominously.

"They will hold. We have to get into the tunnel. Anything else is secondary."

The car dashed past a sign proclaiming local speed limits, and they all held on as it swerved left onto a narrow track between some warehouses. In moments, they were passed them and out in the countryside again, tearing up the middle of a field deep with wheat.

"Look there," Eva said, pointing. "They've constructed a new road."

"Going exactly where we need to," Swanson agreed.

"This must have been one of the excavation routes. All the rock had to go somewhere."

The car turned left onto the new track, leading them into the woodlands and onto the same road that ended in the recent ambush. There was no sign of anything on their end.

"The ambush must have been farther down."

"They assumed we would go by the shortest route," Madden said.

"You hope speed was in their mind," Swanson added in a quiet tone.

"Squad one, come back please?"

The radio emitted nothing but static.

"Do you want us to go after them?" Gila said over the channel, and Eva burst with pride at the bravery of her friend.

"No. We have our own focus. Let's just hope they are still about to occupy whatever caught them."

While still fast, there was a hint of hesitancy about the speed they travelled through the forest. Eva stared ahead, trying to spot any signs of combat. The road was pristine.

"There, to the right," Madden said, suddenly animated. A track disappeared into the foliage and they followed it. The track opened out onto an asphalt track eaten up by the mouth of a huge concrete-framed tunnel.

"Orpheus," Eva breathed.

Swanson had already opened the door of the car, and they got out in quick order. The vehicle behind, a small troop carrier, had stopped, and Gila joined them while half a dozen troops reported to the agent accompanying them.

"Two here, the rest with me," he ordered, and picked up an assault rifle from the vehicle. "We will try to secure the place for you, slow them down a little."

"Good luck," Eva called as the group ran down the tunnel ahead of them.

She turned to Madden, who stood staring at the entrance to the tunnel as if entranced. His eyes were wide, almost aglow with an inner light as he looked at her.

"What is it?"

"I have no idea," he replied, clearly mystified. "There's a sensation here. It's glorious, and yet terrible at the same time. I should fear it but Nina's below. Questions are going to be answered down here. It's time to end this."

CHAPTER THIRTY-THREE

THE CONCRETE TUNNEL STRETCHED OFF INTO INFINITY, bending out of sight as it doubled back on itself, descending into the depths of the Swiss underground.

Eva did her best to keep pace with the men, but both she and Gila began to lag behind an entranced Madden, who strode ahead with a sense of purpose Eva had rarely seen since before is abduction in Egypt. He had truly embraced his fate.

"Madden, wait," she called as he began to disappear, and instantly he stopped, her husband returning to her in body and soul.

"I'm sorry. Whatever is going on is drawing me to it." He looked around at the tunnel. "Strange though. I feel as if whatever is happening could occur as easily here as it could down there."

"But Nina isn't here."

He smiled, and hugged her with such tenderness her eyes began to well up; such moments had been few and far between. "Still, here we are, yet again. I feel it's our lot in life to crawl through tunnels."

Madden looked down the tunnel, his face yearning to be there. Eva felt a tinge of guilt for holding him back.

"Did you find anything else out about Orpheus, and the connection?" She asked Gila, hoping to divert everybody's attention.

"He was Thracian Royalty, and an ancient Greek legend. It was said he was an incarnation of the god Dionysus. His wife was Eurydice, daughter of Apollo."

"The god of the sun," Madden chipped in.

"More specifically the god of light. Orpheus was a gifted musician, and his songs were of such beauty, when those he spurned took umbrage and attacked him, their weapons refused to touch him. His song had power.

Eurydice was killed when bitten by a snake, and such was the level of Orpheus' mourning, and the sweetness of his song, the gods allowed him to enter the underworld to reclaim his wife. He was bound by the tenet that when he found her he must not look upon her face until they had reached the mortal plane. Orpheus distrusted Hades and as they reached the portal, turned to look. His wife was there and was banished back to the underworld.

In time, Orpheus was himself slain by Maenads during a Bacchic orgy, and thus reunited with his wife. The parallels between the story and what we could find are uncanny. Orpheus is well named if it indeed provides access to the underworld. It was said by some Orpheus was killed for mocking the gods. Is mocking God not what Asmodeus does now? Do his actions not make a mockery of faith? The very belief in a higher power is at once confirmed and also derided. If they can open a portal to Hell, what is the Almighty doing to prevent it?"

"Maybe he's working through us," Madden said, his voice very strange, lower pitched than usual.

"If God chose a mortal, why not my ex-demon of a husband?" Eva asked nobody in particular. "If you have been to Hell and back, you understand the stakes."

They continued down the tunnel in silence, following the bend to the left until it was clear to Eva they must be at least underneath the entrance. The tunnel straightened, and in the distance, an enormous door was visible. Something was piled in front of it, but from this distance, it was impossible to make out.

Madden picked up the pace, and Eva and Gila kept with the men this time, as exhausting as it was. A tunnel with the potential for leading one to Hell was not a place to be alone.

As they neared the closed door, the mass in front began to gain definition. Black, pointed protuberances, shiny in places, reflecting the light of the tunnel. Around them, more black, duller and flat. On the outside, black spheres.

"This isn't good," Swanson warned, and broke into a jog. Madden followed, seemingly slowed by Swanson's pace, but content to stay with him.

"I can't," Eva gasped when Gila looked at her.

"Then we stay together. There's nobody behind us."

Up ahead, the men had reached the pile. Swanson knelt to examine the contents while Madden remained standing. By the way he was facing, Madden was clearly not inter-ested in the floor, but whatever was behind the door.

Swanson blocked most of the pile as Eva caught up.

"What is it?"

Swanson's voice was somber, "The squad of agents, or at least what's left of them."

He stood to reveal the grisly sight; the dull parts of the

pile were kevlar armor the spec-ops had been wearing. The pointed sections were the muzzles of their guns. Most horrible was what surrounded the pile. The severed heads of the entire team, the necks cut by something sharp judging by the way the still-helmeted men were arranged upright. Blood had pooled underneath the heads, and was smeared on the floor in a trail leading to the doorway. A bloody invitation to proceed.

Once upon a time, Eva might have emptied her stomach at such a scene, but not now. She viewed it dispassionately. They had her daughter. Her only concern was the next barrier, not violent warnings.

Swanson pulled an assault rifle from the pile, causing the disturbed pile to collapse.

"You think a gun will make any difference?" Eva asked him. "We weren't far behind, but we heard no combat, not a single shot."

Swanson held the rifle halfway down in one hand, regarding the weapon. "Maybe not. Who knows? If this is our end, I want to go down fighting by any means possible. They won't conquer me."

"Remember who's in there, Swanson. Nina isn't bulletproof."

Eva stared at the door; her three companions joined her. There was an air of hesitancy as all watched the door.

Madden squeezed her hand and smiled. He leaned over and brushed her lips with a kiss. "I love you, Mrs. Scott. Thank you for this adventure." Madden stepped forward and heaved open the door to the Orpheus sensor.

Eva squeezed through the gap Madden had created only to be greeted by another scene out of nightmare, and at once, she had the answer to the question of where the bodies had gone. The Orpheus sensor loomed high over them, the octagonal shape and its subsections reminding Eva of an enormous clock. The room was cuboid in shape, maybe fifteen feet in each direction. The gantry climbed scaffolding up to the center of the machine, and on it, the naked bodies rested in pieces, torn limb from limb, blood dripping to the floor, entrails hanging in morbid decoration from the steps.

Atop the gantry, a figure crouched, gnawing on part of one of the bodies. Noticing them, it stood. Stripped to the waist, and covered completely in gore, Brian gazed down at her.

"Brian... What have you done?"

The hellbounce once her husband, captor, and tormentor threw back his head and laughed.

"One thing your pet tutor did not tell you was after his wife died, Orpheus became a degenerate, a sodomite of the deepest perversion. I can merely attempt to emulate the acts he was driven to perform."

Enraged, Swanson raised his gun.

Eva noticed the act in her peripheral vision, for, at that moment, a presence came to her, one she had not felt since the day before, when her child was still with her.

'Mother, come.'

Nina was near and she needed them. She was in danger.

"Swanson, wait!" Eve threw a hand out to forestall him. "Look about you."

Swanson paused and did as bidden. "Where are they?"

"Exactly. This isn't quite what it seems. You kill him and we lose our only chance." Eva glared up at Brian. "What have you done with her, you son-of-a-bitch?"

"Your bastard child? She is beyond you now, my wife."

"I am no wife of yours. I was never your wife. Not in any way making any sense."

Brian belted his trousers up, and Eva was profoundly grateful they hadn't interrupted him earlier. "Perhaps not, but that doesn't matter now."

"Tell me, why aren't you with them? Are you not important enough to warrant a spot at the head of all tables? Are you not trusted, or merely another delay?"

Brian grinned, teeth as covered with gore as the rest of his upper torso. "Me, a delay? Do you hope to enrage me? That time is long past. I am a fountain of rage, I pulse with it. You wouldn't even be here were it not for me."

This caught Eva on the hop. "I don't understand."

Brian started to descend the many steps, and stopped about a quarter of the way down, still far above them.

"You were not meant to be delivered to the Convocation. They took it upon themselves to detain you. My master wanted you scared, off balance. He did not want you trapped."

It hit her like a blow to the stomach. "You. You were the one responsible for the portal destroying the mansion. All those innocents killed."

Brian roared with laughter, an insane gibbering noise. He flexed his muscles and raised his arms to the ceiling. "Them, innocent? You see the good side of far too many people, Eva. You always did. To a one they reside in the deepest pit of Hell, awaiting my master's return. A return you will be too late to witness. My forces allowed you to escape. My forces destroyed the abominations in wait at the facility on the lake."

"Your forces allowed me to give birth to our daughter," Eva said, indicating Madden, who watched Brian like a hawk. The anticipation rolled off her husband like fog down a hill.

"Your forces were so important they have been taken away from you, as has your weapon. Where is the knife, Brian? Not trustworthy enough for a minion are you?"

"The Well of Souls has another task, bigger than all of us: they're gonna cut her open and gut her like a pig, Eva."

"Won't happen," Madden cut in.

This caused Brian to regard him as one would a rival, a look she had seen her mortal husband give many a man who had dared even to speak to her in the past. Finally, Brian paid attention to his rival.

"They need her as much as they don't need you. Impure. You're a degenerate mongrel."

"I CAME BACK FROM HELL A GOD!" Brian roared.

"You came back impure. Whatever brought me back was genuine. They needed the blood of another mingled with whatever dark tar passing through their veins to recall you and consequently your own 'minions'. Is the unsatisfied hunger why you feast as you do now? Because you are depleted? Did you go against the orders of your masters, dog? Are you worthy only of the scraps they drop from their table?"

The confidence exuding from Madden was quite over-powering to Eva. She began to feel as she had once done back in the bar in Worcester, yet there was no false sense of lust overpowering her. Madden was deliberately goading Brian, and it was working.

"Doesn't it wind you up to see me with her? Don't you feel somehow inadequate we had a child as a result of your own master's doing? You were too socially impotent to be able to undertake the act yourself."

Madden turned to Eva, and leaned in. "He doesn't know what's coming," Madden whispered in her ear. "I have a feeling I do."

Madden kissed her thoroughly, turning Eva's legs to jelly. She gasped as he let her go and turned back to Brian.

"Yum. You want to taste that peach? You have to go through me."

Brian's answering roar of rage made Eva duck, her hands over her ears. He didn't stop roaring as he rushed down the remaining steps. As he neared the bottom, the noise became deeper, more primal. To Eva's horror, his face had distended in the same way any hellbounce she had seen before had done.

"You won't get through the door," the deeper voice growled, and as Brian hunched, his skin began to split, and a larger being burst through. Humanoid, bulkier, looking like muscle and sinew attached to bone with no skin; the being discarding the shell of Brian had eyes of complete white, and tatters of what passed for hair on the back of the skull. It was an incomplete being, and it roared at him with semi-formed vocal chords, a strangled mess of a noise.

Madden shoved hard on her shoulder, sending Eva stumbling back toward the entrance.

Losing her balance, she fell and landed awkwardly on her side.

In front, Madden squared up to the creature, looking up at the malformed face.

The creature reached back, and punched Madden with a clubbed fist as hard as it was possible to do so. Bones were crushed in an instant, the noise impossible to miss. Madden's limp body sailed through the air just past where Eva now lay. In an instant of despair, their life together flashed before her eyes: Moynagh's, the first night. Finding him alive on Gehenna. Their wedding day, his face when he first saw Nina. If a moment could last, she would have grabbed on and existed there forever.

But then the unthinkable happened. The body stopped in mid-air, and his arms and legs shot out. He screamed in triumph before dropping. Madden landed on his feet, arms stretched to either side of him.

Madden turned to her and winked. He removed the bandage and turned his shoulder to her. The skin was whole, not even a blemish from the bullet wound remained.

"How..?"

"The portal's open, Eva. I'm back, baby! The game's changed: time to fight fire with fire."

"Hurry, they could cross at any time,"

Madden winked. "Trust me."

The Brian-beast roared once more, the muffled bellow sounding like a voice from a head tied under several sheets. It began to stomp quickly towards them, one leg dragging, fluid oozing from its joints onto the floor.

"Come on," Eva heard Madden growl under his breath.

The creature reached Madden and swung for him with its gnarled club of a hand.

Madden ducked underneath and threw a punch into what passed for a midriff. The creature threw its head back and screamed in pain, its middle turning white.

Mist came off Madden's hand, and he looked at it in disbelief. "The cold hand, what am I becoming?"

"Madden!" Eva screamed, "Nina!"

Ceasing his self-examination, Madden sprinted away, climbing the steps to the gantry as easily as Brian had descended them.

"You want to end me," he taunted from in front of the sensor, "here I am. Come get me."

The nightmare-made-flesh gurgled in response, fluids now leaking excessively from every joint. Eva stayed motionless in the hope it would be distracted.

The creature had no time for her, and belying its apparent state of undoing, rushed the scaffold, clambering up even as flesh began to unravel and sinew got caught in the construction.

It reached the top and fell over the railing, its body threatening to fall apart completely.

Madden picked it up with the cold hand, his fingers digging deep where the throat should be. The creature retched, spewing a viscous fluid over him, but Madden stayed resolute. In a herculean effort, he shifted his stance and threw the creature over him into the sensor. Genuine or not, the sensor was pulsing with electricity, and as the body touched, sparks flew out, the current searing flesh as the leaking fluids conducted it.

"Madden!" Eva screamed, and rushed for the gantry with Swanson and Gila close behind. By the time she had reached the top, the creature had dropped back to the walkway, smoking from a myriad of fatal wounds, frozen from the contact with Madden. Yet still it breathed, the death rattle obvious.

Eva stayed well back, but the creature lifted its head, eyeless sockets black and charred, and appeared to look at her.

"No portal," came Brian's voice, strangely lucid despite his transformation. "You are too late. Hell and Earth are about to become one. See you on the other side where you belong."

With one last gurgle, what remained of Eva's former husband dropped back, the flesh unravelling before her eyes and dropping through the holes in the metal walkway to the floor below.

Madden turned to Eva and opened his arms. She ran into them, sobbing, but at the same time close to becoming overpowered by the vibrancy emanating from him.

"Hellbounce," he said, looking at the malformed remains of Brian. "Sooner or later, you always lose control."

"*Mother, help!*" Came the call so loud in Eva's head she repeated it aloud without thinking.

Madden turned to her, his face questioning.

"The door! She's still here!"

CHAPTER THIRTY-FOUR

"Time slowed for Eva. She willed it to do so. Her daughter was merely feet away, but with the doorway sealed, she may as well been on the other side of the world. Free of demonic infection, the Orpheus sensor continued to hum with power, and the thought struck Eva.

"It's an electromagnetic lock."

Madden turned to her, his eyes shining with his reborn self and sense of purpose. Eva realized she actually preferred him this way. His look was questioning.

"In banks they have mechanical locks, and they have electromagnetic locks as a failsafe. You can drill through whatever you like, but if only power can move a door, you're screwed."

Swanson pulled out his phone, intent upon getting more answers.

Madden ignored him, looking at the hand he had used to punch Brian's demon. "I can feel it getting worse. Slowly, but faster every time I use it. The cold is spreading." He flexed his fist. "Ah well, not going to live forever."

Madden turned, placing his hand on Orpheus.

"No!" Eva screamed, but he just pushed harder.

Unlike the reaction to Brian, as there was no fluid the sensor did not react, and the wiring turned frosty as Madden persisted, tendrils of ice spreading in a spider web across the surface. After a few seconds, the frosty wiring terminated and the ice came together in a smaller octagonal version of the larger portal. The center of the Orpheus sensor powered down and started to move forward, hinged on the left.

"Orpheus *is* the door," Gila said, amazed.

They stepped back, allowing the sensor to swing open as far as it could. The door proved to be several feet in thickness, only allowing a gap large enough for one person to enter at a time when it concluded its ponderous movement.

Eva followed Madden through the gap and down a short hallway. The scene meeting them as they emerged into a far larger room was one out of a terrifying memory.

Directly in front, a portal swirled. Emitting a sullen red glow, it fought to redden the bright white of the floodlights pointing directly back at it. Fully as big as the portal in Afghanistan, it must have been over ten feet in diameter. The portal swirled lazily, already stable, a scarlet-tinged cave viewable through what looked like a rippling lens. The portal was framed by a circular metal framework this time, instead of the fire and accompanying vapors that had threatened to overwhelm before. Six massive bundles of cables attached to this, the power source of the true Orpheus.

"This is where the power ends then," Swanson said from behind her. "It doesn't need to go anywhere. It feeds the portal."

Eva had lost interest in the conversation. There was only one thought on her mind.

"Nina, where is she?"

Her companions stopped, and looked down from the walkway they had emerged. There were figures visible in front of the portal.

Forgetting any worries about personal safety, Eva dashed down the steps to her left, and ran across the floor of the enormous cavern hollowed out from the rock beneath CERN. It must have been a hundred feet across, so small were the characters in front.

And then it dawned on Eva. She couldn't feel her daughter any more. Elaine was standing in front of the portal.

Or was she?

"Elaine, you don't have to do this," Eva called, pleading.

Seeing she was being addressed, Elaine managed a smirk, her face looking somehow watery. She held a small figure aloft, again mewling in distress, limbs moving independently of each other.

"Oh my God, no. No! Nina!"

Eva tried to run headlong for the portal, but strong hands grabbed her and kept her immobile.

"Madden, no! They have our daughter! They have my baby girl!"

"Eva, stop. Think about what you are trying to do."

A wave of betrayal hit her when she realized Madden wasn't joining in the rush for their daughter. Betrayal threatened to become hatred.

"You bastard," she spat. "You would let them take her. When I say I would go to Hell and back for my child, you can damned well believe that is *exactly* what I mean!" She started to struggle again.

"Eva, no! This is exactly what they want you to do. Look at them. Feet away but it's so much more profound. Why would they send Elaine with her if they were planning to slaughter Nina. They need somebody to look after her, to care for her. They want us to take her back."

A rumbling chuckle echoed around the portal. From one side, Asmodeus emerged, still the armor-clad hellbeast he truly was. His red eyes seemed so much more malevolent in the light of the portal.

"Whosoever said one had to go to Hell to learn true wisdom was either a prophet, or an imbecile. Yet here you stand. What are you, mortal?"

"I am no mortal," Madden said, and rushed Asmodeus.

However, this was no imperfect hellbounce he was facing, but one of the Seven, the demon caste Lords. If such a maw could be said to sneer, Asmodeus' face did so as he backhanded Madden, sending him hurtling back almost to Eva's feet.

"It is clear you are also no prophet," Asmodeus concluded, the tone of his voice dripping disdain. "Do you think the meager powers granted to one as insignificant as yourself would come to even a fraction of what I can bring to bear?"

Asmodeus thrust a hand in their direction and Eva dropped to the ground, her middle on fire. She screamed, a wordless noise, and Madden joined her. The odd thing was amongst the pain, she wanted Madden with such overwhelming desire. The look in his eyes indicated the very same; this was Asmodeus, and the pain was lust. As such, it could be controlled. Eva closed her mouth, refusing with a herculean effort to touch her husband, lest the spell work its magic and take hold once more.

Eva climbed to her feet, her loins tight from the ecstatic trembling. "You have no power over me. Not anymore."

"Perhaps not. I do not need it. My plans have thus far all come to fruition. I no longer need you. But cross the threshold if you will. I am certain you will be satisfied with the outcome."

Eva knelt to see to Madden, who lay prone on his back. "Are you all right?" she whispered.

"A tad full of desire. Demon Lords have a different effect on their minions. I'll live."

"Not for long," said a female voice, sounding strangely crystalline, the syllables tinkling around the cavern. Eva turned to see the woman they had met as Florentina, the woman who had fed a small child to a frenzied cannibalistic orgy, the woman who was the demon Lord Belphegor, ascending the walkway to the portal. One of her arms was completely white, the crystalline frost having spread up one side of her face. Both her eyes had become translucent, frozen cataracts replacing the pupils. In her frozen hand, she held the glass knife Eva had found in Qena, the same blade responsible for carving her arm open on Gehenna. The blade of the knife was held tight against Swanson's throat.

"Lost something?" She sneered.

Eva turned back to where they had entered; there was no sign of Gila.

Madden rolled to his feet, a dangerous glint in his eye.

"I wouldn't move," Belphegor pre-empted him.

"Kill me," Swanson growled. "Madden, don't stop."

"Hush pet," Belphegor purred. "Madden knows the reality of the situation. He knows what I wield. The Well of Souls is aptly named, for it retains the essence of every being it tastes." Belphegor pressed the tip of the knife on Swanson's throat, causing a single drop of blood to bead on his skin.

"Now it knows your essence. I won't just kill you, mortal. I will use this as a conduit to bring you back as one of them. You will lose your mind, and your free will. Can you live with your choice, knowing what it could cost you? See The Well of Souls is not of this realm, banished from our domain millennia ago. But now it has her blood on it, allowing us to do what has never been done. This will open the Gates of Hell from the other side. You will be powerless to stop us. Your impurity has tainted this Holy relic and now the impossible becomes reality."

Casting Swanson to one side as if he weighed nothing, Belphegor turned to the portal. Swanson's body hit the wall and crumpled to the ground, a motionless pile.

"Stop her," Eva begged Madden, who launched himself once more at the walkway.

Once again, Asmodeus blocked him, this time grabbing Madden as he tried to dodge past, and holding him aloft with one hand. "Not until she is through. I'll squeeze the life out of you and we shall see what demon emerges. Only then will I destroy you."

Atop the walkway, Belphegor began to push the dagger into the portal. There was resistance, the liquid glow intensifying around the dagger, sending streaks of blood-red light shooting about the aperture. Belphegor pushed harder, and the red light became white. The portal began to give.

"It's working!" Belphegor began to giggle, pushing harder. The knife was halfway through now, and Eva watched helpless. Gila was nowhere, Madden was caught, and Swanson was unconscious or even worse.

"Join her," Asmodeus crooned, his voice a compulsion. "Reclaim your daughter. You can see her; take the steps and cross the threshold. Your little Nina awaits. Nobody will take her from you once you are in my domain. All I ask is a drop of blood from you both. One precious drop, and you are both free."

"Yeah, free to end our existence your prisoners as you inhabit the earth. No deal."

The knife had passed. The portal quietened as Belphegor passed through. Turning, raising the blade in salute, Belphegor indicated Asmodeus should join her.

"No matter. You will join us. The dagger, the scroll and the sacrifice; all are in my domain. Your only remaining decision is how you die. Here, or in my domain, but rest assured they will come for you. Stay here, and I can promise you this: Your daughter. Your baby girl will die screaming by my hand as I employ the Well of Souls to flay the skin from her flesh. While you cower here on the mortal plane, I will torture her in ways you cannot comprehend. As she fades from existence, I will ensure she knows you are responsible for her condition and then I will turn her."

Asmodeus' mouth widened in the approximation of a grin. Eva knew he had her. Any mother would give the ultimate sacrifice for their child. Alone, she had no choice.

"It is not a death and return from your mortal world. Any soul in Hell is already dead. I will turn your precious child and she will become a pureblood demon, not a minion confined in a mortal shell. I will train her, nurture her, and instil in her the desperate need to fulfil her destiny by killing the one who gave her life, then abandoned her. When we return to conquer, your own daughter will hunt you down and end you."

"Enough," Eva said. What else could she do? "I'll come."

Asmodeus trembled, one clawed hand involuntarily reaching up towards her. "Of your own free will."

"You leave me no choice, but yes. My blood for Nina's life. Just let me say goodbye to Madden and I'll join you."

"Take all the time you want, child of David. It has no meaning where you will go."

Asmodeus turned to the portal, moving towards the threshold.

Eva ran over to Madden and knelt by him. He was out cold, in a heap beside Swanson. She stroked his face.

"I hope you can forgive me someday for what I have to do now. I know you would do the same. I love you, Madden."

Madden stirred at the sound of her voice, but did not waken.

Having said all she could, Eva pulled her wedding band from her finger and placed it on his palm, closing his fingers around it. She leaned over and kissed him, preparing to take the first steps to her doom.

Asmodeus had reached the portal, and glanced in her direction. Apparently satisfied she was compliant, he turned back.

"Home!" He declared, and pushed into the portal.

Eva followed the rippling form of the demon, the sullen red glow of the cave filling her vision, her daughter waiting in the arms of her nemesis.

A noise from behind her caused Eva to stop and turn. Gila stood in the middle of the cave, Swanson's assault rifle raised towards Eva.

"Eva, get down. This is our only chance!"

"Wait, Gila. No!"

Not listening, Gila squeezed the trigger, and the gun spat a volley of bullets up past Eva, striking one of the relays powering the portal.

Eva watched in mute horror as the only way into the domain holding her daughter began to destabilize. The rippling became a swirling, and just for one moment, cleared so she could see her baby daughter one more time. Nina, intentionally or not, reached forth with one hand. Elaine's face was a mask of horror. Something was very, very wrong.

'*Find me,*' came the thought in her mind, meek and pleading. Nina had reached out with a final plea. Eva dropped to her knees, numb.

The portal built up momentum now it was no longer stable. Within the aperture, Asmodeus had turned, and was now attempting to re-enter the cave. His form was clouded by the swirling mass, but as he pushed through, it was clear what had caused the look on Elaine's face; Asmodeus reached through with one hand, and the flesh was hanging off. Torn, ripped asunder by the forces within the portal. Asmodeus leaned forward, building pressure, his face a flesh-ribboned skull, red eyes glowing within.

"You... can't save... her..." The skull croaked, armor being stripped by the portal even as he stepped partially back into the cave. "I... will... have... my..."

The rotation of the portal increased, the red becoming white-hot, and burning Eva's face. Asmodeus let out a high-pitched scream of such utter pain, for just a moment, and then the portal winked out.

What had passed back into the cave dropped to the floor with a fleshy thud. Asmodeus had only passed halfway. The remaining part of the skull stared at Eva, the red eye faded black.

A whining began to sound, building in volume.

"Come on!" Gila shouted, bringing Eva out of her stupor. "You hear? That's the sound of blowback for all the energy being directed here. There is nowhere for it to go now the portal's closed."

"You have lost my daughter," Eva whispered.

"Not yet. There is another way. But there won't be if we don't get out of here. Help me get the men awake. This entire place is going to collapse!"

Eva saw Gila wasn't kidding: the power relays adjacent to the portal were already glowing white, and the walls around them were cracking.

They ran to the slumped form of the two men and pulled them up. Madden leaned heavily on her shoulder, but step by step they made it closer to the door.

Eva had throbbing aches in her shoulder and back from the weight of her husband, but she dragged him onwards. The whining became painful, and as the power relays erupted with blue bolts of electricity, she stumbled on with her eyes closed. The eruption became a louder noise as the floor began to shake, and a roaring accompanied the concrete falling from the ceiling. Ahead of her, Gila dragged Swanson to safety, leaving her to do the same with Madden. Somehow, she made it up onto the steps, and through the door.

"Close it!"

But she was too late. The power relays exploded, causing the ceiling to fracture, and collapse in chunks. The door swung to with obvious reluctance. A blast hit the door, the ground beneath their feet lurching, knocking everybody flat. The lighting failed and rocks continued to fall. Eva curled up into a ball, protecting her head with her arms. In the darkness, Hell seemed the only place left with any hope.

EPILOGUE

On a cliff jutting from a mountainside, Belphegor regarded her domain. It had been far too long. In the distance, minions flew through the sky on their transporters, the seven great cities with their sky-piercing towers the home for their respective castes glowing in the distance. It was all so temporary, even in a place without time. Already, the white was showing from the nexus. Ice gripped the mountainside, something alien to anybody who did not remember their mortal existence; Belphegor had seen it in abundance.

Forgetting the vista, she regarded her own form. The crystalline matrix had covered most of her body, accelerating these last few moments. She turned her hand, watching the tentacled form as it swirled beneath her skin.

'*With this, I make thee truly immortal*' a voice whispered inside her head.

"I accept it," she purred, and spread her arms wide.

The being formerly known as Belphegor retained just enough awareness to behold the tentacles erupting from her midriff as a new being was born. Once banished, now returned, always vengeful.

Dear reader,

We hope you enjoyed reading *Hellborne*. Please take a moment to leave a review in Amazon, even if it's a short one. Your opinion is important to us.

https://www.nextchapter.pub/authors/matthew-harrill-horror-author-bristol-uk

Want to know when one of our books is free or discounted for Kindle? Join the newsletter at

http://eepurl.com/bqqB3H

Best regards,

Matthew W. Harrill and the Next Chapter Team

ABOUT THE AUTHOR

Matthew W. Harrill lives in the idyllic South-West of England, nestled snugly in a village in the foothills of the Cotswolds. Born in 1976, he attended school in Bristol and received a degree in Geology from Southampton University. By day he plies his trade implementing share plans for Xerox. By night he spends his time with his wife and four children.

http://www.matthewharrill.com/

BOOKS BY THE AUTHOR

The Arc Chronicles

Hellbounce, Book 1

Hellborne, Book 2

Hellbeast, Book 3

The Eyes Have No Soul

Lightning Source UK Ltd.
Milton Keynes UK
UKHW022301080321
380016UK00014B/1924/J